Dragon Blade

Dragon Blade

THE BOOK

OF THE ROWAN

Andre Norton &

Sasha Miller

TOR®

A TOM DOHERTY ASSOCIATES BOOK

NEW YORK

DRAGON BLADE: THE BOOK OF THE ROWAN

Copyright © 2005 by Andre Norton & Sasha Miller

A Tor Book
Published by Tom Doherty Associates, LLC
175 Fifth Avenue
New York, NY 10010

Tor® is a registered trademark of Tom Doherty Associates, LLC.

ISBN 0-765-30747-2

Printed in the United States of America

Acknowledgment

Many thanks to Patricia Gaderborg, who first thought of the Dragon Blade, and was gracious enough to provide a sketch of it.

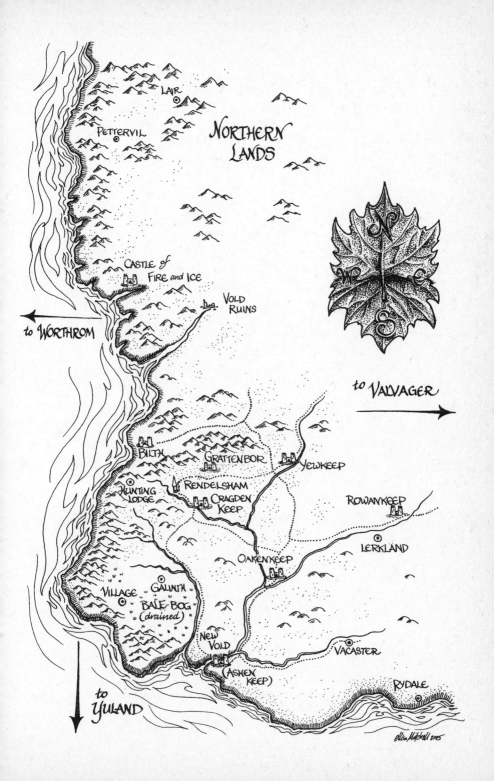

ᛏᚺᛖ ᛋᛟᚾᚷ
(The Song)

Thrice brave Ashen, valiant NordornQueen,
Courage and beauty blended in one.
Joins her true lover, Gaurin NordornKing,
She will not have him battle alone.
Stalwart Gaurin, praiseworthy NordornKing,
Faces unflinching the danger unknown.
His greatest weapon, steel-slender NordornQueen;
They live forever in story and song.

Dragon Blade

Prologue

In the Cave of the Weavers, the Youngest of the Three paused in her work, rose from her seat, and took a step back to survey the Web Everlasting, as was her wont. The artist in her was very pleased; what they had wrought in that portion of the Web where lately there had been such a difficulty now lay clean and smooth. Always the Youngest Sister strove for harmony in their work.

But wait—something appeared to be amiss at a point where the design had not yet fully taken shape. She moved forward to examine it more closely. One thread of the completed work had emerged, working its way forward and growing in the process. Even now it was in the process of snarling itself around others. It was quite large, harsh to touch, and would form a fearful tangle by the time the Three reached it.

Oh, no, she said to herself. Then, aloud, "Look, Sisters. I fear we have another problem in the making."

"How many times do I have to tell you? The concerns of mortals are not our business," said the Eldest, more than a little sharply. "I thought we had settled all that." She touched the spot on the Web where four very differently shaped golden leaves from four species of trees had settled themselves into the weave and become a part of it.

"So we did," the Youngest agreed, "but this is different."

The Middle Sister shifted in her seat so she could get a clearer look at the spot the Youngest had indicated. "She is right," the Middle Sister reported. "Here is a growing tangle of white—quite a nasty snarl, really. I can trace the thread to this section, where the great battles were fought that freed the land." She touched the knot of white threads. "Wait. The snarl doesn't trace *from* this spot, but *to* it instead. And there is another as well, arising from the south. It is very ancient. Both are." She looked up. "It is clear that there is yet something to be done before peace can come to the Land of Ever Snow."

"Still, that is none of our concern," the Eldest retorted waspishly. Yet she, too, examined the bunched-up ball of white threads that looked as if something in its death throes had thrashed about. "It is not of men, but it is for men to learn of, and to remedy. They will address it in the fore-decided time, and live or die in the trying."

"I pity them," the Youngest murmured. She was the most sentimental of them. Though generally her sisters tolerated this trait, today the Eldest did not.

"Leave it!" she snapped. "Have you learned nothing?"

The Youngest Sister was properly abashed. She had always wanted to rush ahead, to find out what lay in store for those whose lives weaved in and out of the Web of Time and even to *change* it if she thought her elders were not looking. She had thought this her secret; now she knew that her sisters recognized this trait in her, too.

"We have work enough here for our hands," advised the Middle Sister. She was ever the calm and practical one, not as sentimental as the Youngest, nor as irritable as the Eldest. "Do not trouble yourself with the future. I keep telling you, work for *today*. When tomorrow is ready, it will tell us. You know that."

"I know," the Youngest said. "I remember. But it is hard when I am forbidden to care about them. They are brave, but so frail, so short-lived. . . ."

"I hate having to repeat myself," said the Eldest. "The affairs of mortals, frail and fleeting as they are, must not concern us."

"We will see what happens in good time, Sister," the Middle one of the Three said, as she had so often in the weaving of this portion of the great Web. "You must be patient."

"When I look at that horrible tangle, I see great danger to one who has been staunch and steadfast throughout," the Youngest said, scarcely above a murmur, "and to those who love each other. I cannot help it that these people have—have interested me."

"And they still do. In observing how they love each other, you in turn have come to love them," observed the Middle Sister, "though it is forbidden."

Ashamed, the Youngest could only nod.

"Put this 'love' away at once," the Eldest commanded sternly, "or I will send you off until this section is in the past, woven and unchangeable. You put all in danger, and I think it is possible that you yourself have created this very tangle."

The Youngest bowed her head at the rebuke. "I will strive earnestly to put away the concern I have for them," she said meekly. "Please do not banish me. Instead, let me work on the spot that troubles me, the way you have in the past. Let that be my punishment."

For a long moment the Eldest just stared at her. Then she nodded brusquely. "So be it," she said, "but be assured that we will both be watching you closely. Your weakness is a danger not only to these mortals you have grown so fond of, but to us as well—yea, unto the Web Everlasting itself!"

The Youngest moved back to her seat and, as unobtrusively as possible, drew a fold of her garment over her head, hoping to hide her countenance from her sisters. She accepted the truth of their words as she had more than once in the past. Yet, in spite of her promise, she could not remove all traces of compassion for the mortals who had bravely arisen to face the horrors in the snow and who now would be called upon to face yet another challenge, perhaps the hardest of all. She touched a spot where several threads wove around each other—one a bright green thread, another of radiant blue, one of a lighter blue, and one of gold. A fifth emerged, mixing blue and green. She ran her fingertips over this one and felt it throb with life.

Then, lest the permission to continue work on this puzzling section of the Web be rescinded, the Youngest shrugged the fold of her garment off her head once more as she glanced back along what had been completed and was now beyond change. All lay in order, lives and deaths, and even Kingdoms' rise and passing recorded. Through the centuries the Three had worked generally in harmony, but the events of the recent past had put a terrible strain on their tranquility.

The Youngest resolved to find the strength to suppress the pity she had felt for the actors in this terrible drama, ever since the first unfolding of the illicit love that had begun it all, that had brought the person represented by the bright blue thread into being. That she not be sent into exile after all, she would offer no mercy to those who were doomed and above all would not meddle with the design or try to change it lest all be destroyed.

Then, the Youngest began working over the area where this latest white tangle had arisen from the myriad colors, as if from a deep sleep. Under her patient fingers, it began at last to take form and shape. Grimly, she kept what she discovered to herself, for indeed, it was the worst of any of the calamities that had befallen the mortals whom she had come—she admitted it, but to herself only—to love.

And as always, the living continued to believe that they were free to make decisions, to act as they deemed fit, even as their threads passed through the fingers of the Weavers.

One

*A*shen NordornQueen, great with child, stood on the balcony clinging to the half-completed residential wing of the new Castle of Fire and Ice, while she watched the Sea-Rover ship maneuver its way past a large ice floe that could, if the captain were unwary, rip the bottom out of the vessel. The floe had only recently separated from the great ice river that lay opposite the castle site, at the end of the deep, water-filled fjord another ice river had gouged hundreds of years before when the world was new. She regretted not having seen the ice fall, for that sight never failed to fascinate her. However, judging from the cracking and booming rising from this ice river, more would surely follow, and soon.

She pulled her heavy cloak closer about her, grateful for the wulvine fur rimming the hood. Frost would not cling to such fur, and at this time of the year, everyone's breath could clearly be seen on the frigid air.

Construction had halted temporarily on the castle when the masons reported their mortar freezing before it could even be applied to the stones. The latest level of stonework that had been achieved lay under a blanket of hay and manure, to keep it warm, and the workmen had returned to their homes. On the first day that water didn't freeze in the washing basins, they would begin again. It was very important to all that the new castle, a replacement for the old Palace of Fire and Ice, be completed as speedily as possible.

As the Sea-Rover ship approached, Ashen could make out the banner flying from the highest mast, blue-green with the device of a crashing wave. That was Rohan's badge! Doubly pleased, she turned around that she might go to greet him and nearly ran into Gaurin.

"I saw it, too," he said, smiling. The lines at the corners of his eyes crinkled, a pleasant sight that always warmed her heart. A few strands of white glistened in his honey-colored hair, just at the temples. "We shall go down together."

He offered her his arm, and she took it not only as a courtesy but also because her steps were slow and her balance uncertain these days.

"Thank you, Gaurin," she said.

"How goes our son and heir?" he asked, placing a gentle hand on her belly.

As if the child could hear, it delivered a mighty kick that almost knocked Ashen off her feet. "He is impatient to be born," she said, a little wryly. "I do not think it will be long now." Indeed, she thought she had been feeling slight contractions since morning. But as she was still, by her reckoning, a week away from her time, she ignored them. She didn't want to create a great confusion for nothing. It would not be the first time a woman had had false signs of this nature.

For answer, he kissed her; then, with him carefully helping her with each step, they descended into the Great Hall, one of the few completed portions of the castle, where Gaurin bade her wait and let their visitors come to them. She handed her cloak to a steward.

Ayfare hurried through the door bearing a platter laden with covered dishes, cups, and a steaming pitcher. She who had once been Ashen's personal maid back in Rendel, later the head house-keeper of the Oakenkeep when that became Ashen's property, now was the Chatelaine of the Castle of Fire and Ice.

"Sit, sit!" she exclaimed. "You're too close to your time to be climbing up and down those stairs all day!"

"I only went up to watch the Sea-Rover ship come in," Ashen

said as she accepted the steaming goblet of snowberry juice lightly mixed with wine that Ayfare handed her. Nevertheless, she half sat, half fell into the chair Ayfare offered her. The Chatelaine, perhaps out of habit, began setting Ashen's headdress to rights and pushing strands of silver-gilt hair back in place. "Rohan is here. I saw his ensign flying from the mast."

"I don't care if the Dowager Queen herself was swimming in from the ship," Ayfare retorted, "your health and well-being come first."

"I tried to tell her as much," Gaurin said, "but she wouldn't pay any heed. Let us hope she listens to you."

Ashen looked at him, overcome anew with the love she had felt for this splendid man from the first moment she had seen him. "The sunburst at midnight," he had called the overwhelming upsurge of emotion that had arisen between them, and the feeling had grown, if possible, even stronger over the years.

"I hardly think the Dowager Ysa would be swimming in that frigid water just to see me," she told Ayfare, trying to be stern but unable to keep her lips from twitching with a suppressed smile. "Nor do I think my daughter, Queen Hegrin, would allow her to be so foolhardy even if she were inclined to such folly."

"Be that as it may," Ayfare said with the manner of an old friend who was allowed to take liberties, "the first boat is already here. Furthermore, I know there was at least one woman on board, and one you know, too."

"Who is it?" Ashen asked. "Oh, please don't tease me! Tell me who it is!"

"That I will not do," Ayfare retorted, her own eyes dancing merrily, "for I had to promise on Nalren's head."

Ashen nodded. Like Ayfare, Nalren had come with her to the NordornLand and, like her, he had exchanged his position as High Steward in the Oakenkeep for that of Seneschal in the Castle of Fire and Ice. The rumor—which Ayfare steadfastly denied—was that the two were, if not betrothed, at least on the brink of it. That this mysterious visitor had extracted an oath on Nalren's head suggested that the rumor was true.

"I will at least greet them standing," Ashen said. She set the goblet aside and struggled to her feet. Gaurin stood ready to lend her assistance, but she had told him that in this regard, her own efforts were better than his help. If she tottered and threatened to fall, then was when he could be of the greatest service. "Let them come in, and quickly! I am all eagerness to hear of what has been happening in Rendel."

Just at that moment, the door to the Hall opened, bringing with it a gust of chilly air. Rohan of the Sea-Rovers and of Rendel entered, random flakes of snow swirling in his wake, dusting the red-gold of his hair.

"Ashen!" he exclaimed. "It's been so long!" He covered the distance between them in a few long strides and swept her into his embrace, kissing her heartily on both cheeks. "I thought you would have dropped the brat long before now," he added teasingly. "Can't get close enough to hug you properly. Sir." He turned to Gaurin, and the two men likewise embraced, kinsman to kinsman.

"Well met, Rohan," Gaurin told him. "But we were told that there was someone else with you."

"Oh, there is, there is." The twinkle was plain in Rohan's eye. "She wanted to prolong the mystery just a little more. She'll come in presently."

Only partially in jest, Ashen aimed a blow at Rohan, which he easily dodged. "Tell me now!" she said. "Is it Hegrin? Or perhaps Anamara. What are you hiding from me? If necessary, I'll go and see for myself—"

A trilling chirp interrupted her and to Ashen's astonishment, Weyse came bounding into the Hall, straight for her, and, without the least regard for the dignity of the heavily pregnant Nordorn-Queen, the odd, unearthly little creature climbed up her dress to nestle into her arms with a happy sigh.

"Weyse!" Ashen exclaimed. "That means that—"

"That Zazar is close behind," the Wysen-wyf said, as she entered the room in Weyse's wake. She was puffing a little from the climb up the steps from the ward. "Could you possibly make this place a little harder to get to?"

Hurriedly, Ashen handed the little creature, half again the size of a house cat, off to Rohan, and took a few awkward steps toward the woman she had long referred to as her Protector.

"Oh, stay there, stay there," Zazar exclaimed impatiently. "I don't need any help."

She kissed Ashen on the cheek—an unexpected gesture—and Ashen was shocked to discover that Zazar had grown so stooped she had to reach up to do it.

"Indeed you don't," Ashen said. "It's just that I was so glad to see you, when I never expected it."

"I told you you hadn't seen the last of me," Zazar returned airily. "Don't stand in my way, girl. You're blocking me from the fire."

Barely hiding his smile, Gaurin stepped forward and gave Zazar his arm so he could escort her to one of the high-backed chairs, reserved for honored visitors. "Come, Ayfare, serve our guests and let them warm themselves."

Ayfare smiled in turn, removing the covers from the platters, revealing slices of roast fallowbeeste on new bread, accompanied by a steaming tureen of lentil soup. Without any further ado, both Rohan and Zazar fell to eagerly. Ashen seated herself, and Weyse returned to her arms.

"There's hot food for those with you as well," Gaurin said. "We started the soup to heating when your sails came in sight."

"Who else was on board?" Ashen asked. Shifting Weyse a little, she accepted a fresh goblet of the hot snowberry juice from Ayfare. "Anybody I have known? That little man who always had a drum with him—"

"Kasai," Rohan said around a large mouthful. "No, he's back at New Vold. When Grandfather died, a lot of the spark just went out of him. But you probably remember Harvas. He's still captain of *Spume Maiden* even though he could have moved up to the flagship by now if he wanted it. Says she's been lucky for him."

"I can't imagine a Sea-Rover journey without a Spirit Drummer on board." Ashen moved a little as Ayfare set a bowl of the hot soup in front of her and a portion in another bowl for Weyse, setting it aside to cool a little. The little creature climbed out of

Ashen's arms and hunkered down to eat when she could do so without scalding herself. "Or, for that matter, imagine Kasai without a spark. He read for me once, you know."

"He's given it up, and handed his drum on to a younger man, Frode. I haven't yet had the occasion to test him out as to how good his readings are. Incidentally, I have the gifts I promised you when you got to be royalty, Gaurin. The Rinbell sword for you, and a special gift for Ashen as well." Rohan glanced at her, smiling mischievously. "That one is full of mystery. I think you'll like it, and the sword, too. And, of course, baby goods. Lots of them. Anamara insisted."

"We'll have a look at all of your gifts later," Gaurin said. "Right now, we're rejoicing in your safe arrival at the Castle of Fire and Ice."

"And how do you fare, Ashen?" Zazar asked around a mouthful of meat. "The babe is about ready to drop, isn't it?"

Ashen felt herself blush. "I am very near my time," she replied modestly.

Zazar swallowed, snorted with laughter, and wiped her mouth on her sleeve. "I should know!" she said derisively. "I all but had to arrange the whole thing for you."

Even Gaurin raised his eyebrows. "I didn't know it was your doing," he said with a wry smile. He held out his hand to Ashen, who took it. "It seemed to me that this was a matter that concerned only my lady and me."

Zazar laughed again. "Well, if I hadn't put a little pinch of something special in your soup, maybe nothing at all would have come of your time in the Snow Fortress during that fierce war against the Great Foulness. That is where it all began, you know."

"And why," Ashen said, fascinated in spite of herself, "did you think this needed to be done?"

"Any fool could have seen it," Zazar replied, pushing her bowl aside, "and so that means that you didn't. From the moment I first laid eyes on your kinsman, Hynnel, onetime NordornKing, I knew that he would never live to reclaim his throne. That left only Gaurin with a good enough claim to it. And, as I believe he might have told you, a king needs an heir." She shrugged. "You were being laggard in your duties. As I recall, you rushed right off to correct your tardiness. But it was much too late by then, of course, this getting of an heir being under way already."

Gaurin laughed aloud. "Well, however it came about, it seems to be no more than a few days before we'll find out if the midwives' predictions are correct. They say it will be a boy."

Zazar looked at Ashen with a critical eye. "Most likely. Very well, if you're finished, girl, take me to your chamber, where I can have a closer look at you. Just a few days, eh. Well, dismiss your midwives, for I am here, and in good time as it happens." She arose from her chair, took Ashen by the hand, and pulled her to her feet as well. "Come on, come on, we've no time to waste."

"This way, Madame Zazar," Ayfare said hastily, rushing forward to escort the two women.

Ashen had only a moment to be taken aback by the way her Protector showed complete disregard for both her condition and her position as NordornQueen before she found herself being dragged, almost bodily, toward the stairs. Halfway up, she stopped, doubled over with the first real twinge and knew that, once again, Zazar had been correct. Her time was upon her.

Without willing it, she moaned. Zazar turned and stared at her intently. Then she jerked her head toward the men still sitting at the table, nonplussed by what was happening.

"We need help," she said.

Almost running, Gaurin quickly crossed the distance between them and took Ashen in his arms. Gratefully, she allowed him to carry her the rest of the way as her body began to labor in earnest.

Nearly two months after that tumultuous day when Rohan brought Zazar to her, Ashen sat contentedly watching her infant son as he slept. As if he sensed her presence, he opened his eyes. Unlike other babies, he didn't start crying at once but only looked at her solemnly. Nonetheless, she began gently rocking the cradle he lay in.

"Ah, you're awake, are you," she said in a low, soothing tone, as if he both heard and understood her. "Then you know what a big day tomorrow is. Oh, yes. Tomorrow your father and I will have our official coronation, and you'll be given your name and a tiny crown of your very own because you are the Prince of the Nordorners and everyone will be very happy."

The baby unexpectedly gurgled and kicked his feet, disturbing the blanket that covered him. Ashen tucked him in again and continued her monologue.

"Everyone will be there. Your kinsman Rohan has had time to send *Spume Maiden* to New Vold so Harvas can bring Anamara here for the ceremonies, and your brother-in-law Peres will be there, your sister Hegrin, too. Oh, isn't it wonderful that you have a real king not only for a father, but for your sister's husband? What a lucky little boy you are! And the Lord High Marshal, Protector of Rendelsham, will be there and his wife, my best friend, who is your aunt too, in a way and there will be such fine presents for all. . . ."

She talked on, enjoying not only the way the baby seemed to be listening to every word but also the anticipation of Gaurin's coronation day. And hers, of course.

Though the Castle of Fire and Ice was still incomplete, it was now filled with important people who had made the cold journey to honor the new rulers of the NordornLand. Yuland, far across the southern sea, and the wealthy island Kingdom of Writham, to the west, had sent ambassadors and representatives. Even if the nursery that housed her infant son had been chilly, Ashen would have been warmed by the thought of the high regard in which Gaurin NordornKing was held by the entire world.

Rohan had been of immense help while the NordornQueen was recuperating and the NordornKing swamped with duties and responsibilities. He had assumed the bulk of the detail work of sending out the necessary proclamations to surrounding nations, of overseeing the completion of at least one wing of the castle to house the expected dignitaries, of clearing an area in the immense ward where great—and comfortable—pavilions might be erected for those who wanted more luxury than the cramped guest quarters could presently provide. Other guests of high blood would make do with what the castle could offer, but Rohan also made arrangements in the town that was beginning to arise outside the walls, for extra lodging where it could be found.

Somehow he had also managed to find a moment to send Harvas for Anamara and their son, young Obern, who was of an age to take his first uncertain steps, and also Beatha, once Hegrin's nursemaid and later elevated in stature to nurse—the proper companion for unmarried young ladies. Now that Hegrin was a crowned queen herself, she was under the supervision of tutors and guardians selected by the Council of Rendel and Beatha retired from her duties. Ashen had every confidence that Lord Royance, Head of the Council, would have selected wisely for her daughter's company.

The Rendelian royal couple had chosen to occupy heavy wool pavilions, and Ashen noted that there were two—one for each of them. She spared a moment to be grateful that those in charge of the King's and Queen's upbringing—they were but children on the verge of young adulthood—had proven wise enough to have them postpone the physical side of their marriage for a few years. In this arrangement she suspected Lord Royance's hand as well.

She glanced over to where Zazar and Beatha sat. Beatha would brook no thought of anyone else tending to Ashen's new child and so was enormously grateful to have been sent for. Retirement didn't suit her. She had been at loose ends and so had accompanied Rohan without hesitation. Any complaint she might have now was that she had not been sent for earlier and, now that she was here, Ashen wondered the same thing.

For once Zazar seemed content not to occupy her old hands with any sort of task, but Beatha was busy with the last-minute embroidering of yet another row of ornamentation on the child's naming-day robes. The silver thread glinted in the light.

"Surely this baby will have the finest and most beautiful garments in the history of the world, if you have your way about it," Ashen commented, smiling. "Even more so than Hegrin."

"My Hegrin wasn't born a princess," Beatha responded as she snipped off a silver thread. "And it was a waste to dress her in fine clothing when she kept ruining it, climbing trees and generally acting worse than any boy. I predict that *he*—" she indicated the baby with a nod of her head "—will turn out to be much better behaved."

Ashen laughed openly, and even Zazar smiled. "They're all different," the Wysen-wyf said. "Ashen had her moments as well."

"How good he is," Ashen said, looking at the baby who had fallen asleep once more. "How I wish—"

"Wish what?"

Ashen turned to Zazar. "It's so strange. I lost Obern's child, and then, when I married Gaurin I had Hegrin soon after, but it was so long before there was another. I wish I could give Gaurin more children." She looked back at the baby, hoping to hide tears that had, unaccountably, filled her eyes. "To pin all our futures on this one frail life . . ."

Zazar stirred in her chair, slightly disturbing Weyse, who was dozing at her feet. "If that's what you want, Ashen, then that is what you shall have. Now that I am with you, that is."

"What do you mean?"

"Beatha, would you mind to leave us for a while?" Zazar said. "I'm about to tell Ashen something very private. Please don't get your feelings hurt."

"If you say so," Beatha responded. She gathered her embroidery and prepared to go to her own private quarters adjoining the room in which they all sat.

"It's all right," the Wysen-wyf assured her. "In fact, it's something you'll like in the long run."

Beatha merely shrugged and left the nursery. The set of her shoulders stated quite plainly that whatever secret Zazar was preparing to tell Ashen would be hers, sooner or later, particularly if it involved Ashen's children.

🌶

"Do you remember," Zazar said, when Beatha had closed the door behind her, "when you were so sick after you were taken to

Rendelsham Castle, after you miscarried your first child?"

"Yes," Ashen said. "I should have gotten better quickly then, but I didn't."

"You came very close to dying," Zazar told her, "and it was my fault that I wasn't there to save you. But Obern did. He discovered that you were being poisoned—"

"*What?*"

"Yes, and by your half brother, King Florian."

Ashen sat without moving, shocked, but finding this news no news at all. "He always hated me. I don't know why. Rohan told me in a letter about some potion he had found among Obern's belongings that he poured into the bay and it poisoned fish."

"That must have been what he used, that Obern found and hid lest someone else use it to work even more mischief. Ashen, Obern loved you very much, in his own way. He gave his life to save yours and to avenge the injury to you and to his honor."

"Yes, I know." Ashen's cheeks grew hot. "I—I never fully appreciated him, not after I—"

"After you met Gaurin," Zazar finished for her. "You felt as if you were betraying one with the other, and were never quite certain who was the betrayed." She leaned over and picked up Weyse, settling the odd, furry little creature on her lap. Weyse sighed heavily and went back to sleep.

"Yes," Ashen said. "It was very difficult—for all of us."

"Well, things happened so swiftly I couldn't manage to counter the damage Florian's evil actions had done you in time for you to bear Obern the child he wanted from you. He died first. But I could do it for Gaurin." Zazar turned very serious. "The concoction Florian poisoned you with almost destroyed your capacity to have children, Ashen. It was only through my actions that you had Hegrin and, later, your son when it became clear to me that you were destined to become NordornQueen and you had a duty to provide an heir."

"But how—"

"How what? That I knew you would be NordornQueen, or how I helped you become pregnant?"

Despite herself, Ashen smiled a little. "You've always known what would happen to people long beforehand. I meant, helped me have my son."

Zazar shrugged. "I've already told you," she said airily, almost the same as she had always been before age had begun to overtake her. "I slipped some mixtures of my own into your food." She favored Ashen with a wickedly gleeful grin. "Not Gaurin's, though I teased him about it. I didn't have to put anything into his victuals to make him want to do his duty. Unless I guess wrongly, he's never been remiss in that area."

Now Ashen's face flamed in earnest. "I should be furious with you," she said. "I only wish that you had told me what you were doing when Hegrin was born. Gaurin and I could have had several more children by now."

Zazar shrugged. "Hegrin was handful enough, and it seemed that you and Gaurin were content." She grew serious once more. "You have no real idea what a strain childbearing puts on you. Your mother died having you, you know, and you have inherited her frail bones and fragile constitution."

"Nevertheless, I would have more. If I can. I would be glad of a whole houseful of children."

"Well, as to that, let me have a look at you."

Before Ashen could protest, Zazar had arisen from her chair, placed Weyse in the warm spot, and conducted Ashen over to a small bed set there for Beatha in case the infant prince were sick with the colic or some similar ailment. "Disrobe," she told the NordornQueen, "and lie down. Just your dress—you may leave on your petticoat. I need to touch your skin."

Automatically, Ashen obeyed. The Wysen-wyf poked at her abdomen with her strong old fingers, put her head against Ashen's chest to listen to her heartbeat, flexed her knees to test the strength of her muscles. She lifted Ashen's eyelids and stared at her eyes, opened Ashen's mouth to examine her teeth, gums, and the color of her tongue, and sniffed her breath. She even peered into Ashen's ears and felt her skull.

"Sound enough," she declared once the examination had been concluded. "More so than I had reason to hope."

Ashen began putting her clothing to rights again. "Then you'll give me more of that potion, whatever it was—"

"No potion. Just certain herbs, at certain times."

"More of the herbs, then. You'll do this?"

"Yes. I judge that with my help you'll be fit to bear one more child, and perhaps two. Then you must resign yourself to having no more."

"Four children," Ashen said softly. "Four children with Gaurin as their father. With what you have told me, it is as much as I could hope for."

"Of course it is," Zazar said with a derisive snort. "By all rights, you should have been dead several times over!"

A bell sounded from somewhere in the distance.

"That was the signal for the midday meal. Well, girl, are you going to stand there mooning all day over babies you don't even have yet, or are we going to go eat?"

Two

The coronation and naming day dawned bright, clear, and unexpectedly mild, a good omen some said. Every turret in the castle was aflutter with the pennons of noble guests, making the otherwise grim and forbidding structure gay and inviting.

Ashen, the knowledge that she was to bear Gaurin at least one more child warm within her, descended the great staircase with Zazar beside her. The Hall was already crowded with guests both noble and common. Rohan spotted her first and raised a cry of greeting. Anamara, standing beside him, gave her a shy but radiant smile. Many goblets were raised to her and Gaurin, who had been occupied in a moment of private conversation with Esander, the priest who had come with them to the NordornLand, hurried to her side.

"How beautiful you look, my Ashen," he said.

Ayfare had, indeed, taken time from her other duties to attend to her, and had outdone herself in turning Ashen out to perfection. Like Gaurin, she was dressed in the purest of white garments woven of snow-thistle silk. This was the light, nearly weightless fabric Ashen had first become acquainted with, in Gaurin's tunics, when the women of Rendel were preparing their men for the coming war with the forces of the Great Foulness.

Snow-thistle silk was spun from fibers gathered from the pods of certain plants that grew only in ground covered deeply with snow. The land of Rendel had certainly been cold enough for the plants to flourish, but no one had thought to bring any with them when first they had fled as refugees ahead of the armies the Great Foulness had mustered. No one in Rendelsham had been able to come close to making the silk, let alone duplicate it.

Ashen understood now the appeal of snow-thistle silk, and why it was so valuable, used to keep huntsmen and soldiers warm at need. Only the wealthy nobles could afford the finest grade of snow-thistle silk for their clothing. It had taken countless pods to yield enough fibers for the dress she wore and many long hours at the spindle and later with skilled workers laboring at the loom. Lesser grades of the fabric, just as warm but not as beautiful, were used for ordinary clothing or the blankets hunters and soldiers wrapped themselves in when they slept under the sky.

Even the wool spun in the southern lands was no equal in fineness and delicacy to that from the colder climes. She herself had a wool shawl like the ones Gaurin had once described to her—so sheer, yet warm, that it could pass through the circle of one of her finger-rings.

She touched the silver embroidery that adorned the white dress; matching motifs covered Gaurin's doublet, and their son's naming-day robes as well. Snowflakes glittered and sparkled everywhere the light touched—a fitting symbol for the King and Queen of the Nordorners. She had been apprehensive that the white and silver, with her pale skin and silver-gilt hair, would make her look ill, but with just the lightest touch of rouge to lips and cheeks, they didn't. Her mirror told her that she shone like polished silver as well.

Gaurin's garment bore also an embroidered snowcat wearing a silver collar, and her Ash badge—flame rising from a vessel of pure silver—adorned her skirt. Their son's robe had no individual emblem worked on it, for he had not yet received his various titles.

"There is a little time before the ceremonies, so come and see our gifts," Gaurin said, offering Ashen his arm. "We have them set aside for all to admire."

They nodded to their guests as they made their way through the crowd, stopping often to speak with old friends and with representatives of foreign lands come seeking cordial relations with the newly reclaimed NordornLand. Ashen spotted Hegrin in the crowd and would have gone to her, only the young Queen of Rendel shook her head, smiling. Today was Ashen's day. Later, at the feast, she and Gaurin, according to Nordorn custom, would occupy separate tables. Hegrin would sit on one side of her, and her best friend, Rannore, on the other, with Anamara beside her. King Peres and the Lord High Marshal and Protector, Lathrom, would occupy similar places of honor with Gaurin, and other nobles seated according to rank.

It was as Gaurin had said; in a small room just off the Hall, tables groaned beneath the weight of the outpouring of gifts from nobles and the common people alike. She spotted Rohan's gift at once—there was no mistaking the peculiar, watery sheen of a Rinbell blade—and beside it, a beautiful box with dragons inlaid in the wood, outlined in silver and thickly set with what looked like precious white stones. It was the size of a jewel chest, or perhaps a box a lady might use to store her writing papers, quills, and ink. She longed to examine it more closely, but there was no time.

"That must be Anamara's gift," she said to Gaurin. "I remember I was just on the verge of finding out what it was when our son announced that he was ready to be born."

"Yes, it is," he replied. "Rohan forgot to show it to you, in all the confusion. And later, everything got put aside as it arrived, and not brought out for display until today."

"It's overwhelming."

They strolled down the row of tables, admiring one beautiful article after another, all considerately marked with the names of the givers, until they approached a good-sized chest occupying the very end of the last table. This one was open, and inside were heaped coins of all types and values. Even as Ashen watched, a townsman, obviously dressed in his finest, bowed to them and added a few more to the pile. Ashen looked at Gaurin with a question in her eyes.

"This is from our ordinary citizens," he told her, "the ones who could never afford a standing cup or a game set made of precious gems. However, even the poorest can give up a coin. And though

I never made any mention of it, this idea has caught on among our merchants and other ordinary citizens." He leaned closer and spoke so only she could hear. "They have no idea that this gift is, possibly, even more valuable than all these glittering, useless treasures they all admire."

Ashen nodded her understanding. Gaurin was a wealthy man, having inherited his father's estate, and she herself was not without resources; nevertheless, both their purses had grown lean in financing the rebuilding efforts that had occupied them since their arrival. Gaurin did not want to draw upon the NordornLand treasury until there properly was one, and she agreed. The coins would be put to good and immediate use.

Ashen was drawn to the box decorated with the jeweled dragons that Anamara had sent her, but she had no time to examine it closely. A bell from outside the main castle sounded, coming from the small, perfect, almost completed Fane across from the entrance to the Castle of Fire and Ice. It was the signal to all that the coronation and the naming ceremony were beginning.

Because all the Nordorn regalia had been lost or destroyed with the fall of Gaurin's uncle, Cyornas NordornKing, the new rulers had to make do with what was available. The only remnants were a handful of brilliant red gems called fire-stones that had been found buried in the rubble of the ruined Palace. They were thought to have once adorned Cyornas's crown, though no trace of it had ever been found. New crowns had been commissioned, and one of these gems had been set into Gaurin's, another into Ashen's, a third set aside for the young Prince's coronet. The rest, save for two, had been inlaid into necklaces of state for the two sovereigns.

The procession, previously planned and the participants informed, formed at once, and the rest of the guests drew back to give them room. There was no State Sword, but Rohan took up the Rinbell blade and carried it. Gaurin's signet ring, bearing his badge of the snowcat, now rested on a velvet cushion, borne by Lathrom, Lord High Marshal of Rendel. Ashen wished she had a royal signet as well, so that Anamara could carry it, but she had not thought to order a new one made. Until this day, her seal had borne the Ash

Tree rising from a flame, surrounded by the canting pun, "Without flame, there can be no Ash." It had been suitable for her in Rendel, at the Oakenkeep, but she needed something more regal as NordornQueen. Instead, Anamara bore Ashen's necklace of state. Gaurin's kinsman Cebastian walked beside her, carrying the other.

In a particularly graceful touch, the new royal couple's daughter and son-in-law, monarchs in their own right, carried the Nordorn crowns. These were of silver, and the fire-stones blazed in the center of the bands that would rest on their heads. Above these bands sleek columns rose, surmounted by high spikes adorned with delicate crystals carved in the shape of snowflakes that gave off rainbow colors, much like those hidden in the depths of the bracelet Gaurin had given to Ashen on the occasion of their first meeting.

She was wearing it now, the artifact of Gaurin's house, once belonging to his father, which she had found during a perilous adventure in the old Bog of recent memory, in Rendel. She touched it, and Gaurin smiled at her. They both knew the bracelet's power. If she wore it and thought of him in need, he would come to her side no matter the difficulties and obstacles he must overcome; in turn, wearing it, she had discovered that she knew when he was in danger and so would go to him likewise.

Then, hand in hand, they walked out of the Great Hall of the Castle of Fire and Ice, across the ward on a carpet of scarlet wool, to where the good priest Esander waited for them.

Because of the mildness of the day, the ceremonies would be conducted on the porch of the Fane, where everyone who could crowd into the ward could see and hear. There had not been a coronation in the NordornLand for as long as anyone could remember, so Gaurin and Esander had conferred long and put together a ceremony between them.

"Simplicity, please," Gaurin had said. "We are as good as being on a rough frontier, for all the turrets and towers of the castle, and as I intend to be a king who works hard for his people, I would have no great pomp or ceremony."

"It will be as you wish," Esander had replied.

And so it was. With dignity, but keeping the solemnity of the moment, the good priest anointed each of them with fresh oil, touching them on forehead, hands, and heart. He placed Gaurin's crown upon his head, then Ashen's upon hers. The royal couple turned and faced those waiting, to be greeted with a tumultuous cheer.

When he could make himself heard once more, Esander said, "There is another important ceremony for us to celebrate today, good people. Our new King and Queen have a Prince, not yet named. Let him be presented forthwith."

At these words, Beatha, carrying the infant well bundled up against the cold in snow-thistle silk and scarlet wool and accompanied by Zazar, emerged from the castle door and walked across the same carpet his parents had but recently trod. "He is here," she said, when she had reached the step to the Fane.

"By what name shall this child be known?" Esander said.

Gaurin took a step forward. "Henceforth, this child of our bodies, our heir, shall be called Bjauden NordornPrins."

Something like a sigh went through the waiting crowd. "Thus shall it be," Esander proclaimed. "Welcome, Bjauden NordornPrins, heir to the throne of the NordornLand."

Ashen smiled; she and her husband had settled on giving the baby Gaurin's late father's name well before he had been born, but according to custom had never spoken it aloud from the moment he emerged, almost as solemn as he was on this occasion. He didn't cry even when the chilly oil touched his forehead, or when Zazar placed a circlet worked of silver thread and ornamented with red beads upon his head.

Then it was time for the great feast to begin. Castle servants, under Ayfare's stern and watchful eye, had been setting up the trestle tables from the moment the last observer had filed out into the ward to watch the coronation. When Ashen and Gaurin reentered the Hall, they were greeted with the sight of tables laid and ready, each covered with snowy linen, and with platters already being brought in to serve the guests.

Without any great fanfare, they laid aside the new crowns of state and donned simple silver diadems in their place. Each bore a crystal snowflake with a fire-stone at its heart and, except for size, were identical. Gaurin had made it plain that Ashen would rule side by side with him, as Queen Regnant, her powers equal to his. Little Bjauden, being much too young to be exposed for long to crowds and feasting, regardless of his demeanor—so much older than one might expect—was taken back to the nursery.

Ashen and Gaurin made their way to the twin daises, across the Hall from each other, where they would sit for the coronation feast. They smiled at each other and took their seats.

Immediately, the Hall was filled with the sounds of people finding their own places, calls for meat and drink, joyous shouts of friends calling to one another from one table to the next. Page boys began circulating through the Hall, bearing great platters of meat delicately seasoned and steaming even in the comparatively warm air. Ashen took a slice of roasted waterfowl and a helping of preserved fruit onto her platter.

"It's a wonderful day, Ashen NordornQueen," said Rannore, once a queen in her own right. King Peres was her son, but her titles had vanished. She now was but the wife of an honored knight, though acknowledged the bravest in all of Rendel and charged with its defense in time of peril.

"Am I allowed to still call you 'Mother'?" Hegrin inquired from Ashen's other side. Her eyes twinkled with mischief. "Or must I say that mouthful every time I tell you good morning?" She also helped herself to a large slice of the waterfowl and an even larger helping of the sweetened, preserved fruit.

"You could call her 'Madame Mother' as I do," Anamara commented from her seat just below Hegrin's.

Hegrin giggled aloud.

"Becoming Queen of Rendel hasn't done a thing to improve your sense of decorum," Ashen noted, smiling in spite of herself. "Or, for that matter, your overfondness for sweets."

"My ladies make me eat what you'd call 'sensibly,'" Hegrin retorted, "meaning just a little sweet after meals, but today is special."

"And my son, your lord King husband?" Rannore said. She also was smiling.

"Oh, he never has had the taste for sweets that I have," Hegrin said. She smiled, the dimple at the corner of her mouth showing. "Sometimes, though, he gives his share to me."

"I take it, then, that it is a happy match?"

Hegrin turned her clear gaze on her mother. "Yes, it is a happy match. We grow fonder of each other by the day and long for the time, fast approaching, when we shall reach our majority and can fully become husband and wife."

"Then I am happy for you," Ashen said.

She turned to her friend. "And you, Rannore? How does your daughter Laherne?"

"She thrives," Rannore said happily, "and Lathrom dotes on her. I hope, though, for his sake, that our next will be a boy, as yours was."

The fashions of the time, high-waisted and full of skirt, could have masked even an advanced pregnancy. Even if Rannore's dress hid it, the telltale glow to her face proclaimed her condition clearly. Ashen squeezed Rannore's hand. "I am surprised that you would risk travel at this time."

"I think I am stronger than you in that regard," Rannore said. "I have seldom felt as well as I do now. And in any event," she continued, "how could I miss your coronation?"

"What did you bring as your coronation gift?" Hegrin asked around a mouthful of preserved fruit. "Lord Royance said a silvergilt basin would be appropriate. I have no idea what use it could possibly be. He asked me to convey his regrets, by the way. What did Granddam Ysa send?"

"One like it, only larger," Anamara said a little wryly. "She had it sent all the way down to New Vold with her note of regret for not attending, and insisted on my bringing the useless thing along with me."

"I suppose that was to make up for not digging herself out of Yewkeep long enough to come here," Rannore commented. "We sent the new NordornKing a set of the finest armor the Rendel smiths could devise, the match to Lathrom's best, and inlaid with silver and gold. And for the new NordornQueen, twenty ells of fine linen to be used as she wills. It's bound to be warm in this country, eventually."

Ashen laughed aloud. "As Gaurin predicted, I have grown to love the cold and the snow," she said, "and will miss it when it departs for our very brief summer. But your gift is very much welcome."

Finally, the feast ended and the musicians began to play, signaling that the dancing was about to begin. By the rules of etiquette, Gaurin and Ashen would lead the first galliard. Then they would be free to dance or move about the room as they pleased.

Ashen was eager to take another look at the bejeweled Dragon Box that Anamara had sent her, and so, as soon as she could, she made her way to the room just off the Hall. She went straight for the box. The complicated clasp puzzled her for a moment, but then she solved the riddle and opened it. The lid sealed tightly, proof against damp or rot.

Instead of the quills, ink, and paper she had expected to find, the box was empty save for a letter written on heavy paper, and sealed with wax. She recognized the impression on the wax as Rohan's personal signet, a circle inside which waves crashed against the edges of the border. It had come from an amulet Zazar had given him, and which he had taken for his badge. But why would he have put a letter inside Anamara's gift and not handed it to her at once?

She broke the seal and opened it. The writing and the signature at the bottom showed it to have come from Anamara. She must have borrowed Rohan's seal, not having one of her own. Ashen made a mental note to provide her with one, even before her own lack had been taken care of. Then she began to read.

Greetings, Madame Mother.

Not only my dear husband and yours fought hard against the Ice Dragons of recent memory, and those who rode them and those who followed them, but you yourself entered the battle and for that the people you saved will ever hold your memory dear.

This box that you presently hold in your hands is an artifact from the ruined city of Galinth, even now rising from its long slumber. I visited there, curious to see with unshadowed eyes the place where I stayed when I was still under the spell of the Sorceress. There I found this and knew it could go to no one save you.

Ashen remembered the ruins of Galinth well, having visited there many times both before she left the Bog to go to Rendel and the life there, and after. She read on.

Those who are uncovering the wonders of the lost city were reluctant at first to yield the Dragon Box to me, but when I told them who it was for, and for what occasion, they gave it me gladly. And so it now rests in your hands.

Bog-men—though they no longer look or act like the low savages they once were—and men of Rendelsham work side by side. One of them, a man called Tusser, actually put the box in my hands, for you. "Show this to my Lady Ashen and tell her that I am still hers to command," he told me. Another, a Rendelian scholar, told me that in the time period this dates from it was the fashion for boxes of this kind to contain a hidden mechanism. If you could find the proper spot and pressed on it, a tiny spring would open a false bottom to reveal a hidden compartment.

I did not attempt to find or open the secret compartment, preferring to save this surprise for you, the guardian whom I love and revere, and to whom I owe so much.

It was signed with Anamara's name and a little drawing of an ash leaf. Her new seal would be—what? Ashen smiled, an idea coming to her. Anamara must have believed, Ashen thought, that she would not be coming to the Castle of Fire and Ice when she gave it to Rohan to be conveyed north.

She beckoned to a page who was standing guard in the room full of treasures and he sprang forward at once.

"Your command, NordornQueen?"

"First, find the best sealmaker and tell him I wish to commission a seal for my daughter Anamara. The device, a snow rose superimposed on an ash leaf. Tell the artisan to set everything else aside if necessary, so he can have it ready before she departs for her home. Then, please have this box taken to my private apartment," she said.

"Your commands will be obeyed." He saluted and hurried off to find a maid to deliver the article as requested, and to find the artisan to carve a seal for the NordornQueen's kindred.

She gazed at the jeweled dragon ornamenting the lid of the box. Now she could see that the stones were pearls, opals, and moonstones set in silver tracery, and tiny fire-stones formed its eyes. A hidden compartment might also explain the box's unexpected weight. She longed to pursue the mystery but put her curiosity aside for the moment. She would not abandon her duties toward her honored guests to indulge herself.

Then she went back out into the Hall once more where the celebration looked nowhere near ending any time soon.

Dawn was beginning to turn the eastern sky pearly gray before the last guest went to bed, allowing Gaurin and Ashen to do likewise. Ashen was so tired she could have fallen asleep, still standing, on the spot.

"Leave it," she told an equally weary Ayfare, as they surveyed the state the Hall was in. "There is time enough later to clean the place."

"No," Ayfare said firmly. "You forget, when the guests wake up they will be wanting food and good service without a second thought as to how this miracle is accomplished. It would reflect badly on you if they were greeted with the destruction they created."

And so saying, she began to direct maids, who set to work at once clearing away the remains of the feast, taking up soiled linen to be washed, gathering platters and utensils to be cleansed. Others she put to work sweeping up the debris that littered the floor save for where the dancing had taken place.

"Go, go," she directed Ashen. "We both have our duties. Yours is to greet your guests when you see them again as if you were so royal you have no need for sleep. Mine is to make all ready for that occasion. I'll rest later."

Seeing the sense in Ayfare's statements but concerned for her well-being at the same time, Ashen started for the great stairway that led to the royal apartments. From habit, she looked for Gaurin, remembering belatedly that he would be bidding their guests a good night. Instead, she caught a glimpse of the Seneschal, Nalren. Though she might be forced to abandon her friend to her duties, Nalren was not; he had already summoned pages and manservants to take over the heavy work from the tired women.

Gaurin appeared at her side. "Perhaps the next celebration we'll be holding at the Castle of Fire and Ice will be a quiet wedding between two of our most trusted and valuable servants," he said softly.

"If it will bring her only a portion of the contentment I have found with you, then I will be glad for it."

Then Ashen allowed him to help her to their apartment and to their bed. She scarcely remembered pulling the coverlet over her before it was full morning and time to take up her duties again.

It would be several days before she had the opportunity to examine the Dragon Box, and she was hard-pressed to curb her impatience. Fortunately, only a few of the guests from other lands would be staying on past the coronation day; most expressed regret at the necessity of returning to their homes.

"Seldom have I seen greater hospitality, even though your castle is not complete," the ambassador from the island Kingdom of Writham stated, and the ambassador from Yuland, who would be traveling with him on the same ship, nodded agreement.

"It is plain that the NordornLand is in good hands once more," the Yulander said.

Both bowed low and took their departure.

Queen Hegrin and King Peres left as well. Rendel could not long afford to have their monarchs absent, even with Lord Royance at the head of the Council table. Ashen hugged both of them close.

"Let us have visits back and forth very often," she said. "Peres—I call you that, not as King of Rendel, but as my daughter's husband and my son-in-law—I confess that I was against this match at first. You are both so young. But Hegrin tells me that you are happy, and that is enough for me."

"And for me, Ashen NordornQueen," Peres told her, his youthful voice cracking. Manfully, he strove for a deeper tone. "Let us never forget that our bonds of friendship go as deep as our ties of kinship."

"Well said." Gaurin held out his hand, and the King of Rendel grasped it warmly. "Though between us there is no need for words on paper, nevertheless, I will draw up a treaty to show others how firmly our two lands are joined."

"It is well thought on, Gaurin NordornKing," said Peres. Then he turned to Hegrin. "Alas, we cannot stay the tide. Come. Do not weep. We will all be together again as soon as we can."

Ashen embraced Lathrom, and then Rannore, who would be accompanying the Rendel monarchs. "Let what was said apply equally to you, my friends."

"Can it be else?" Lathrom said, his deep voice rumbling in his chest. "Gaurin NordornKing, know that, with my own lord's permission—" he nodded at Peres, who inclined his head in return "—if it haps that you should find yourself in peril, if a remnant of the late enemy's evildoing should remain and arise to bring you harm, then I am yours to command, as I ever was."

"Thank you," Gaurin said.

They were all at the top of the stairway that clung to the side of the cliff on which the Castle of Fire and Ice stood. From far below, someone on the ship bearing the Rendel royal emblem raised a shout. "Tide's beginning to turn!"

"We cannot stay the day." Lathrom turned to Peres. "Look carefully and watch out for Queen Hegrin, for the way is steep. I will go before you and conduct your lady mother, my wife, lest she fall."

"I need no help," Hegrin said, laughing, her voice carrying clearly on the chill air. So saying, she lifted her skirts, leaped ahead of Lathrom despite his attempt to catch her, and scrambled nimbly down the stairs ahead of them all.

"And to think, I was about to cry," Ashen commented.

Nevertheless, a few tears escaped unbidden as she stood watching until the ship bearing her daughter, her son-in-law, her best friend and her husband Lathrom had cleared the fjord and turned south, on its way back to Rendel. She wiped them away resolutely.

At last all the guests had departed except for Rohan and Anamara, all the gay pennons struck save theirs. Ashen sent word, asking them to meet her and Gaurin within the hour, in the sitting room of the private quarters she and Gaurin shared. "I thought, since this was Anamara's gift, and there is a little mystery involved with it, it was only fair that she and Rohan be with us when I open it," she explained to Gaurin.

"I confess, I am curious as well," Gaurin replied, "though the matter had to be set aside for a while."

While they were waiting for Rohan and Anamara to arrive, Gaurin, at Ashen's direction, set the Dragon Box on a table and opened the lid.

"I can't explain why I am so drawn to this out of so many gifts we have received," Ashen said. She ran her fingers along the edge of the box, noting where the ancient artifact had suffered slightly with the passing of the years. There was something—"Gaurin, look!" she exclaimed. "Here, where there is what seems to be a chip out of the wood."

"Perhaps that is the spot where the hidden spring is located."

She tried pressing on it with her fingernail, then with the tip of a hairpin, to no avail. At that moment, there was a rap on the door, and Rohan and Anamara entered.

"Playing with Anamara's trick box, I see," Rohan said, smiling. "I don't think there's any truth to that story, but it was amusing, and the thing is pretty, I have to admit. Too bad the Ice Dragons we faced were such ugly beasts, and not a gem among 'em. Otherwise, we'd all still be squabbling over the treasure."

"Oh, Rohan, you never take anything seriously," Anamara said. She turned to Ashen. "I received your gift today! Thank you. It pleases me well. Also, I'm glad you like my gift to you. And I am gladder still that you chose to try to solve its riddle with both of us close at hand."

"You, my Anamara, just you," Rohan said. "I don't care about riddles. But I could do with a little heated wine."

Gaurin touched a bellpull and a maid entered, to be dispatched speedily to provide the beverage. "We're running a little short," the NordornKing admitted, "but I am told that the new wine from the vineyards around the Oakenkeep is excellent."

"While you're waiting for it, let me send you a dozen casks from the stores at New Vold," Rohan said.

"And in return, I'll provide you and your lady with enough snow-thistle silk for garments for both of you and your son."

"Done, sir!" The two men shook on the bargain.

While this pleasant banter had been going on, Ashen had pulled a chair close to the table and indicated that Anamara should join her in examining the Dragon Box. She tried probing anew on the supposed chip she had located earlier. Then a portion of the wood finish—a veneer—flaked away, leaving a bright gleam. "Gaurin!" she exclaimed. "Oh, do look here!"

He examined the spot she indicated. Then he began to smile. "Rohan, Anamara, you have given us more than you knew, in terms of sheer value," he commented. "The Dragon Box only seems to be made of wood. Beneath the finish, it covers what looks to be pure silver."

"What?" Rohan exclaimed incredulously. "And to think, when I arrived here with the gifts, I just tossed the box down to Grof in the boat taking Granddam Zaz to shore, thinking it would float if he missed. This treasure might even now be lying at the bottom of the fjord!"

"The lid seals tightly," Ashen said. "But you could have taken better care."

The two women had been taking turns carefully picking away the wood sheathing on the interior of the box. Partially revealed was a smooth surface of silver, with an embossed seal stamped into the side just under the hinges.

By this time, both Gaurin and Rohan were peering over their shoulders. "The spring is in the middle of that design, unless I miss my guess," Gaurin said.

Ashen took up the hairpin she had been using earlier and probed in the area. All four were rewarded with the sound of a muffled *click!* and the false bottom of the chest loosened visibly, enough that it could be pried up so the compartment beneath lay revealed. In it lay two articles—a bracelet composed, oddly, of nine tiny teeth strung on a thin chain, and what seemed to be another letter, folded tightly but bearing no seal.

"Oh, do read it, Madame Mother!" Anamara exclaimed, her eyes sparking with excitement.

Ashen set the bracelet aside, wondering what it was and why someone had taken the trouble to hide it for so many years. Then she caught her breath as she took out the ancient piece of parchment. Trying to ignore the tingling in her fingers, she smoothed out the creases, touching it as little as possible. The letters were incomprehensible to her.

ᛗᚠᚾᛋ ᛋᛗᚠᚱᛋ ᚠᚷᛩ ᛈᚺᛗᛏ ᚷᚠᚠᛁᛏᛏᚺ ᛈᚠᛋ ᚠ ᛋᛩᚾᛏᚷ ᚾᛏᛗ
ᛈᛩᚾᚱᛁᛋᚺᛁᛏᚷ . . .

"The language must be very ancient. I think I have seen it before, but I cannot read it," she said. "Call for Zazar."

The Wysen-wyf came bustling in presently, frowning as she was told of what had been transpiring. "You should have consulted me in the first place," she said gruffly. "I could have solved your mystery in much less time."

"Ah, yes, Madame Zazar, but then my Ashen would not have enjoyed figuring it out for herself."

Zazar scowled at Gaurin. "Hmmph," she sniffed. "Well, then, let me have a look at it."

She peered at the old document, and the scowl gradually left her face. "Interesting," she said, as if to herself. "Interesting indeed."

"What is it?" Ashen asked.

"Even if you can't recognize the letters you can almost read it, in the small drawings to the side of the writing," Zazar said. She took the hairpin from Ashen and began pointing out the illustrations for the text. "Many years ago, when Galinth was a young and flourishing city and true kings ruled in Rendel, an old and powerful male Dragon arose and, in his wrath, laid waste to the Land of Ever Snow to the north." She glanced up. "That would be the old name for the NordornLand. A brave knight conquered him in battle—see here?—but he died as well. To honor this knight, smiths versed in the magical arts fashioned a fabulous sword from the creature's scales."

"I've never heard this legend," Ashen said.

"Nor I, though it refers to my homeland," Gaurin commented, intrigued.

"There's more." She returned to the parchment, tracing the words and drawings, half-reading, half-paraphrasing. "Ice Dragons, unless they are deliberately hunted down and killed, are well-nigh immortal. At the time this document was written and hidden away, the female still lived though it was thought she had hidden herself and escaped into deep sleep, unable to bear her grief for her lost mate. This legend, as you call it, Gaurin, goes on to say that only this sword, the Dragon Blade, will slay the Mother Ice Dragon. Unfortunately, nobody knows where her lair is, and furthermore, the Dragon Blade has disappeared." She looked up at her fascinated listeners. "That's all the parchment says."

"But not all there is to the tale, I'll warrant," Ashen stated. "Gaurin, do you think—"

"—that the Great Foulness awoke this Mother Ice Dragon and caused her to create the ones we faced in the recent war?" His expression was very serious. "It is entirely possible."

"Then," Rohan said slowly, "what we fought were merely—youngsters." He shuddered in spite of himself.

"Again, young Rohan, it is entirely possible."

"You have solved one mystery only to uncover a deeper one," Zazar commented. Her expression gave away nothing.

Ashen studied the Dragon Box again. Pearls and moonstones—these were Ice Dragons depicted on it. It could not be a coincidence. "Gaurin, I must go to Galinth," Ashen said abruptly. "And I must take Zazar with me. Will you go?" she asked, turning to the Wysen-wyf, who nodded.

"If you hadn't spoken first, I would have insisted," Zazar said. "I had already determined to go from the moment I put my hand on this parchment and knew its Power."

"I felt it, too," Ashen said. "A tingling in my fingers." She wiped her hands, scarcely aware of what she was doing.

"There's bound to be something that later scholars discovered about this. Can you think it was really an accident that Anamara came into possession of the Dragon Box or that she chose it for your coronation gift?"

"No, I do not. It was as if we were meant to find it," Ashen said. "I think it is a warning—but from where or from whom, I do not know. I do propose to find out, however."

Gaurin thought for a moment, his brow creased. "I find that I agree," he said finally, "for this might represent a renewed danger to us all if the Mother Ice Dragon is still abroad. Sorely though you will be missed, my NordornQueen, it is upon my shoulders that the rebuilding of the NordornLand must fall. Bjauden is old enough that it will do him no harm if his mother is absent for a while—a short while, I hope."

"As do I," Ashen said. She turned to Rohan. "You planned to sail with the morning tide. Will you take me and Zazar with you?"

"Of course, Ashen," he said.

"We will be ready at dawn."

Three

*G**aurin notified his young kinsman*, Cebastian, now holding the post of commander of the House Troops of the NordornQueen, to assemble a small contingent of guards. At dawn, he and six Nordorn soldiers were waiting when Ashen and Zazar embarked on *Spume Maiden* to return to Rendel.

Under ordinary circumstances, Ashen would have enjoyed the voyage down the coast to New Vold. The weather was fair, without the danger of early spring storms, and as they sailed south to sunnier climes, she could see the color of the water changing from frigid gray to a more moderate blue. Also, she was always glad to be in the company of her foster son, Rohan, and the daughter-in-law she had come to respect. Rohan and Cebastian spent a great deal of time together, being friends from the time when both were young knights-in-training, in the Dowager Queen Ysa's Great Levy. Also, there was young Obern, who could be thought of as Ashen's first grandchild, though she had not yet passed her thirtieth year.

The first few days of the journey proved stressful. The NordornQueen had her heart in her throat, constantly alert because of the utter fearlessness of the toddler. He would race from railing to railing, often falling on his plump bottom, always laughing and daring to stagger on, on some errand known only to infants of his age. He had been put into the little leading-strings harness that children of this age customarily wore, but seldom was anyone holding the other end of the rope. Ashen could clearly picture the little boy falling overboard and being lost forever.

Today, the sun being out and the waves calm, she and Zazar were sitting in chairs placed for them on the deck. She had relaxed formality enough that she had laid aside the elaborate headdress, and now her pale hair was covered by a veil. The fresh sea breeze rustled both veil and hair most pleasantly, and Ashen found that she had missed this sort of freedom. Anamara was still below, giving instructions to the cook for refreshments to be brought to them, and Weyse had found a place to hide from the vigorous attentions of Obern, who was fascinated by her.

"Oh, don't fuss so," Zazar told Ashen, a trifle complacently, Ashen thought. "The Sea-Rovers are smarter about their children than you give them credit for being. If that child is going to fall into the ocean, better he learn caution now, while there's a way to fish him out quickly."

That very thing happened just as Zazar was speaking. A scream—more of outrage than of fear, Ashen thought—a splash, and then two Sea-Rovers, laughing uproariously, were vying for the line and the privilege of rescuing their Chieftain's young son from the chill water.

"What say we drag him along for a while?" one of them said, grinning. "Just pull him up enough so he skims the waves? Give him a taste of ship life, it will."

"If it was yours, I'd say yes and not even pull him up," the other retorted.

Other seamen had gathered around these two, and they joined the laughter, enjoying the joke. Ashen started to rise from her chair, and Zazar put her hand on Ashen's arm.

"Leave be," she said. "They know what they're doing."

Still laughing and offering wagers as to how many more times it would take, dunking the boy, until he learned caution, the men pulled him up and onto the deck once more. Now Obern found his voice and began to wail—but again, Ashen noted that his cries seemed to be far more of outrage than discomfort, though he had to be chilled through.

Anamara appeared on deck with a Sea-Rover close behind carrying a tray. Unhurriedly and displaying little concern, she took Obern, now wrapped in a makeshift towel, and started toward the door leading to the Chieftain's quarters. "Hush now," she told Obern. "You aren't hurt." Then, to the other women, she said, "I'm going to put him down for a nap now, after I get him into dry clothes."

"Well, she certainly doesn't seem to be alarmed at any of this," Ashen commented.

"No point in it," Zazar said. "If you want my advice, don't borrow trouble and let her bring up her brat her own way, which seems to be as the Sea-Rovers do."

Ashen bit back any further remarks she might have been inclined to make and turned the conversation to lighter topics.

The remainder of the voyage passed with little incident, and no repeat of young Obern's getting a thorough dunking. Perhaps, Ashen thought, he had actually learned his lesson. She did not allow herself to think that there might be some merit in the way the Sea-Rovers dealt with obstreperous children, but she did note that Weyse had cautiously come out of hiding again.

As the ship made its way down the coast of Rendel, Ashen could see for herself the changes that had been wrought when over a year earlier she, Zazar, and the Dowager Ysa had faced down the Great Foulness and, as far as anyone had ever been able to ascertain, destroyed him. The events of that day remained hazy in her mind for she had been taken over by a Power she had never even imagined could exist.

There were still cliffs along the coastline in this area, but they were considerably less lofty than before, and the waterfalls that continued to drain the land were sweet and wholesome, with no smudge of the decaying life that had spread out over the sea before. The slumbering beauty of the land was awakening, and Ashen enjoyed watching the scenery as, dreamlike, it floated past.

The entrance of the Sea-Rover ship into the sheltered bay at New Vold provided another pleasant sight, for the countryside, where she could glimpse it, was now fresh and green. The snow and ice that had clogged it for too long had disappeared, and all around there were signs of the land's rebirth.

"And yet I long for the NordornLand," she murmured to herself, "and its crisp, chill air."

"You're its queen," Zazar said. "You have to like it."

Ashen turned to the woman she had, for years, thought of as her Protector. There was the merest hint of a twinkle in Zazar's eye, and so Ashen knew she was being teased—something she was still far from accustomed to, from the Wysen-wyf. "For that reason and more," she said with some humor. "It is now my home. And yours as well."

Zazar sniffed. "Wouldn't have been for long if it weren't for that fabric your women weave—you know, the stuff that keeps me warm."

"Snow-thistle silk," Ashen said. "We've got several lengths with us as well, for gifts."

She was wearing ordinary garments made of this miraculous fiber, warm enough at need but never too warm, as were Zazar, Anamara, young Obern, and even Rohan, wherever he might be. She had glimpsed him but seldom on the voyage, for he was kept busy elsewhere. He took his duties as Chieftain of the Sea-Rovers very seriously and, she was pleased to note, the people whom he commanded seemed to lack little of the respect he was due. He was, at last, settling down and, she knew, she had Anamara to thank for that.

In a remarkably short time, the little ship was docked and its passengers on dry land.

"Will you stay a while, Madame Mother?" Anamara inquired. "We can put an entire tower of New Vold at your disposal."

"Thank you, but I feel I must get about the errand that brought me here," Ashen replied. "Perhaps, after I have learned what I can at Galinth, my mind will be easy enough that I can accept your offer."

"Until then."

Rohan supplied horses for Ashen, Zazar, and her Nordorner escort. Zazar decided to ride rather than trudge stolidly as was her long custom, prompting Ashen to vow to keep an even closer eye on the woman who had reared her. I will go north to Rendelsham, Ashen thought, before our return. There she could have another day or two in her daughter's company and, if she were lucky, could persuade Zazar to allow Master Lorgan, the most skilled physician in Rendel, to have a look at her.

Also, having seen glimpses of Rendel from a distance, she wanted to witness at close hand the renewal that the three women—Ysa, Zazar, and Ashen, each holders of their own sort of Power—had brought to the land. It was likely, she thought, that the effects of the terrible cold would linger, and Rendel would remain in an eternal springtime with no extreme in the seasons. Vanished, however, was the lingering and persistent chill that had plagued the Dowager so heavily and had prompted her to keep a fire ever roaring on the hearth.

As if she could read Ashen's thoughts, Zazar broke into Ashen's reverie. "Ysa remains in seclusion at Yewkeep, according to what I've heard," she said. "Retired from the world."

"She has earned her ease," Ashen said, "and I do not plan to interrupt it."

Zazar laughed outright. "We'll see," she said. "My guess is that she's 'retired' behind a thick veil to hide the wrinkles her magic spells kept at bay too long. And I'd wager she hasn't learned to love you any better, even after all that's happened."

"As you yourself instructed me, don't borrow trouble," Ashen retorted. "I have still to visit the Oakenkeep to see that all is in order. Then, the sooner I am at Galinth, the easier I will be." She touched a leather packet, which contained a hastily drawn copy of the document she had discovered in the false bottom of the Dragon Box.

The little company jogged along the road that paralleled the River Rendel, separating the land that had used to be known as the Bog from the lands around New Vold, which bordered those surrounding the Oakenkeep. For years the now-vanished marsh wilderness had been Ashen's home.

As they entered Oakenkeep territory she noted that here, too, all was neat and well tended. Cebastian nudged his mount until he was riding next to her. "In all the time I lived here, the land never looked so good, nor the new crops so vigorous," he commented.

"It is good to see prosperity returning," she replied. "I feared all of Rendel had taken permanent harm from the hateful efforts of the Great Foulness and his minions." Privately, she rejoiced as well for the revenues from her lands that would shortly begin flowing into her privy purse—money that would go far toward rebuilding another part of the world that the Great Foulness had corrupted, her now beloved NordornLand.

The little company spent one night at the Oakenkeep, then began to journey westward toward a ford in the River Rendel that would lead them swiftly to Galinth.

To Ashen's surprise and pleasure, she discovered a stone bridge being constructed near the ford, which would improve access from the eastern portions of Rendel. "The Bog must be unrecognizable," she said to Zazar.

"Mostly, it is," the older woman replied. She shifted Weyse in her arms. "You're heavy," she told the sleepy little furred creature.

"Here, give Weyse to me for a while," Ashen said. With a contented sigh, Weyse snuggled into the NordornQueen's arms and began to snore softly.

Zazar began shaking her right hand, trying to restore circulation. "There's still plenty for the new Wysen-wyf to do. Not everybody welcomed the Change when it came."

"Then there really is such a person."

"Of course. Chances are they haven't built new roads yet, and the best way to Galinth goes right by the village and my old hut. I'll introduce you. Her name is Nayla."

When the company arrived at the village, Ashen had the odd feeling that here scarcely anything had changed. Wisps of smoke still rose in the still air from the cluster of huts, and outside the one where she had grown up, a woman stirred a kettle. The familiar, noxious smell told her that it was mollusk glue, such as the villagers had always used to repair the thatched roofs of their dwellings.

The woman glanced up, unsurprised at the sight of the former Wysen-wyf, accompanied by a woman richly clad and carrying a sleeping unworldly creature, and, in her train, a troop of armed men, appearing before her door. "Greetings, Zazar," she said. "And those with you."

"Greetings in return, Nayla," Zazar said. She slid down from her saddle. "Still having trouble with that roof, I see."

Nayla shrugged. "There are those as would build in the new style, heavy stone walls and wooden roofs, but I like the old ways. I could use some new thatch, though."

"D'you have any soup made? Or are you going without while you use the kettle for other purposes?"

At that, Nayla gave a grin. "I've come up in the world. Two kettles now. This is the old one and yes, there's soup. Wager my noodles will stand up to yours for tastiness, too." She glared at one of the soldiers. "You, there. Come stir the glue and don't let it separate, or it'll be ruined, and you'll have to go gather the makings for a new batch. The rest of you, come inside and eat a bite."

As the company dismounted and followed the new Wysen-wyf into the hut, Nayla nudged Zazar in the ribs. "I'll relieve that fellow out there in a while. Let him think he'll go hungry. Do him some good, I'll wager. Now, what brings you here, in the company of this fine lady? Ashen, is it? The one you reared? She's come up in the world, too."

"Yes, it's Ashen, but Outside, you'd have to bow and curtsey and call her NordornQueen. Ashen, this is Nayla."

A little at a loss, Ashen had the absurd feeling that she should be the one to bow. She held out her hand to Nayla. "It is good to meet the one who is the successor to Zazar," she said.

"Hmmph," Nayla responded. She stared at Ashen's out-stretched hand and, after a moment, touched it with her own. "Well, sit down. I don't keep any finer store here than Zazar did, so you'll just have to make do."

The Wysen-wyf bustled about, ladling soup thick with tart, edible sourgrass and noodles into bowls for everyone. "Here, take this to the lout stirring the glue," she said, handing a bowl to Cebastian, "and take your turn with the paddle."

He cast a wry glance at Ashen, then ducked out of the hut to do as he was told. There was no gainsaying a Wysen-wyf, young or old, his glance told her, and suddenly Ashen felt at home.

"Please," she said, "tell us of what has been transpiring in . . . I suppose you can't really call it the Bog anymore."

Nayla shrugged. "It is as you see," she said. "Things are better than they were, mostly. The people are free of a long shadow that they labored under for generations, but it has left its mark."

"Yes, I noticed that that part of Rendel I have seen also bears traces of what it lately endured, and that was for a much shorter time than the Bog has been in existence."

"Having land that can grow food, fresh water instead of brackish, and being free of Gulpers is a boon, but some will still long for the old ways," Zazar commented. "Only to be expected. Bog-men, many of them, had iron skulls." She slurped noodles.

"Many of them still do," Nayla said unconcernedly. "The older ones know what it was like before, but the youngsters are the ones who complain and moon about for the former days. Fools, all of them. I'll always have plenty to do."

"I can't imagine a world without a Wysen-wyf in it," Ashen said politely.

Nayla stared at her over the rim of her bowl, mouth corners turned down. "Pretty manners, is it?" she said sharply. "Better than having an oaf as NordornQueen, but with me, speak your mind, girl."

Ashen smiled. "Now I know that you are the Wysen-wyf indeed," she said. "And that what remains of the Bog, and of the Bog-men, are in good, tough hands."

"I told you so," Zazar said, her tone almost too low to be heard. Then, louder, "Have you been practicing what I taught you, Nayla? Mixing the potion and adding castings from the Web of the Weavers?"

"Yes. It is good you chanced by, Zazar. It was very . . . unusual. Both my kettles are in use, or I'd show you how I did it." She turned to Ashen. "You'll just have to take my word. There are new things, not all favorable, coming into your life, Ashen NordornQueen."

"What sort of things?"

"Can't say."

"Can't—or won't?" There was a hint of sharpness in Ashen's question that she couldn't quite suppress.

"Don't trifle with me, girl! I said 'can't,' and that's what I mean. There were omens, and all I can do is tell you about them. Now, forewarned, you can keep a sharp eye out. Thank the Powers that Zazar had the wit to bring you to me. Otherwise, I can see you'd have ridden right past on your high horse and never known about it."

"I apologize. Please," Ashen said, "tell me of what you have seen."

"That's better," Nayla sniffed, somewhat mollified. "A *person*, man or woman I do not know, will be at that big stone box where you live up north, and there will be upset. That's all I know."

Ashen knew better than to question the Wysen-wyf further. A worthy successor to Zazar, she might be entirely capable of delivering a sharp slap for Ashen's impertinence, her queenly station notwithstanding. "Then I will be careful of all who come to the Castle of Fire and Ice," she told Nayla, "and I am grateful for the warning."

"It's more than I can do, these days," Zazar commented. She turned to Ashen. "I gave Nayla a great deal of my Power, you see. Now, with what she's told you, I wonder if I didn't grant her too much of it."

Nayla gave a snort of laughter. "Not likely!" she said derisively. "You've forgotten more than I'll learn over the next century! Get off that soft cushion you've been resting your backside on and start practicing again. You're far enough away now that we won't interfere with one another, and surely this girl can afford to buy you a kettle. I'll provide you with a box of Web threads. A fresh supply has come my way. Cost dearly, too, and trade-pearls are hard to come by these days."

"Then, please, allow me to provide you with coins," Ashen

said. "That much, I can do. And new thatch, and anything else you need."

"Thanks," Nayla said shortly. "I'll make a list and get it to you before you return north."

Ashen put aside her worry over what the new Wysen-wyf had told her as she rode toward Galinth. Time enough to consider Nayla's words when she arrived in the NordornLand. Now, she was engrossed in the changes that had come to the Bog.

Where there had once been narrow paths skirting pools both deep and shallow, the lurking places of hideous creatures, the old roads had begun to emerge once more to be cleared of the deep mire that had covered them. Ashen remembered a time when she had been in peril and had relied on stepping-stones just under the surface of the water to escape from an island on which she had been cornered by those who might have caused her harm. The pools and the island had long since vanished, but here and there stone columns remained, marking where great houses had once stood. Pavement formerly overgrown with slimy moss and clods of coarse grass now led straight and true to the walls of the lost city of Galinth.

Ashen gasped when she saw it. The walls gleamed in the sun, and she marveled. If Galinth was this beautiful now, in its ruin, how much more so it must have been when it was at the height of its strength and glory! What, she wondered, had caused the downfall of such a mighty citadel?

Once there had been a double gate; she could see the rusted hinges at either side though all traces of the wooden doors these hinges had once held had long since vanished. Close by she glimpsed the stone figure of a giant lupper that had frightened her, many years ago, when she chanced upon it as she fled from one like it in flesh. She became aware that men were approaching from the city, through this empty gate, and she set aside her memory of the fearsome stone statue.

"Greetings, honored strangers," said one of the men. He was

very tall and lean, with a snowy beard that reached almost to his waist. "I am Master Emmorys, and I have the honor of heading the scholars who delve here." He indicated the men with him. "This is Berrore, and this—"

One of them interrupted Master Emmorys, his mouth agape. "It is Ashen! Ashen NordornQueen! Does you remembers me?"

Ashen stared at him uncomprehendingly for a moment before she recognized who he was. "It is Tusser, is it not?" Ashen replied. "Of course I remember you. How well you look." Indeed, his appearance had altered even more than from when she had last glimpsed him, his posture straightening after the Change as all the Bog-men became less bestial and more human.

"Now I works alongside Master Emmorys," Tusser said proudly. "I have learn—learned to read and write, and Master Emmorys depend on me."

Emmorys bowed low from the waist. "Greetings again, Ashen NordornQueen. We had heard we could expect you, but not the day nor the hour. Will you come inside?"

"Gladly," Ashen responded. "I am most eager to discover what you have learned about everything in general and a few things in particular."

"Then we will be glad to share our knowledge with you. It is seldom that anyone other than those whose interests lie solely with the past come and visit us."

The party dismounted and followed the elderly scholar inside the city. Glancing around, Ashen could see that many of the buildings, rescued from the mire in which they had been encased for untold years, were now habitable. Two such buildings, across the square, were even now being prepared for the use of the newcomers, judging from the numbers of people going in and out.

"It is good to see Tusser at work on your worthy endeavor," she said.

"He is invaluable. There is no one like Tusser to sniff out exactly where to set the workers to dig next," Emmorys said, glancing at him with fond respect. "It must come from having lived a lifetime in the Bog."

"I like learn," Tusser said. "Like old city becoming new city again. Much honor to Bog."

"People will journey from everywhere to see, once we have completed our task," Emmorys said. "Your quarters are not yet finished, but I will be happy to offer mine until they are. Will you rest after your travels, Ashen NordornQueen, and later we will talk about these particular questions you have?"

"I am not tired," she said. She held out the leather packet to Emmorys. "Herein lies a document bearing the source of the questions. It was found in an, an artifact that came from here."

"It will be my privilege to examine it straightaway, and give you answer as soon as may be."

Ashen glanced around. "Thank you. While I wait for your reply, may I examine what wonders you have discovered?"

"Please, start in yonder building, where we have stored a number of treasures, one of which in particular will be interesting to you," the elderly scholar said, eyes twinkling.

"Cebastian, set the men to helping those who are making available space for us. Zazar, take your ease if you're of a mind to. As for me, I will go with Master Emmorys, for I am all eagerness to gaze upon these wonders he spoke of."

"It goes against my grain for you to move about, even in this place, without escort," Cebastian said. "Also, it is Gaurin NordornKing's order that I accompany you wherever you go."

"And whatever it is you are looking for, I wouldn't dream of being somewhere else when you find it," Zazar said. She put Weyse down, and the little creature, awake at last, scampered off immediately as if in search of the places she had once been accustomed to go at will.

"It is good to have loyal people around you," Emmorys said. "Come this way, and I will show you the treasure I told you of."

They entered a long building, cool and with a lingering trace of dampness remaining in it. Despite the lack of windows, it was brightly lit with the kind of bone lights Ashen was familiar with from the burial chamber she had discovered in the ruins years before, and also in the hidden library under the Great Fane of the

Glowing in Rendelsham. The room was lined with tables on which had been spread artifacts uncovered by the workmen. Some of these items lay on other tables, where other scholars examined them, making notes and drawings. Emmorys nodded to them as he escorted the three people along the room. Engrossed in their work, the scholars barely acknowledged the fact that they had a visitor, let alone royalty, as they returned to their work.

"Here are our great treasures," Emmorys said, as they approached a smaller table.

On it lay two jeweled boxes, similar to the one Ashen had received but bearing different designs, along with bits of broken jewelry and, on a pillow, four rings set with great carved gems that glowed in the light. With wonder, Ashen gazed upon a ruby as big as her knuckle, and an equally impressive emerald. A third ring bore a golden topaz the size of a grape that looked as if it had gathered all the light of the room into its depths. But it was the fourth ring that made her gasp aloud.

It was an enormous sapphire set in heavy gold. The urge to reach out and take it was almost overwhelming. Resolutely, she clasped her hands behind her back.

"Yes, Ashen NordornQueen, we have discovered the signet rings of the Four Great Houses of Rendel, placed here for safekeeping during some ancient time of peril and strife, then lost when a mystery yet undiscovered caused the land to engulf the stronghold of Galinth. The one you look upon was made for Aldrin of Ash, and his name is still engraved inside the band. Now they belong to the heads of those Four Houses, and it is my honor to present the first of these to the heir of the House of Ash."

With that, he picked up the sapphire ring. As if in a dream, Ashen removed her old signet, bearing the Ash Tree rising from a flame, surrounded by the canting pun, "Without flame, there can be no Ash." She held out her right hand, and Master Emmorys slipped the sapphire on her middle finger.

At first it was far too large for her, but to her surprise, it snugged down into a perfect fit. Dazzled, she stared at it, turning it this way and that to examine the details of the intaglio carving, still as sharp as the day the genius craftsman had first taken up his drill.

A large letter "A" in ancient script was entwined with leaves of an ash tree that resembled tongues of fire. Beyond the bezel holding the stone, the gold setting was also fashioned in the shape of ash leaves, and this bezel bore not the canting pun Ashen was familiar with, but the ancient motto of the House of Ash—"Loyalty ever binds me." Though worn, the band of the ring was still thick and sturdy. It should have been too massive for Ashen's slender hand, but it looked, somehow, *right*. She found the weight of it to satisfy some forgotten need, as if it had returned after too long an absence.

She became aware that Master Emmorys was speaking again.

"The other rings are likewise engraved with their owners' names—Bartholo of Yew, Javis of Oak, Tybalt of Rowan. There is no dispute that of the few remnants of the House of Ash, you have the most standing. Some controversy remains, however, regarding to whom the other rings belong. Let me have your thoughts and see if they correspond with the majority."

"The House of Rowan is almost as barren as is Ash," Ashen responded, through lips that felt stiff and unused. "Yet there is an undisputed head—Lord Wittern, grandfather to King Peres. He was full of years the last time I saw him, and might be retired from public life by now, in which case the ring should go to his heir, the Lady Rannore, Peres's mother."

"That is the conclusion most of us have reached. What are your thoughts concerning the House of Oak?"

"Peres can claim unbroken and undisputed descent from a long line of Oak kings. It is to him that the ruby signet of Oak should go."

"Agreed. And what of Yew?"

Ashen finally looked up from the sapphire adorning her hand. "Yew has its strongest sprig in the person of the Dowager Queen Ysa," she said. "I'm certain she would cherish this artifact of her House."

Behind her, Zazar snorted in derision. "She always did have an eye for fine jewels," she commented. "She might not appreciate the importance of this one, but I'll lay a wager she can tell you to the last grain of gold how much it is worth."

"You do the Dowager an injustice," Ashen protested. "She was always deeply conscious of family."

"So much so that she. . . . Well, never mind," Zazar said. "Take the lot, girl. You can dole 'em out as we pass through Rendelsham, and then give Ysa's to her when we get to Yewkeep."

Startled, Ashen turned to stare at Zazar. "Yewkeep?" she demanded. "When did our plans change and we decide to go to Yewkeep?"

"You need to, now, to give Ysa her bauble," Zazar said with a shrug. She looked away, trying to keep her expression bland, but Ashen could see the amusement in her eyes.

"If I may speak," Cebastian said diffidently. He was having a hard time keeping his features appropriately neutral. It could even be thought that he too was amused.

"I suppose it is another order from my husband," Ashen said.

"Yes, Madame. Gaurin NordornKing bade me instruct you, if circumstances sent you to Rendelsham, that instead of retracing your steps to New Vold and journeying home by ship that I was to find sleds and dogs to pull them and thus return home more quickly by way of the ferry across the Sea-Rovers' Fjord. But he said not to mention this if it were not necessary."

"I see," Ashen said. She sighed. "Thank you. Both you and Gaurin have had great foresight, to look after my well-being."

"Madame." Cebastian bowed low.

She turned to Master Emmorys. "Sir, have you any objection to my removing these priceless objects and carrying them away with me, to deliver to their rightful owners?"

"None, Ashen NordornQueen. In fact, it seems to me that this is a perfect disposition for them."

"In that case, Cebastian, I charge you with their safety until they are in those owners' hands." She glared at Zazar, who refused to meet her eyes.

"I will find a fine case, suitable for holding such precious things," he said.

"No, that won't do," Zazar said. "Master Scholar, have you got any rags? Clean rags if you've got 'em, but dirty would do as well if not better."

For once startled out of his composure, Emmorys raised his snowy eyebrows. "Why—why yes, I suppose we do. Yes, of course there are rags."

"Then bring some. Cebastian, you've got a jar of smut—boot-black—with you, right? Well, then, press these things down into the jar, wrap it in rags, stuff it in the bottom of your saddle-bags," Zazar said.

"Madame Zazar—"

"Don't be a noddle-noodle," Zazar retorted. "Who would look for priceless jewels hidden in boot-black? Oh, take the case if you must." She shrugged. "Fill it with bits of broken stonework or any other trash that strikes your fancy. Then if it gets stolen, there's only the case lost. And the gems will clean up with a little work."

"I would never have thought of that," Emmorys said.

"Of course you wouldn't." Zazar smiled suddenly. "I can hardly wait to see the look on Ysa's face when she has to pry her nice emerald out of the smut."

When they had left the building housing the treasures of Galinth, Ashen found a moment in private with Zazar.

"How dare you say that I will take that wretched emerald to Ysa in such a way that I couldn't decline!" she said furiously.

"I have a feeling that you need to see Ysa," Zazar replied. "I was having some fun at your expense the other day, true, but I sincerely believe that her fate is intertwined with the mystery of the Dragon Box."

"I don't see how."

"I don't, either," Zazar admitted. "But it's how I feel, and you know I'm never wrong."

And so, Ashen had to accept it, unpleasant though the prospect of seeing Ysa again might be.

Four

Ashen stayed at Galinth for a week, wandering through the reclaimed ruins where she had once lived briefly. It was difficult, in places, recognizing the areas she had come to know. She realized that only the topmost portions of many buildings had been visible; the rest, surprisingly undamaged, had lain beneath the ground until the Change had caused the earth to crack and fall away as Galinth arose from its deep sleep. Most of the restoration crew's work involved digging away what still clung to walls and clogged interiors. Only a few places remained still buried. Each day brought new discoveries, new pieces of knowledge to be assessed and placed in the mosaic with that which was already known.

The catacombs, identified for her by Gaurin when they had visited there in the company of Zazar and Rohan, were now neatly cleared of all debris and the coating of moss and lichen that had stained the alabaster. The floors had been swept clean as well, and the pile of dust that had been all that remained of Gaurin's father, lost so many years ago, removed. She asked a worker about it.

"Aye, Madame," the man replied. "Was plain that used to be somebody fine until he met his end here in the Bog, bits of bone and a scrap or two of red cloth too fine for common folks. We gathered all and put it in yon urn." He indicated a gracefully shaped container now occupying a niche in the wall.

"Thank you," Ashen said. "He was—I suppose you could say a kind of relative, though I never met him."

She stood in silence for several moments, contemplating Count Bjauden of the Nordorners and his fate, before paying her respects to his memory. Then she moved on. There was never an end to the wonders of Galinth.

On an impulse, she next sought the stone figure of the giant lupper that had so frightened her, many years before.

The ground around it had risen and made smooth the area in which it stood. The moss, lichen, and bindweed that had covered it had been removed and the markings incised across the rounded belly cleaned out. If she had expected it to be less fearsome, resurrected from its ruin, she was mistaken. It still reared up on its more powerful hind limbs, while the forelimbs rested on the huge swell of its belly, and the large, bulbous eyes yet gleamed brightly yellow. The vertical pupil of each eye still reflected the shade of welling blood. She shuddered.

"Afraid of guardian, eh? Gulper." It was Tusser, who had come up beside her. "Right to be. He stand—stood there many years, and we have learn what he was for."

"Please, tell me!" Ashen exclaimed.

"He watchman," Tusser said, proud to show off his knowledge. "I tell you I learn read and write. I read you what it say across his belly: 'Approach with clean heart and know you are see—seen beforehand, stranger and friend alike.' "

Ashen gazed at the figure and at the writing.

ᚠᚲᚲᚱᛟᚠᚲᚺ ᛈᛁᛏᚺ ᚲᛚᛗᚨᚾ ᚺᛗᚨᚱᛏ ᚨᛁᛗ ᚲᛁᛟᛈ ᛏᚺᚨᛏ ᛃᛟᚾ ᚠᚱᛗ ᛋᛗᛗᚨ
ᛒᛗᚠᛟᚱᛗᚺᚨᚾᛗ ᛋᛏᚱᚨᛁᚷᛗᚱ ᚨᛁᛗ ᚠᚱᛁᛗᚾᛗ ᚨᛚᛁᚲᛗ

This was the same kind of writing as on the parchment that had prompted her to come to Galinth! Suddenly Ashen remembered when, many years ago, Zazar had brought her here and left her for a while. Then she had searched behind a tall pile of mats for sitting and sleeping and found an assortment of clay plates that were not scratched, but had oddly shaped drawings and symbols embedded in their surfaces. These symbols. This must be the ancient language of Galinth as well as the Land of Ever Snow, known now only to a few.

She stared at the yellow, red-slitted eyes, thinking. "Then," she said slowly, "this was a device that, somehow, showed an image to those inside of any who approached these city walls. Through the statue's eyes."

"Yes!" Tusser cried triumphantly. "Eyes see, those inside see. It still work, too, after all these years, only nobody left inside to see until Master Emmorys come."

So that, Ashen thought, also explained the alarming semblance of life she had discerned in those crystal orbs embedded in the image's head. She had felt that she was being observed, and, in truth, she had been.

"A small mystery solved at last," she said. "Thank you, Tusser."

Eventually, Master Emmorys found a moment's respite from his duties so Ashen could sit down with him and talk. At her direct command, Cebastian left her alone in the room the old scholar used as an office, though he stationed himself just outside the door.

It was just the sort of place she imagined it might be—a cabinet of cubbies holding bits of carved stone, a table cluttered with stacks of meticulous drawings, the entire room filled with the musty smell of age. She liked it, and the aged Master sitting across the table from her as well, the copied document before him, weighted down by a large candelabrum, probably another unearthed treasure.

"I am amazed that you allowed such an artifact as the Dragon Box to leave Galinth, just as a present to me, coronation day or no," she told him. "Thank you for it, and for everything you have done for me."

"Tusser felt—and so did I—that if the Dragon Box belonged to anyone, that person was you. Think of it. You and those with you fought and vanquished six Ice Dragons! That is no mean accomplishment. Without you, it would have been for naught. After all, you, according to the prophecies, were the Changer, and the Change you wrought was, indeed, great."

"The Dragon Box will, of course, be one of the great treasures of the NordornLand. You do know that under the veneer, it seems to be made of solid silver, don't you?"

"I suspected as much, but hadn't had time to verify."

"It was. It isn't the artifact's intrinsic worth that brings me here, however. We found that document, of which you have a true copy, under a false bottom in the box."

She went on to tell him how Zazar had translated it for her, and of what else had been discovered.

"Interesting. And a bracelet, you say, made of small teeth?" the old scholar said.

"Yes. I thought at first they might have been children's baby teeth, but they could just as easily have been from something else. The shape wasn't quite right."

"I would like to have seen them."

"It never occurred to me to bring them to you. I put them in my jewel chest, though, where they will not be disturbed. Do you think there is any significance to them?"

"It is possible. But it is also something that does not concern me now. According to this document, the ancient female, the Mother Ice Dragon, must still live, and those children of hers the Four Armies fought so valiantly must have been, as your husband surmised, youngsters, just a few years out of the egg. Where else could they have come from? Since only the Dragon Blade is capable of slaying her, it seems that someone must now go and find it, and then put an end to her before she produces more to plague the land. How may I be of further help?"

"I was hoping that more information had been unearthed in Galinth that would point the way."

"We are finding more daily," Emmorys told her, "but so far, nothing that would be of great help to you. I am sorry."

"Please, don't be. My sojourn here at Galinth has been most satisfactory, and informative."

"If we unearth anything else concerning Ice Dragons, or the

Dragon Blade, please be assured that we will send it to you at once."

"Again, I thank you for your courtesy."

❧

"Where's Weyse?" Ashen asked, as they were preparing to depart.

Zazar shrugged. Again she was mounted, though she had made the trip between the Bog and Rendelsham many times on foot and thought nothing of it. "She's somewhere. Probably looking over old haunts, the way you were doing. When she gets bored enough, she'll find us, never fear."

"Very well," Ashen said. "Cebastian, are you ready?" She put a small emphasis on the word "ready."

"Aye, Madame," he replied. He touched his saddlebag, and she nodded her understanding. The priceless rings were safely in his possession.

"Let us be off, then." She gave the signal, and her little company began the next leg of its journey north.

The distance between Galinth and Rendelsham seemed much shorter than it ever had before. They traveled along a new road, part of the network of such roads linking every part of Rendel. Either Peres or the Council were being very diligent in their care and restoration of the land. Travelers were also abroad, and if any were robbers in disguise, they gave Ashen's party a wide berth, not wanting to tangle with Cebastian's well-armed men.

Before long, Cragden Keep, the great fortification that defended the capital city, Rendelsham, loomed before them. Ashen knew the place well. It had been to Cragden Keep she had been brought when she had first been taken out of the Bog by Count Harous, once the Lord High Marshal of Rendel. Only a scarce handful of others besides herself knew of his treachery and ignoble death; as for Rendel, Harous had an undying place as one of its national heroes. Now Sir Lathrom, husband to Ashen's closest friend, held the post of Lord High Marshal as well as that of Protector of the King's Person. No hint of treachery would ever attach to his name, baseborn though his origins might be, Ashen knew, else Rannore would never have married him. As husband to the King's mother and therefore his stepfather, his loyalty was beyond question.

Too bad, Ashen thought, that Harous had not had such ties. He had only the ambition to claim her, then merely the bastard daughter of the old King, Boroth, and half-sister to his unworthy son and successor, Florian, hoping to use this blood tie to pry Florian off the throne. Harous had ever been a schemer, and it had been his undoing.

The daunting gate was shut. It probably indicated that Lathrom and Rannore were not in residence, but to make sure, she turned to Cebastian. "Please have one of the men go and make inquiry." At his questioning look, she added, "I have no wish to waste any more time if Rannore is not here, what with Rendelsham just a short distance away."

"Yes, Madame," Cebastian said. "Hensel, you heard the NordornQueen's command."

Obediently, Hensel put spurs to horse, clattered across the drawbridge, and drew up at the small door in the gate. He knocked, and eventually the door opened. In a few minutes, he returned.

"As you thought, my NordornQueen, nobody's home," Hensel reported. "They're to be found inside the city."

Ashen breathed a sigh of relief. "Then let us continue and so meet them there."

Without fanfare, Ashen and her companions entered Rendelsham and made their way to Rendelsham Castle. It had always resembled a fanciful concoction created by some pastry chef, now more than ever. The walls had been freshly whitewashed and they fairly glittered in the sun. The little entourage drew up at the doorway to the small fortification located at the base of the ramp that led up to the castle. At one time it had been Harous's town house; now it belonged to Lathrom.

Rannore welcomed them inside. "Will you stay with me," she said, "however long you remain in Rendelsham, or will you continue on to the castle?"

"To the castle, I think," Ashen said. She glanced sideways at Zazar. The old Wysen-wyf looked tired.

"Of course. You didn't spend nearly enough time with Hegrin. Will you go on at once, then? If so, I'll go with you and pay a visit to Master Lorgan."

"Is anything wrong?"

"No. He just wants to see me now and then."

"Of course there's nothing wrong with this girl," Zazar said, eyeing Rannore up and down. With the privilege of old age and her former position as the Wysen-wyf of the Bog, she laid her hands on Rannore's belly. "Fairly leaping about, isn't he," she commented. "You'll want an elixir to calm your stomach so he won't kick out everything you swallow. I could mix it for you, but I'd need some ingredients."

"All the more reason to pay a call on Master Lorgan," Ashen said. This was going to be easier than she thought. She needed only a moment to inform Master Lorgan of her concerns about the possibility of Zazar's declining health, and he would do the rest. And all under the guise of mixing a stomach remedy for Rannore. "We'll all go," she said to Zazar.

Rannore did not care to ride, nor did she like the sedan chair that was offered to her. The three women set off for the ramp on foot, with Cebastian and his men, leading their mounts, behind them.

"How fares Lord Royance?" Ashen asked. "There was so much commotion when last I saw you, that I had no chance to inquire."

"He fares surprisingly well," Rannore replied, "though he sometimes goes into his privy chamber each day after the midday meal for 'meditation.' It refreshes him for the afternoon."

Zazar laughed. "We all grow old, sooner or later," she said. "Even I." She shot a sharp glance at Ashen. "And no number of visits to a physician will cure it."

Ashen, recognizing that none of her careful plans had gone unnoticed by her Protector, forbore to make comment beyond saying, "I am concerned for your well-being."

Zazar sniffed. "I was looking out for *that* long before I ever heard of you, girl." Then she laughed.

The stay at Rendelsham Castle turned out to be shorter than Ashen would have wished, had circumstances been different. But they weren't, and she didn't need Zazar—for whom Master Lorgan prescribed a tonic, then pronounced her in excellent health for a woman of her years—to tell her of a foreboding in the north. She hoped it was only the dread of a visit to the Dowager Ysa that was making her uneasy.

Having been made aware of the import of Ashen's errand, Peres and Hegrin greeted her formally in the Great Hall. To her pleasure, Lord Royance as well as other members of the Council attended at the meeting. As Rannore had told her, he had aged somewhat but still looked hale and in good fettle.

She presented to King Peres the ruby signet engraved with the Oak badge—a bear, standing erect within the letter O in the same ancient script as Ashen's ring over a circle of oak leaves, and in the bezel, the motto, "Strength prevails." Lord Wittern, as she had guessed, had now retired from public life and so to Rannore went the topaz. It was carved with a capital R and the rose that appeared on the Rowan badge; inside the band was engraved the name of its former owner, Tybalt. Its bezel likewise bore Rowan's motto, "Here find all peace."

"These are princely gifts indeed, Ashen NordornQueen," Peres said. "I will strive to live up to the example set by my renowned ancestor, Javis of Oak. All the old stories have it that the Great Signets had been lost forever."

"So many thought. But look you. Here are two, and on my finger is the third." She held her right hand aloft, and the sapphire glinted richly in a beam of light from a high window.

"No one is better suited to wear that ring than you, Ashen NordornQueen," Royance said. He quirked one snowy eyebrow and Ashen could read his unspoken question: And the fourth?

She smiled at him. Before she departed from Rendelsham she would be certain to show him the huge emerald that, as far as she knew, was still lodged in the jar of boot-black in Cebastian's possession. Her smile deepened. Somebody was going to have to clean it up before Lord Royance could be expected to examine it, and she had exactly the right person in mind for the task.

True to Zazar's prediction, the first thing the Dowager Queen Ysa did, when Ashen presented the emerald Yew signet to her, was hold it up to the light to see the clarity and quality of the stone. Zazar sniggered, loud enough to be heard, and Ashen dared not look in her direction.

"You said something?" Ysa inquired.

"Just something in my nose, maybe a little dust, and it was trying to make me sneeze," Zazar replied blandly. "Nice stone, isn't it."

"Yes, it is, but what it stands for is most important." Ysa slipped the ring on her finger, admiring it. "To think, this once adorned the hand of the great Bartholo himself."

Like the other three, the stone was set in a bezel, and the design bore a circle of yew leaves, with a bow superimposed over the letter Y. On the bezel was engraved the Yew motto, "This ever I defend."

Ashen couldn't help noticing how the Dowager's appearance had changed. Two deep lines marked the space between her eyebrows, and these, where the pencil had worn thin or been carelessly applied, were threaded with silver hairs. Ysa's eyes had faded. Where once they had been the cold color of a sword blade, now they were a watery blue. Lines had etched themselves around her mouth, bravely painted scarlet, and her forehead was deeply scored. Her jaw was still square, however, with little sagging of the flesh that covered it, and Ashen thought how much more suitable this face would be viewed under a war-helm frame than peering out from the lady's coif she wore.

Her figure was still arrow-straight, and though she might have begun taking on weight, her appearance was far from that of an old woman. Her Gracious Highness, the Dowager Queen Ysa, widow of one King, mother of another, granddam of the present King of Rendel, First Priestess of Santize, was still a formidable force to be reckoned with.

Dragon Blade

"I am very glad you came to visit me on your return to the Nor-dornLand, Ashen," the lady said, as gracious as her title. "I find that, in my self-imposed retirement—a kind of exile, you might even say—I miss the company of those whom I have come to esteem and ad-mire. So many have departed this life—Boroth, Flavian, Harous, my dear friend Marcala. In some ways I miss her most of all. Feminine companionship was never something I sought, but now that I am bereft of it, I find that there is a lack in my life that only the presence of other women—or one special woman, a true friend—could fill."

A sense of foreboding filled Ashen. "I am sorry for your many losses," she said politely. "I know how fond you were of Marcala and how grieved you were about her terrible illness."

Perhaps Ysa really had persuaded herself that the Countess of Cragden's dreadful accusations of Harous's treason and treachery were but the products of a mind temporarily deranged by fever. She was fully capable of this kind of self-deception. With appre-hension, Ashen awaited the Dowager's next words.

"Because of this, I have made up my mind to accompany you to the new Castle of Fire and Ice, and there make my residence," Ysa said. She actually smiled. "Once I craved solitude, but I find that it is lonely here at Yewkeep—more so than I thought possible. It will do me good to be among the young and the active once more. Also, I would like to see your new son. He is, after all, almost my grandson."

"Your—your grandson," Ashen repeated, not believing the word.

"Of course," Ysa said blithely. "You are the child of my late hus-band. I always thought of you as my daughter. And so, I will reside with you and that fine man you married and your dear little son, as close kindred. Oh, but it will be good to get back into the world again—though the NordornLand can't be called 'in the world' ex-actly, can it, isolated as it is. Tell me, Daughter Ashen, however do you manage to keep warm in such a chill clime? Ah, it must be the snow-thistle silk like the length you so kindly presented to me. I remember how we all suffered so badly during that time when the seasons had all become one, and that one deep winter . . ."

Ysa prattled on, happily talking about her proposed new life at the Nordorn Court. Ashen glanced at Zazar, but the former

Wysen-wyf was no help. She seemed almost as nonplussed as Ashen herself. She merely shrugged. Get used to it, the gesture informed her, for that is how it must be.

"You are," Ashen said, hoping the lump in her throat didn't make her words sound false, "most welcome at the Castle of Fire and Ice, and an apartment will be made ready for you and for your household. It will be our privilege and our honor, Gaurin's and mine, to have you reside with us for as long as shall please you." She swallowed hard. "Madame Mother."

The ruse had worked, Ysa thought with relief. She would be departing the Yewkeep forever, possibly within a matter of hours. She forced herself to think about that terrible episode when, using her books and hoping once more to summon a little flying servant like the long-departed Visp, she had instead disturbed a sleeping evil trapped beneath the foundation stones of the southernmost tower of Yewkeep.

That tower had rocked and threatened to fall when the entity, whatever it was, had first stirred, and Ysa feared that it would burst forth then and there, a new manifestation of the Great Foulness, so recently defeated. But then she recognized that this was an ancient thing, one long dormant, and that if it bore any kinship with His Putrescence, as the old witch from the Bog called him, it was only that they were both pure evil.

Further, she sensed a great and gnawing *hunger* when this entity stirred, one that filled her with the greatest terror she had ever felt, even when facing the Great Foulness. She had sensed hunger about that one as well, but his had been lust for power and for aggrandizement. This was different. It was personal, and she knew herself to be the target for her presumptuousness in awakening it.

Ysa had come as close to panic as she ever had in her life. Ashen's visit was so fortuitous it had to have been arranged by some Power that still loved her. Even if it meant feigning affection for the whey-faced little snip she still disdained as the living proof of her husband's infidelity, the Bog Princess who had risen far above her station, Ysa must leave the Yewkeep immediately and hope that the evil would lapse back into the horrid slumber from which it was so perilously close to awakening.

As if to make a bad situation worse, there was a smell. At present, it lurked in corners and along corridor walls near the south tower, so faint that one could encounter it and, unless one knew better, mistake it for something unpleasant but natural.

Surely, with the Castle of Fire and Ice so many leagues distant, she could manage to leave this noisome creature, this entity, whatever it was, behind to slip back into what might well have been a sleep a thousand years old. Or, she thought practically, perhaps, if it awoke fully, it would attach itself and its unnatural hunger onto someone else.

In either case, she would be safe. In the Nordorn Court, she could find something with which to occupy her hand and mind. Surely there were currents and ripples to be explored among those who made up the nobility, courtiers, staff, hangers-on. She would undoubtedly find much to interest and entertain her there.

She had begun making preparations from the first moment she had learned from the messenger Lord Royance had sent from Rendelsham, notifying her that the NordornQueen was to pay her a visit. Her favorite ladies, Gertrude, Ingrid, and Grisella, were even now busy packing clothing and goods, books and artifacts, everything that would make Ysa's life more bearable once she was back into a real court with real intrigues to be explored.

Ysa smiled. Indeed, she looked forward to having much with which to occupy herself.

She refused to consider that she might be leaving the Yewkeep behind to fend for itself if whatever it was that Ysa had roused from its long slumber should rise up in earnest and break free from its prison. Instead, she comforted herself with the thought that even if this horrible-smelling thing did waken and try to follow, surely it would stop, baffled, at the shores of Sea-Rovers' Fjord, the great gulf of ice-filled water that separated Rendelsham and the NordornLand. Then it would realize its quest was doomed to failure and perhaps wander off somewhere and die.

Five

Now, on the journey home with Ysa's being added to Ashen's company, there was no longer the possibility of continuing overland, or, even if they had not had the Dowager's entourage and many bundles of belongings to burden them, of using the ferry across Sea-Rovers' Fjord. Unaccountably, though the season for it was yet early, ice clogged the stretch of water separating Rendel and the NordornLand. A ferry passage would have presented an unacceptable risk though had it been frozen solid, they could have driven across on sleds, as Ashen had done once before in Royance's company.

Cebastian sent his swiftest rider, Braute, hastening back the way they had come, bypassing Galinth, on down to New Vold. There, he would request that *Spume Maiden* once more put out to sea and meet the Nordorners and their guest—and their guest's great volume of belongings—at the indifferent harbor that served Castle Bilth.

Ashen was not even close to getting over her dismay at the prospect of the Dowager Ysa taking up residence in the Castle of Fire and Ice.

"How could you let this happen?" she said to Zazar, furious but careful to keep her voice low.

"I had nothing to do with it," Zazar retorted. "You are the NordornQueen. You could have told Ysa to stay put where she was, and nobody would have gainsaid you."

"That wasn't possible, and you know it."

"No, I agree; it wasn't. However, unless I miss my guess, there is somewhat more to this than one of Ysa's whims. There is something *wrong* with the Yewkeep. It smells wrong. Perhaps she's dug up some old evil and wants to run away from it. That would be just like her."

Ashen sighed. "Whatever the matter may be, I may as well make the best of it, at least for the time being. Perhaps Ysa will decide she doesn't like the NordornLand and will go back to Rendel again."

But in her heart of hearts, Ashen knew this would not be the case. There was surely nothing for the Dowager in Rendelsham, with Peres so firmly taking command of his kingdom and discouraging the sort of intrigue that had amused Ysa for so many years. Ashen could only hope that her own open disapproval of such meddling would make Ysa less inclined to stir up the kind of trouble she reveled in.

While they were delayed, a messenger—a Bog-man—came with a small package for Zazar. She opened it eagerly to find the box of Web threads Nayla had promised to send. "Well, at least one good thing has come of our forced wait," she commented.

Harvas, captain of *Spume Maiden*, made no comment when he saw the sort of cargo he was being asked to convey. He merely turned the corners of his mouth down, quirked one eyebrow at Ashen, and gave orders for his men to set to the loading. "We'll have you back home in good time," he told Ashen. "Good thing I was ready to go back out again anyway, to see what I could find that's interesting."

Behind Harvas, a small man began stroking a drum.

"That's Frode," he said, jerking a thumb in the Drummer's direction. "Go speak to him, and maybe he'll give you a reading if you speak to him nice enough."

The new Spirit Drummer. Ashen remembered what her late husband Obern had told her of the Sea-Rovers' ways. Frode's presence and that of Säugle, the Wave Reader, indicated that Harvas was planning a freebooter mission. No wonder he hadn't been put out at being asked to return to sea so soon.

"Greetings, Frode," she said to the Spirit Drummer. "I knew your predecessor, Kasai. He read for me once."

"Came true, didn't it," Frode commented. "Well, let's see what the drum has to say for you, NordornQueen."

He began stroking it in earnest, drawing out a throbbing rhythm that made Ashen's skin tingle slightly. Then Frode closed his eyes and seemed to be listening to something that only he could hear. He began to chant in a low voice pitched for her ears only.

"Told you, yes, Wysen-wyf, that upset lies in the Castle of Fire and Ice. You take with you one who carries unrest with her like her handbag, but there is more, yes, more, waiting. Beware, Nordorn-Queen, of false friends, true enemies. Beware."

He undoubtedly referred to Ysa, Ashen thought. Nayla had mentioned her, too. That was no news. But who else?

Then the drumming ceased, and the Spirit Drummer awoke. He grinned at her. "Don't know what I said. Hope it was helpful."

"Perhaps, when I understand it, it will be," Ashen responded. "I thank you in any event."

"My privilege."

Spume Maiden might have known the route by heart with no need of Harvas's hand at the wheel. In a remarkably short time, the sails were down and rowers at work as they entered the deep fjord where the Castle of Fire and Ice stood atop one cliff, and a river of ice flowed from the one across the water from it. Ashen shaded her eyes against the glare, noting that work was already well under way on the walls of the city that had been planned to occupy the land beyond the castle. Cyornasberg, it would be called, to honor the brave old NordornKing who bought time for his people to escape by facing the Ice Dragons alone.

Dragon Blade

A faint gust of wind caught Ashen's banner, a circle of flaming ash leaves on a blue ground, where it floated from the highest mast. A horn sounded, echoing and reechoing from the cliffs. Lookouts from the shore raised the cry. At the Castle of Fire and Ice the NordornQueen's standard bearing the same insignia was quickly raised on a staff on the highest tower, signaling that she had at last returned to her land. Even Ysa, standing at the rail near Ashen, seemed impressed.

"Such a to-do," she commented. "Is that how they do things in the NordornLand? I think I shall have a standard made as well, with my new Nordorn device on it."

"Of course, Madame Mother," Ashen said. "All highborn visitors—and residents," she added hastily, "are entitled to this sort of display."

Ysa shaded her eyes with her hand. "I see a green one flying next to yours, or it would be if there was a better wind. Gaurin's, I suppose. And whose is that beneath it?"

Ashen likewise stared at the strange standard, straining to make it out. "I do not know. I cannot recall ever having seen it before."

"Well, no matter," Ysa said with a shrug. "Mine will go in that place when it is finished. After all, I outrank anybody else who might live here. Except the NordornKing and his consort, of course."

"NordornQueen," Ashen corrected, but Ysa wasn't paying any attention.

Let it go, she thought. These little slights of Ysa's were as natural to her as breathing.

Already *Spume Maiden* was reaching its familiar moorage, letting down an exceptionally long anchor chain. The men began readying the first of the boats that would bear Ashen, those with her, and, later, Ysa's many belongings to shore.

As the anchor dropped, a breeze caught both standards and lifted them so they could be read. The unknown standard was dark crimson, and the emblem on it a wulvine. Nobody bearing that cognizance had been at the coronation celebration. Ashen was curious about the noble to whom it belonged. She would find out soon enough.

While Ashen had been away on her errand to the south, a new-comer presented himself to the NordornKing's Court. He arrived in the Great Hall accompanied by only two retainers, but his bearing was such that he might have commanded an entire retinue of supporters.

His clothing was of deep crimson trimmed in gold braid, bespeaking a man of upper rank. Involuntarily, Gaurin thought of the garment of like color that his father had been wearing, many years ago, when he had met his doom. His skeleton had still been arrayed in the mouldering remains when Ashen had led him to it, in the ruined catacombs of the half-buried city of Galinth.

"Greetings," Gaurin said courteously. "Come, sit, warm yourself by the fire." He nodded at Nalren, and the Seneschal immediately turned to give quiet orders to a servant to bring heated wine and food. Another servant set up a small folding table between the two men. "Please let us know the errand that has brought you to the Castle of Fire and Ice."

"Shall I be modest and reserved and bring it out piecemeal, or would you prefer that I be direct?" the stranger replied. He smiled as he took the seat indicated for him. He had a charming smile.

"Be direct by all means."

"Then what brings me here is kinship. I am Einaar of Asbjørg Isle."

"I know of the place," Gaurin said. "It lies not far off from our shores, but somewhat farther north, as I recall. But you spoke of kinship. I am not aware that any branch of my family hails from Asbjørg."

"Nor did any before, some four-and-twenty years ago, Count Bjauden of the Nordorners, nephew to Cyornas NordornKing, did come to our shores. There he met my mother, a princess in her own right, and won her heart." He arose from his chair and bowed, smiling even more charmingly. "The result, as you see, stands before you."

For a moment Gaurin could not move, from sheer shock. He should have retired from the Hall, out of earshot of anybody who happened to be there as witness, but the words had been said openly and it was far too late. Well, better now to have an old half secret out in the open, rather than a subject for gossiping tongues.

He did some rapid calculations in his head. That would have been the time shortly after his own mother, Hegrin, had died giving birth to a stillborn child, when Gaurin himself was yet a boy. Bjauden had grieved so deeply that even Gaurin, kept isolated as he was, had known of it. The Count had gone away from the NordornLand, it was said, in an effort to assuage that grief. From the looks of the stranger standing before the NordornKing with an air that bespoke of his confidence of being accepted without question, he had found some success in that endeavor.

"I see you here in my Court," Gaurin said now, slowly, "but I do not see any proof of your claim."

"You knew our father better than I did," Einaar replied with a shrug. "He was a man of honor. Do you not think he would have left some token of his regard for Princess Bergtora, my mother?"

Einaar reseated himself and motioned to one of his companions. The man stepped forward, carrying a small chest, which he opened and placed on the table for Gaurin's inspection.

Inside, Gaurin found a folded piece of paper—a letter, most likely—and a ring. Unwilling yet to read the letter, he picked up the signet ring and examined it. A thrill of recognition went through him. The ring bore a large fire-stone engraved with the device of a snarling snogpus, in the southern realms called a snowcat, the emblem of Bjaudin's house, and when Gaurin had grown to manhood he would have claimed this signet as his own, but it had never been found. To see it now, here, in the possession of someone who was a complete stranger—

He looked up and eyed this stranger anew. Yes, if he searched the other's features, he could see some slight resemblance to Bjaudin. But Einaar was dark of eyes and hair, and his skin was the tone known as "olivista." Both Bjaudin and Gaurin had blue-green eyes and hair the color of honey.

"I confess," Gaurin said, "that I might see a shadow of my father's features in your face. But that could be only a trick of the light. The ring is a different matter. You say my father gave it to your mother?"

"He did, when he learned that I was on the way. Also, he gave her the letter that accompanies it."

Now Gaurin reached for the letter, unfolded it, and began to read.

> My Bergtora.
>
> I must leave Asbjørg, and with it, my heart. If only circumstances had been kinder to us, we would have been wed and I would have taken you back with me to the NordornLand. Now, however, Cyornas NordornKing summons me to an errand vital to the very survival of our people. I have been chosen to go as emissary to the lands to the south, in hopes of finding a place of haven for those of our people who have not the heart to remain in the face of the danger that is hard upon them. The danger is such that if there be a place of safety, or relative safety left in this world, it is the Isle of Asbjørg, and here I would have you remain and wait for me.
>
> When I return, I will come for you and for our child and, whatever perils we might yet encounter, I will stand as a fortress against them. In anticipation of this day, I grant him his own cognizance, a wulvine on a dark crimson ground.
>
> Your Bjauden.

Gaurin folded the letter and returned it to the box, hoping that the disquiet he felt did not show on his face. "Why," he began, and had to clear his throat. "Why did my father not wed your mother before he left Asbjørg?" He left unvoiced the question of how Bjauden could have fallen into another alliance so quickly following the death of his wife, Gaurin's mother. Such things, he knew, happened with some men, but he never imagined that his father—their father, if Einaar's story were true—could have been one of them.

"Ah, well, as to that." Einaar took a long swallow of his wine. "Excellent vintage. My mother found our father extremely attractive, and she set her cap for him. She was quite frank about it when finally we spoke of the matter. She was betrothed to the Baron Yngvar of Asbjørg, a very rich noble some years older than she, and the dissolving of this betrothal would have taken a great deal of time. Among us on the Island, such a betrothal meant she was as good as wed already. Perhaps she didn't care as much for the Baron as she did his wealth. She never said. She, er, forgot to tell our father about any of this until he was ready to depart. At any rate, to make a long story short, our father left Asbjørg, and to save her shame, my mother married her betrothed and became Baroness Bergtora. In the fullness of time, I was born, Yngvar gave me the modern form of his own name, and reared me thinking I was his true son. Last summer he died full of years and still unaware of how he had been cuckolded. Mother and I had the little talk I mentioned, she gave me the tokens you see, and then she sent me off to find the half-brother who is now the NordornKing, the mightiest noble in the land. I think she had some thought that I might make my way here much more advantageously than I ever could on the little Isle of Asbjørg. It seems that Father—I mean, Baron Yngvar—wasn't as wealthy as Mother thought. I inherited his title, of course, but in her eyes I would be a burden to maintain, should I stay with her." Einaar's tone held more than an edge of bitterness. He took another drink from his goblet. "Please forgive my lighthearted manner of speaking about weighty and sometimes painful subjects. You understand, I hope, that I try to hide the shame and disappointment of the circumstances of my birth, which my mother had kept secret from me as much as from Baron Yngvar. He was a good man. I wept when he died."

"Your candor must have cost you some pain as well," Gaurin said, still somewhat at a loss as to how best to handle the situation.

"It is only because of our newly discovered kinship that I dare be so frank." Einaar leaned forward in his chair, and his expression now became serious. "Look you. Your tasks in rebuilding the NordornLand are great, so heavy that they would crush a lesser man.

I could be of help to you. I am in no way your equal as a warrior; the sword does not come naturally to me. However, I have some talent for administrative work. I could find a place on your Council, perhaps. Please allow me the opportunity to be of service."

Gaurin sat a long while staring into the fire, thinking about what he had just been told and the proposition he had been given. He fingered the ring with the snogpus blazon. Everything this newcomer said fit like pieces of a puzzle. Even his coloring, so different from his own, was understandable. The people of Asbjørg tended to dark hair, and Princess Bergtora had most likely been a raven-tressed beauty. Then he arose from his chair, and Einaar did likewise. "I will accept you as my blood kindred," he said, his voice firm and clear, "and likewise your offer of aid. From this moment in addition to being Baron Einaar of Asbjørg, you are also Count Einaar of Åsåfin, my friend and my brother in whom I trust." He picked up the ring with the snogpus blazon. "This will I keep as a token of my—our father, but to you I grant the device as he specified, a wulvine on a field of crimson. He was always reckoned wise; he must have foreseen the struggles that lay ahead of you. The wulvine is a canny creature that survives against many odds."

Einaar bowed low. "My heartfelt thanks, Gaurin NordornKing. I accept the device, the title, and most of all, your friendship and confidence with humility."

"You will find a place in my Court, in my Council, and in the hearts of both me and Ashen NordornQueen," Gaurin said gravely. "Accept now the kiss of kinship."

So saying, he embraced Einaar and, according to Nordorn custom among close kindred, kissed him on the lips.

Thus it was that Ashen found Count Einaar, lately of Asbjørg and now of the Nordorners, standing beside her husband when she, accompanied by Zazar and the Dowager Queen Ysa with her ladies in attendance, entered the Castle of Fire and Ice.

At a word from Ashen, Ayfare hastened to oversee the castle women-servants in making ready an apartment for their royal guest. The Seneschal, Nalren, now was occupied in the preparations for dinner for the growing Nordorn Court. He and Ayfare had exchanged dubious glances but had turned to their tasks without comment. Ashen had no doubt that Ayfare, at least, would remedy this reticence once they were in private. The Dowager Ysa was no favorite of Ayfare's because of her shabby treatment of Ashen.

"What a wonderful, romantic story!" Ysa exclaimed when the formalities of greetings had passed. She settled herself in the most comfortable chair in the little room just off the Hall, where the innermost circle of the Court waited for dinner. She was freshly attired in deep green velvet, and had even pronounced herself satisfied by her new quarters. Her ladies, excluded from the intimate gathering, would take their places at one of the lesser tables later.

Ashen was still a bit at a loss herself as to exactly why—and how—Ysa had decided to make her home in the NordornLand. Zazar was no help. The Wysen-wyf now occupied her own chair, stroking Weyse, who had magically appeared out of nowhere and was watching Ysa flirt with Einaar.

"How exciting it must be to have lived a life that one might have read about in a book!" Ysa was saying. She smiled as if trying to summon a dimple, and tilted her head coquettishly. "And to think that we two, cast adrift in the world to make our ways as we might, ended up here, in Gaurin's kingdom. And Ashen's, of course," she added, simpering in the NordornQueen's direction.

If this didn't stop, Ashen thought, she would be inviting Count Einaar to her bedchamber within the hour. She remembered Rohan's comments about how the Dowager had ever had an eye for young men and had keenly enjoyed their company, but until now had never seen this for herself.

"If you are to be a permanent part of our household, Madame Mother," she interjected, "then, like our new brother Einaar, you must have a new title. Here, you should not be merely a Dowager Queen, but something better—loftier. Something that looks to the future, rather than what is past."

To her relief, Ysa took no offense. Perhaps it was Einaar's presence that softened her mood. Instead, she seemed interested.

"A new title? For a new beginning, and a new life. Yes, yes, dear my Daughter Ashen, that is a good idea." She turned to Gaurin. "What think you?"

Gaurin smiled. "My Ashen was ever wise. There is a fine manor in the province of Iselin, a few leagues distant, and there I will create a duchy. Shall you now add 'Ysa, Duchess of Iselin' to your many other titles and become a true Nordorner?"

Ysa clapped her hands delightedly. "I like it well! And my device?"

"I will think on that, to select one best suited for you."

And so saying, Gaurin turned the talk to other matters as the NordornKing and the NordornQueen dined with their newfound kindred. The Hall was full, with many richly dressed men and their equally sumptuously attired ladies occupying places at the tables just below those of the sovereigns. The Hall was filled with warmth, a trace of smoke from the fire, good smells of roasted meat, clink of knives upon platters as the diners fell to heartily, the sound of many voices.

A plaintive yet lilting air of melody began from somewhere. Ashen looked around and saw one of her new ladies seated on the musicians' platform, holding a curious stringed instrument flat on her lap, on which she strummed rather than plucked the plangent melody. Thus accompanying herself, she lifted her sweet, pure voice, and began to sing in a language Ashen did not understand. Ashen remembered she was Tordenskjold's niece, though she could not recall the young woman's name. She turned to Gaurin.

"It is the Nordorn tongue," he told her. "We are very lucky that Lady Pernille has an interest in the old music and the talent to perform it for us. This is an ancient melody, known only as the Song, and it had almost been forgotten when I was a child. Now, it seems that an aged master has come to us. He knows it all, and is teaching a new generation. Lady Pernille is one of Oskar's most apt pupils."

"What is it about?"

He smiled. "It has many verses. This one is a love song." He began to sing along with Lady Pernille in the common language, but softly, so as not to compete with her. "Ah, sweet maiden, look to your lover; soon he departs across the land. Ah, fleet moments, hearts will discover; lifetimes dancing hand in hand."

Couples were beginning to get up from their places and join the twin rings that had formed in the center of the hall, ladies inside and gentlemen outside. The dance was simple—three gliding steps to the right, clap hands and spin; four gliding steps to the left, then the couple took each other's hands and turned about. Thus the dancers slowly progressed, in the direction of the sun's yearly course, around the circle.

The music, so artless and in such contrast to what Ashen had come to appreciate in Rendel, touched a place deep inside her. She patted her foot to the rhythm, as irresistible and steady as a heartbeat. Gaurin took her hand and without a word, they joined the dancers.

Throughout the rest of the meal, couples entered and left the ring as they chose, while the music continued without end. The old master joined Lady Pernille on the platform. Sometimes one, sometimes the other, sometimes together, they sang many verses of "The Song."

The evening grew late. The fire burned down and was banked for the night by the stewards and, contrary to the usual custom, even the men who liked to drink far into the night left the Hall. Ashen thought she knew why. The Song, with its hypnotic, repetitious strain, satisfied some deep longing, even for those who customarily sought this satisfaction in vast quantities of ale.

The NordornKing and NordornQueen had long ago formed the habit of retiring to their private apartment relatively early in the evening after the formal dinner had ended, and so they bade the members of their Court a good night. Hand in hand, they ascended the stairs. It seemed to Ashen that she still danced, pacing each step with the rhythm of the Song that wound its way through her head.

When Gaurin had closed the door behind them, he folded Ashen in his arms. "How much I have missed you."

"And I you. I never expected to see this new brother of yours when I returned, though. It was quite a surprise."

"Not only to you, my Ashen," he responded wryly. "However, his credentials were persuasive. I have given him the title of Count and granted him the county of Åsåfin as his demesne but foresee that he will be of more use to us here, than in some seat at a distance from the Court. When it comes to surprises, however, little did I expect to find you accompanied by your sometime enemy and constant source of irritation."

"Well, Einaar, if he is as good at administrative work as he claims, will be kept very busy."

"He has shown himself to be both thorough and reliable in several tasks I have set him, as a test," Gaurin told her. "He has proven his worth, and I have grown to trust him."

"For that I am glad. And Ysa, if she can leave him alone long enough for him to fulfill his office, will find plenty to occupy herself with as well." Ashen smiled. "I think I will assign her the task of composing protocol for the Court. She'd like that."

Gaurin kissed her. "And so she would. That should keep her occupied, and there is a growing need for such a service."

They seated themselves at a little table to share a slim flagon of wine before they went to bed. Gaurin poured a measure for both of them.

"Much more than the arrival of your brother has changed at Court, I see," Ashen observed. "The courtiers. The music. There were many new faces in the Hall at meat tonight."

"With the castle almost completed, the new city walls are going up swiftly. Many of the landholders have come to see what we will do." Gaurin tasted his wine, then set his goblet aside.

"Indeed. The building of Cyornasberg proceeds apace."

"I find that a Council is a necessity, and such a Council I have begun to gather. I have been creating a new class of nobles, for it is through them that our ravaged country will best be reclaimed, even as in Rendel. Baldrian of Westerblad, Mjødulf of Mithlond, Svarteper of Råttnos, Tordenskjold of Grynet—all hold the title of Count now, and are members of my new Council. You saw them with their ladies, all but Baldrian. He is a widower and I think every woman at Court has decided she should be the next Countess of Westerblad."

There had been a rush of introductions. Names and faces swam together for Ashen, indistinguishable one from another. "I hope to be able to sort them out quickly," she said.

"You will," Gaurin assured her. "Håkon of Erlend, Gangerolf of Guttorm, and Arngrim of Rimfaxe are now barons, with more to follow. These are what we call jarls—nobles—and their fathers were at Cyornas's Court. If I have chosen wisely, they will each oversee their counties and baronies and thus good government will once more come to the NordornLand."

"You could be no less than wise, and your actions seem a sound approach to me."

"I can only hope so. Now, good my Ashen, tell me of what you learned in your visit to Rendel. In particular, there is a sapphire on your finger that I never saw before."

Ashen handed him the Great Signet ring for his inspection and informed him of what the old scholar, Master Emmorys, had told her.

"I could not help noticing it while we were at table," he said, as he returned the ring to her. "Nor could I help noticing that Ysa— the Duchess Ysa," he corrected himself with a smile, "wore one similar except set with an emerald."

"Yes. Hers is the signet of the House of Yew. Peres now wears the ruby signet of the House of Oak, and Rannore the topaz of the House of Rowan."

"How fortunate that these priceless artifacts were found once again. But there was no further word of the Mother Ice Dragon, no information unearthed in Master Emmorys's inquiry?"

"None. I am sorry."

"Don't be, my Ashen, for I have news of the beast that came to me in your absence."

Ashen set her goblet aside also and leaned forward to listen more closely as Gaurin began to tell her of what he had learned.

Away in the far north wilderness lived the Aslaug, remnants of the original inhabitants of the NordornLand, who had been there even before the Nordorners had come. Always these Aslaugors had existed in an uneasy peace with both with the Nordorners and with the Fridians, an almost subhuman race akin to those who had once inhabited the Bale-Bog of Rendel. Indeed, some Aslaugors under the leadership of the man who called himself Baron Damacro in alliance with the Fridian leader, Chaggi, had taken up arms with the entity known as the Great Foulness during the late war. Chaggi had survived the final battle; Damacro had not.

The Fridians, brought forward swiftly in their development from the Change wrought by the destruction of the Great Foulness, still preferred to live apart. The Aslaugors, however, had now united their disparate septs under one leader, whom they called the Great Aslaug Chieftain. Further, they had lately begun to seek alliance with the Nordorners, as if seeking expiation for their error in fighting against them under an unworthy leader.

This new Aslaug Chieftain was a woman, Öydis, reputed to be wise as well as tough enough to go to war under her own banner if need be. It was from Öydis that the main pieces of information had come concerning what was happening in the far northern regions, including tantalizing scraps of tales about the Mother Ice Dragon, and she had used these as the opening move in negotiations for furthering a peaceful accord between the Aslaugors and the Nordorners. On the basis of this, Gaurin had granted her safe conduct to enter the Castle of Fire and Ice in person, for more detailed negotiation.

Ashen discovered that she had pressed her hands to her mouth in growing horror and disbelief. "Then the tales are true," she said faintly. "Somehow, against all reason, I had hoped it was just a fantasy—"

"Alas, it is not. Öydis herself is due to arrive in person within the week," Gaurin said. "Therefore, your arrival back home is most timely."

"Much is timely." Ashen's head was spinning. She must confer with Zazar and who else? Not Ysa. Perhaps the good priest,

Esander, who might have run across something about the Ice Dragons in the vast library beneath the Great Fane of the Glowing in Rendelsham Castle. "Oh, Gaurin, what are we to do?"

"Naught until the morrow, at the earliest," he said. "With the new day will come new hope. I will not act hastily, or without due consultation with those around me. I have learned well the lesson of bringing weighty matters before a Council. Among us, we may devise a plan to combat the Mother Ice Dragon without endangering all around us. Until then—"

He arose from his chair and held out his hand to Ashen. She took it, knowing her fingers were icy from fear and dread. This must have been the source of the repeated warnings she had received, the latest from Frode, the Spirit Drummer. Beware, NordornQueen, he had said, of false friends, true enemies. But who was friend, false or nay, and who the enemy? She went into the shelter of Gaurin's arms, and he gathered her against the warmth of his body.

Six

To Ashen's relief, Ysa—*Her Grace*, the Duchess of Iselin, as she reminded everyone she encountered—took to the position of Arbiter of Court Protocol with alacrity and great enthusiasm. She might have been born to the task. In no time she was immersed in determining what was the proper Court dress—which bore a marked resemblance to the dark blue of the Rendelsham Court—and which noble took precedence over another.

"That's a relief," Ashen said to Zazar.

"Don't allow yourself to become complacent," the older woman warned. "I've known Ysa for many years longer than you have, and it is never a wise thing to ignore her, or to leave her to her own devices unsupervised. In Rendelsham, this wasn't easy to accomplish, for she wielded great power both by the force of her personality and by virtue of the Four Great Rings she wore. Here, however, you are Queen, and she is your subordinate. Never forget that."

"I will take your advice to heart," Ashen said. "But I am still relieved that she is settling in and not showing any inclination to meddle in things that do not concern her."

"Not yet, anyway."

With that, Ashen had to be content. She found that Ysa's new project meant that she herself was caught up in details she cared little about, but which the Duchess was constantly bringing to her to resolve.

One of these details concerned the somewhat delayed arrival of the Great Aslaug Chieftain, Öydis. She could not be expected to cleave to the new Court protocol as set out by the Arbiter, and Ashen warned Ysa of this.

"Oh, I know, I know," Ysa said airily. "I am not inflexible, you know. I'm sure that when this Öydis—what kind of name is that, anyway?—arrives and sees what state we keep here, she will be glad to use the services of the seamstress I will assign to her."

"And perhaps not."

"In which case, good manners forbid that anyone even mention the matter, just as good manners insist that Öydis conform to our customs."

Ysa's lecture was interrupted by the trumpets announcing a newcomer.

"That is surely Öydis," Ashen said. "Come. We must hasten to welcome the leader and emissary from the Aslaugors."

With Ysa almost at her elbow, but trailing her sufficiently that she could not be accused of trying to usurp the NordornQueen's place, the two women, accompanied by Ladies Ingrid and Gertrude, made their way quickly toward the Great Hall. Cebastian and two of Ashen's House Troops fell into step behind them. The six ladies Ysa had selected as Ashen's personal attendants scurried in their wake.

"I see that you are well protected in your residence," Ysa said, glancing at Cebastian. "I think I'll send for Lackel. He's retired now, but he was once head of my personal House Troops, even as this young man is for you."

"Of course," Ashen said, not really paying attention. She smoothed her skirt, grateful that Ayfare had insisted she put on her necklace of state when she dressed for the day. Now as she hurried toward the Hall she donned her silver circlet adorned with the snowflake set with the crimson fire-stone, wishing she had a mirror to make certain she had not put it on askew. Her ladies rushed to her, and she felt almost panicked by the attentions of so many women. At least she knew their names now. Ladies Frida, Elibit—nicknamed Bitteline, "tiny one" as she was the most diminutive of the lot—Amilia, Ragna, Dinna—about whose light morals some unsavory rumors had begun to circulate—and, of course, Lady Pernille, who continued to entertain them all at dinner. She had come to wonder when Pernille ever ate.

Ysa dropped back a step to look at Cebastian more closely. "You look familiar. Have I met you before?"

"Indeed, Madame. I came to Rendelsham from the Oaken-keep, part of Your Grace's Great Levy in Rendel to be trained in the art of war. Rohan and I shared quarters."

"Oh. Of course."

Thanks to the hindering ministrations of her ladies, Ashen barely had time to take her place beside Gaurin before the trumpets sounded again, a different note, announcing the Aslaug Chieftain's approach. She was greatly interested to see this woman, with her reputation of being both wise and tough. Once the formalities had been completed, they would all retire as soon as possible to Gaurin's new Council chamber and hear what she had to say.

There was a commotion at the door when it had closed behind Öydis and her retinue, as if someone had wanted to come with her and had been excluded. However, this detail was almost lost to Ashen, swallowed by her great curiosity concerning their visitor.

If she had been expecting a kind of wild, northern beauty, these fancies were quickly dashed. Öydis was well into her middle years and, if she had been comely when she was young, she retained little trace of it now. She had flung back her cloak, and the armor now displayed from under it did nothing to conceal the fact that her figure was square and heavy. She strode toward where the NordornKing and the NordornQueen waited and bent her knee slightly in a gesture of obeisance that was clearly for appearances only. This one, Ashen knew instinctively, would never acknowledge even the Nordorn royalty as higher ranking than she. Despite—or perhaps because—of this, the NordornQueen liked what she saw of the tribeswoman.

"Greetings, Gaurin NordornKing and Ashen NordornQueen," Öydis said. Her deep voice carried easily throughout the Hall.

"And a thousand welcomes to you, Great Aslaug Chieftain," Gaurin responded. "We welcome that the day that has brought you to our Court."

"You might not be, once you hear what I have to say to you." She laughed, giving a quick glance around at the courtiers who seemed taken aback at her bluntness. "Oh, keep your swords sheathed. I have no intention of starting a new war—at least not with the Nordorners—in spite of the visitors I bring." She nodded at one of her escort, who opened the door again. The noises outside had increased until they indicated that someone—or, perhaps several someones—were intent on breaking down the barrier if it were not speedily removed.

Two pairs of war-kats came bounding into the Hall and made straight for the royal couple. Ashen recognized them at once, as did Gaurin.

"Rajesh and Finola!" he exclaimed.

"And Keltin and Bitta," Ashen said.

Both of the males came to a respectful halt half a pace distant from the humans' legs, but Bitta moved close to Ashen, stood up, and placed one front paw on the NordornQueen's knee. Thus braced, she held up the other to be massaged, as Ashen had been accustomed to doing when the young war-kat had been injured during the war with the Great Foulness.

As for Finola, she veered off and headed for Zazar, who was holding Weyse. The little furred creature struggled out of Zazar's arms and tumbled into Finola's embrace. The two immediately curled up together, and Finola began washing Weyse's head. Both filled the air with trills and purrs of contentment.

"Thought this might be the case," Öydis commented, as both her escort and members of the Nordorn Court looked on in astonishment at the exotic, fabled creatures rumored to be fierce and untamable. "It's obvious they know you well. Picked them up along the way—or, rather, they picked us up. Don't know how they knew where I was going."

"Strange indeed are the ways of war-kats. They often sense what we mere humans can't." Gaurin gestured Rajesh to him and fondled his ears. The war-kat leaned against him, eyes closed in contentment. His deep, rumbling purr added to those of Finola and Bitta. Keltin also began to purr as Ashen put her hand on his head and began stroking the silky white fur.

"There is no peace in the far reaches of your land, Gaurin NordornKing," Öydis said somberly, breaking into that comforting sound.

"The presence of our friends is proof enough of that, even if the errand that has brought you to us had not been known to us," Gaurin said in agreement. "We did receive the letter you sent. We will discuss grave matters, you and I, Öydis, with our Council. But first—" He caught the eye of one of the house stewards, still goggling at the war-kats. "See to it that our visitors have food and drink, all of them. Öydis, please take what time you need to refresh yourself."

"No need," Öydis responded. "I am an Aslaugor of the Aslaugors and no weakling who has to lie down and rest every hour. However, a draft of wine—or better, beer or ale—would go well."

"Then let us set ceremony aside and go at once to the Council chamber, where new ale will be waiting for you." Gaurin raised his brows in Nalren's direction.

The Seneschal bowed, acknowledging the silent order. He also took charge of the other steward, who seemed reluctant to approach the war-kats of such fierce reputation.

"They won't hurt you," Zazar said, amused. "Not unless you threaten Gaurin or Ashen."

"Come, Rols," Nalren told the man. "Pick up Madame Zazar's familiar and all will follow you without question."

A little fearfully, Rols extracted Weyse from Finola's embrace. "Follow me, and we will find meat for you," he told them, voice trembling in spite of his obvious efforts to put a brave face on his duty.

To the relief of everyone not familiar with the ways of war-kats, they obeyed. The courtiers gave them a wide path, and as the war-kats padded after Rols toward the door leading to the service rooms, Gaurin and Ashen arose from their chairs.

"The Council chamber lies opposite," Gaurin said. "Please. Let us be your escort. As I said, we keep little ceremony here."

He and Ashen led the way, Öydis beside them, accompanied by Zazar. On their heels came Einaar, followed by the heavyset Tordenskjold. The other three counts were close behind—Mjødulf, blade-slim, with an air that bespoke of keen intelligence; Svarteper, a doughty warrior as dark of visage as Einaar; and handsome Baldrian, whose nickname, Ashen had learned, was "the Fair." Trailing them all came an Aslaugor carrying a large bundle.

Then, uninvited and most unexpected, someone else swept ahead of all these nobles to walk immediately behind the monarchs. A cloud of perfume announced the presence of Her Grace, the Duchess Ysa who, to Ashen's consternation and displeasure, seemed to have awarded herself a seat at the Council table unasked.

"Protocol, gentlemen," she said to them, smiling blandly. "We must remember who takes precedence here."

Ashen glanced at Gaurin; he gave her an almost imperceptible shrug in return—the increasingly familiar acknowledgment that there was little that could be done about Ysa.

She shook her head slightly, frowning.

He leaned down, and whispered in her ear. "Let her be. Her whims are as strong as iron," he said. "I think I'll grant her the device of a Terror-bird and not tell her what it really is."

Ashen bit back a burst of laughter. Well, she thought, let Ysa sit at the table if she wished. She was experienced in statecraft as none of them were; but with no depth of knowledge about Nordorn affairs, at least she wasn't likely to do any great mischief.

Inside the Council chamber, Ashen discovered Nalren putting small painted placards at each chair. They were beautifully lettered with the occupant's name and also bore a colored drawing of his or her arms and device, in case that person could not read.

Gaurin, as Head of the Council, would sit at one end of the table, with Ashen opposite him. As was fitting, Öydis would be seated in the middle, the place of honor. Without great surprise, Ashen noted that Ysa's card had been placed directly opposite Öydis's. The Duchess's presence, therefore, had been carefully arranged—by her.

Zazar would sit at Ashen's right hand. Einaar occupied that position at Gaurin's end of the table, with Svarteper of Råttnos at Gaurin's left. He was, Ashen knew, the most likely candidate to be named Lord High Marshal, and, it would seem, the Duchess Ysa had now added her tacit approval to the selection. As if such were needed or even wanted, she thought with a flash of resentment.

She stifled it quickly. There were far more important matters to consider than the haughty Duchess and her preoccupation with making certain her rights and privileges were fully acknowledged. Perhaps by chance, perhaps not, Mjødulf of Mithlond was on Ashen's left. The rest of the Council had been placed along both sides of the table apparently at random, as their positions in Council were equal.

Empty chairs stood along one wall. The barons were not included in this privy meeting, though they would, of course, be informed of its import later.

Ysa was speaking. "Later, of course, there will be chairs carved with your devices for those permanent members of the Council, but for now, the cards will do."

"Thank you for your efforts, Your Grace," Gaurin said courteously.

The heavy-muscled Aslaugor who had followed Öydis placed the bundle beside her chair and left the room, pulling the door closed behind him.

The NordornKing sat down, and Ashen did likewise, knowing that even Ysa wouldn't breach protocol enough to seat herself before both sovereigns had done so. When all were settled at the Council table and Nalren, accompanied by Rols—who seemed to have survived unscathed his encounter with the war-kats—had begun serving heated wine, fresh ale, and Ashen's preferred snow-berry juice, Gaurin turned to Öydis.

"Now, please, Great Chieftain," he said. "Be frank with us. What news do you bring us from the northern reaches of our land that we do not already know about?"

✣

Mincing no words, Öydis confirmed every rumor about the Mother Ice Dragon.

Quiet for many years, perhaps mourning the mate killed by the brave knight mentioned in the letter retrieved from the Dragon Box, under the influence of the entity known as the Great Foulness, she awoke, left her lair, built a nest, and laid six eggs—the ones that hatched into the Ice Dragons fought against with such loss and difficulty by the Four Armies. The question of how, without a living mate, she could accomplish this went unanswered; no one had the inclination—or courage—to investigate the secret ways of Dragons, and so this riddle remained unsolved, and largely ignored. Most people simply put it down to magic.

Some Aslaugors had brought Öydis certain tokens—fewmets; gnawed bones, some animal, others possibly of human origin; a broken tooth from an extremely large creature; some fragments of a large shell.

Others claimed to have seen a creature, the description of which sounded like the Ice Dragons the Four Armies had fought, only immensely bigger—and more dangerous. Apparently, she was still wakeful. Further, she had continued laying even more eggs, and they had begun to hatch. Some of the Aslaugors, knowing what depredations these hatchlings would visit upon them, formed search parties. They fought and killed every hatchling they could find—no easy task, according to the survivors.

Those Aslaugors who claimed to have actually glimpsed the Mother Ice Dragon told tales of her size and strength that brought gasps of fear from around every hearth. No one was safe even in the farthest reaches of the NordornLand, where the Aslaug had lived for years uncounted.

Andre Norton & Sasha Miller

"I bring proof of my word," Öydis said, when she had finished her tale. She picked up the bundle her companion had left beside her chair and put it on the table. Then she opened it and drew forth several items, placing them on the polished surface.

There was a sound of indrawn breath from all the Council members. Even Ashen found herself drawing back in her chair, horrified. It was one thing to listen to a woman war-leader tell tales that were, on the surface, unbelievable and quite another to be confronted by the tokens that erased every doubt and made it cold reality. The gnawed bone, the broken tooth, the malodorous fragment of icy blue shell that could only have housed a dragon hatchling—all stood silent witness that Öydis's words were true.

"We'd have brought the fewmets as well, but I figured you wouldn't care for the smell," the Aslaug Chieftain said. "The shell stinks enough." She smiled grimly.

"Thanks for leaving the dragon dung behind," Zazar commented. "I'm grateful. No need to dirty the place with it. We believe you."

Even she seemed a little less composed than usual. As for Duchess Ysa, she had turned her head away and was pressing a kerchief soaked in perfume to her nose.

"Your tale only confirms the pieces of information we have put together from other sources," Gaurin said. "Now, the question becomes, what service can we be to you?"

"Isn't it plain, NordornKing?" Öydis said. "We need help in ridding the world of this plague, once and for all. You are the source of that help. You must aid us; it is your destiny."

"Now comes information that you do not, as yet, have," Gaurin responded. "My beloved NordornQueen—" He nodded at Ashen, and all eyes turned in her direction. "My Ashen has but recently returned from a journey to the site of Galinth, the ancient, lost city of scholars in Rendel, seeking to learn more about a certain document found in a gift given us for our coronation. This letter tells of a sword, perhaps imbued with magical qualities, made of scales from her mate. It is said to be the sole weapon that can vanquish this Mother Ice Dragon."

Öydis nodded, her eyes lighting up. "I know of it! There's a little verse. '*Naught but Nordorn-crowned, Can wield sword of dragon spawn.*' But—You were searching for knowledge of it? Don't you possess it?"

"Alas, no." Gaurin got up and began to pace. "This has occupied my thoughts ever since the first hint came to me that the matter of the Ice Dragons had not been entirely been settled. For that reason only I agreed that my NordornQueen should go to Galinth; at least, to the south, she would be safe if the threat posed by the Mother Ice Dragon should come upon us at the Castle of Fire and Ice in her absence. Like my predecessor, I was prepared to fight and, if necessary, die defending what is mine, even without the Dragon Blade."

Now it was Ashen's turn to gasp. Her heart lurched, suddenly feeling too large for her ribs to enclose. The room began to waver in her sight, and a buzzing arose in her ears.

Zazar quickly snatched Ashen's kerchief. She rummaged in her sleeve, pulled out a vial, and doused the kerchief with a sharp-smelling substance. "Your face has gone much too white. Don't you dare faint," she whispered, managing to make it as stern as a shouted order. "Here, smell this. Much better than perfume."

Obediently, Ashen held it to her nose, inhaled, and began to feel a little steadier.

"Well, now, that puts a different light on the matter," Öydis said. "I thought—I hoped, even expected—that this sword would be part of the Nordorn royalty's treasure. It never crossed my mind otherwise. I assumed that you had it, and all that was keeping you from marching out at once and putting the Mother Ice Dragon to death was that you knew nothing of our danger." She shook her head, as if in disbelief.

"Would that that were the case, mighty Chieftain," Gaurin said. "But my Rinbell blade will suffice." He reseated himself and looked around the table at his Council. "Now that we all know the situation, I would hear from each of you. Einaar?"

"I would say, send a token force and search for this fabled sword. Once it is in your possession, then you can make other plans."

"Thank you. Tordenskjold?"

"Much the same. My lands border the Icy Seas, and I've got a good relationship with the Sea-Rovers. I say, sail north rather than go by land. It will take less time."

"A sound suggestion. Svarteper?"

"Go in force, NordornKing, by land or by sea, it doesn't matter. The Aslaugors will join you. If this Dragon Blade exists, and you find it, well and good. If not, the Aslaugors will still join you. Between them and the men I can levy, we will have a force sufficient to slay the Mother Ice Dragon." He took a gulp from the goblet of wine before him.

"Thank you. Baldrian?"

"I can bring up a levy of borderers to add to those that Svarteper can muster. I stand ready to march at your command."

"Your loyalty is noted. Mjødulf?"

He shifted in his chair, and Ashen turned likewise to look at him, wondering if his appearance of intelligence had any basis.

"I have listened and find that all these suggestions have merit, Gaurin NordornKing," he said. "And so, I would counsel that they all be used."

A murmur went around the table. "Impossible," Ysa muttered, loudly enough to be heard, but not so softly that she could be ignored.

"Please elaborate," Gaurin said.

Mjødulf leaned forward, his slim, aristocratic fingers laced, reflected in the highly polished surface of the table. "Look you," he said. "Consider the war-kats so lately arrived. Would they have come if they did not, in their mysterious fashion, know there would be need?" He turned to Svarteper. "You say that it matters not if our forces go by land or by sea, and I agree. Therefore, I suggest that we enlist the Sea-Rovers as allies, as Tordenskjold counseled. Then, I propose that we divide our men and send part overland and the others in Sea-Rover ships." His thin lips turned up a little. "The Aslaugors are our allies, by right of inheritance as well as by kinship, and I suspect it might go hard with them to be left out of what might be a good fight."

"And who would lead these two armies?" Tordenskjold demanded, glaring at Mjødulf. "Certainly not you."

"I would suggest you for the sea forces," Mjødulf replied. He turned to Gaurin. "Was not one of the Four Armies in the late war led by Admiral-General Snolli?"

Gaurin nodded.

"And was not he lost in battle? Then honor him by awarding Snolli's title to Tordenskjold and send him to make alliance with your foster son Rohan, the Sea-Rover Chieftain. As for the land contingent, everyone knows that Svarteper is the natural choice to become Lord High Marshal of the NordornLand. He might even persuade a few Fridians to join him."

All eyes turned to Svarteper in silent approval.

Ysa had become interested in spite of her initial skepticism. "Of what benefit would splitting our forces be?" she asked.

"Your Grace shows a keen appreciation of strategy. What escapes one arm will not evade the other," Mjødulf replied. He arose from his chair and bowed to Gaurin, who nodded in return. "All this is just my thought, and in all particulars dependent on what you decide, NordornKing." Then he sat down again.

Gaurin appeared lost in thought. Ashen turned to Zazar, who jerked her head in Mjødulf's direction and nodded, more a movement of her eyebrows than anything else.

"Good head on that one," she murmured. Then she raised her voice for all to hear. "I have a question."

"Please, speak, Madame Zazar," Gaurin said.

"If all these brave fellows are so eager to ride off to war or climb in a ship and sail away, then who's to be left to defend Cyornasberg in case some enemy decides to rise up and attack while we're vulnerable?"

Einaar spoke before Gaurin could say anything. "I will volunteer to stay behind and guard Cyornasberg," he said. "I cannot measure up to any of you around this table—even the women—as a warrior." A ripple of amusement ran through the Council members, and Öydis laughed out loud. "But what skills I do have I will gladly put to use in Gaurin NordornKing's absence, should he decide to embark on this adventure."

"I think I have no choice but to do it," Gaurin said heavily. "The Mother Ice Dragon is a menace to the Aslaugors, and will become, in time, an even greater menace to us and also to those lands to the south. She has no reason to love the Rendelians or the Sea-Rovers, or even those people lately of the Bog, who managed to kill one of her brood as well." He gazed at Ashen. "All have spoken here save you, my NordornQueen. Have you no comment?"

"Only that I wish with all my heart that it would not be necessary for you to take up this heavy task. But I know also that you will not flinch from the burden."

"It is a stalwart queen that we have, gentlemen," Gaurin said. His voice was full of pride. "I have decided. We will, indeed, take two forces, but relatively small and carefully chosen. The remainder we will leave behind, in reserve, to guard our city and our castle. Go and start summoning your levies, for I wish to leave as soon as possible."

Ashen arose from her chair, and all the men did likewise. Belatedly, Öydis and Ysa stood as well. Only Zazar remained seated. She groaned, plainly using her age as her excuse for what would otherwise have been bad manners.

"Even as you march off to do battle with the Mother Ice Dragon," Ashen said, "so shall my task and that of our brother Einaar be to preserve and defend Cyornasberg and, with what other help we can muster, the NordornLand as well."

Brave words, and false, she thought, trying to keep her lips from trembling. How I wish he did not have to go.

Seven

I hate it!" she cried passionately to Gaurin, when they were finally in their private quarters. "How can I let you venture into danger alone?"

"I will not be alone, my Ashen," he said. "Remember, we will be assembling both an army and a fleet, with Rohan's marines. We will keep close to the shore as long as possible, before turning inland to stable the horses and hire dogsleds. Rohan and Tordenskjold will be our supply source so that we may march light and swiftly." He looked aside. "In any case, it is my duty."

"Duty," Ashen repeated, trying to keep resentment out of her voice. She sighed, knowing that it was in times like these that the burden of kingship grew heaviest. "Let us hope that such duty does not fall also on Peres and Hegrin."

"Just so," he replied. "And that is one more reason why I must go. To protect you and our children."

Ashen's hand went, involuntarily, to her belly. Her courses had not come upon her; could she have conceived again so quickly? Gaurin spoke of protecting their children. Yet she could not tell him about the possibility of another child, lest his resolution waver after all. She turned the gesture into one of smoothing her skirt.

"Then I must turn my ladies to helping prepare what will be needed by the men of the Court," she said.

"Staunch Ashen," Gaurin said approvingly.

At least she had some reprieve. It would take Tordenskjold time to journey back to New Vold—again in *Spume Maiden*—and then there would be further delay before he returned with whomever Rohan could muster to send. Harvas could barely conceal his disgust at being further delayed in his freebooting errand, but took it in good enough part when both Tordenskjold and Gaurin paid him for the passage in Nordorn gold.

Four weeks later almost to the day, Ashen, certain now that she was carrying another child, watched from the balcony of the residential wing while three Sea-Rover ships sailed into the deep fjord that served the Castle of Fire and Ice as a harbor—minus *Spume Maiden*. Ashen recognized the old *GorGull* and *Stormbracer*, but not the third vessel. They tied up at buoys that had been set for just such a purpose.

She hurried down to the Hall to join Gaurin in greeting the captains and other visitors when they had made their way up the steep side of the cliff and into the castle. Zazar would not be present, being in bed with a cold and warmly surrounded by Weyse and all four of the war-kats who had, unaccountably, decided to take up residence with the old Wysen-wyf. Ysa, however, came bustling along in Ashen's wake—no doubt to oversee the protocol such occasions called for. Öydis was already there, eager to meet her allies in the proposed undertaking against the Mother Ice Dragon.

To Ashen's surprise and pleasure, there were more new arrivals than anticipated. Not only Rohan accompanied the new Nordorn Admiral-General Tordenskjold, but several of her friends from Rendel as well—one in particular.

"Rannore!" Ashen cried. She rushed forward even as Rannore hurried toward her, and the two ladies embraced with deep affection. "Oh, how glad I am to see you! But how could you be spared your duties at home?"

"My husband, the Lord High Marshal and Protector of Rendel, would not be left behind if there is even a hint of danger to our country," Rannore said, her eyes twinkling.

Lathrom came up beside her and bowed to the Nordorn-Queen. "She insisted," he said, his deep voice rumbling in his throat, "and I could not gainsay her." He gazed at his wife fondly. "Greetings, NordornQueen. Your glowing beauty grows with every passing year."

"And to you greetings, likewise." She clasped Rannore's hands. "And the children?"

"Safe and well, at Cragden Keep."

Ashen turned to Ayfare, who seemed as pleased to see Rannore as she. "Can you have the largest guest apartment prepared for the Lord High Marshal and his lady?"

"By the time you have greeted all your guests, it will be ready and a fire lighted," Ayfare replied. She glanced at a couple of her maids, who scurried off at once to obey, as if they were more in awe of the castle's Chatelaine than they were of the Nordorn-Queen. "Also, I have water heating so that our guests may refresh themselves as they will. Nalren is already busy with other room assignments."

"Thank you," Ashen said.

At that moment, Rohan nearly swept her off her feet in an embrace. "Greetings!" he cried. "Anamara sends you her best. She would have accompanied me except—" He broke off, and to Ashen's surprise, blushed.

"She is with child again," Ashen said.

"Well, yes. It happens, you know." Rohan shrugged, blushed deeper, and kissed her hand before joining Gaurin in helping get all the newcomers settled, each according to their rank.

Ashen heard the Duchess Ysa's exclamation of pleasure, and turned to see her giving a warm greeting to a grizzled veteran accompanied by half a dozen armsmen in Rendelian livery, none of them young. That, Ashen thought, would be Lackel, brought out of his retirement to serve once again as head of Ysa's personal House Troops that she had awarded herself.

Ashen sighed. Then, as was her duty, she entered the general confusion and began to welcome all the newcomers, high and low. When these proprieties had been satisfied and the men had begun to talk of war among themselves, she turned to Rannore, and they made their way toward the great staircase.

"You see how it is," she said. "All they want to do is make plans that don't include women. Well, except for Öydis, and she's no proper woman, as you and I understand womanhood. I'll tell you about her later. Even Gaurin is too busy to explain to me the plans the men are making. How much do you know of this errand to the northern wilds?"

"Enough," Rannore said. "Perhaps more than you."

They entered the apartment, where stewards and maids busied themselves with carrying and stowing the belongings of Sir Lathrom and Lady Rannore. Gratefully, the two friends found a secluded spot close to the fire where they might talk in relative privacy.

Four vessels, Rannore told her, had set sail from New Vold, putting in at the little harbor serving Rendelsham to pick up Lackel by the Duchess Ysa's orders and, as it happened, Lathrom and Rannore as well. Three had sailed north from there, but Harvas, perhaps gratefully, had given his farewells and departed at last on his mission of freebooting before he could become enmeshed again in the problems besetting the Nordorn kingdom.

Of these three remaining Sea-Rover ships, *Stormbracer*, the largest and slowest, would be the one designated to carry supplies for both the land and sea forces. The new ship, *Sea Witch*, had been chosen as the flagship for Admiral-General Tordenskjold. Rohan would stay with reliable old *GorGull*. He and Tordenskjold had decided between them that if the land army were slow, they would sail ahead and scout out the territory. In any event, the excursion would commence no sooner than a week from their arrival at the Castle of Fire and Ice.

"So soon," Ashen murmured.

"So soon."

🙠

Much too soon for Ashen, resigned as she had thought herself to Gaurin's setting out on the quest to find and destroy the Mother

Dragon. He would be well accompanied; a hundred men, hand-picked from the levies of the Nordorners, would be going with him along with the Aslaugors and the marines the Sea-Rover ships carried. There was something nagging at her memory, a detail that had been all but forgotten in all the excitement of mustering men from the outlying lands around Cyornasberg, the training, the settling of the army into makeshift barracks, the arrival of the Sea-Rovers and their ships, the preparation for their departure. Though she ruled equally with Gaurin, she knew that in practice her new brother-in-law, Einaar, would be dealing with the day-to-day matters. Without much success, she tried to ascertain what, if anything, he planned to do in Gaurin's absence.

"It will come as it may," Einaar told her, with grave courtesy. "No one can see that far ahead. We will simply handle matters as they arise, and hope for my brother's swift return."

To that, she had no answer. So, she set it aside, along with the vagrant memory, being taken up with other, more pressing duties. Whatever she had forgotten would come to her, in its own time.

She did note that Einaar slipped easily into the role he had requested and Gaurin had given him. He was now, in fact if not in name, Head of the Council even as her old friend Lord Royance was, in Rendelsham. However, Royance had the advantage of long years in service through more than one monarchy, whereas Einaar was still untried. Without any great surprise she observed that the Duchess Ysa was beginning to take it upon herself to instruct him in various political matters, well beyond any Court protocol.

At least it kept both of them preoccupied and out of the way. Even if Ysa were plotting any more mischief, the way she delighted in doing, it could be easily undone.

However, that too, she thought, would wait until Gaurin's absence, when she would be able to turn her attention to what her "foster mother" was up to.

Delay though she might wish, the day came when all was in readiness and Gaurin all impatience to depart. "The sooner I am gone

Andre Norton & Sasha Miller

and have accomplished the errand so needed by us and by our allies, the sooner I will be returned, my Ashen," he told her. He caressed her cheek.

She knew he was truly concerned for her, and yet his attention strayed. In his mind, she knew, he was already riding forth on his favorite warhorse, a great bay stallion named Marigold. Nordorners had a habit of calling their fierce steeds by mild, innocuous names—the braver the charger, the sweeter and more innocent the name. Marigold was a very fearsome beast indeed, and nobody but Gaurin could ride him. When he trotted, he lifted his forefeet high, proudly dancing along his path. When he galloped, he carried all before him from the sheer strength of his charge. Ashen knew that with Marigold fighting for him, Gaurin had a much better chance against the Mother Ice Dragon than alone and on foot should he encounter the beast quickly. She also knew, however, that the farther north he traveled, the deeper the gathered snow and the thicker the ridges of ice, the less effective a warhorse would be. Then Gaurin would have to give up this ally and travel by dogsled.

Emotions warred within her. She wanted simultaneously for the Mother Ice Dragon to be found not far from Cyornasberg and quickly dispatched, and for her to be laired up many inaccessible leagues distant.

If only the creature would go to sleep again, Ashen thought, and let this danger pass. But eventually, someone would have to go against this grave peril, and Ashen knew, even as she wished otherwise, that it had fallen the lot of her husband and no other.

She could delay the parting no longer. Outside the plaza where she stood with Gaurin and the war-kats, the hundred Nordorners were lined up and ready, and with them the Chieftain Öydis and those Aslaugors she had brought with her. More would join the little army later, in the event they switched to dogsleds for swifter travel in the snowy regions of the north. At that point, Marigold, too valuable to trust to a hired stable and who, furthermore, would tolerate no stabling but his own, would be returned to Cyornasberg, along with Firefly, Svarteper's roan charger. With them would come news of the Nordorners' progress and possible success in tracking the Mother Ice Dragon. Also, there would be a personal message from Gaurin to Ashen. Already she anticipated reading his words and knowing that he was safe and well.

The ships had already raised anchor and sailed out of the deep harbor of Cyornasberg Fjord. They would lie offshore, to pick up the land army and pace them as they traveled north. A young trumpeter blew his horn, joined by others in a brave challenge—the signal to depart. Gaurin mounted Marigold, the war-kats yowled, and with brave banners flying and Lathrom, equally well mounted, by the NordornKing's side, the army set forth. All the nobles rode, if not trained chargers, then sturdy mounts; the armsmen marched to the beat of a drum. Öydis took her place on Gaurin's left, equal to equal. A large Aslaugor rode just a pace behind her, obviously her second-in-command.

Ashen left the plaza and, accompanied by Rannore, Einaar, the Duchess Ysa, and Zazar, who had finally arisen, still sniffling, from her sickbed, watched from a high balcony as long as they could. Just as Gaurin's spring-green pennon vanished from view, she felt the first faint flutterings in her womb. She closed her eyes, miserable.

"Come and have something warm to eat and drink, sweeting," Rannore said. "It is hard, I know, and no less so for me than for you."

Ashen looked at her friend. "How selfish I am. I had all but forgotten that your husband is with mine, at his right hand."

"And Öydis at his left," Zazar said. "He's well protected."

"Of course, he is!" Ysa exclaimed. "Isn't this what men love to do—march off to war? I saw it many a time when Boroth was alive, and he always came back to me."

Zazar quirked an eyebrow, and the unspoken thought hung in the air, almost clear enough for Ashen to read—*more's the pity.*

"These ladies are right," Einaar said. "Let them care for you now, while your husband, my brother, the NordornKing, takes care of those many other lives the Powers have entrusted to him."

With a sigh, Ashen acceded to their entreaties and returned to the relative warmth of a castle that seemed very empty now, to endure as she might until her husband's return. There were domestic matters to attend to, perhaps enough to keep her occupied so that she would not utterly despair in his absence. On the morrow, she would start with learning what Ysa had been up to while Ashen was preoccupied. Also, there was the question of the "wrongness" Zazar had noted at the Yewkeep. Ashen had, in her spare moments, tried to put that uneasiness out of her mind, only to discover that she could not. It was never wise to disregard any of Zazar's warnings, and this, delayed though it might be because of other, more pressing problems, was one. Now seemed as good a time as any to explore the matter.

She called Ysa into her presence chamber, thinking about how many times she herself had been similarly summoned when Ysa had been in power in Rendel. Then, the Queen, later the Dowager, had never hesitated to display her power and remind Ashen of how she was but a pawn to be used at Ysa's whim. How many times had Ashen resented this but been unable to protest?

Now, her title of Duchess notwithstanding, it was Ysa who lacked the power that Ashen possessed. It was a great temptation for the younger woman to respond in kind, but she suppressed it. There was nothing to be gained by making an even deeper enemy of the Duchess than she had always been. As to whatever was troubling Ysa, Ashen sensed—from where she did not know, for she had not discussed it with Zazar—that it was working its way to the surface. She hoped to draw it out of the Duchess, if not during this interview, then soon.

Ysa swept into the room in a cloud of perfume and a swirl of snow-thistle silk skirts, as green as the emerald signet on her finger. "Ah!" she exclaimed. "Heated wine. And minced-meat pies. How thoughtful of you, my dear."

"Providing warm food and drink for honored guests is a pleasant custom. As for the cold weather, I have grown to love the climate that others would call harsh," Ashen responded, "but possibly you have not yet had time to do so. Come. Warm yourself. Let us converse. We have scarcely had time to do so in private since we learned of the Mother Ice Dragon."

"Thank you." Ysa seated herself in one of the four chairs drawn up close to the fireplace and helped herself to a pastry, heavy with finely chopped fallowbeeste meat mixed with fruit. "You are very kind. More so than—"

"More so than you have been to me?" Ashen finished for her. "Come, Madame Mother, you may be frank. What's past is past, and we all do what we must, at times, whether it is to everyone's liking or not."

"Well," Ysa said around a mouthful of pastry, "I admit I had wondered if you held it against me, your first marriage to Obern. I planned it, you know."

"Obern was the logical choice for me to marry," Ashen replied. "He was a good man, in his way. I mourned him when he died, even as I mourned your son, my half brother. That was a tragic incident, their deaths at each other's hands. It should have brought us closer together."

"And would have, at another time and in another circumstance."

Ysa was beginning to relax, Ashen noted. She smiled and helped herself to one of the minced-meat pies as well, wondering at how easily she could be in the company of a once-powerful woman against whom she was entitled to hold a blood grudge and know that she could afford to set it aside. Later, if needed, it could be resurrected once more. Ashen realized she had, indeed, come a long way from being the "Bog Princess" Ysa had once called her.

"Are you happy and content?" Ashen inquired. "Do you have everything you need? Is there anything I can do to make your life more comfortable?"

"I am very comfortable, Daughter Ashen," Ysa replied. "With my ladies, my honor guard, my pennon with the device the NordornKing granted me flying from the tower just beneath your own, my role in the Court, what more could I want, as my days begin to draw to an end?"

Ashen laughed lightly. That had been a minor item of contention—whether Ysa's pennon outranked Einaar's. "You are far from being at the end of your days!" she said. "And yet, I think there is something you are not telling me—something I felt when we were at the Yewkeep to deliver the Great Signet of your House into your keeping."

Ysa, perhaps unconsciously, fingered the enormous emerald she wore, symbol of the House of Yew, and she glanced at the matching signet on Ashen's finger, the sapphire carved with the seal of the House of Ash. "It was uncommonly generous of you to give it to me," she said. "You could just as easily have put it into the treasury at Rendelsham Castle, or even left it at Galinth."

"But I didn't." Ashen leaned forward a little, daring to push Ysa a little. "Come, Madame Mother, if there is something yet to tell me in private, please feel free to unburden your heart."

Ysa sighed heavily. "You are correct, Daughter Ashen. There is something, and it matters not if others besides we two know of it. It is women's business, and we are a castle of women now, Einaar notwithstanding. Let him do the things that concern men, while we deal with what I have—quite accidentally, I assure you—unleashed."

"I have asked Lady Rannore and Zazar to join us, a little later," Ashen said. She nodded gravely. "Let them come now, if they will."

She touched a bellpull, gave instructions to the maid who answered the summons, and in a very few minutes both Rannore and Zazar had joined Ysa and Ashen in the presence chamber. Rannore curtseyed to Ashen and to her former mother-in-law and sat down beside Ashen. She placed a small box beside her chair.

Without any ceremony, Zazar plopped herself into the remaining chair between Rannore and Ysa, waved away the offered plate of minced-meat pastries, and reached for the hot wine. "This feels good on a sore throat," she said hoarsely.

"Are you sure you did not catch a fresh cold while we were all outside?" Rannore asked.

"No, I'm well enough," Zazar said. She coughed. "Greetings, Ysa. Are you well?"

"Yes," the Duchess replied. "In body. But in spirit. . . . Well, that is why Daughter Ashen has called you, kin and close as kin, to listen to what I have to say. I must confess a possible misdeed, and ask for help."

Zazar coughed once more but, at a warning glance from Ashen, said nothing as the Duchess Ysa began her tale of the mysterious entity that she had unwittingly evoked from under the foundations of the Yewkeep.

The wine grew cool. Rather than interrupt Ysa's telling, Ashen set the pitcher on the hearth close to the fire to warm it again.

Zazar had been listening closely. "And you say you felt hunger from this, this whatever-it-was that you awakened? And that it was personal, directed at you alone?"

"Yes," Ysa said. "At first I was terrified that it was a new manifestation of the Great Foulness. But then I knew that it was far, far more ancient than he. More ancient even than the Mother Ice Dragon, perhaps. All I sought was another little flying servant, another Visp. But this thing *knew* me from the first. It wants me, and only me, to slake its hunger."

"And, knowing this, still you came to Cyornasberg," Rannore murmured disbelievingly. She twisted her own signet, the beautiful topaz, and it caught the light like a ray of warm, southern sunshine.

"I hoped it would be baffled by the great icy gulf separating Rendel from the lands to the north, the one where the Sea-Rovers' strongholds once were."

"And now you aren't so sure, are you?" Zazar snorted, coughed, and blew her nose. "When are you ever going to stop your meddling in things that are beyond you?"

"I swear that I have not lifted a hand to magic since that moment, nor will I as long as I reside in the Castle of Fire and Ice," Ysa said solemnly. She held her hand up, bearing the emerald signet that glinted in the light. "I swear by this, the emblem of my House."

"That is a heavy oath, and so I believe you," Ashen said. "But I, too, wonder, like Zazar, what now leads you to think that this entity has not given up its pursuit of you."

"I don't know," Ysa admitted. "I only know that it has weighed on my mind more than it should have. I had hoped it had gone back under the foundations of Yewkeep and into the sleep from which I awakened it, but I now think that is an idle wish."

"Well, there's nothing to be done about it until it shows up at the castle gate, knocking for entrance," Zazar said brusquely. "Unless, of course, you want to return and let it take you."

Ysa paled visibly. "No! Please!" She lifted her goblet of wine and drained it at a single gulp.

"There is no question of Madame Mother's returning to Rendel or to Yewkeep," Ashen said. Her pity had been stirred. No matter Ysa's past misdeeds, this was different. "Now that we know—or, at least, have an idea—of what we might be facing, we can be better prepared for it."

"Well," Rannore said. She still looked shocked. "If this is an occasion for confessing, may I add mine?"

"Of course, my dear friend," Ashen said, taking her hand. "But I doubt that anything you might have done could come close to what Madame Mother has told us."

"No, nothing like that. I have something for you."

She took the box from beside her chair, pushed the tray of now stale pastries aside, and placed it on the table. The box was made of plain wood and bore no distinguishing mark or symbol. "This was sent me by Master Emmorys. You remember him."

"Of course I do! What is it? Has he found more jewels belonging to the Four Great Houses?"

"Nothing so grand. It is a document he discovered in his research. As he had learned I was coming here, he sent it to me to bring along, but the messenger arrived after we had left Rendel. I received the parcel but two days ago. You have been very occupied ere now, and I didn't wish to intrude."

Ysa stirred, but Ashen held up her hand, and she subsided again.

"The original remains at Galinth," Rannore continued, "but this, he said in an accompanying note, is a fair copy. He told me nothing of what it contained, only bade me see to it that you received it. I do not know what the document contains, for it was sealed by Master Emmorys himself, as you will see. Please forgive my tardiness in giving it to you, but he did not stress any urgency in his note. I hope it is only one of those matters that scholars find important."

"There is nothing to forgive." Ashen opened the box and drew out a thick, folded parchment.

As Rannore had said, it was wrapped in scarlet ribbon and sealed front and back. She broke the seals, unfolded the parchment, and laid it on the table. It was a map. She knew the writing on it. Like that on the papers that had been found in the elaborate silver box that had been Anamara's coronation present to her, this was in the language of Galinth.

ᚺᛖᚱᛖ ᛁᛋ ᛏᚺᛖ ᚹᚨᛋ ᛏᛟ ᛏᚺᛖ ᚳᚨᛁᚱ ᛉᚠ ᛏᚺᛖ ᛗᛉᛏᚺᛖᚱ ᛁᚳᛖ
ᛗᚱᚠᚷᛉᛏ. . . .

"Zazar, please take a look at this."

The old Wysen-wyf hitched her chair closer to the table and peered at the map. "Here is the way to the cave—no, the lair—of the Mother Ice Dragon. Beware of hatchlings for she feeds them on man-flesh—" Zazar skipped past some of the writing to another line, written with great care and in red ink.

ᛁᚻ ᛏᚺᛖ ᚳᚨᛁᚱ ᚳᛁᛗᛋ ᛏᚺᛖ ᛗᚱᚠᚷᛉᛏ ᛒᚳᚠᚹᛖ.

"Here, the map says, is where the Dragon Blade is to be found." Zazar looked up and met Ashen's stricken gaze.

"The lair," Ashen said through numb lips. "The Dragon Blade lies hidden somewhere inside the depths of the Mother Ice Dragon's lair."

"No wonder no one has ever been able to find it," Zazar said.

Rannore was looking both puzzled and alarmed. In quick, terse terms, Zazar and Ashen, taking turns, informed her of the legend of the Dragon Blade and how only that weapon was reputed to be able to kill the Mother Ice Dragon.

Rannore's voice shook. "Gaurin is incredibly brave—"

"Or incredibly foolhardy," Ysa finished for her. She turned on Rannore. "If he had had this information before he started out, he would not even now be marching to his doom, you foolish, thought-less girl! How dare you endanger the NordornKing this way—"

Ashen slapped her hand on the arm of her chair. "That will do, Madame Mother," she said sternly. Somewhat to her surprise, Ysa closed her mouth. "Didn't you listen? The delay was none of her doing! Do you think that Rannore would deliberately put Gaurin, let alone Lathrom, in more danger than they are already? I do not." She put emphasis on the words.

The women sat in silence for a few minutes. Suddenly a course of action sprang into Ashen's mind as cold and as clear as clean wa-ter abruptly crystallizing into ice.

The NordornQueen spoke once more. "I know what I must do," she said. "All is far from lost. It is obvious that I must take the map to Gaurin, that's all. He will know what to do then."

Ysa and Rannore raised a protest almost in one voice.

"You can't go!" Rannore cried. "It's much too dangerous! It's only a legend that this one sword is needed. After all, the knight who killed the Mother Ice Dragon's mate didn't have a sword like that!"

Ysa flicked the map with her fingernails. "Send a rider! Let someone else track him and carry this wretched thing to him, and then let him decide," the Duchess said. "It's not our concern."

"Everything that happens in the NordornLand is my concern, if not yours," Ashen replied. "And Rannore, how could I not dare danger if it will help Gaurin in his quest? I speak to you all now, not as foster daughter nor as treasured friend, but as Nordorn-Queen. This is something given to me to do, and only I can accom-plish it. This I know, but cannot explain. Rannore, you will stay here. Madame Mother will work with Einaar, maintaining the peace and security of the kingdom."

"And what am I supposed to do?" Zazar demanded. "Stay in my room and blow my nose?"

"You are old, Zazar," Ashen said as kindly as she could. "Such a journey would be too hard on you, and you have been ill."

"And getting better."

"I had hoped you would lend me Weyse. There is a loving con-nection between her and Finola. It is probable that snow may render the trail unreadable, especially if they have gone inland. Perhaps this connection will draw me in the direction I must go."

Ashen did not mention the iridescent stone bracelet, which she also planned to take. Using it brought its own risk, though, for even as it could prompt her which way to go to find Gaurin, if she were in danger he would know. It would create an unstoppable compulsion in him to rush to her side, perhaps to his detriment.

"Weyse won't go with you, not without me," Zazar retorted. "So I must bundle up my sick *old* bones and go anyway."

Ashen thought a moment. "Then you will ride as far as we can. I will have snow-thistle blankets made for us like Gaurin and his men carry, stuffed with silk lint, to keep us warm at night. You will be taken care of, and if you object, you will stay behind—with Weyse—and I will find my own way or be lost and die in the attempt."

"Very well, Ashen," Zazar said with unwonted meekness. "I will do as you command."

Ashen breathed a silent sigh of relief. This had been the most difficult of her instructions, for she had never seriously thought Zazar would agree to stay behind, the state of her health notwithstanding. She would insist if she were lying on her deathbed. At least, this way, there would be both her and her House Troops to care for the aging woman. Now, if the other two acquiesced—

Both Ysa and Rannore were staring at Ashen, as if not believing what they had just heard.

Rannore recovered soonest. "I will do as you require, Ashen NordornQueen," she said, "asking only that when you return you bring word of my husband, as dear to me as yours is to you. Further, I will send for my children Laherne and Viktor, and put them in the nursery with Prince Bjauden and look after them all. Also, I will assist Madame Mother insofar as I am able, in maintaining the peace and tranquility of Cyornasberg."

"Thank you." Ashen turned to Ysa. "And you?"

"Of course, of course. I will do as you ask, and gladly." Ysa shuddered a little. "Only I still think you are going off on a dangerous, harebrained errand when someone else would gladly do it for you."

Eight

*R*ohan **spent as much time** or more aboard the *Sea Witch* as he did the sturdy, reliable old *GorGull*. This was partly because he wanted to keep close contact with Admiral-General Tordenskjold. In an odd way, the older man reminded Rohan of his grandfather Snolli, whose title Tordenskjold now bore, except that on his worst days Tordenskjold was the soul of geniality compared to Snolli on his best days.

Also, he was intrigued with the new vessel. The art of ship-building had advanced considerably since the *GorGull* had first slipped into the icy waters of Sea-Rovers' Fjord in northern Vold, the hereditary home of the Sea-Rovers. *Sea Witch* looked fit for any project she would be put to, whether freebooting, carrying cargo, or warfare.

"Can't wait for this dragon-slaying to be done with so you can take her out roving, can you?" Tordenskjold said, laughing. "Oh, you needn't pretend otherwise. That's what Sea-Rovers do even when their wives are expecting. Y'see, some of your folk stayed behind when the great exodus began. Before your time, I imagine. Or you were still in swaddles. They sought refuge with my father, and I got to know their ways, at least a little. Hand me that far-see glass, would you?"

Rohan obliged and Tordenskjold put it up to his eye. "Need to make sure we don't outpace our land troops," he explained.

"The Sea-Rovers would rather sail on ahead and be waiting for them when they arrive for their camp at night," Rohan said.

"That's one way to do it," Tordenskjold replied. "They're making good enough time despite the brokenness of the coastline, so I'd rather keep them in sight as long as possible. Let us sail slowly— for us—and then we'll send *Sea Witch* out ahead, scouting every evening. After all, what good's a combined sea and land expedition if they don't keep in close contact with each other? Eh? Tell me that."

Rohan just shrugged. He knew that Tordenskjold had a lot to teach him, and he wanted to learn. The Admiral-General had reminded him of something, though, and he was abashed that Anamara's delicate condition was something he had not thought of since weighing anchor, back at Cyornasberg. Well, he thought, if I'm a Sea-Rover, then I must be one to the bone. Hers is women's business, and I am about men's business. So has it always been.

"Well, I'll tell you," Tordenskjold continued, sounding a bit testy. "It's what we do. It's our business."

Startled, Rohan thought for a moment that Tordenskjold was reading his mind. "I—I don't understand, sir."

"We're the lifeline for the men ashore," Tordenskjold told him. "We're the reserves the NordornKing can't take with him because the country can't sustain them. Oh, yes, I know, the Sea-Rovers have their ways, and they would rather be in the van of any battle instead of being the second wave. The second wave. That's a good one." He laughed at his own joke, his good humor completely restored. Then he clapped Rohan on the shoulder so vigorously he nearly knocked the younger man off his feet. "It's the fortunes of war, Chieftain. The fortunes of war. We all have our parts to play, and this is ours."

"Yes, sir," Rohan replied. Surreptitiously, he rubbed his shoulder. "I'll remember that."

"Then get you over to the *GorGull* and make sure those eager warriors of yours know it, too. And come back when you can. I enjoy our little talks."

※

Despite the haste of her preparations for her journey to take the map to Gaurin, Ashen found time to consult in private with Count Einaar.

"With my husband and me absent, both the guardianship of young Bjaudin and the governing of the NordornLand will fall to you," she told him. "You are the sole adult relative either of us has, to our knowledge, though your relationship and mine is through marriage. Therefore, we must rely on you perhaps more than you had anticipated when first you came to Court."

Einaar bowed, hand to heart. "I cannot deny that this is an unforeseen circumstance. Yet, I will do my best to you, to my brother, and also to Bjauden NordornPrins. I do think, however, that your, um, foster mother might have aught to say to that."

"Yes. The Duchess Ysa." Ashen thought a moment. Then she made her decision. "I have no idea about what ceremony might be involved here," she told Einaar, "but Gaurin and I rule here as equals. And so, because of your close kinship with the King, I hereby elevate you to the title of Duke Einaar of Åsåfin and the NordornLand. That ought to settle any problems that might arise with the Duchess."

Einaar bowed again, even lower. "Thank you, Your Majesty." A smile crossed his face, his expression so like Gaurin's when something amusing struck him that any doubt Ashen might have harbored concerning his kinship vanished. "There will, of course, be the question of precedence."

Ashen tried to bite back laughter, unsuccessfully. "Thank you for that. With all my worries, any levity is welcome. I do not envy you the struggle." She became serious again. "As brother to the King—"

"—even on the wrong side of the blanket, as they say."

"Even so. As brother to the King, you are a duke by right of birth. Gaurin would have corrected this in due time. It just comes a little sooner, because of circumstances."

"Will you draw up letters confirming me in my title, and also as guardian and Lord High Protector of the NordornPrins?"

"Of course," Ashen said. "With a badge of office also as Head of the Council. We must have stability in Cyornasberg, and you must be the one who maintains it until Gaurin returns."

"And his NordornQueen with him." Respectfully, Einaar raised her hand to his lips and kissed it. "Rely on me, my sister and my Queen. All will be well, I pledge it on the honor of—I started to say, on the honor of my mother, but that would not be the best of pledges." He laughed. "On the honor of my fathers, then. Both the one who sired me and the one who reared me."

"With such a promise, I will be content," Ashen said.

The newly created Duke bowed his way out of Ashen's presence chamber, and she turned to other matters. She touched a bell, and a steward appeared.

"Please ask Madame Zazar to come in," she said. She wanted to see for herself if the elderly woman was truly up to the trip, or if she had simply been putting up a good front. She knew she needed Zazar with her.

"It's about time," Zazar grumbled as she entered the room. "I've been sitting too long on a hard, narrow bench outside the door. So you had business with Einaar, eh? He looked pleased and perplexed all at the same time when he left."

Ashen told Zazar what she had done, and the old Wysen-wyf's expression changed gradually from one of disgruntlement to amusement.

"That ought to keep Ysa busy for weeks, trying to figure out just who goes in front of whom," she said with a chuckle. "Keep her out of mischief, too, is my guess." She favored Ashen with a shrewd glance. "Or maybe into different mischief."

"It would be better if Ysa would simply accept her new life as it has come to her. But she cannot help being what she is any more than the Terror-bird on her badge can help being what it is," Ashen replied.

Andre Norton & Sasha Miller

Zazar shrugged. "Let her try her wiles on Einaar. It will keep her out of Rannore's way, and also out of the nursery. With all her grandchildren in one spot. . . ."

"I hadn't thought of that. In my concern for Bjaudin's safe-keeping, I had forgotten that, by her odd sense of family, she would consider Rannore's children her kindred as well."

"She's quite the matriarch." With a gesture, Zazar dismissed the subject of the former Queen of Rendel and turned to other matters. "Now, to you. I'm well enough, thanks to this new Court physician of yours, Master Birger. His medicines taste foul, but they break up chest congestion. My worry now is centered on you."

"How so," Ashen said, instantly on her guard.

"You're with child," Zazar said bluntly. "All your ladies know, of course, and the word is sure to spread."

"I will order them to keep silent."

"Oh, that will make you more fit for this hazardous journey, I'm sure!" Zazar exclaimed with more than a little sarcasm. "I meant your fitness for what is sure to be required of you."

"I was with child when we faced the Great Foulness," Ashen pointed out.

"I know. I've often wondered if—"

"If what?"

"Nothing. The child is just old for his age, that's all. He seldom laughs or gurgles or does the things a baby does. I think if some-body handed him a book, he'd read from it straightaway."

Ashen laughed. "He's solemn, that's true, but he's perfectly normal. He does laugh, and he does gurgle, and he cannot read a word!"

"Never meant to imply there was anything wrong with him. Well, since you're so set on going on this errand, you were wise to have me along so I can keep an eye on you. Oh—speaking of being wise, the priest Esander wants to have a word with you. He's out-side bruising his backside on that hard bench. Talking with him was all that kept me from dying of boredom waiting for you to de-cide you had time for me."

Ashen sighed. Zazar was, indeed, recovered. "Please ask him to come in," she said. "It would help much if you could oversee the gathering of those supplies we will need for our journey."

"Oh, I'll get out of your way," Zazar said, not bothering to try to conceal a smile. "See you at meat tonight."

She left and, the next moment, Ashen's old friend Esander from the Great Fane of the Glowing in Rendelsham entered. For the sake of this friendship, he had come with her to the Nordorn-Land. He bowed respectfully.

"You have something for me?" Ashen said.

"I think so, Madame," he replied.

"Then be at your ease and tell me." Ashen moved toward the chairs next to the fireplace and at her gesture he came forward and took a seat facing hers. "I am sorry not to have consulted you ere now. In all the ado concerning the Chieftain Öydis of the Aslaugors, I had to set other matters aside. And now—" She held out her hands in a gesture indicating that her actions had not entirely been of her own will.

"No apologies necessary, my NordornQueen," Esander assured her. "I had the leisure to pursue matters that might be of some help to you."

"Then please, let us remedy my tardiness. Tell me what, if anything, you have discovered."

"As you might know, when I came to the NordornLand, I brought with me a number of books, duplicates of many that lie in the hidden library under the Great Fane. You yourself have read some of them."

"Yes. Those you gave me, I brought with me. Others that you lent me, I read and returned."

"Between your books and mine, we have accumulated a respectable library ourselves, in our own Fane, by now. Among those books in my possession are several having to do with the history and lore of the NordornLand."

Ashen leaned forward. "Then you know of the legend of the Dragon Blade?" she asked eagerly.

"Yes. Also, I know the ancient language in which these legends are written." Esander could not repress a smile. "Madame Zazar came to me after that first time when she deciphered for you the document hidden in the silver box your daughter-in-law gave you as a coronation present. She was reluctant to admit it, but her knowledge had grown rusty, and if it hadn't been for the pictures accompanying the text, she would have had to admit she might not have accurately read it."

Ashen smiled in return. "She hates having to admit failure."

"She remembered quickly enough, with my help. That was what piqued my interest in the Nordorn books. And also, there is always gossip. The story of your intent to take the map so carefully copied from the one uncovered at Galinth to your husband. . . . Well, the entire castle is talking of nothing else."

Ashen sighed. It was impossible that such an undertaking remain a secret. "Was there anything in your books about the monster Gaurin is set to destroy?"

"Yes." Esander settled himself more comfortably in his chair and accepted a goblet of snowberry juice that Ashen offered him, from the pitcher being kept warm on the hearth. "It is stated that dragons, when they grow old enough and wily enough, acquire the capability of human speech. The dragon the brave knight killed is said to have taunted him mercilessly."

"Let us hope that this is not the case with the one Gaurin is seeking. Surely, being female, she will be of a—a softer nature."

"Alas, no, my NordornQueen. The Mother Ice Dragon is entirely evil—worse, if possible, than her mate. It is said that she abstains from devouring men's flesh only so she can feed it to her hatchlings and thus develop in them an early taste for it."

Ashen could not repress a shudder. "Did Gaurin know this? Is there some way he can avoid. . . . No. Certainly he knew. Öydis would have informed him, out of my hearing. Nor would he avoid the danger, for he is bound to protect his people. And me."

"Just so, Ashen NordornQueen. And just so you are bound to help him in any way that you can, to make his task even slightly easier."

"Now I am glad that I did not consult you earlier, for if I had known this, I would certainly have made it even more difficult for him to ride away on his errand. And this would have been unbecoming."

"How may I help you now?"

"I would have you implore the Powers to lend any assistance that I might deserve, unworthy though I have shown myself to be. And further, I would have you take the NordornPrins under your tutelage and protection so that you, along with Duke Einaar—"

"Duke?" Esander raised his brows slightly.

"Yes. I have elevated him to that title and also made him Head of the Council and the NordornPrins's guardian in the absence of both Gaurin and myself. I would have you quietly oversee Duke Einaar as well, if you will accept this duty."

"With all my heart, Ashen NordornQueen. But you have made no mention of a certain high-placed lady."

"Yes. The Duchess Ysa. Well, she is as she is. I can only hope that she will not seize on this opportunity to begin more of her plotting and scheming as she has done throughout her life."

Esander smiled a little. "Let us hope that instead she finds suitable occupation in trying to outshine Duke Einaar in precedence and pride of place."

"That was my intention." Ashen stood, signaling that the interview was nearly over. "I know that you have no authority to turn these two from a course that might have a bad outcome for the kingdom, but if you see trouble on the horizon—trouble that, for once, does not involve Ice Dragons—you can surely send word to me somehow, and, somehow, I will find a way to avert it."

Esander bowed. "I will help in any way that I can, though I might easily be crushed between these two powerful people."

In an astonishingly short time, the general preparations for Ashen's journey north were complete. Now she stood in her chamber, her jewel chest open, pondering what, if any, of her personal belongings and ornaments she would take with her. Zazar's precious box of castings from the Web of the Weavers was already in the chest, to be locked away safely while she was gone. She caught sight of the bracelet of nine tiny teeth strung on a thin chain, found in the Dragon Box. She had nearly forgotten it.

Another bracelet, however, the one made of iridescent stone, definitely would go with her, though Ashen would not wear it unless at great need. She put it into a wooden box equipped with a hasp and a peg to close it. The great crown? No, but she would take the simple silver diadem she customarily wore when she appeared in the Hall. She touched the crystal snowflake with a fire-stone set in its heart. Yes, somehow, this seemed fitting. She took Gaurin's diadem also from its resting place in his own chest and put it into the box with the bracelet and the precious map. The rest of her jewels were useless frippery, more easily left behind than the box of Web threads Nayla had sent to Zazar. However, when she began to close the chest she stopped.

The first jewel she had ever owned caught her eye. It was a necklace made of a gold circle set with a large sapphire. On either side of this circle, a gold chain, set with smaller stones, was attached so it would hang straight around her neck. Though she had many other jewels now, she had never dreamed of setting this one aside, because the centerpiece of the necklace had once been a brooch belonging to her mother, Alditha.

Harous, the former Lord High Marshal of Rendel, had found it—Ashen preferred not to think about the circumstances—and had it made into this necklace for her. Around the circle, the letters could still be read: "Without flame, there can be no Ash." Nor had Gaurin, generous and noble, ever objected to her keeping a valuable bauble given to her by another man.

Moved by something as inexplicable as her urge to undertake this errand, she fastened the necklace around her neck and slipped it inside the tunic she wore. The snow-thistle silk—cut high at the throat and long enough to brush the tops of her fur-lined boots—hid the bauble completely. She felt a little silly for taking the necklace, but no one would ever need to know that she had, at the last, given in to love of foolish, feminine ornamentation. Not even Zazar.

The great sapphire signet ring of the House of Ash would

definitely not go, nor would her marriage ring. Both were much too valuable to risk losing. She dropped them into the chest and closed it firmly. Ayfare would put all to rights, then see that it remained locked securely until she returned.

Ashen fastened her cloak. It was likewise of snow-thistle silk and for protection against the icy rain, the silk had been mixed with fine wool in the weaving and lined with fur. Then she inserted the peg into the hasp that closed the wooden box, put it into a carry-sack, and left her chamber.

Outside, Zazar waited in the inner keep, mounted on a fine mare that stamped and snorted, impatient to be gone. In the panniers on her saddle, Ashen knew, Weyse would be comfortably ensconced on one side—no more carrying the little creature in the Wysen-wyf's arms, not on this long a journey. Fortunately, Weyse didn't seem to have any objection. The other pannier would be stuffed with herbs and other implements of Zazar's former craft.

With Zazar was Cebastian. As commander of the House Troops he led ten picked men—the six who had accompanied her on her journey to Galinth, and four more whom she did not yet know. They also bore panniers on their saddles carrying what each man deemed he would need in addition to the food and other supplies that loaded the short line of pack animals. She stowed the carry-sack securely in one side of the panniers on her saddle, under a stack of snow-thistle silk garments—mostly tunics for extra layering; also included was a knitted coif that covered most of the wearer's face. When a hood or cowl was pulled up over this, it provided surprising warmth. Knowing that Zazar would have scorned such as "soldier's garb," Ashen had put one for her into her own pannier.

Before she mounted, she spoke to each of her House Troops in turn. "Greetings, Cebastian. And to you also, Hensel, Braute, Nels, Arild, and Dunder. Alas, I do not yet know the names of the rest of you."

Cebastian bowed. "Allow me to make them known to you. Egil, Fjodor, Goliat—he's the big one whose horse is threatening to collapse under his weight—and Jesper."

The men chuckled at his jest, Goliat the loudest. "I asked for a plow horse, gracious Majesty, and they gave me this yearling colt!" he said, and the laughter rose even louder.

"Then, Goliat, you give me an assist into my saddle, and we're off," Ashen said, her own lips turning up in a smile.

Goliat proved to be as strong as he was large. He dismounted, put his hands around Ashen's waist—fingers almost meeting—and without any discernible effort, lifted and placed her on the chestnut gelding that had been chosen as her mount.

Gathering her reins, Ashen turned to look back at the steps of the castle. Beatha had come out, carrying Bjauden NordornPrins, to bid her farewell. Flanking the nursemaid were Rannore, whose own children had not yet arrived to be added to the population of the nursery, and the Duchess Ysa. Beside them, a little removed, Duke Einaar stood.

"Fare you well, Ashen NordornQueen," Einaar said. "May you be gone quickly, and even sooner returned to those who love you, with your husband by your side."

"Let it be so," Ashen replied soberly.

She dared risk a farewell glance at little Bjaudin, hoping she would not mar her façade of bravery by bursting into tears. She had to firmly put aside all thoughts of this child and the one growing within her as well, or all would go for naught, she knew. Beatha held Bjaudin's little hand up, causing him to wave good-bye to his mother.

"There, there, sweeting," Beatha said. "Don't be so solemn. Mama will be coming back very soon, and in the meantime there's pudding."

Ashen turned and dug her heels into the gelding's side. The rest of the company fell into line, Zazar and Cebastian only a pace behind her. She scarcely saw the castle gate as they passed through it, nor the wide main street of Cyornasberg. By the time the tears had cleared her eyes they were well out into the countryside, traveling north through the land she had claimed as her own, but which she had not, until now, actually visited.

That night, they rested in a tiny village where the occupants seemed overawed at playing host to such exalted visitors, the second time in a fortnight. The next evening, however, they camped on the side of a wooded hill, close to a freshet of water that seemed to fall directly from an ice river. Since the air was unexpectedly cold, Ashen was grateful for the fire and for the hot food the men were preparing for their supper. She and Zazar kept their cloaks about them and watched while sipping from mugs of hot broth as the men built double lean-tos such as the one Ashen had occupied on her journey from Rendelsham to the Snow Fortress during the late war. One shelter was set apart a little from the rest; this would be the women's. The men took care that the surface on which she would lie was thick and springy. There was plenty of room both for her and Zazar, along with whatever items they wanted to keep near them. Ashen's thought was of the box containing the map and the diadems. The men were also laying a little fire-ring in the shelter, she observed, in case the snow-thistle silk sleeping cover proved inadequate and she wanted to kindle a fire as well. The smoke, she knew, would escape easily through the roof of the makeshift dwelling where the sloping sides nearly met. The boughs were fresh and green—she inhaled their fragrance with pleasure.

Such, Ashen knew, would be their routine nighttime preparations throughout their journey until they came to Pettervil, where the horses of Gaurin's company would be stabled. Cebastian had commented that they were likely not only to reuse some of the boughs of the NordornKing's camps but also to meet his returning messengers on the road before long.

On the route they now traveled, following the shore, villages or even isolated houses were very seldom to be seen. *Seters*, stone and wood houses built specifically for sheltering travelers, were few and far between. Inland, there were farms and holdings aplenty, and *seters* as well. The shore route made for faster travel, but nobody wanted to live where the winds scoured the unprotected and deeply riven coastline. Travelers who wanted to go swiftly hugged the hills as much as they dared, while still keeping the cold gray water in sight.

"Have you journeyed in this part of the country?" she asked Cebastian.

"No, Madame. I left the NordornLand when I was barely old enough to walk," he said. "But since our return I have listened well to those who stayed behind, hidden from the Ice Dragons that were Cyornas NordornKing's bane when the Great Foulness escaped his bonds and destroyed the Palace of Fire and Ice. I learned much from others during the late war. Also, I can read the land, and I know that we ride swiftly, almost in the hoofprints of those who went before us." He smiled at her.

Ashen nodded. It brought her comfort and even security to know that the traces of Gaurin's passage were so close. She could almost feel his presence.

The men were finished with their tasks and, while waiting for their dinner, joined her around the fire. To her surprise, the sounds of music filled the little glade where they had made their camp.

One of the men—Fjodor—held a small version of the instrument Lady Pernille was accustomed to play at meat in the Hall. She recognized the tune. It was "The Song," though she did not know this verse. He seemed as if composing it as he sang. Others of the men offered suggestions. Some were accepted, others were not.

"What are they doing?" she asked Cebastian. "What is it Fjodor is trying to sing?"

"It is a new verse of the Song. They have the first two lines, and are arguing about the rest. It seems there is difficulty in finding a suitable rhyme." He sang it to her softly in the common tongue. " 'Thrice-brave Ashen, Valiant NordornQueen.' " His light baritone was very pleasant.

"Thrice-brave?" Ashen said. "How so?"

"You are a woman about an errand that would daunt most men. In addition, you are but new-come to the NordornLand, so your courage and loyalty are even more remarkable. Also—" Abruptly, his face flamed scarlet.

"Also what?" Ashen made it an order, not a question.

"Also, we know that you are with child."

Zazar, sitting just within earshot, snorted loudly enough to be heard.

"And how is this known?" Ashen's voice was cold. "I ordered my women to say nothing."

"Forgive us, gracious NordornQueen," Cebastian said humbly. "Your ladies know, of course, and Braute has formed a, a liaison with Lady Dinna. There was, I suppose you'd call it, pillow talk. This was before you instructed your ladies to keep silent. Neither of them meant any harm." He gazed at her, and she could see the loyalty and admiration in his eyes. "Thus are you thrice-brave, and many times over that beloved, my NordornQueen, even revered. There is not a man among us who would not gladly die in your service."

Abruptly, he rose and went out of the circle of the firelight. The old Wysen-wyf moved closer to Ashen.

"He speaks the truth," Zazar said. "I heard them talking while they were building the shelters. I don't think a man among them had a thought about keeping you back. No, they see this foolhardiness of yours as bravery beyond measure. But that's men for you." She hawked and spat into the fire. "They confuse foolhardiness with bravery. Guess it's even luckier that you dragged me along on this idiot's errand."

Ashen was silent throughout supper, speaking only when it was necessary. She was greatly disconcerted, finding it difficult to come to grips with the way her House Troops—and, she must suppose, the rest of the NordornLand, once the story gained wide publication—considered her a kind of national heroine, worthy of a verse in "The Song."

The men banked the fire for the night, and according to trail custom, everyone retired to their shelters. An early night made for an equally early departure. Ashen found that her bedding had already been laid out for her and a small fire already laid in the stone circle, with flint and steel close at hand.

Ashen removed her cloak, then her boots, surprised to find that in spite of their fur lining her feet were cold. She took off her outer garments and folded them. Beneath everything she wore a snug-fitting short tunic and leggings knitted, not woven, of the finest and purest snow-thistle silk, and these were what she elected to sleep in.

Without comment, Zazar likewise disrobed, rolled up in her coverlet and was asleep almost before she laid her head down. Her breath puffed frosty in the chill air. Weyse was already beside her, not under the coverlet, snoring softly.

Ashen slipped under her own covers and curled up, pulling the top layer over her head so that her breath warmed the little air space that was left. She was astonished at how quickly the snow-thistle silk gathered her own body warmth and returned it to her. Gradually, she relaxed and stretched out.

Making sure she could sense the cold air in the breathing space of the cocoon she had made for herself so she would be in no danger of suffocating, she fell asleep. She hoped she would not dream of heroism or the exalted opinion her men held of her, and which she felt she certainly did not deserve.

Nine

*D*uke Einaar was seething, and trying hard not to show it. Her ladyship, the Duchess Ysa, had to be the most infuriating woman—his mother excepted—he had ever known.

"I see no reason why my banner should fly beneath yours," the Duchess was saying yet again. "We may be of equal rank at least here in the NordornLand, but as I understand it, you held no title at all in Asbjørg Isle, or none to make mention of. Whereas I. . . . Well, my titles were numerous and varied, not the least of which being that I was at one time Queen of Rendel. My lord Duke, frankly, you must admit that I outrank you."

"With all due respect, and just as frankly, I admit no such thing, Madame," Einaar returned smoothly. "I am Baron of Asbjørg by right of birth, and hold my title of Duke of Åsåfin and the NordornLand by grant by Their Gracious Majesties. But let that be as it may. This is a new life for you and, in its own way, for me as well. The past is gone. For good or ill, we can no longer draw upon it, much as we might like to." That last had an unintended touch of malice. Einaar hoped Ysa wouldn't take fresh offense.

Instead, she looked away and shrugged. "I cannot deny that we cannot relive our past glories. But my banner should still fly above yours."

Einaar came close to losing his patience and decided to be truly frank with her. "Madame, let me remind you that, in the absence of both the NordornKing—my brother—and the Nordorn-Queen, I govern by right of being named Lord High Protector. To me is given the guardianship of the heir, Prince Bjauden. To me fall the duties and responsibilities of maintaining the peace—such as it is—of this young realm. Can you say as much?"

To that, Ysa had no answer. Einaar knew a brief moment of chagrin for having shamed her.

"Come, Madame," he said, holding out his hand to her. "You are both formidable and powerful. I would not have you for an enemy, so let us be friends. Look you: I shall cause two staffs to be erected, and your banner and mine will fly as equals, side by side. What say you to that?"

She looked up at him, and her expression caused his chagrin to turn to pity for this aging woman who had once been so mighty and who now was fighting to retain any and every shred of youth and dignity she could muster.

"That is most fair, my lord Duke," she said, her voice low but with the slightest trace of tremor.

He kissed her outstretched hand, glad to turn to other matters. "I called you so that we might consult about the young Prince's maintenance and upbringing. Is his nursemaid suitable? Is he being taught early those things he will need to know when he comes into his inheritance? I confess, these are women's matters that I had never thought about until Ashen NordornQueen unexpectedly conferred upon me the office I now hold. Therefore, I must rely on you, my lady Duchess, to inform me." He gave her his most charming smile.

"As to that," Ysa replied, "from my best knowledge, my grandson—" she put the slightest emphasis on the word "—is being looked after well enough. Beatha also reared my granddaughter-in-law when she was a babe, and save for an unfortunate overfondness for sweets and a tendency to act like a hoyden on occasion, Hegrin seems to be fitting into her role as Queen of Rendel. With me and Lady Rannore, whose own children will be arriving any day, to oversee Beatha, I think we can safely leave the Prince's welfare to her."

"That is excellent news. I had not heard that Lady Rannore had sent for her children, though."

Ysa warmed to her news-telling, and Einaar began to relax. Perhaps the Duchess could become an ally rather than an adversary after all. He offered her a goblet of warm snowberry juice lightly mixed with wine, and she accepted it graciously.

"Oh, yes. The children are well on their way now to Cyornasberg. And I approve. Prince Bjauden is a solemn child, and we— that is, Lady Rannore and I—think that having other children around will help make him more cheerful." She sipped from her goblet. "Lady Rannore is mother to King Peres, you know. Another of my grandsons."

"How fortunate to be the matriarch of such an illustrious family," Einaar said.

"Ah, yes. However, I do miss—"

"What, Madame? Come, now that we are friends, hold nothing back. What do you miss?"

"I miss the gaiety and life of the Court at Rendelsham. You Nordorners are dour in comparison. There is so little gossip, so little intrigue. If it weren't for Lady Dinna—"

"What of Lady Dinna?"

"Very light of morals, that one. I understand that she has a child that nobody speaks about, and yet she continues to warm the bed of any man who takes her fancy."

Einaar regarded Ysa through wary eyes. He himself had had a brief alliance with Dinna, before he learned of her growing unsavory reputation. Now he was paying court to Lady Elibit—Bitteline— though very quietly lest her reputation, too, be tarnished. "Surely this is but idle gossip," he said to Ysa. "Nothing for us to concern ourselves with."

"Yes, but for one who was accustomed to grander matters, it serves as diversion. When I was Queen of Rendel, there were wars both against invaders and civil, with noble vying against noble. We had the Bog-Men to contend with. Refugees from this very land, fleeing the Great Foulness. Why, it was only with my help that the Great Foulness could be vanquished! Is it any wonder that I find too much tranquility to be burdensome?"

"Your life has, indeed, been filled with great strife and excitement. A lesser woman would seek this tranquility with gratitude, but I can see that you are far too vital to take to it tamely." Einaar smiled, feeling that he now had an insight into Ysa that he could turn to his advantage. "Shall we equip you with sword and armor, and send you off to vie with Öydis to be Great Chieftain of the Aslaugors?"

Ysa laughed. "What a spectacle that would be!" she exclaimed. "No, my dear Duke, I always preferred to stay within the safety of my chamber, making plans and sending others out to do my bidding."

"And to calm the frictions that inevitably arise between one noble and another," Einaar supplied helpfully.

"Indeed. That was, I flatter myself, an area in which I truly shone."

"Our realm is young, as I said, still being rebuilt. There has been little time for noble to begin warring against noble. However, knowing where your talents lie, you could be very helpful by getting to know our counts and our barons so that you may foresee where problems may be expected to arise. What say you to that?"

"It sounds interesting," Ysa said. "Also, there is something else."

"Tell me."

"You have a long head and can see past the day, that is plain. Even as we must look ahead to future problems among the Nordorn nobility, we must prepare for the worst regarding this errand that has taken Ashen and Gaurin away from Cyornasberg."

"The worst being?"

"Gaurin and Ashen could both perish, leaving the Mother Ice Dragon still at large. Then the NordornLand would not only be without their rulers, but also the peril from this dreadful creature would be even greater than it is now."

Einaar sat back in his chair. He hadn't expected Ysa to take this disastrous view, in light of the various prophecies and the strength of Gaurin's invading force. Not to mention that Ashen carried with her the key to locating the only weapon that, according to lore, would destroy the Mother Ice Dragon.

"Madame, you astonish me," he said.

"I speak no treason—but we must consider all the possibilities, including the unpleasant ones," Ysa replied. "I learned to do that through hard and bitter experience."

"And what does this experience tell you, supposing this horrible situation comes to pass?"

"It tells me that Prince Bjauden is far too young to be proclaimed king. It tells me also that you are the only logical claimant to the throne, one who could bring strength and stability to the land when both these would be most sorely needed."

"Set aside my nephew in favor of myself?" Einaar's head was spinning. The audacity of the woman! Still, he had asked for her frank thoughts in the name of friendship. It behooved him to listen and, from them, learn what he might be facing with her growing influence among Nordorn nobility. "I could never do that."

"You might have no real choice."

"I could hold the throne only until Bjauden comes of age."

"Yes, that is one approach," Ysa agreed. "He seems healthy enough, but sometimes children do die, you know. Unfortunate, but true. Again, one faces unpleasant possibilities. In such a case, you would be called upon to hold the throne permanently."

"Your gloomy and dismal predictions have cast a pall over my good humor," Einaar said.

"Predictions? No, my dear Einaar," Ysa replied. "Possibilities only, which must be considered and every eventuality foreseen and planned for. Perhaps only Gaurin will perish; perhaps Ashen will die. Perhaps one or both of them will be gravely wounded and rendered unable to continue in their royal duties. We must gird ourselves and plan for the full range of eventualities. However, like you, I have every confidence that Ashen will locate Gaurin, give him the map to the Mother Ice Dragon's lair, where he will locate the sword and dispatch the beast speedily. They will return in triumph to great acclaim, and your title of Lord High Protector of the Heir will become an honorary one only. Yes, this is what we all hope for."

"Indeed." Einaar was not reassured. Despite Ysa's protestations that her words were not treasonous—and at first blush they seemed only good, hard common sense—the hidden meanings in what she was proposing could tempt a lesser man than he. Her meaning was plain. With the Duchess's aid and advice and just a little effort of his own, he might take the throne for his own in his half-brother's absence. And Gaurin, if he returned, might have difficulty in reclaiming it. Einaar could scarcely encompass the thought. After all, he had sworn an oath. And yet, oaths had been set aside before; this he knew from his childhood.

He wondered how to end this interview gracefully and was on the verge of rising from his chair to signal that their meeting was ended when there was a rap on the door. Jørgen, one of the two companions who had accompanied Einaar to Cyornasberg, now elevated to the rank of secretary, entered and bowed deferentially.

"A ship approaches," he reported.

"A Sea-Rover vessel?"

"No, Your Grace. By its lines it looks to be a private pleasure craft. It bears on the stern a red ensign bearing the device of a flying silver war bird."

"Lord Royance's badge!" Ysa exclaimed. She turned to Einaar. "That must be the *Silver Burhawk*, the yacht he has talked about building for—it must be going on twenty years—completed at last! There never was the occasion or leisure before now, for we were too taken up with the Great Foulness and the dangers he represented to Rendel." Then she addressed Jørgen directly. "Does a similar ensign fly from the mast?"

"No, Your Grace. That one is dark gold, with the device of a sword and shield."

"Lathrom's insignia. Then Royance is not aboard, but has made his yacht available for the transport of the Lord High Marshal's children," Ysa exclaimed. "He had ever a generous heart, especially when it came to young people."

Einaar noted that Ysa seemed pleased at being able to show off her knowledge of Rendelian matters, even after being away from Court so many years.

"This is a happy day. I must go and start writing letters thanking Royance and inquiring after my grandson and my granddaughter-in-law," Ysa continued. "Please, Your Grace, excuse me." She rose from her chair and, with the nod that protocol required, sailed out of the room.

"Make certain that everything is prepared for the arrival of Lady Rannore's children," Einaar said to Jørgen.

"All has been in readiness for days, sir, and the lady informed. She and the nursemaid and others of the women wait even now for the boat to arrive at the quay."

"Good. Thank you."

Jørgen paused. "Sir, by your leave, there is more. I did not wish to disturb the Duchess with what might be bad news."

"What is it?"

"The ship also flies a distress flag. It is very small, and easy to overlook, but the lookout has sharp eyes."

"Thank you for this information. I will see to the reason for such a signal straightaway."

Jørgen bowed again and left the room, closing the door behind him. Einaar rubbed his temples. Obviously the ship itself was not in danger. Therefore, its captain brought news of something else, another peril as yet unknown.

He had hoped not to be called upon to face this sort of worry, not yet if at all. He likewise rose and fastened his cloak, making certain that the wide chain bearing his badge of office lay straight across his breast. First things first, and duty above all. He must interview the ship's captain in private. Time enough to go and pay his official respects to the Lord High Marshal's children and rejoice with their mother on their safe arrival. In a way, with the arrival of these children—a girl and an infant boy, so he understood—he now assumed the duty of Lord High Protector to them as well. And put Lathrom of Rendel in his debt. . . .

Yes, he did have more than enough to think about in such time as was given him to do so.

The countryside through which Gaurin traveled was growing more and more difficult for the horses. Fire mountains, many with glowing peaks, dotted the landscape, and rivers of molten rock had hardened in the snow, creating rifts of sharp-edged rock that could catch a horse's hoof and result in a broken leg.

So far, they had managed to avoid the worst of these but soon, he knew, the company would have to abandon their mounts and go on foot. They now had halted to eat and also rest the horses, letting the animals drink from one of the many snow-fed streams.

"Where lies this village with the stabling that you spoke of?" he asked Öydis.

She gazed northward, surveying the countryside with her hand shading her eyes. "Pettervil. Just a little way farther, we'll find an opening in the high hills along the coast. There's an anchorage, but not a port. We turn inland there, and the village is half a day's march on foot. Less time if we're riding."

"We will reach that point, and there bring our shipboard companions ashore to conference as to how best to manage the stores and supplies we will need on our further journey."

"If you'll take my advice, we'll send a man to Pettervil and bring back sleds. We'll load 'em up there on the shore, march to Pettervil, leave the horses, and not waste time going back and forth."

"It is well thought on, Öydis," Lathrom said.

"They'll be expecting us," the Chieftain said. "I left word with them when I came down from the north."

"What sort of village is Pettervil?" Gaurin asked.

"Fridian, mostly," Öydis said, around a mouthful of dried meat. "These Fridians are more civilized than most. They never took part in the late war though there are rumors they supplied food and horses to Baron Damacro and some of his men. A few Aslaugors live on farms outside the village, or have trade in it. They all live together in peace." She grinned suddenly. "Unless a fight breaks out."

Gaurin smiled in return. "So has it ever been." Swinging himself into Marigold's saddle, he gave the signal for the company to mount again. The sooner they reached the rendezvous point, the closer he would feel to the actual search for the Mother Ice Dragon. Everything so far had just been preamble.

When they reached the notch in the hills about which Öydis had spoken, they began to set up a camp in as heavily wooded an area as the site afforded while waiting for their shipboard allies to arrive. Gaurin selected a messenger, but Öydis sent one of her own men off to the village instead.

"They might not take well to a stranger coming in and making demands," she explained. "No matter if they already know to expect it, or that he bears a letter with your seal, Gaurin Nordorn-King. They can be a suspicious lot." She grinned again. "Not many of 'em can read, anyway."

"As you think best, Öydis," Gaurin responded.

"We are in my land now," Öydis said, turning serious. "No matter that you reign; here, I rule. And here, I do know best. You will do well to recognize that and follow my lead in all things, as far as you are able."

"I welcome your experience and value your friendship and the firm alliance between your people and mine," Gaurin said.

"Good. That shows uncommon wisdom, for a man."

A sudden commotion caused Öydis to turn. "Ah," she said. It seems that our wave-soaked allies have arrived. The first part of them, anyway. The leaders. They'll be wanting to sit on their backsides and talk while the men bring the supplies ashore. I hope your fellows and mine can find enough boughs to make shelters for all of them. The woods are scanty around here even in the spot you picked."

She strode off to see to this errand, and Gaurin smiled, shaking his head a little.

"Quite a woman, isn't she?" Lathrom said.

Gaurin looked at him; he, too, was smiling. "Indeed she is, though I must say I prefer the valor of my Ashen to her kind."

"As I prefer my lady Rannore's," Lathrom responded. "Still, Öydis is the one I would have at my back in a fight."

Andre Norton & Sasha Miller

"Agreed." Gaurin couldn't help thinking of how Ashen had fought bravely, in her own way, for the destruction of the Great Foulness, and how it had almost been her doom. This time, he thought, there would be no need for her to take the field, and for that he was grateful. He could protect and keep safe the slender, fragile woman he had loved from the moment he first saw her, silver-gilt hair glowing in the sun and making it into a royal diadem dazzling to the eye. He had felt such dismay when he discovered that she was newly wedded to another man that it had sickened him. Again, he silently thanked the Sea-Rover Obern for defending her at the cost of his life, when she had been in such dire peril from her half-brother and his schemes that had come so close to killing her by slow poison. To think that her life had rested on the blade of Obern's sword—

"You were worthy of her, Obern Sea-Rover, especially at the last," he whispered to himself. "And so have I always striven to be, and to protect her even if my own life should be forfeit."

Then he, too, turned to his tasks of getting his men settled in their temporary camp while they made final preparations for the next—and, he hoped, last—stage of their journey.

Ashen opened her eyes to find Weyse comfortably curled close beside her, washing her face and paws, and Zazar busy heating something over the small fire she had kindled.

"About time you woke up," the Wysen-wyf said. "Tired out from all that riding yesterday, weren't you. Well, drink this. It will help restore you."

A twinge of morning nausea gripped her. The last thing she wanted was food or drink. Nevertheless, Ashen moved Weyse aside so she could sit up and accept the mug of steaming liquid. She sniffed at the steam. It smelled of herbs and of the tart, refreshing sourgrass Zazar had always added to the noodles she used to make, back in the Bog. "What is it?"

"Never you mind. Just drink it down." Then Zazar softened a little. "It's to strengthen and restore you, like I said. And also to make sure that the burden you carry—" she reached out and touched Ashen's abdomen "—stays where it belongs."

"I see. Did you think there was any danger of it?"

Zazar shrugged. "Why take a chance? The first day, we didn't travel all that far, and you could rest in a bed. Yesterday was more difficult. Anyway," she continued, "I said I'd keep an eye on you, and this is one way of doing it. Now drink. Or I'll get Goliat to pour it down you."

Ashen had to smile. The concoction wasn't nearly as unpleasant as she had feared it would be. She swallowed it all, including the bits of herbs that had not been ground so fine they were almost dissolved in the liquid. The nausea vanished as if it had never been.

"Thank you," Ashen said. "I do feel better now."

"Good. Ready to face another day in the saddle?"

"Every step brings me closer to Gaurin with the information he must have if he has any hope of succeeding in his errand," Ashen said.

Someone cleared his throat just outside the shelter. "Here is hot water for washing," Cebastian said.

"You can hand it in," Zazar said. "Nobody's modesty is going to be offended."

Nevertheless, without peering inside, Cebastian set the vessel down where the inhabitants could reach it. The sound of his footsteps receded. Zazar retrieved the hot water—rapidly cooling in the crisp morning air—and both women washed as quickly as they could before they dressed.

Outside the shelter, Nels, who seemed to have a talent for it, was preparing their morning meal. Ashen was apprehensive, fearing that there might be more singing and more reference to her valor and bravery. However, to her relief, the men treated her with no more deference than her station called for. Perhaps Cebastian had noticed how uncomfortable she had been the night before and had cautioned the men accordingly.

Soon all traces of their camp, save for a pile of branches, had been cleared away, and they were once more mounted and traveling northward, following the NordornKing's route toward his fateful meeting with the Mother Ice Dragon.

If Einaar had been provoked with Ysa previously, he was downright livid now as he and Kensel, the Sea-Rover captain of Royance's pleasure yacht, conferred in private. Determinedly, he set his anger aside. He would deal with it—and with Her Grace—later.

"Oh, the word's out all over, how her ladyship stirred up somewhat she shouldn't have, back in Yewkeep," Kensel said. "The poor folks she left behind hid theirselves, the lucky ones, while Old Slimy—that's the name they gave it—went squelching around, looking for food. It likes human flesh."

"Were there any survivors?"

"Enough to carry the nasty tale," Kensel said. "Lord Royance knew of it, o' course—he knows everything—and when it looked like Old Slimy was headed for parts north and not Rendelsham, then's when he give me the word and I put up the little signal flag so's you and me could talk about it before letting the word out, so to speak." Kensel took a deep draught of the strong wine Einaar had ordered brought to the little room where they sat, secluded from the rest of the Court.

"And you're certain that the Duchess was aware of this?"

Kensel laughed heartily, wiping his mouth with the back of his hand. "O' course she knowed! She's the one what started it from where it was sleepin' who knows how long, with her spells and her books, and set it on the hunt. Why d'you think she run away like she did, to live with the lady she'd despised ever since she heard tell of her?"

Fascinated, Einaar poured more wine, and, obligingly, Kensel related the whole tale—possibly accurately—of Ysa's less-than-cordial relationship with Ashen. A number of pieces of a puzzle Einaar hadn't known existed fell neatly into place.

"Lucky for her ladyship, Old Slimy sticks to the land," Kensel commented. "And it moves slow, so they say. Even so, sooner or later it will make its way around Sea-Rovers' Fjord; and then you can expect a knock on the castle gate."

"I thank you for this information," the Lord Protector told Kensel. "It is very valuable to me. You shall be suitably rewarded."

"I never turn down a reward." Kensel grinned. "Oh—nearly forgot." He rummaged in his clothing and from some secret recess brought out a small book, obviously very old. "Lord Royance, he bid me bring this to the priest what runs the local Fane."

"Esander?"

"If that's his name. Lord Royance thought it might be useful to him."

Einaar accepted the book and placed it on a nearby table. "I will personally see that Esander gets it," he said. "I will also give orders that your reward be made ready for you to receive whenever you want it."

"Sooner is always better than later," Kensel said.

He got to his feet, and Einaar forbore to object to the man's not waiting to be dismissed. He might yet prove to be a continued source of valuable information.

"I would request that you tarry until I have had time to confer with Esander," Einaar said, "for perhaps this will affect the content of certain letters that must go back to Rendel."

"Oh, no worries on that score," Hensel said airily. "Coin in my pocket and a town full of cold Nordorn women waiting to be warmed up—you can trust I'll find enough to keep me nicely occupied!"

With that, he left the private chamber, swaggering with something more than the usual gait of a seaman on land. Einaar sat in silence for a moment before reaching for the book. He examined the writing, but could not read the text. It was in a language unknown to him. Finally, he slipped the book into his doublet and reached for his cloak, hanging on a nearby peg. Something told him that it would be better, more politic, for him to seek out Esander rather than have the priest summoned to an audience. Such instinctive feelings he never ignored.

Luckily, he found Esander unoccupied. At Einaar's request,

they went into the priest's private chamber, where Esander was accustomed to consult with those who came to him asking advice. Einaar quickly outlined what Hensel had told him. Then he handed the volume to Esander.

The priest opened it at once. His customary serious expression grew even more so as he scanned the title and the first few pages. "If I am correct, this is a history—lore, actually—of the creature Hensel called Old Slimy. It will take some study, for my knowledge of this language is meager. May I call upon you, say, tomorrow?"

"Please do, good Esander. I have a feeling that much import is to be found in the book you now hold."

"As do I, my lord Duke. Until tomorrow, then."

"I am at your service."

It was not mere courtesy on Einaar's part. He was, indeed, at Esander's service. Esander might well play a crucial role in dealing with this monster that Ysa had unleashed upon the world.

Also, he would have time in which to deal with her ladyship and what he now recognized as her tissues of half-truths, if corroboration of what Kensel had told him could be found. He was grateful that his anger, unabated, had had time at least to come off the boil. If ever there was an occasion for him to keep a cool head, this was it.

Ten

he effectiveness of Duke Einaar's tactic regarding the
Duchess Ysa quickly became clear to him. He invited her
into the privacy of the small room beyond his main audience
chamber.

"And have you thought on what we talked about before?" she
asked. "Plans must be made should the need arise that you assume
a higher position in the kingdom. I will help you—"

"Later, Madame," he said. "I will hear more of this, but now
there is a gravely important matter to be considered."

The woman seemed to wilt before his eyes as he continued,
coldly and without emotion, concerning the creature she had
awakened from its unnatural slumber. Ysa swayed in her chair,
fumbled a small bottle from the purse at her waist, and breathed
deeply from its contents.

"I—I didn't know," she said, her voice hardly above a whisper. "I
thought perhaps with me gone, it would simply go back to sleep.
Not bother anybody."

"Madame, you were rash and unwise," Einaar said. "Nothing of
this nature will tamely go back to its bed, once aroused. No wonder you were all eagerness to be gone from the Yewkeep."

"Well," Ysa said, visibly struggling to retain some shred of dignity, "I had grown tired of being stuck away like that, out of sight

and memory of everyone, and then, when Daughter Ashen paid me a visit to give me this—" she held up her hand so Einaar could not miss seeing the emerald ring "—I took it as a sign. A new life, a new beginning."

"Far away from the thing the people call Old Slimy."

Ysa shuddered. "Surely it has another name."

"Probably one even worse," Einaar said. His eyes narrowed. "But why did you feel such urgency, I wonder. Could it have been that you felt the malice of this creature directed at you personally?"

His guess had hit the mark, squarely in the gold. Ysa shuddered again and turned pale.

"You are perceptive, my lord Duke. Indeed, I felt that it was seeking me out, that it hungered for my blood, my flesh. But I never dreamed that it would venture beyond the borders of Rendel."

Einaar allowed himself to utter a harsh laugh. "And did you think there would be signs posted—'This far and no farther'—to keep it back? Madame, in addition to being rash and unwise, I must add that you have acted extremely foolishly."

"I admit it, and I yield myself to your mercy, Einaar. Please believe me when I say that I never wanted—never anticipated—that matters would come to this. Never."

"I will believe you, for it is beyond reckoning that anyone would deliberately act otherwise." Einaar noted with some satisfaction the look of relief that flooded Ysa's features. "However, intent or not, the result is the same. We have to face this thing and, it is to be hoped, destroy it. Later, we may discuss your plans and the eventualities should my brother and sister not return, for that is only sensible. Go you now and reflect on these matters while I confer with the priest Esander. He may have aught else to report on the beast. Lord Royance sent a book on the subject."

"Grattenbor, Royance's demesne, lies farthermost north in Rendel. If anyone would know of the creature, it would most likely be he." Ysa straightened, almost herself once more. "I give you great thanks for your mercy toward a woman who allowed panic and fear to get the better of her good judgment. And I am certain that with your wisdom and guidance, we will find a way to be rid of this approaching danger."

And save your precious skin, Einaar thought. Still, he rose to his feet and held out his hand to help Ysa to hers. With full courtesy, he kissed her fingers. "When I have learned more, I will so inform you."

They emerged into the main room. She left much more subdued than when she had arrived, her emerald-colored snow-thistle silk skirts rustling. At his worktable, Einaar began to address some routine matters that must be attended to at once despite the peril Ysa had brought on them.

Esander appeared more promptly than Einaar expected. "The book was most illuminating," he announced.

"Come, be at your ease and tell me of what you learned."

"I spent most of the night translating from Lord Royance's book," Esander began. "This creature is very ancient, but that we knew already. It was abroad in the land many centuries ago, when the Four Great Families of Rendel were in their full strength. And it wrought great havoc before it was contained."

"Tell me of these Great Families. Remember, I grew up on Asbjørg Isle and know very little of mainland affairs."

"Four Great Families, clans I suppose you might call them, symbolized by four great Trees—Oak, Yew, Ash, and Rowan. Four such trees stand in the courtyard of the Fane of the Glowing, at Rendelsham. When the Foulness in the north awoke, the trees began to sicken. Now they are in full health once more, but I fear this will not last once the Arikarin, a kind of troll-slug for want of a more translatable descriptive, accomplishes its mission of destroying its awakener. Then it will doubtless turn its attention toward the remaining descendants of the ones who confined it—the Lords Tybalt, Aldrin, Bartholo, and Javis."

Einaar digested this news in silence. "Arikarin. I know aught of trolls—after all, I am Nordorn-born—but I have never heard of this one."

"The word translates as 'the Eater,' or possibly 'the Last.' Even when it first pushed into the affairs of men it had largely been forgotten. Uztinov of Yew was the ruling king then. As the foundations of a larger Yewkeep were being extended, he caused them to be excavated exceptionally deep at one point, and there, with the aid of the heads of the other Families, he was able to confine the Arikarin, paving over it. It lay slumbering in its prison for many hundreds of years until the Duchess Ysa inadvertently awakened it."

"And how did the other Families lend this aid?"

"The book relates—it is hard to separate fact from legend at many places—that they did it with the aid of their signet rings set with gems. Supposedly, the light from these gems put it into a trance that rendered it helpless. King Uztinov forbore to kill it outright, but the book gives no reason why he showed it such mercy." Esander shifted in his chair. "I must tell you, my lord Duke, that another four Rings of Power figured large in Rendel's recent past. They were simple things, made of rainbow metal inlaid with wood, decorated with golden replicas of leaves of the trees they represented. They were worn first by King Boroth, and then by Queen Ysa to whom they mysteriously transferred themselves. Through these rings she wielded the Power that strengthened Rendel as it prepared for the final struggle with the Foulness. When the danger had passed, the rings fell into dust. The golden leaves blew away and disappeared. It is said they lodged in the Web of the Weavers."

"Ysa wears another ring now, an emerald. I heard that it was unearthed at the lost city of Galinth."

"Yes, the emerald, the Great Seal of the House of Yew. Ashen NordornQueen wears the sapphire, emblem of Ash. Lady Rannore, as the ranking noblewoman of Rowan, likewise wears the topaz. It can be no coincidence, my lord Duke, that three of the four Great Rings, with their rightful owners, are here in Cyornasberg, just as the Arikarin approaches."

"You forget one thing, Esander. The NordornQueen may have taken her ring with her on her journey northward. With only two of these legendary rings in our possession, even if this preposterous tale is true, it seems to me we will have to fight the Arikarin with the strength of arms."

"I had not forgotten. I have known Ashen NordornQueen for a

long time. The ring would not have aided her on her errand, and so I think she would have left such a valuable article safely behind. Send for Ayfare. She will be able to tell us."

Einaar touched a bellpull, and when the steward arrived, did as Esander requested. In a very few moments, Ayfare entered the room. She stood calmly, hands folded, waiting.

"The priest Esander tells me that you would know aught of the NordornQueen's signet ring, the sapphire she brought back from Galinth. But you are the Chatelaine, not her maid," Einaar said. "Nevertheless, I will ask. Did she take it with her?"

"I was my lady's maid long ere she elevated me to my present position, and there is none else who can do for her as well as I, sir," Ayfare said. "When I was putting all to rights, I found her ring in her jewel chest. I locked it away safely, and here is the key." She indicated one of many she wore on a ring depending from a chain hanging from her waist.

"Thank you. You may return to your duties now."

Ayfare curtseyed and left the room. Einaar turned to Esander.

"Three rings are better than two," he said. "It comforts me to know the signet of the House of Ash is here, even though the heiress of that house is absent. I confess I believe we will have to battle this thing with sword and spear. Still, the book could be right. We need every aid we can summon. We must find the fourth ring even if the effect is only to hearten our armsmen."

"The ruby, emblem of the House of Oak, is currently on the hand of King Peres of Rendel. We will have to ask King Peres to come to our aid."

"I will write the letters at once and send them swiftly on Lord Royance's pleasure yacht, the *Silver Burhawk*."

"With luck, the message will get there and King Peres will respond to our need before the Arikarin begins to assault the walls, seeking—seeking whatever it is the creature wants."

"Think you've found a way to battle Old Slimy, eh?" Hensel said. He grinned. "Well, luck to you. You'll need it."

He accepted the packet of letters from Einaar, including those Ysa had given to the Duke to be delivered to her grandson and the Rendelian queen. With the barest of salutes, the captain of Lord Royance's yacht took his leave.

An hour later, from the window of the audience chamber, Einaar watched the graceful craft depart Cyornasberg's deep harbor. How long, he thought, before it will return, if it ever does?

He had been thinking hard and deeply and had come to a tentative theory regarding the Great Signet rings of the Four Houses. He needed to consult with the Duchess, but even more than that, he needed additional information. Jørgen and Frikk had blended in well with the retinues of the nobles in and around the Castle of Fire and Ice. Surely they could pick up something useful. Further, Frikk was one of those people who could strike up a conversation with a paving stone and come away with news of who had been treading on it lately.

Quickly, he called them into his chamber and sent them out on their errand. Then, on impulse, he sent for Ayfare again. If she had been Ashen's personal maid for so many years, surely she would know the truth of how matters had stood between Ashen and Ysa.

She entered through the servants' door, bearing a tray with a pitcher and two goblets, with a plate of cakes as well—an unaccustomed addition. "Only I can prepare the snowberry juice and wine to suit Her Grace's rarefied tastes, and it is known that you and she will meet within the hour," she told him.

It was a good sign that Ayfare appeared better disposed toward him than previously, but it still took a while to get past her reluctance to talk of her mistress. Once Einaar convinced her he had only Ashen's welfare in mind, she relented enough to verify and corroborate his feelings about her ladyship, the Duchess Ysa, combined with what Hensel had told him.

"You are to be commended for your discretion," Einaar told the Chatelaine. "It does you good credit."

"I have been with my lady since we were both little more than children, set adrift in Rendelsham to be ground to powder between great nobles if we were unlucky, to make our way as we could, if we were fortunate. I have always been my lady's friend and she mine, despite the difference in our stations."

"My kinswoman Ashen NordornQueen is lucky to have a friend such as you."

Ayfare curtseyed—with a bit more deference than before, it seemed to Einaar—and then left by the inconspicuous side door. Ysa was already a little past the hour designated his interview with her, giving Einaar only a moment to gird himself. He discovered that he was tired even before he began. Resisting the seductive suggestions the Duchess presented to him required much effort, but he was beginning to think that, with luck, she could prove very useful to him—if he could manage to steer a course without being wrecked on the rocks and crags of her barely submerged schemes.

Then he heard the self-styled gracious lady approaching in full array; he could hear the footsteps of her House Troops, her chattering with her ladies, taking leave of them, and even thought he could smell her perfume and hear the rustling of her skirts. Today, he noted, as she entered his audience chamber, she was attired in deep crimson—his color. Perhaps she thought to ingratiate herself by a subtle show of allegiance.

"Madame," he said, rising and bowing to her.

"My lord Duke," she responded, inclining her head. "I see that the *Silver Burhawk* has sailed away."

"The quicker to return," he said. They took their customary seats beside the fire. "Lord Royance sent me a book in an ancient language; our priest, Esander, translated it for me. It contains much that we must know about the Arikarin—that's Old Slimy, also known as the Eater. Esander described it as a kind of troll-slug. Most unpleasant. Did you actually see it?"

"No. I but felt its presence. Most unpleasant, you say? That's mild. I found it malignant in the extreme." Ysa reached for the goblet of snowberry juice mixed with wine Ayfare had prepared for her.

"I daresay a troll-slug would be malignant, if what else learned about it proves true. More important, however, I wanted to talk with you about Rings of Power."

Involuntarily, Einaar thought, Ysa's hands clasped, and she

rubbed thumbs and forefingers where the wooden rings must have once rested. Einaar fancied he could still see the marks they had left.

"There were such rings," she said, "but they vanished when peace came to Rendel."

"I think they were symbols—substitutes, if you will—for the Great Signets that were lost."

Ysa gasped. Again, she rubbed thumbs and forefingers. The emerald glittered on her right hand. "But how—"

"No one knows how the Powers work their marvels. As I have come to understand the story, the Four Houses were either at war or in eclipse, and the signets lost forever as far as anyone knew. The substitute rings came to the ruler of Rendel in the time of its greatest need—first to King Boroth and then, when he was found to be in decline, to you as the one most fit to wield them."

"Where I used them to such good effect as I could, as long as it was given me to do so."

"There was never a question that you did otherwise." Einaar poured himself a draught of the beverage. "Look you, and tell me what you think." He went on to tell her the tale of King Uztinov of Yew and how the light of the four Great Signets had subdued the Arikarin and imprisoned it deep beneath Yewkeep. "Now," he continued, "I think the four Rings of Power you wielded to such good effect were not only mere substitutes, but, indeed, the spirits of those signets."

Ysa was regarding him intently, and he could see that his words were having an effect. She touched the emerald she wore, twisting it on her finger as if to verify its existence. "If you are correct," she said slowly, "these spirits of the Great Signets were sufficiently weakened that it took all of them to grant their wearer enough Power that one of these such as is on my hand might command. I had always wondered why it required four of them, and also why they disappeared so mysteriously when their task was done."

"And so my theory."

"Naturally, they came first to Boroth as head of the House of Oak and also because he was the king. Then, to me as queen and also the highest-born member of the House of Yew. We were entitled to two of the Great Signets, and their Power." She stared again at the emerald. "If only one knew how to wield it. . . ."

"That secret has yet to be uncovered," Einaar said. "At least, no word has yet come to me. I take it, then, as one who once wore the spirit rings, that you find my theory believable."

"And without flaw," Ysa said. She appeared to be almost in a trance, captivated by the flashes of green light the emerald emitted as she fondled it. Oddly, she raised the gem to her lips and tasted it with the tip of her tongue.

"Because we do not have the secret of unleashing the Power in the ring that you wear, and also because the legend states that it took all four to subdue the Arikarin, I have sent for your grandson, who wears the ruby signet of the House of Oak. The other two are already here in Cyornasberg. Esander does not think it is an accident, and neither do I."

"No, it is no accident," Ysa murmured. "Nothing could be so fortuitous."

"All we can do now is await the arrival of King Peres and hope that is before the Arikarin is sighted. As I am assured it will approach from land, I will set extra lookouts on duty." He allowed himself the luxury of a cold smile. "The creature is rumored to avoid water; otherwise, it would have been here long since. There is the ferry across the Sea-Rovers' Fjord, but perhaps the Arikarin hasn't the wit to use it. It is to our advantage that it has been forced to go the long, tedious way around the Sea-Rovers' old lands."

Ysa held up one hand, waving away his words, while she massaged her temple with the other. "It is too much. No more, I beg you. Forgive me."

The woman did look more than a little ill.

"Forgive me, Your Grace. Shall we turn to lighter, more interesting topics? Perhaps we could discuss those contingency plans you spoke of before. I find myself very intrigued."

"Another time, please, my lord Duke. I confess myself dumbfounded. Again I must go into seclusion to ponder on what you have told me."

Ysa recovered quickly. Only a day had passed in relative peace before she was back in Einaar's audience chamber pursuing that subject and others with renewed vigor.

"Now, even more than before, we must be prepared for any possibility," she said, "even the unthinkable—that we should not prevail against the—what did you call it?"

"The Arikarin. The Eater."

"Yes. The Eater. There must be letters written, wills drawn, pleas for help sent to Yuland and the island Kingdom of Writham. If I remember correctly, your former home, Asbjørg Isle, was allied to Writham."

"Writham considered Asbjørg Isle to be a vassal state. The people of the Isle did not concur, but since Writham was far more powerful, they did not see fit to press the matter."

"This gives us more advantage about requesting aid," Ysa went on. "We must use everything that can be brought to bear, for we do not yet know the extent of the danger we face."

Einaar laughed. "Nor will we, until we see the Arikarin coming over the horizon, and it is eye to eye with us."

"Then it will be far too late to summon help," Ysa said, her tone more than a little sharp. "Forgive me for saying so, my lord Duke, but you demonstrate that you know little of statecraft."

"Oh, your suggestions have good merit, Your Grace. I crave your forgiveness. It is ever my way, when tensions and tempers are running high, to take refuge in humor that is sometimes apparent only to me." He stifled his laughter and brought himself under control with an effort. "When the ship from Rendel returns, we will consult with our allies. Then there will be time enough to send out calls to Writham and Yuland."

"Very well," Ysa said, mollified. "This is a time of stress for everyone. As long as I know that you are considering my suggestions, I will be content."

"For the time being."

She gave him an odd look, then nodded. "Indeed."

He was finding a certain amusement in Ysa's ambitious plans for placing him, a bastard half-brother, on the throne in Gaurin's— or young Bjaudin's—stead. With the capable Duchess, so skilled in intrigue, thinking she would be guiding his every move, of course.

"It was in my mind to call a Council meeting with those counts who did not ride out with the NordornKing, and also the barons whose lands lie to our east. Fortunately for us, Arngrim of Rimfaxe and Håkon of Erlend are in the city, supervising the building and furnishing of their town homes. Gangerolf, who, I am given to understand, cares nothing for such things, is still in Guttorm un-less the messenger I sent has arrived already and he is on the way. In any event, he will be here quickly enough to attend this meet-ing. I will rely on them for the majority of the armsmen we will need in the coming conflict."

"You seem to have everything well worked out," Ysa com-mented, "leaving nothing for me to do."

"What I have described is nothing more than my duty and re-sponsibility. However, there is much for you to do, and will be more later. For now," he told her, "you will oblige me by seeing to it that the preparations for our royal guest, your grandson, are ade-quate. He is sure to bring with him a retinue—secretaries, tutors, manservants—and I thought one floor of the west block of the castle—"

"Not the south? The evening sunlight may be too bright."

"The south block is where I have my apartment. Like this chamber, it has a view of the water and, from my bedchamber, the ice river. Therefore, it is hard to heat. I don't mind, being inured to the cold, but a young man who has lived ever in the south might find it too chill. The east block might do, but it is from that direc-tion the Arikarin might be expected to come. I would not have King Peres alarmed without due cause."

"I had thought . . . I will give orders that the arrangements be made accordingly," Ysa said.

She looked a little put out. Einaar hid a smile. Ysa's own quar-ters were at the corner where the east and south blocks met, and doubtless she had thought to lodge Peres where she could have easy access to him and thus influence him toward whatever additional schemes she might be hatching.

Within two days all preparations were made, and, within two more, the trim little yacht was sighted entering Cyornasberg harbor. Ayfare's household staff rushed to put the finishing touches on the greeting feast already being prepared.

According to protocol, all the nobles who remained in the city gathered to greet the King of Rendel. On the main landing of the stairs leading to the Great Hall, Arngrim, Gangerolf, and Håkon stood to one side of Einaar, while Ysa, Mjødulf, and Baldrian flanked him on the other side. All wore their coronets of rank and the symbols of their offices hung from great gold or silver chains across their breasts. As the castle gate was flung wide, those waiting had full view of the visitors.

To his surprise, Einaar noted that an elderly gentleman accompanied the youthful king, in addition to the attendants he had expected. The man's white hair blew in the breeze.

"Lord Royance!" Ysa exclaimed. She laid her hand on Einaar's sleeve. "That's a surprise. He is your counterpart—both Lord High Protector of the King's Person and Head of the Council. He is perhaps the most powerful man in Rendel, the King excepted. I thought perhaps he had retired from public service. This must be an important occasion, to bring him out of Rendelsham."

Einaar looked closely at this great lord, about whom he had learned much from Jørgen, Frikk, and their agents. It was Lord Royance who had defied Ysa when she was still Dowager Queen and had conveyed Ashen northward to the encampment known as the Snow Fortress, for what purpose Einaar had not yet learned. The NordornQueen and NordornKing had an uncommonly close bond uniting them, but surely that hadn't been enough to cause her to risk such a perilous journey merely to be in his company. The Duke put that question aside; it would be answered in due time, if it were important enough.

"Go you inside and see that all is in readiness," he instructed those with him. "Her ladyship the Duchess Ysa is in charge, not only for her kinship with the King, but also for her knowledge of such matters." Then he hurried down the steps so that he could personally welcome the royal guests even before they entered the castle gate.

"My lord King Peres!" he exclaimed.

He strode toward the newcomers and opened his arms in greeting and the youthful king increased his pace likewise. As kinsman to kinsman, they embraced.

"Your Grace," Peres responded with a smile.

"I am Einaar, your uncle of Åsåfin," the Duke said, "lately come to the NordornLand, after your visit for my brother's coronation." He eyed Peres up and down. "But they told me you were but a lad! You are very tall for a boy. Near grown-up, is my guess."

Peres's smile widened. "I think I like you already, Uncle. Allow me to present Lord Royance of Grattenbor. He is almost my uncle as well."

"I give you good greetings, Duke Einaar," Royance said. His tone and manner were formal, but not unfriendly.

The two men bowed to each other. Royance, too, wore his emblems of rank though Peres didn't. Einaar glanced at the rest of the retinue—guardsmen, a scholar or two judging by their sober robes, a physician. Secretaries, body servants. It was a good thing, he thought, that an entire floor had been set aside for the Rendelians. They would need it.

Peres turned to address the young courtier who stayed near the Rendelian king, almost in his shadow. "Tamkin," he said, "please oversee our establishment in our quarters."

"My lord," Tamkin replied, bowing. He turned at once to obey Peres's instructions.

"He was my personal body servant in our childhood, and now is my dear friend and protector," Peres explained. "He has earned my trust and regard."

"It is always good to have one such as he in one's service," Einaar replied. He glanced from the King to Lord Royance. "Come, my good friends. A welcoming feast awaits us all. And then, later—"

Lord Royance lifted one eyebrow and nodded almost imperceptibly. Einaar's estimation of the old gentleman went up a notch.

Later, we two will confer privately, that gesture said, and all without a word spoken aloud. Here, Einaar thought, was one wise in the ways of statecraft. One to whom he might even open his heart and mind in matters beyond the danger currently approaching—a steel-spined aristocrat through and through.

The Duke found that he very much wanted to speak openly with a man of this depth of experience—something that he had come to realize he lacked.

He nodded to Royance in return. Then they all entered into the warmth of the Great Hall.

Eleven

The Nordorners placed their camp just inside the fringe of trees at the base of the mountains, a little south of the notch opening inland to the town of Pettervil. There they could build adequate shelter for those who had no tents. A hunting party had brought down some fallowbeeste, a welcome addition to their dried provisions, and the fresh meat was even now being portioned out for the men's evening meal.

This camp would last longer than their previous ones. Gaurin wanted to get their stores and equipment ashore and into temporary storage, where the various goods could then be sorted and allocated as to what the men would carry themselves and what would go by dogsled. Some would be left behind, for the villagers, to help build their goodwill.

One of the Nordorners, Rusken, a man with an uncommon touch with horses, led Marigold past on the way to the enclosure the others had hastily erected for the animals. There they would be fed, watered, groomed, and allowed to rest for a day or two. Affectionately, Gaurin slapped Marigold on the flank, and the horse tossed his head and whinnied.

"Good lad," Gaurin said. "I shall miss you in days to come."

The horse whuffed, and Rusken pulled on his reins. Reluctantly, Marigold allowed himself to be urged on. Keltin and Rajesh,

who had formed a fondness for the great stallion, trailed close behind. Later, they would sleep in Marigold's stall, all three animals
keeping each other warm.

Gaurin surveyed the countryside. Here the land was not as
deeply gouged and riven as the territory he and his men had just
traveled through. Those who lived in Pettervil had chosen their anchorage well. If he looked closely, he could even see, leading inland, what could be called a road in good weather. Down this road
he would ride Marigold, there to leave him temporarily in strange
stabling, before he could be taken back to Cyornasberg. Gaurin
made a note to assign Rusken to that task; Rusken had proven one
of the few people Marigold would abide being near him or allow
the liberty of leading him.

Gaurin anticipated that in another hour the camp would be
completed. Fires were already lit so the men could prepare their
meals and find warmth in which to rest. Gaurin knew that he and
Lathrom, along with Svarteper, Tordenskjold, and Rohan would
confer well past their bedtime in Gaurin's tent.

And Öydis, of course. Despite her reputation as a fighter and
her position as Chieftain of the Aslaugors, he still had difficulty
forgetting that she was a woman who scorned being treated as anything but a warrior.

Suddenly, wild yells erupted from the trees behind them and
before anyone quite knew what was happening, the camp was being overrun. There seemed to be no end to the numbers of men
carrying spears, clubs, and a few swords charging toward them.
Even as Gaurin stared, horrified, three of his soldiers fell before
they could bring their weapons to bear.

Lathrom's deep voice was already booming through the camp,
rallying the soldiers, and Svarteper was only a heartbeat behind
him. The Sea-Rovers needed no urging but rushed forward, shouting fierce war cries. Even the archers did not stand back, as was
their wont, but ran toward the invaders, pausing only to fire and
snatch another arrow from their quivers before firing again. Finola
and Bitta uttered their own war cries and sprang toward the conflict. Rajesh and Keltin, being closer to the battle, were already

there, snarling defiance. Screams from enemy throats told of the success of their efforts.

Gaurin put two fingers in his mouth and whistled shrilly. From somewhere in the melee came an answering whinny, and Marigold galloped toward him. He swung himself into the saddle and drew his Rinbell sword in the same motion. Marigold reared, slashing the air with ironshod hooves, and came down with a jarring thud that shook the earth.

Dimly, he was aware that Svarteper had likewise managed to mount Firefly and was already laying about with a heavy war mace. He saw neither Lathrom nor Tordenskjold. Rohan would be with the Sea-Rovers. He caught a brief glimpse of Öydis, on foot, laughing as she fought, her teeth gleaming in the firelight. She struck a two-handed blow with her battle-ax and her enemy fell, cloven nearly in twain.

She noticed him in turn. "Damacro!" she shouted, as she dodged a blow.

Instantly he understood. Baron Damacro, the Aslaugor whose allegiance was with the Great Foulness in the late war. This must be the remnants of his force, still fanatic in their opposition to any Nordorner they encountered. And here he had led an entire army of Nordorners—an irresistible target. Gaurin dug his heels in Marigold's sides, shouting a war cry as he brought his sword down in full force.

Man and stallion fought as one. Marigold screamed his own challenge, lashing out with lethal hooves and teeth, while Gaurin's Rinbell sword filled the air around him with death for any who foolishly ventured too close. An arrow whined past, too close to his head, and he realized, belatedly, that the enemy had archers, too.

"Take them out!" he cried to a Sea-Rover, by the badge he wore, the leader of their bowmen. The man's face was familiar, but he hadn't time to search his mind for the name.

"Already done, NordornKing!" the Sea-Rover shouted in response. At his signal, a veritable hail of arrows winged in the direction from which those of the enemy had come. A few outcries, and the enemy arrows ceased.

Dordan, Gaurin thought. That's who he is. A good man.

Suddenly, the battle was all but over, the rogue Aslaugors defeated. Their lines broke, and they retreated, their attack dissolved in utter rout. Marigold reared once more, trumpeting a challenge echoed by Svarteper's Firefly, but none of the attackers dared face it. A few Sea-Rovers began storming into the gloom of the trees, after the Aslaugors.

"Don't follow!" Öydis shouted.

"Aye, the Chieftain is right!" Marshal Svarteper bellowed, keeping Firefly in check only with an effort. "They'll pick you off one by one in there! Let them go, let them go!"

Reluctantly, the Sea-Rovers—Rohan among them—turned back. "We could finish them here and now," he protested as he joined the other leaders.

"It would be your finish more likely," Tordenskjold told him bluntly. "Put up your sword. We know the Aslaugors best. Let us guide you now."

"Very well, but let it be known that this is not our way," Rohan said through gritted teeth. He turned and addressed his men. "Back to the camp, lads. We'll deal with these fellows later. If at all," he added in a low voice, as if to himself.

"Never you fear, youngster," Öydis said, amused. She dealt him a comradely buffet on the shoulder that nearly knocked him off-balance. "We know how to take care of outlaw bands like this one."

Gaurin whistled, a different signal from the one that had brought Marigold to him. In the distance, the war-kats howled an answer, but did not return immediately. The Nordorners heard one scream from an enemy throat, followed by two more almost as one, then a fourth before the war-kats came trotting back into the camp, looking extremely pleased with themselves.

When he knew that these invaluable allies were safe and unharmed, Gaurin dismounted. "Let us see to the welfare of our men, then meet in my tent. We have much to discuss, more than before."

Their casualties proved to be light, after all, despite the fury and suddenness of the attack. Two of the three Gaurin had seen fall were dead, the third wounded badly enough that he would have to stay behind in Pettervil, but for the rest, there had been only minor injuries once they had drawn weapons. All of them— Nordorners, Sea-Rovers, Aslaugors, the handful of Rendelians— seemed in high spirits, despite so many of the enemy having escaped into the gathering night, and had even now turned to preparing their food. Satisfied, Gaurin made his way to his tent, where his companions awaited him.

Entering, he caught the smell of fallowbeeste stewed with wild onions, and his stomach growled. "Thank you," he said, smiling, as he sat down at the little table and accepted a generous helping. "A fight always awakens an appetite in men—in everyone, even if there was no clear-cut victory."

"You and Rohan and your 'victories,'" Öydis said. She ladled a spoonful of stew into her mouth. "Let me worry about that small matter. Tomorrow's soon enough for it anyway."

"Very well," Gaurin said. He applied himself to his bowl; his had not been a mere jest. He was genuinely hungry.

The rest of them were devouring their meals as well, including the war-kats, who were enjoying generous trimmings from a fallowbeest carcass, gnawing some of the large bones. In a short time the people had set the bowls aside and begun the conference that had been delayed by the unexpected attack.

In the Castle of Fire and Ice, another feast was drawing to a close. Einaar was pleased; Ysa had accomplished her hostess tasks well.

Jugglers, mimes, acrobats, and a man with trained dogs that jumped through burning hoops drew applause from those watching. When the entertainers were finished Lady Pernille took her accustomed seat on the platform and began the Song. The noise in the Great Hall quietened as the newcomers listened, enthralled. Oskar, the aged master, took up a flute to complement the melody. When Lady Pernille's fingers tired on the stringed instrument, Oskar played for her and occasionally sang with her, his old

Andre Norton & Sasha Miller

voice quavering but still strong enough to reach everyone in the room.

As had become customary, Nordorn couples arose from their places, formed a circle in the center of the Hall, danced the simple, elegant steps a while, and then returned to their seats.

Impulsively, Peres held his hand out to Lady Rannore, who was seated at the high table, but not next to him. "Come, Madame Mother, will you dance?"

Rannore's smile was radiant enough to outshine the flambeaus lighting the room. "I will, and right gladly," she replied.

"And you, my lady Duchess?" Royance inquired gallantly. "Will you do me the honor?"

"Of course," Ysa replied.

Einaar glanced around. The NordornQueen's ladies had all been seated at a lower table, across from Ysa'a ladies. Elibit gave him a small, secret smile. Amilia was already in the circle with Fredrikke, eldest son of Baron Gangerolf of Guttorm, and Frida was accepting the hand of Nils, another of the Baron's sons. Now all Einaar had to do was wait until Ragna had been claimed by Axel of Westerblad, the young man who was so desperately—and amusingly—smitten with her. Then he could claim Elibit's company without creating undue comment by the gossips.

Dinna was nowhere to be seen, and, Einaar noted, neither was Blåmann, a jarl connected to Baron Håkon's household. He had a feeling that neither of them would appear again before morning.

Stifling the flash of chagrin at how he had been so easily seduced into Dinna's bed, he approached Lady Elibit. "Will you dance, lady?" he said, knowing the answer.

She blushed and took his proffered hand. He longed to hold her in a close embrace though she was so tiny he feared he might crush her. Even her little hands were lost in his.

He stayed with her as long as he dared—Court wag-tongues were always so eager to start rumors of liaisons—and then, from duty, danced with the Duchess and with Rannore. Courteously, he partnered each of the other Court ladies in turn, noting that both

Peres and Lord Royance were doing the same. Even Tamkin, base-born though he was, had no trouble finding a partner. This portion of the entertainment, he judged, was a complete success. Ysa looked pleased as well.

At last, the flambeaus began to gutter. Peres looked visibly tired, yawning, with dark shadows under his eyes. Einaar rose to his feet and rapped on the table for attention. Master Oskar signaled to Lady Pernille, and they brought the Song to a close.

"Our guests are weary," Einaar said. "Let us not prolong the pleasures of the evening, tempting though it is. Tomorrow we will all gather in conference and so I bid you all a good night."

The Hall filled with the rustling noises of people rising from tables and preparing to go each to his or her own lodging. As Einaar had expected, Royance sent his young charge off to bed, accompanied by Tamkin and his body servants, the Duchess Ysa solicitously and unsuccessfully trying to take charge of the undertaking. Now he stood nearby, as if waiting.

"Will you share a late-evening goblet with me, my lord?" Einaar said politely.

"It would be my honor and my pleasure," the old gentleman replied.

In a very short time, the two men were seated in the small room off Einaar's chamber, where a fire had been lighted and the flagons filled.

"This is very like to my suite in Rendelsham Castle," Royance commented. "It's always good to have a place where one can confer in private, I find."

"I have looked forward to a confidential talk with you, sir, ever since I saw you approaching the gatehouse," Einaar replied. "I never dreamed you would come in person to the NordornLand. I thought you would remain in Rendelsham, since so many of its important people are now absent."

"I almost stayed behind, but Queen Hegrin has, with the current emergency, developed remarkable maturity in a short time. Even old Wittern, with the help of his second-in-command, Edgard, has come out of retirement to sit on the Council. My kinsman,

Nikolos, is well trained in my duties, and I have complete confidence in him. Also, Lathrom's deputy, Steuart, can manage very well in the Marshal's absence if necessary. These are all young knights I have watched coming along from their days as fledgling cadets, during the former Queen's Great Levy."

"I envy you such a number of good and competent people," Einaar said. "We have not yet acquired this depth of strength."

"Your land is ancient, but your country is yet new. It will come, with careful management." The old gentleman leaned back in his chair and regarded Einaar with a keen eye. "Now, tell me. First, what is the situation here, and next, what has our former Dowager Queen, the Duchess Ysa, been up to?"

Einaar discovered he was not as startled by this blunt question as he might have been. Royance had the knack of making it seem they enjoyed the ease of long and intimate acquaintance. Wasting no words, he outlined for Royance the discovery of the Mother Ice Dragon's presence, Gaurin's expedition northward to destroy the menace she presented, the finding of the map that had led Ashen to follow. Then he turned to Ysa's part in awakening the Arikarin, her reticence in admitting what she had done, and, before he could call the words back, her tempting words and near offer concerning the succession.

Lord Royance listened to all with scarcely a change of expression. "How like her ladyship," he commented. "And you, my lord Duke? What say you to the prospect of easing your brother off his throne in his absence and ruling in fact as well as name?"

Despite himself, Einaar was startled at the calm baldness with which Royance phrased his question. "I—I don't quite know what to say."

"Of course you don't." Royance helped himself to another flagon of wine. "Ysa is most accomplished at presenting outrageous schemes in such a way that they seem the very soul of reason. So here, with you. You are still young, Einaar, but I have known Ysa for many years, known of her dabbling in spell casting, watched her at her schemes and machinations, and I am not bragging to say that I have foiled a large number of them personally."

"Did she put me under a spell then?"

Royance laughed. "Of sorts. As easily as she awakened the Arikarin she was able to arouse a longing in you of which you had previously been unaware—but then, dangling a crown before someone's eyes is certain to find a positive reception. Power, or the promise of it, has seduced more seasoned men than you."

It was as if a fog had lifted from Einaar's vision, and he could see clearly after a long darkness. It was almost startling in its suddenness. "Yes, this lure of power can blind someone to everything else. But now I know how to answer your question." He arose from his chair and addressed Lord Royance with full formality. "I was close to being foresworn, but I am my brother's true man, and will fulfill my trust faithfully to him, to Ashen NordornQueen, and to their heir, Prince Bjaudin, as long as there is breath in my body. I cannot swear that the Duchess Ysa's blandishments won't find a response in me again, but with you to guide me I feel that I can resist the call to take power that is not mine. This I swear anew, as I did to Gaurin NordornKing, on the memory of the father who sired us both, and the father who reared me."

"Good man." Royance smiled. "And honest, not to swear to that which you may not be able to fulfill. Now, let us consider how best to turn the Duchess's schemings to our own use."

"You mean, make her think she is succeeding?"

"Best her at her own game. It is plain to me that she longs for another kingdom to rule and has chosen you as her tool with which to accomplish this aim. I think this is something unknown even to her; I daresay you've noticed that Ysa is very good at overlooking unpleasant facts when it suits her. So it ever was. Perhaps, between us, we can get her to reveal herself in such a way that she cannot ignore it, and in that manner she will finally learn that this sort of meddling cannot be tolerated. It will be good for the repose of her restless spirit if she can be brought to accept this lesson."

Einaar sat down and took a deep breath, feeling as if an enormous burden had been lifted from his shoulders. Despite the many dangers still facing the NordornLand, he was heartened by Royance's words. "How glad I am that you are here, Lord Royance," he said. "Had you not decided to accompany King Peres and had we not had this private talk, I shudder to think of what might have befallen because of the Duchess's idle actions."

"Never think Ysa idle," Royance cautioned. "Unless she has changed drastically, she always has a purpose for everything she does. In this instance, I believe it is her aim, whether she acknowledges it or not—or even recognizes it—to rule the NordornLand as she once did Rendel, and that is no small matter. We must also grant that her motives be good ones, for she has always genuinely believed that she was the most fit for governing whatever and whenever the occasion arose—and, to give her her due, generally, she was correct."

"A complicated woman," Einaar said.

"Beyond the depth of most men. You are to be commended for merely venturing near the abyss, not tumbling in." Royance finished the contents of his flagon and rose from his chair. "Now I can bid you good rest with a heart not nearly as heavy as that I bore before we spoke."

Einaar likewise got to his feet again and bowed low to the old gentleman. "And I as well," he said. "Thank you, sir. You have my undying gratitude and friendship. I bid you good night."

Thick snow was beginning to fall, making the trail Ashen's company followed more difficult to keep, although they knew by continuing along the coastline they would not become lost.

"Isn't it early for such a heavy storm as this?" Ashen asked Cebastian, brushing snowflakes from her eyelashes. The wind had begun to blow, making her hug her cloak even tighter about her body.

"Yes, it is," he said, "but you must remember, my Nordorn-Queen, the farther north we travel, the more we must endure the cold and sudden storms such as this one. The days are long and night is slow to fall. In full winter, such travel would be impossible, even for those who live here year-round."

"Gaurin and his companions must be suffering."

Dragon Blade

Cebastian smiled at her. "Not yet, my NordornQueen. Remember, he has many wool tents with him, so he is even better able to endure than we, and we have yet to complain of more than a bit of chill. When we catch up, you'll see."

Nevertheless, when they stopped to rest in what the men called twi-night, Ashen noted that while their dinner was cooking, Cebastian had the men build shelters for the horses as well. Above, flashes of colored lights like curtains could occasionally be seen in the northern sky.

"Good thing I have Weyse with me," Zazar grumbled, when the women had retired for the night. "Else, I would never be warm. She's taken to sleeping under the covers, you know." The old Wysen-wyf kindled the little fire and began to brew a hot drink, different from the morning potion she had continued to prepare for Ashen. When it was steaming, she poured it into two mugs.

"We'll soon catch up with Gaurin," Ashen said, accepting her mug gratefully. "Then we can give him the map, and return home once more."

"After you've assured yourself he isn't frozen solid," Zazar said sharply, but with a trace of humor.

"Well, yes," Ashen admitted, smiling a little. "Am I foolish to feel so?"

"No," Zazar said with a sigh. "Merely foolish to risk yourself on this journey. But I've told you that before."

"Something I cannot explain drives me onward," Ashen said. "You of all people should understand this sort of thing."

"Oh, I do, I do. That's why I dropped my objections, and even the reason I let you drag me out into the snow and the cold when I should be seeing to it that Beatha is performing her nursemaid duties properly. Not sure she hasn't frozen her brain and forgotten everything, and I'm sure she needs my direction."

Ashen's heart cramped. "I had vowed not to think about Prince Bjauden, lest such thoughts turn me from my mission."

"I'm just an old woman being cross," Zazar said, but her tone had softened. "Days that don't end, night that won't fall. It's my right to complain."

Now Ashen was certain that Zazar was teasing her. But to what purpose? "Complain all you will," she told the Wysen-wyf. "It's a longer journey back than it is ahead of us, so you might as well make the best of things since you won't be returning alone. Also, I heard the men talking, and they expect to reach the road inland to Pettervil perhaps tomorrow. We travel faster than Gaurin can, with his large company, and it may even be possible that he will still be there. If not, from there, we can pick up his trail easily. So no more complaining from you, if you please. Or even if you don't."

At that, Zazar actually chuckled. "You're coming along, girl, if slowly," she said. "I like the stiff backbone you're daring to show me. Now get you to sleep. I'll bank the coals to get a little extra heat in here without too much risk of burning this place down around our heads. We're bound to have a hard push ahead of us tomorrow, as set as you are on getting to Pettervil almost before you left home."

Outside, the snow was still falling, even thicker than before. Flakes drifted through the top of the shelter, and the air was chill enough that some did not melt until they fell, sizzling, onto the grayish coals. Even though full night was a long time coming in this time of twi-night, the cold continued to deepen. Despite the added warmth the banked fire provided, Ashen felt the chill pressing down on her through the snow-thistle bedding. Both women put on extra clothing and spread their cloaks over themselves as well, to keep out the wetness as the snow eventually melted, and for any possible additional warmth. Tomorrow, Ashen determined, she would get out the knitted coifs and make Zazar wear hers, by force if necessary.

At last Ashen fell into an uneasy sleep, disturbed by dreams of an unconquerable Ice Dragon towering over six motionless people and four war-kats facing her. As if selecting tidbits from a tray, it extended its long neck toward them, one by one, and daintily opened its mouth—

It seemed but a few moments before Zazar was handing her her morning tonic. Ashen drank the hot potion in grateful silence, knowing better than to mention anything about her restless night, lest Zazar, Cebastian, and the House Troops, who had professed themselves willing to die in her service, hinder her from what she felt was the last stage in her journey. Weary or not, she would present Gaurin with the map that might, if the legends proved true, lead him to the only chance of conquering the Mother Ice Dragon.

At the Nordorners' camp, the weather turned foul overnight, with heavy, blowing snow that piled up deep drifts. Despite his impatience at the delay it would cost him, Gaurin welcomed it, knowing that a repeat of the attack of a few hours before was very unlikely.

With the morning, the leaders of the company joined him for the heated remnants of the previous evening's stew plus the last of the roasted fallowbeeste, still on the bone. A pitcher of the bitter morning beverage the Aslaugors had an unaccountable fondness for, preferring it to the customary ale, steamed in the chilly air, ready to be poured into mugs.

His commanders entered his tent, brushing heavy snow from their garments. They threw back hoods, took off their knitted coifs, and found their places at the table.

"I have decided what we shall do," Öydis announced, falling to the meal as heartily as she had the night before.

"Oh?" Gaurin said. "Then pray inform us."

"Don't be so high-and-mighty," Öydis said, grinning. "You're the NordornKing, but I remind you, you're in my country now. You may reign, but here, I rule."

Gaurin swallowed the rash, irascible words that sprang to his lips, knowing the woman was well within her rights to claim precedence. He knew also that his irritation was not her doing but rather his chafing at the delay. "I accept your correction," he said.

"Good." Öydis tossed a fallowbeeste bone, still with scraps of meat on it, through the tent opening. "That's for your pets. Now. While the rest of you were sleeping, I was up and about, making sure that we weren't attacked again in the night. Frankly, I don't trust any sentinel other than myself. The snow stopped for a while and the lights in the sky were brilliant, almost bright enough to read by. While I was patrolling, I got the lay of the land and how we had been ambushed, and even a good estimate of how many there were in the fight—about twice our number. It was easy, to see that they anticipated just where we would make our camp, and all they had to do was wait until the right moment. I think they expected us to break and run, and now they're holed up somewhere, making new plans."

"You think they'll come after us again?" Tordenskjold asked.

"If they're anything like the people we fought during the late war, you can wager your entire estate on it," Rohan said. "They're single-minded that way. Furthermore, they were clever enough to design a trap for us that nearly worked."

"Was that Damacro's plan?" Öydis asked.

"It's hard to say," Lathrom replied. "The Baron was in no shape to be interrogated after the battle ended; his head was off, you see." He went on to describe the desperate battle in the narrow valley against Aslaugors, Fridians, and Ice Dragons, and how the Sea-Rovers had come close to disaster by being lured into attacking the camp behind the lines, only to find themselves attacked instead. "If Gaurin NordornKing hadn't left the valley fight in my charge and gone to their relief, young Rohan wouldn't be here today."

"Sounds like Damacro's doing," Öydis said.

"We learned something that day," Rohan said, "but I have no clear idea how to apply the lesson."

"No need to worry about it," Öydis assured him, "because I do." She turned to the other men around the table. "Here's my plan. You know Patin, my marshal."

"No, I don't think so," Gaurin said.

"Of course you do," the Aslaugor Chieftain told him. "He carried that great stinking bundle into the Council chamber the first time we talked."

The hulking Aslaugor who had been at Öydis's right hand then, and since. "Ah, now I remember him," Gaurin said. "I was not aware of his name or his rank."

"He's my son," Öydis proclaimed, with more than a touch of

pride. "Not a finer warrior, except me, to be found in the whole of Aslaugor territory."

"You're a widow then?" Svarteper inquired politely.

"Never married. That doesn't matter," Öydis continued impatiently. "What I've decided, with this change in the weather, is to station you and the men, except for a few of Patin's men, at Pettervil. There you will remain in reserve and also as bait."

"For the rogue Aslaugors to nibble at?" Tordenskjold laughed richly.

"Just so." Öydis emptied her mug of the hot beverage in a single gulp before refilling it. "Patin will take his Aslaugors and go out looking for the renegades. I say we should all get to Pettervil as quickly as we can. He'll let 'em chase him toward the village. Then you can all enjoy a much better battle than the little skirmish last night."

"And what shall I be doing in the meantime?" Gaurin inquired, interested in spite of himself.

"Going about your errand, of course. Look you. You brought too many soldiers with you—or not enough. You already know something of Damacro's strategy. He liked to hold back half his force or more in reserve, so you can double the number I estimated. One of his lieutenants must be leading this rabble and using Damacro's methods."

"They did seem to be following some kind of a plan, rather than its being a random attack," Svarteper commented. "Despite the confusion, it seems to me they were too well organized for that."

"Against the village, I believe they'll go full out in an attack, smashing hard with everything they've got. If my guess is right, the men in Pettervil will be outnumbered at least five to one. Possibly more." Öydis turned to Gaurin. "Speed's your friend, Nordorn-King, and you'll travel both better and faster with just a few companions. Perhaps only one dogsled with food and other supplies. You'll be safer, too, leaving your men behind to keep these renegades busy and off your trail. If you're worried that the men will object to your going on ahead, this will keep them too busy to do anything about it, you can count on that."

The Chieftain sat back in her chair, waiting for the response, her entire attitude proclaiming that she expected it to be favorable.

Gaurin fought a fresh burst of annoyance, admitting that he was impressed with the depth and thoroughness of her planning. "Your arrogance borders on insolence, Madame Chieftain," he said. "But you are, as you have oft reminded me, the ruler here, and also you know your people far better than I. So I will consider your proposal."

"Of course," Öydis returned blandly. She didn't allow even a hint of a smile to cross her features, but the twinkling in her eyes gave her away. Plainly, she was amused.

"There's merit in what the Great Chieftain suggests," Lathrom said, "as long as I am one of those who accompany Gaurin NordornKing."

"And I!" Svarteper exclaimed.

"I won't be left behind," Rohan declared.

"Oh, yes, you will be," Tordenskjold said. "You and I have ships to command and touchy Sea-Rovers itching for a fight to hold in check. They won't be happy when they find out they're to be confined inside the town. And you, too, Svarteper."

"The Lord High Marshal's place is beside his king," Svarteper stated. His tone was belligerent. "I'll fight anybody who tries to keep me from his side."

Tordenskjold snorted. "Oh, of course you'd do that. And take yourself out of the real battle? This decision isn't yours to make," he said bluntly. "I see the Chieftain's plan plain even if you don't. The Lord High Marshal's place is where his king decides to put him. Somebody has to be in charge here, a Nordorner whose authority will not be questioned, and that's you. I think we'll all serve him better by removing such obstacles as renegade Aslaugors from his path. And by being ready, in reserve, when he should call on us."

Öydis shrugged. "Fight it out among yourselves," she said. "No more than five men, total, should go on with Gaurin NordornKing, though. Including me, of course. And his pets."

"It would be folly to leave you behind," Gaurin said. He made his decision. "Very well. Our army includes men from the NordornLand, Aslaug, Rendel, and the Sea-Rovers. Of the three presently decided who will journey on—you, Lathrom, myself— we represent the NordornLand, Aslaug, and Rendel. I propose adding Dordan the archer from the Sea-Rovers. Who shall the other two be?"

"Take my son Lars," Svarteper said. "He's all but my second-in-command. If I have to stay cooped up waiting for some battle that may never happen, I'll feel better if Lars Svartepersson is with you."

"Granted. And the sixth?"

"Well, I have a suggestion," Öydis said, "and this time it really is just that. I've been in this part of the land, yes, but I admit I'm not familiar with the places where we'll be traveling. If we're lucky, and he's in town, I'll be able to contact a Fridian scout once we get to Pettervil, one I know and who can be trusted. Ueli knows the country even better than I do."

"Then please make inquiries as soon as this storm abates enough that we can move on inland and put our people into better quarters." Gaurin arose, indicating that the conference was ended. "The more swiftly our picked band travels, the more quickly we shall return."

"And the sooner we will all be in the Blue Snogpus—that's the local public house in Pettervil—toasting our success," Öydis said.

Her statement, Gaurin thought, was unnecessary and detracted from his own. She merely wanted to assert her authority by having the last word. It annoyed him all over again but on consideration, he decided it would be wise on his part to let her have it.

Twelve

The storm kept Ashen's company huddled inside their shelters for two days. She couldn't help but notice that Weyse, content until now as long as they were traveling northward, grew increasingly restless. From time to time she would leave the relative warmth of the shelter Ashen and Zazar shared and eventually return, whimpering, covered with snow and half-frozen. Then the women would rub life back into the strange little creature and tuck her under a coverlet until she got warm again.

"She wants to be on her way to find Finola," Zazar commented.

"We'll be moving as soon as we can," Ashen said, fondling Weyse's round little ears. Fortunately, they were as thickly furred as the rest of her, else they would have been frozen off long ere now. "Little one, I wish you could understand me."

"Oh, she does, more than she lets on," Zazar said. She peered out through one of the curtains the women had rigged to close the ends of their shelter. "I think the snow's going to let up soon, but it'll be even colder for us on the trail than before."

"We might be uncomfortable but the snow-thistle silk will keep us from freezing," Ashen said. She picked up a scarf, designed to be wrapped across her mouth and nose. "Do you remember when you had Rohan creating those lengths of plain silk, to protect the men's faces during the war? He was so annoyed that his broken arm kept him out of the fighting."

"Well, it was good for him. That was his sole magic trick, and I saw no reason for him just to sit on his backside and be lazy when he could be helping even in such a humble way." Zazar rummaged for her own scarf. "These are better, of course, but we didn't have snow-thistles to make fabric from then."

"I hope Gaurin is safe. And warm. And dry."

"Quit worrying, girl. Didn't Cebastian remind you of the wool tents he has with him? Your lord knows what he's about, and he certainly knows enough to get inside in foul weather. Which is more than a lot of men understand," Zazar added.

"You don't especially like men, do you?" Ashen asked.

The old Wysen-wyf sniffed. "Rather, you could say, I don't much like *people*," she replied. "I like them less the longer I live. A few exceptions, but not many."

"Who?" Ashen inquired, genuinely curious. At best, she could learn more of the woman who had reared her, but who remained very much a mystery in so many ways. At worst, it was a topic with which to help pass the time.

"Well, Gaurin. And Rohan, sometimes. Cebastian, a little. Royance. That master of the *Spume Maiden*. He had a good head on his shoulders."

"No women?"

"Hah! Precious few. Being around Ysa has nearly soured me on the lot. Rannore's got some substance to her. Anamara might, given a few years. She's done wonders for Rohan."

"Anyone else?"

Unexpectedly, Zazar grinned. "Fishing for compliments, are you? Well, yes, I admit that I have a certain . . . liking for you, girl. I expect it's because I had to put up with you for so long."

Ashen was glad she had her face muffled in the scarf, so her smile was hidden. "Perhaps also because I didn't turn out too badly?" she said.

"Don't give yourself airs. I don't like you much at the moment, for dragging me out to freeze in a pine-bough lean-to."

Ashen forbore to point out that Zazar had insisted on coming along. Or that she was faring as well as any of them in a shelter designed for use in this climate. She decided to change the subject. "What do you miss most about being back in Cyornasberg?"

"Not much. My own room. My fireplace. My bed. Food that isn't just stewed meat some man prepared without salt or seasoning. What about you?"

"Well, what you mentioned, of course, but I also miss things I never thought I would. Dresses that are pretty as well as warm. Perfume. Hot water to bathe in. Hot snowberry juice."

"You've gone soft!" Zazar scoffed.

Someone cleared his throat just outside. "NordornQueen, Madame Zazar, the storm looks to be almost over, at least enough so that we can travel," Cebastian said. "I know you are eager to be on your way again, so how soon can you be packed and ready?"

"Sooner than your men can strike camp!" Zazar exclaimed.

Her sour mood vanished at once, and even Weyse perked up her ears and uttered a trill for the first time since the storm had locked about them. The Wysen-wyf immediately started scrambling her belongings into a stack to put into the panniers on her saddle, and Ashen did likewise. She inhaled once more the fragrance of the boughs. Pleasant as the scent was, she would be glad to leave it behind if it meant reaching Gaurin that much more quickly.

As he entered the village, Gaurin made a quick but thorough inspection of what Pettervil had to offer his men in the way of defensive positions.

"We regret that we are putting your people into danger," he told the headman, an Aslaugor named Doffen. "We had hoped to bring you some good fortune by hiring your stables for our mounts, but circumstances have turned against us."

"Naught but more of what we've had to put up with of late from renegades under Damacro's lieutenant Asmal," Doffen replied. "They say they're rebels keeping Damacro's quarrel going, but all they really want to do is raid and pillage. Steal our horses.

We've suffered them long enough. If you can put a stop to their doings, I say, go it and that'll be good fortune enough." He grinned. "We'll still charge for stabling your animals, only at a cut rate if you get my meaning."

Gaurin laughed, knowing that the stablemasters in Pettervil would earn every coin they got, several times over, now that Marigold and Firefly would not be returning to their stalls at Cyornasberg. Then he strode off to continue his assessment of what the town had to offer in defense against open attack.

He was pleased to find that Pettervil boasted a wall around what had once been an isolated fort. The old fort grounds had become the village square. Any gate the walls had once boasted had long since disappeared; only the opening remained. Most of the village itself now lay outside these ancient confines. The stables and horse pens were located on the south side of town. They would be difficult for an attacker to traverse, and so offered their own defense.

Some of the houses were built in traditional Fridian fashion— a conical construction of bones and tusks of huge animals, covered with hides. Most, however, had gone to daub and wattle. Perhaps hunting had grown lean and the big beasts hard to track. Perhaps "civilization" was catching up with the Fridians, here in Pettervil at least.

If, Gaurin thought, a stockade fence could be erected around the other three sides of the village, the people could find some protection thereby, retiring behind the fortress walls only if the enemy broke through the outer defenses. They must put together a gate of sorts that might keep them out for a while.

Sea-Rovers were accomplished at making much out of little, so he set Rohan to that task. Men had been very busy bringing supplies into the village by dogsled and by Rohan's order the last loads were piled high with the most sturdy boughs from the camp.

Presently the air was filled with the sounds of stakes being driven into the frozen ground. The thick boughs, woven into mats, would then be lashed to the stakes, forming a dense wall that would stop all but the heaviest stones or arrows. Despite the location of the pens, there was no way to anticipate from which direction the expected attack would come, so the men had to surround the village on all sides as best they could. The village men fell to work beside the armsmen, showing them how the makeshift walls could be set up more efficiently if they were positioned between the houses, letting those structures become part of the barriers.

"Those buildings are apt to suffer," Rohan reported, wiping sweat off his brow. "We thought to protect as many as we could, but the people are all eagerness to help. Wattle and daub is easy to replace, one of the men told me, and it's a price they're willing to pay to be free of the renegades."

Satisfied that the reinforcement of Pettervil's defenses was in capable hands, Gaurin went in search of Öydis, to see if she had had any luck locating the Fridian scout. He found her at the Blue Snogpus at an isolated table, deep in conversation with a person who could be none other than the one she had mentioned.

Öydis glanced up as he joined them. "Have some ale," she said by way of greeting. "Apt to be your last chance for a while." She signaled the tavern keeper to bring a tankard for Gaurin. "This is Ueli."

The little man seated at the table across from her was busy licking clean the last spoonful of stew from the bowl before him. He was dressed in a shapeless tunic and leggings like most people wore, but made of leather rather than wool or snow-thistle silk. The hood of his tunic, rimmed with wulvine fur, was shoved back, revealing a flat, swarthy face decorated with tribal tattoos. He seemed not very impressed by being in the presence of royalty; he didn't acknowledge Gaurin's presence until he had taken a mighty pull from his tankard and wiped foam from his mouth.

"Greetings, NordornKing," he said. "Öydis tells me you want hire me for little trip north. She's close-mouthed about where you go but I got good brains. I figure out. Big thing—you know what I mean, don't want to say out loud—live up there, make more mess than Aslaugor raiders. You go hunt it? Yes? Then you pay me plenty gold."

"Gold you will have," Gaurin said. "Ten gold coins if you can guide me to where this—big thing can be found."

"Nobody better," Ueli returned unconcernedly. "Pay first, though, leave here. Gold no good to take along. Too heavy."

"I'll leave the coins with Headman Doffen," Gaurin said.

"Good. He honest man. But better leave about two-times, mark you, than you pay me."

Öydis guffawed loudly, causing some heads to turn. "He'll settle for one gold coin to pay for the keeping," she told Gaurin, "or he'll answer to me." She laughed again. "How're the defenses coming?"

"Very quickly," Gaurin replied. "And what of Patin? Any news?"

"Gone hunting already," Öydis said. "He'll flush 'em out, never fear. Hope the barricades are up by the time he gets back."

"They'll be ready. All that remains is to gather our six—including our scout here—and slip out under what cover we can manage and hope that all the activity in the village will distract any scouts who might be watching."

"Just so. Your friend Lathrom and Lars Svartepersson are out finding a dogsled to pack with supplies. Dordan is still helping his friends with the barricade, but he'll leave off and join us at your signal."

Gaurin nodded. He arose and went to negotiate with the tavern keeper, Stehmar, to reserve sleeping rooms for his officers and also for food and drink to be kept ready for them, whatever the hour.

By the time he had finished with this task, his small company had gathered. Under the cover of the snow that had begun to fall once more, they unobtrusively left the town and headed northward, accompanied by the four war-kats.

Ashen saw that the heaviest of the snow had abated though occasional flurries still plagued them. However, Cebastian judged that their company was able to travel. They pushed on steadily. When they rounded an outcropping of rock, she was both dismayed and astonished to find that they had been forced to stop just short of catching up with Gaurin. His campsite had lain but a morning's ride distant from hers.

"Where are they?" she said to Cebastian. "The ships are still at anchor, but this place looks well-nigh deserted. There are only a few men still here."

"It looks like they are cleaning the area after loading the supplies from the ships for transport. I will go and find out," he replied, dismounting. He approached the workers and began asking questions.

"There's been a battle here," Zazar commented, looking about. "Recently, too."

"How do you know?"

"I can smell it. Look over yonder. See the spears? That's a funeral mound."

Ashen's heart was in her throat. "Gaurin—"

"Don't be foolish, girl. If he were among the dead, there would be a hubbub the likes of which would reach clear back to Cyornasberg. Strange way for them to strike the shelters, though. Before now, we could always find a great pile of boughs left. You'd think it would be so here, but there's little but needles remaining. Wonder what happened."

Cebastian returned to the impatient women.

"What news?" Ashen demanded. "What of Gaurin? Is he hurt? Where does he lie?"

"Be easy, my NordornQueen," Cebastian told her. "The NordornKing is well and all with him save two who were killed. Yon mound covers his enemies, but more escaped. The Great Aslaugor Chieftain has sent some of her men to keep those busy. Pettervil is even now being made ready for an expected attack from renegade Aslaugors. I don't like taking you there, but I have no choice because we cannot retrace our steps without risking being attacked and overwhelmed. Therefore, it is the safest place for you. We must hurry on to the village."

He nodded at the men. Without a word, Goliat and Fjodor took positions on either side of Ashen, guarding her, and Nels and Arild likewise moved to protect Zazar.

"They'll not get past me," Goliat told both of the women. "In fact, I'd like to see them try!"

Her spirits lifted somewhat, Ashen dug her heels into her horse's sides, and the party rode at a rapid trot toward the village. There, she thought, I will see my Gaurin once more and deliver to him the means of obtaining the Dragon Blade. Just to see him, to know that he is safe—

Then to return home as soon as the danger from these renegade Aslaugors had passed. Had they once been under the command of Baron Damacro? Had they not learned that the war was ended?

No time to ponder such questions. They would be soon answered when reached Pettervil.

As the town came in sight, she saw clearly the preparations being made. Green walls, different from anything she had ever seen, were springing up before her eyes— Suddenly she recognized what they were. Bundles of springy pine boughs, obviously the remnants of Gaurin's camp, made into mats before being lashed into place as barricades.

"Well, that answers that question," Zazar said. "Can we slow down now? I've got a stitch in my side, and Weyse is jounced almost into insensibility."

"Soon, Zazar. Gaurin—"

Rohan caught sight of her from where he was overseeing some of the construction. "Ashen!" he cried. "Ashen NordornQueen, I mean! What in the name of all the Powers are you doing here?"

"Looking for Gaurin!" she shouted in reply, reining in her horse. "Where is he?"

He hurried toward her. "Gaurin? He's—around, someplace. Allow me to help you dismount—if this large fellow with the scowl on his face will let me."

Goliat had put himself and his horse between Rohan and Ashen, an immovable obstacle, staring at the Sea-Rover.

"He won't," Goliat said. He swung himself out of his saddle to lift Ashen as lightly as if she were one of the snowflakes that spangled her cloak. "Here, my NordornQueen," he said, setting her gently on her feet.

"Goliat, this is my kinsman, my foster son. Rohan of the Sea-Rovers," she told the guard. "I would put my life in his hands."

"That task's for me, as long as there's breath in my body," Goliat told her in return. He frowned again at Rohan. Obviously, in spite of the NordornQueen's words, he regarded him with grave suspicion.

"Be that as it may, where is Gaurin?" Ashen repeated, turning once more to Rohan.

"You'd better come with me." He started off toward the center of town, followed by Ashen's company. "Good to see you again, Cebastian," he said over his shoulder. "Sorry about the circumstances."

Puzzled at Rohan's refusal to answer her question, Ashen followed him nonetheless. Presently, they came to a building somewhat larger than the houses surrounding it. Instead of being built sensibly square the way the other structures were, a wing jutted out to the side, with many windows dotting the walls. A sign over the door bore the image of a snowcat, painted blue.

"What is this place?" Ashen asked.

"It's a public house, the Blue Snogpus," Rohan said. "A tavern and also an inn. Center of town activity. I haven't seen Gaurin lately, but if anybody knows anything of his whereabouts, you'll be apt to find them inside."

"I see," Ashen said. "I have never been to a public house before. Do you knock on the door?"

"No, just go in. I've got to get back to work. You've heard about the renegades? Don't worry, we'll keep you all safe. I just hope there's a room inside for you. If not, let Goliat have a little chat with the owner."

Then he turned and was gone, leaving Ashen biting back laughter in spite of herself. "He hasn't changed a bit, not really," she murmured. Surely he had merely been teasing her with his evasiveness. Her present uneasy feeling had no basis in fact.

A little awkwardly, Ashen pushed the door open. Air heavy with smoke from the fire, thickly scented with the smell of old stew and sour ale, nearly set her to coughing. For a moment she wavered, but Gaurin might be just within. Squaring her shoulders, the NordornQueen went inside.

Einaar resisted an impulse to move his chair to Gaurin's position at the head of the Council table even though the Duchess Ysa's up-lifted eyebrow told him that she thought this was his proper place, even to occupying the chair with the NordornKing's insignia carved into the back. He took the place where he had always sat, and glanced around at those in attendance.

King Peres occupied the place of honor at Einaar's right, with Lord Royance at his left, on the other side of Gaurin's empty chair. Ysa sat next to Peres. Count Mjødulf of Mithlond and Count Baldrian of Westerblad were already in their customary seats. The barons, Arngrim of Rimfaxe and Håkon of Erlend, occupied chairs lower down the table. Gangerolf of Guttorm was late. It seemed to be a habit of his, Einaar thought. It was common knowledge he had been tardy even in the building of his town house.

"Let us not wait overlong for Lord Gangerolf," he began. "You all know everyone here—"

Even as he spoke, the door banged open, and Gangerolf strode in. A tall, bluff man, his bearing proclaiming that he was used to being a law unto himself, he did not offer any excuses. Not a sur-prising attitude for one of the independent border-lords, Einaar thought.

"Welcome," he said crisply. "Now we can begin in earnest. There is much to be discussed."

"Mostly it's about levies of men to fight some fool danger on my border, or so I've heard," Gangerolf said. He slammed the door, pulled his chair out, the legs scraping harshly on the polished floor, and dropped solidly into it.

Ysa winced. "It is danger, yes, my lord Baron," she said, "but not a foolish one."

"That remains to be seen," Gangerolf said. He turned to the man seated next to him. "Look you, Arngrim. You've got the repu-tation for breeding the best horses in the NordornLand. I want to talk to you about buying some good animals to keep here in town. You remember Lina, my wife. She told me to ask you."

"That reminds me. Esska wants some, too—a matched pair to draw her sleigh," Håkon said.

"Of course," Arngrim said. "Where's the wine? We'll make our bargain, then drink on it."

Mjødulf pretended to ignore them. Baldrian scowled. His county lay adjacent to the baronies so he was, therefore, charged with keeping them in line. Peres had a disconcerted look on his face at the manners of the Nordorn barons, but Royance was openly amused. Ysa looked as if she had bitten into something sour.

Einaar rapped on the table for attention. "Gentlemen, please." When quiet was restored, he drew a piece of paper closer and began to address the items he had noted. "First, the danger that Gangerolf is so quick to dismiss. For this, I wish to call someone else to describe it." He touched a bell, and a steward ushered yet another person into the Council chamber.

"This is Esander, the priest of the Fane of the Castle of Fire and Ice," he said.

Most of those at the table nodded in greeting; Gangerolf, Einaar noted, looked blank. Obviously he had not yet been to the Fane to make the priest's acquaintance.

"Esander, will you please inform those here present of what we currently know concerning the Arikarin?"

"I obey, my lord Duke, but without pleasure," Esander replied. Then he began the tale.

By the time he had finished, Gangerolf looked as if he were badly in need of Esander's spiritual counseling. Even those who already knew the tale accepted with trembling hands goblets of hot spiced snowberry juice lightly laced with wine and drank, as if to steady shaken nerves.

"Thank you, Esander," Einaar said.

The priest bowed and left the Council chamber. There was silence for a few moments from those around the table. Then the questions began.

"How many men will you be wanting from each of us?" Baldrian asked.

"Aye, and horses. What kind? War-trained, or ordinary riding animals?" Arngrim asked.

"Are you indeed planning to mount an army and ride out against this monster?" Håkon wanted to know.

"Pfaugh," Gangerolf snorted. "I can have a hundred men ready to march within the hour if need be. No need for horses. Riding into a fight is for weaklings, children, and women."

Håkon bristled, and there would have been hot words exchanged if Lord Royance hadn't intervened, just a heartbeat before Einaar could do so.

"I daresay we'll need all our resources before this is over," he told the quarrelsome barons. "And a good use for all, as your people and mine defend your homeland against this creature out of legend however best we may. Pray do not waste time and energy battling each other."

Gangerolf and Håkon arose, bowed to each other, and took their seats again.

"I want you all to draw up proposals for how best to proceed from this point," Einaar said. "We will meet again two mornings hence. Now, I wish us to ponder the question of whether or not to send word to Gaurin NordornKing about this current danger and ask him to return."

"Little to think about. Our king has enough on his hands with his pursuit of the Mother Ice Dragon," Mjødulf observed. "And also, the Court gossip has it that Ashen NordornQueen has undertaken a dangerous journey to join him, for reasons best known to herself."

"Indeed, as you must have noted, her chair stands empty," Einaar said. "The NordornQueen carries with her the key to finding the one weapon that might slay this dragon. Her mission is as perilous to her as his to him. Danger stares back at us, my lords, every way we turn."

"Then leave them to their errands," Baldrian stated. "Time enough to burden them with their new peril, once they return."

Einaar glanced at Ysa, weighing his next statement. "If they return," he said.

The words fell heavily in the sudden silence of the room.

"But that is something we need *not* discuss at this meeting, and, it is to be hoped, a question that will never trouble us," Einaar went on. "Baldrian opposes notifying our king. How say the rest of you? Shall we have a show of hands?"

"I say, leave him be," Arngrim said. He raised his hand.

One after another, the rest of those at the Council table followed his gesture.

"We can handle anything this Arikarin can try to do to us," Gangerolf stated, his voice almost a growl. "I'll lead one division of foot soldiers, and my sons Frederikke and Nils will lead two more. Edvard is still untried in battle."

"My sons Thorgrim and Kolgrim and I will head up three troops of cavalry," Arngrim said, not to be outdone. "How about you, Håkon?"

"I have only a daughter—so far, at least—but I'll put together as many men as I can and lead 'em myself." The baron turned to the two counts who had not as yet spoken. "And you gentlemen?"

"I will send word to begin the muster at once," Baldrian said.

Mjødulf stirred in his chair, his expression thoughtful, and Einaar recalled that he had the reputation of being one with a long head, who could see beyond the morrow.

"You three are true warriors," Mjødulf said. "And Baldrian's loyalty knows no bounds. But you forget that there is more to defend than the countryside. We have both castle and the growing city to look after. I doubt that there are more than twoscore soldiers within these walls."

"That brings us to the last item on my list," Einaar said. "Most of us have families now living in the city who know nothing of these grim matters. In the Castle of Fire and Ice dwell several highborn ladies—" he bowed to Ysa, who nodded in reply "—and we are host to the King of Rendel along with important members of his Court. Finally, in our zeal to protect our loved ones, we must remember that the safety of the heir, Bjaudin NordornPrins, is our responsibility. I want each of you to send a score of men for the defense of both city and castle. These men can serve as reinforcements for those out in the field if necessary, and if the unthinkable occurs and you need to retreat, together we can hold out for a long time behind these walls."

The words he did not say—the doomed survivors, those who would learn to envy the ones already dead—hung as heavily in the air as his previous reference to the possibility that the Nordorn-King and NordornQueen might not return.

"It is a grim situation, gentlemen—and my lady Duchess—and there is no gainsaying this fact. But it is a situation we cannot turn our heads from."

King Peres spoke up for the first time. "Now I regret that I did not bring an army of my own with me," he said. "I can send word—"

"Thank you, but not yet, Your Majesty," Einaar told him. "I hope matters will not come to that. Your presence and that of Lord Royance strengthen our resolve enough, for now." He got to his feet. "Until next we meet, gentlemen. I hope that you have a good report for me then."

"You did well," Royance told Einaar, when they were in the Lord High Protector's private chamber once more. "Very well. I was watching Ysa's face. She nodded approval when you mentioned the possibility that Gaurin and Ashen might not return."

"I hope that was approval of my words and not a wish against our sovereigns." Einaar stared gloomily into the fire.

"Oh, I think so," Royance said. "Even Ysa wouldn't go so far as to ill-wish either one of them. But, as she so cleverly—and truthfully—says, anything might happen, and it pays to be prepared. Just in case." He poured a flagon of strong wine, barely diluted, and drank gratefully. "This goes down much better than insipid, warm fruit juice, though I can certainly see the need for a mild drink with that hotheaded lot of barons you have to deal with."

"That was the Duchess's doing," Einaar said. "She obviously learned of their quarrelsome natures and wished to add no unnecessary fuel to any flame that might spring up."

"Not much worry if you boil the wine long enough, which hardly anybody bothers about these days. They want the extra heat, even if it makes them drunk. How do you manage to have fruit juice this time of year?"

"Snowberries originally grew wild year-round in the Nordorn-Land, even in my homeland, Asbøre Isle. Mother had several bushes in her garden, but they were just ornamental plants. Experts developed even more tasty varieties that are grown as a commercial crop for the juice. We Nordorners drink it by the gallon, sometimes mixed with wine, sometimes not."

"Interesting tale. Maybe I can take some slips back to Rendel, later, see if they survive a milder climate. But to get back to the Duchess, as you commented before, Ysa is a complicated woman," Royance said. "I have never been able to come to a firm opinion as to whether she is a good woman, not scrupling to use evil means when it suited her, or an evil woman pretending to be good. I think more the former."

"As do I," Einaar said. "Well, that's a matter we can set aside for the moment. Now I want to ask you about the wisdom of telling the women residing in the castle, Lady Rannore in particular, about what is facing us."

Royance thought for a moment. "Tell Rannore, if no other. After all, she wears one of the Great Signets. As to the rest of them, I think that knowledge is always better than ignorance when we are face-to-face with danger."

"Then I will call everyone together in the Great Hall, and I will also send out criers to Cyornasberg to inform the people. I only hope that we have no panic at the news."

"The Arikarin is still an unreal peril to the common folk in the town. It's hard to judge what their response will be. Take my advice and also send out small companies of soldiers with instructions to calm the citizens and also to put down any riots or looting if such seem likely to occur."

"I will do this, Lord Royance," Einaar said. "Again, my gratitude for your wisdom and counsel knows no bounds."

For answer, Royance raised his goblet. Einaar likewise raised his, and the two men pledged each other without further words. Then they arose, and when Royance had departed for his quarters Einaar called for Frikk and Jørgen. To these trusted men he delegated the instruction of the criers and also of selecting the steadiest soldiers to follow after them on the morrow. The people in the Castle of Fire and Ice would not have to wait to hear it from the criers, though. The difficult task of relating the news of their danger he would take upon himself, this day.

An hour later, all the people living in the castle, even the blacksmith and the grooms and other servants, both high and low, were gathered in the Great Hall.

To his relief, they took Einaar's announcement stolidly. It was obvious to him that the gossips had been ahead of him, and his news came as no surprise, though there were questions from some of them. He was able to correct a possible few misapprehensions and wild speculations, and thus soothe them as much as possible, under the circumstances.

"I will expect every one of you to perform your duties as before," he finished, "and ask only that you stand ready to give such other aid as might be required of you in times to come."

There was nothing more to be said. Somberly, all of them, Einaar included, returned to their duties.

Later that evening, the Chatelaine and the Seneschal presented themselves at the porch of the Fane of the Castle of Fire and Ice. They clung to each other hand in hand, like troubled children. Nalren rapped softly on the door, and Esander came out to greet them.

"Ayfare. Nalren. How may I be of service to you?" he asked kindly. "Do you need to talk about this calamity that faces us now?"

"There is woe upon woe," Ayfare commented. Her eyes were swollen, as if she had been weeping. "My poor lady—"

"We wish to be wed," Nalren said. "If, as seems to be our fate, we are all to die before long, Ayfare and I will face it as husband and wife."

"So say you as well, Mistress Ayfare?"

"I do."

"I have performed several weddings this afternoon for people of like mind, out here where you stand. You two, however, are special because of your long and loyal service to my lady Ashen NordornQueen, bravest and dearest of women to me. Come you inside the Fane, and there in solemn privacy will I join you both in the here and the hereafter."

They nodded and followed the priest inside, and he closed the door behind them.

Thirteen

*S*tehmar, the tavern keeper, at first regarded Ashen with suspicion bordering on hostility when she asked for lodging. Perhaps, Ashen thought, he imagined she was a light woman, up to no good. His attitude changed instantly to servile fawning when Cebastian made her identity known to him.

"A room, is it, Your Majesty?" Stehmar said, bobbing his head up and down and practically wringing his hands. "Of course! At once! My best! I'll clear out somebody and make him stay with someone else, just for you!"

"I will share my husband's room. Which one is his?"

"Which one?" Stehmar said. He glanced left and right, making himself look shifty, as if something was just now occurring to him. "Which one. Well, NordornKing paid me for all the rooms—that means yours, too, Your Majesty—but I don't know which one he took for himself."

First Rohan acting strangely, and now this fellow. Something definitely was wrong, Ashen thought. There was more here than appeared. "Where did you put his belongings? They have been placed somewhere, haven't they?"

"Dunno," Stehmar said. "You'd have to ask Knud. He does all that."

"No need," Ashen said, smiling grimly. "I'll just knock on doors until I find him."

She drew aside the curtain that separated the wing of sleeping rooms from the tavern itself and almost ran headlong into Svarteper.

"Well met, my lord Marshal," she said. "You can help me. Where is Gaurin's room?"

"A-ashen NordornQueen!" Svarteper seemed so surprised he was about to choke on her name. "What are you doing here?"

"Isn't it obvious?" Zazar said, more than a little acidly. "She's looking for her husband."

"He's—ah, he's not here."

"We can see that," Ashen said. "Where is he?"

"Madame—" Svarteper opened his mouth, then closed it again. "Not here," he repeated lamely.

Svarteper as well. Third time makes it true, Ashen thought. "I take it you have just been setting your things to rights. In your room. The one that Gaurin paid the tavern keeper for. Your room."

Svarteper nodded.

"Then let us go into that room and close the door. Perhaps in this bit of privacy you can remember where my husband is!" Ashen all but shouted the last few words.

"Yes, Madame." Meekly, he showed her to a room located about halfway down the hall. "But is it proper, being in a gentleman's bedchamber and all?"

"She won't be alone," Zazar said. She turned to Cebastian and the guards, who were openly goggling at what had been transpiring. "You can stand outside the door if you're of a mind to, but nobody else is going in except for me."

"And me." Goliat stepped forward as if to accompany them anyway.

"Not you," the old Wysen-wyf said, practically closing the door on his nose. Then she turned to Svarteper. "I'd suggest you tell Ashen what she wants to know," she advised.

"Madame, I can't," the Marshal said, spreading his hands in a helpless gesture.

"You can, and you will," Ashen returned, summoning as much command as she could muster. "I order it."

Only under such order, and reluctantly, did Svarteper tell her of Gaurin's plans. "He left Pettervil while the rest of the army was occupied in strengthening the village's defenses."

"How long has he been gone?"

"That I do not know, Madame. Truly, I do not. But gone he is, with Lathrom, my son Lars, Dordan the archer, and a Fridian guide. And Öydis. She went with him. The war-kats, too, I suppose. Haven't seen them in a while."

"Then I shall follow."

"No, Madame, you cannot!" Svarteper protested. "You don't know the danger!"

"You dare speak of danger that Gaurin is going into, and ask me to stay behind? Do you know what I bring with me?"

"Whatever it is, it isn't worth risking your life for. Hard enough for you to be here in Pettervil where we face an assault at any time. But to let you go out in the open country. . . . No, Madame, that I cannot consent to."

"You have no choice."

Despite her brave words, Ashen knew herself to be at a disadvantage. If she were wearing Court attire, and a crown—even her coronet—she might be able to bend the Marshal to her will. She doubted herself, under the present circumstances. Then Ashen softened her manner. The Marshal was a powerful man, accustomed to command and unused to taking orders from a woman, even a sovereign queen. Perhaps an appeal to his reason would be a better tactic. "I will take you into my confidence. I am speaking of that which is the key to all our survival, even to the Nordorn-Land itself. I have the map showing the way to where the Dragon Blade may be found."

Svarteper blinked as this information sank in. "Then it isn't just a legend."

"No, Marshal, according to the scholars at Galinth, it is real. The map is real also. Now can you see why I must get it to Gaurin?"

"I can, but there is no reason for you to risk yourself further.

You've brought it this distance; now let someone else carry it the rest of the way."

"That I will not do. Gaurin has his appointed task, and so do I. The map remains in my possession until I, personally, give it into my husband's hand."

"Better listen to her," Zazar commented.

"How can I?" Svarteper asked, turning to her with a helpless look on his face.

"Once she's set on something, that's how it will be," Zazar told him. "Anyway, if as you say Gaurin is safer out of town where it's going to get very hot very soon, if what you tell us is correct, that will hold true for Ashen as well."

The Marshal had no reply for that.

"Here is what you will do," Ashen said. "If you have been clever, you will have set aside one of these rooms as Gaurin's so as to arouse no suspicion at his absence."

Svarteper raised his eyebrows, and Ashen knew that he had done no such thing. "No, Madame," he confessed, "but we can say he shares my quarters."

"Stehmar promised me a chamber to myself. It will stand empty, but you will say it is Gaurin's also, to avoid unnecessary complications should someone inquire or enter your quarters unannounced. I will pretend to stay in seclusion. Instruct the tavern keeper to bring trays of food and leave them at the door. Have one of your men take the food and dispose of it—eat it, throw it away, whatever is necessary. I will follow Gaurin's example. Zazar and I will slip away, going quickly and taking only one man to guard us. That way we might travel even more swiftly."

She smiled a little, thinking of Weyse and the little furred creature's longing for her friend, the war-kat Finola. As if Weyse knew her thoughts, she struggled out of Zazar's arms and leaped up onto the windowsill, craning her neck and trying to look to the north. "We need no guide," Ashen told the Marshal. "We'll be following in Gaurin's footsteps and even if snow should obliterate his traces, we have our ways of finding him."

"As you command, Majesty," Svarteper said, bowing his head.

Ashen breathed an internal sigh of relief. She had been afraid the Marshal might detain her, by force if necessary.

"Who do you plan to take with you?" he asked.

"Goliat," Zazar said. "Take Goliat."

"Who's he?" Svarteper asked. "That big fellow who almost broke my door with his nose?"

"The very one." Zazar smiled.

"Well, that much makes me feel better. Maybe you will consent to take my other son, Ludde, as well?"

"I thank you, but no," Ashen said. She turned to Zazar. "Let us go bring Cebastian in here and inform him of our plans. He will not be any better pleased than our Lord High Marshal, but he will obey me because he must." She turned to Svarteper. "Because there is no other way."

"Your Majesty."

It took another direct command and the observation that as commander of the NordornQueen's House Troops, he would serve best by adding his forces to those preparing to meet the renegade Aslaugors before Cebastian silenced his protest.

"It went against my grain, too, young man," Svarteper told him. "But there is something. . . . Well, it's beyond my reckoning."

"Of course it is!" Zazar exclaimed scornfully. "Men, always breaking their heads on what they will never understand. The NordornKing and NordornQueen are both being driven by a Power that even I have some trouble comprehending. Get out of their way and let them follow their own destinies, even as you follow yours. Or risk being crushed by it."

Cebastian bowed. "I will not gainsay you both, Madame. Who else knows of the NordornKing's departure?"

"You mean still here at Pettervil?"

Svarteper was, Ashen thought, undoubtedly very good at leading men into battle, but not noticeably quick of wit in other situations.

"Well, me, of course," Svarteper continued, thinking. "And Admiral-General Tordenskjold. Rohan. We had to let Stehmar, the tavern keeper, in on it, so he could help ward off those who came looking for the king. He sent his man Knud after a dogsled, but I don't think Knud is bright enough to catch on to what was happening. Lathrom and Dordan went with Knud to make sure they got the best to be had. That's it, as far as I know, of those who know the NordornKing is absent."

"And me. The fewer the better." Cebastian turned to Ashen. "Let us send for Rohan. We need him now."

He opened the door a crack, beckoned to one of the men, and sent him out to locate the Sea-Rover Chieftain. In a short time, Rohan knocked on the door and was admitted. Quickly, Cebastian and Svarteper told him of the NordornQueen's plans.

"Just like the old days, eh?" Rohan said. "Baying off into nowhere in the snow. You and Gaurin. Mad, both of you."

"No help for it now," Cebastian told him. "Do you know where to find another dogsled or, better, two so both the women can ride?"

"I can't promise but one. They're in short supply. It'll cause a stir if we load even a single sled outside the Blue Snogpus, though. Let me take care of that part. There's a thick stand of trees off to the north of the village. Ashen, I'll take you, Granddam Zaz and— Goliat, was it?—there when you can slip away without being seen." Rohan shook his head in a resigned way. "I suppose there's no chance of convincing you two that this is a harebrained scheme, is there? No, I didn't think so. Well, I'm off. I'll meet you later."

He left the room, and Ashen caught a glimpse of her House Troops, still hovering outside the door.

"I'll go and see about finding my men places to stay," Cebastian said. "That way, they won't have time to question your whereabouts. I won't give Goliat his orders until the last minute." Then he, too, left. Outside, the people in the room could hear his voice as he began issuing instructions to the men of the House Troops.

"Good man," Svarteper commented to the two women. "If he didn't hold the office he does, I'd like to have him in my command. Well, I was on my way out to the barricade, so I'll leave you to rest now, Madame and, if you can, eat a bite. I hope to see you once more before you depart—if you do, which I hope you will not—but if you are gone when I return, I wish you good fortune and success."

The Lord High Marshal, with courtesy surprising in such a complete soldier, then lifted Ashen's hand to his lips and kissed it.

"Fare you well also, Svarteper," Ashen said. "May your defense of the village be successful and you put down the renegades completely. Know that I am aware of your loyalty both to me and to my husband."

He saluted and, as had the others, left the room. Ashen and Zazar gazed at one another, for once lacking anything to say.

They waited until twi-night, but there was no friendly snowfall to hide what Ashen had come to think of as their escape. Rohan came and guided them out the back entrance of the Blue Snogpus, through the kitchen. The sight and smell made Ashen grateful that she had had no appetite to eat anything from this place.

"I didn't dare delay any longer. So, we're just three people out late, searching for firewood before the fighting starts," Rohan told the women. "Here. Take these baskets. It's what the villagers use for such an errand."

Something smelled unexpectedly good. "What is in here?" Ashen asked.

"Fresh bread. There's a bakery over on the other side of the square. Now let's get going before we're discovered."

At least Zazar looked the part of a villager. Except for her snow-thistle garments, she was dressed very much as she had been when she had come to the Snow Fortress, with a shawl slung over her cloak and tied behind her neck. In this, she carried Weyse and, Ashen suspected, a packet of her precious herbs.

As for Ashen, she had seldom felt so exposed, so vulnerable. At any moment, she feared, someone would come riding across the open area between the outskirts of Pettervil and the woods, and drag her back to "safety" by force. Still, no one did, and the three reached the shelter of the trees apparently without being noticed.

Goliat was already there waiting, with a dogsled. The dogs had been lying quietly, waiting, but got to their feet when they sensed the presence of Weyse. One of them barked, and the other would have set up a racket that would have reached the village if Goliat hadn't shushed them firmly.

"What's that I smell?" he asked.

"Fresh bread," Rohan responded. "Ashen and Granddam Zaz have a loaf each, and I brought some for you. Two loaves. You're a big man!"

Goliat grinned. "Maybe I like you after all, Sea-Rover. You treat my lady NordornQueen well." He reached for one of the loaves and began tearing it into pieces, some of which he crammed into his mouth, and the rest he tossed to the eager dogs. They snapped it out of the air before a crumb could reach the forest floor. "Quiet, doggies," he said, breaking into the second loaf.

Weyse struggled to stick her head out of the shawl in which Zazar had wrapped her. She held out her clever little paws for her share of the delicacy and Zazar tore some off for her. She began to devour it with every indication of satisfaction.

"Can't say taking your—your pet along is a good idea, Madame Zazar," Goliat said.

"She's not a pet," Ashen told him. "She'll keep us on the right path, even if the snow covers my husband's trail."

"I'm more worried about whether the dogs can pull this sled with us two on it," Zazar said around a mouthful.

"They can pull, don't worry," Goliat told her. "These are good, strong dogs. They can manage all three of us in new snow."

"But what if we get into country where the sled isn't easy to maneuver?" Ashen asked. Like the others, she had torn her loaf into pieces and begun to eat. Even without butter or a spoonful of sweet on it, it was delicious. "I saw indications of fire-mountain activity as we journeyed north, and I see no reason to think that we won't encounter more."

"Well, truth to tell, there is, gracious Majesty. We'll get as far as we can. Then we'll leave dogs at the first friendly homestead we find and—" Goliat stopped, obviously unhappy at what he had been about to say.

"And then we go on foot," Zazar supplied firmly, "carrying our belongings on our backs. Don't fret, big man, Ashen here isn't an ice-lily. She's not quite as fragile as she looks. I don't think even you could stand between her and Gaurin, she's that determined to get to him."

"Yes, Madame. Then we go on foot," Goliat said. But he still didn't look happy at the prospect.

"Very well," Ashen said. "I think it's time to depart. Rohan, thank you for all the help you've been to me."

"Maybe we should spend the night here, and get an early start," Goliat suggested.

"No," Ashen said. "I can't."

"I must agree with Ashen," Rohan said. "Gaurin has to be not much more than a day ahead of you. You could make up some of that time, if you pushed on before it's full dark."

"Full dark won't come for hours yet," Goliat said. "Remember, we're in the time of long twilight."

"Good. We will go ahead and hope that Gaurin is not inclined to hurry." Ashen arose and brushed the crumbs from her clothing. She donned her knitted coif, and at her stern glance, Zazar did likewise. The headgear, with hoods pulled up tightly, would keep their faces from freezing. "Rohan, my thanks again. Now, Goliat, you show me where I'm to ride on the sled."

At dawn, Svarteper called a meeting of the officers under his command. One of the houses boasted a second-story porch covered by the overhanging roof, which would have been an ideal observation post, but the owner had, sensibly but unfortunately, from Svarteper's point of view, placed it on the south. It had become more and more plain that they could expect the renegades from the north. Nevertheless, the Marshal stationed a lookout on the porch while he and his officers climbed atop the old fortress wall atop the high point—a gate that was now closed by a green barricade. Out on the perimeter some of the barriers could be set aside if need be, then quickly lashed in place again.

From the wall, Svarteper had a good view of the surrounding

area to the north. He could also see most of the other two sides of the village.

"How have you distributed your forces?" he asked his officers.

"My Sea-Rovers are on the outer perimeter, most of them to the north," Rohan said. "It was a hard task convincing them to wait for the renegades to come to us rather than going out and tracking them down."

Admiral-General Tordenskjold laughed. "I don't envy you your task of leading such a willful lot!" he exclaimed. "But then, all my sailors who could be spared are right out there with them. I think everyone who came with us feels the slight of being set upon last night and is eager to avenge the insult."

"Indeed," Svarteper said. "I have put the Aslaugors in the second rank, on either side of the gate, and stationed my men evenly all along the barricades flanking them. Rohan, send orders that if the renegades look likely to break through the front lines, to let 'em do it. Then your men can turn and we'll catch 'em between our forces."

"Already done," Tordenskjold said. He laughed again. "No need to explain elementary strategy to Rohan or to me. I've been in a battle or two in my time, you know, and so has he."

Svarteper turned to Cebastian. "As outnumbered as we expect to be, we are grateful for your additional men, few though they be in number. I know that they will fight all the harder in defense of the NordornQueen."

"I stationed them as close to the Blue Snogpus as the barricades allowed," Cebastian told him.

"Good. Well, now all we can do is wait."

Off in the distance, movement. Horses, many of them. In a few moments, the sound of the thunder of the animals' hooves on the frozen ground and men shouting with wild excitement reached their ears as the riders approached the village. Svarteper strained his eyes. Five horsemen led the way, coming at a hard gallop, followed at some distance by perhaps two dozen more. But who was chasing whom?

Then his vision cleared. One of the five carried a black pennon

bearing a silver devil-tree badge. "It's Patin," he said. "That's the signal flag I gave him." He cupped his hands around his mouth and bellowed loudly enough so that the Sea-Rovers on the far perimeter
could hear him. "Open the gate! Let him in!"

Then he turned to those who waited with him. "This is it, my
friends. Everyone to your posts."

There were no stairs on the inside of the fortress walls, just
ladders. Rohan and Cebastian were first down. The older men followed as quickly as they could and dispersed. Svarteper at once
made for the village square, where the five Aslaugors were dismounting from their winded horses.

"They're right on our heels!" Patin said, panting. He plucked an
arrow from where it had lodged in his cloak, and grinned. "Cut it a
little close." He slapped his horse on the flank, and it trotted off in
the direction of the stables.

He's his mother's son, Svarteper thought. "We're ready."

"Good. Where are my men?"

"Over here."

"There aren't many horsemen. The main body is on foot.
They'll be here shortly."

That was all the report Svarteper was going to get, for with
those words Patin picked up a sheaf of throwing spears from
where they were stacked and strode off toward his comrades. The
NordornLand Marshal gazed after him for a moment, envying him
the agility and robustness of youth that treated his narrow escape
as nothing. Then he turned to go back atop the wall, from which
he could best oversee and direct the battle. In any other sort of
combat, he would be in the thick of it, but there was too much
danger of confusion that could prove deadly to the defenders. Only
if the enemy came close enough would he go down and join the
battle personally.

He was joined by the lone trumpeter among them, a lad named
Hod, who was not yet old enough to bear arms. "Stay close," Svarteper told him. "Watch and learn. Great deeds are being done this
day."

The renegade Aslaugors charged forward, as if to trample and destroy all the outward defenses. At just the right moment, the Sea-Rovers pulled some of the green mats of the barricades aside. The riders, not expecting this maneuver, couldn't rein in in time before their own momentum had carried them into the streets of the village. Immediately, the renegades were set upon by the defenders, dragged off their mounts, and dispatched, but not without a hard fight. The horses were then turned loose. Most of them, having originally been stolen from Pettervil's stables, sensed the food and water to be had at their old home, and trotted off in that direction.

The defenders had only just cleared away the debris of that first skirmish when the rest of the renegades came into view. As Patin said, they were on foot, but they must have been camped relatively close to Pettervil because they didn't appear tired from a forced march. They formed a line three deep reaching from one side of the village's northern boundary to the other, to Svarteper's best reckoning.

At his signal, Hod blew a call signaling "Hold steady." The Marshal hoped there might yet be talk between the opposing sides and, indeed, two men were coming forward from the line. One of them held a banner. The other would be—what was his name? Asfam, Asmal. Something like that. "Give the call for parley," he told the boy.

"But sir," the lad protested, "isn't that dangerous? Please, no."

"Give the call. It is my duty to bring this to a successful end, and if I can do it without undue bloodshed, I will."

"Yes, sir," Hod said, but his lip trembled. One of the trumpet notes came out mangled as a result.

This is one way to stay in shape, Svarteper thought, as he fumbled for steady footing on the ladder. Going up and down this thing several times a day. Cebastian met him at the bottom.

"Let me go in your stead, sir," he said. "We need you here, safe, to direct the fighting if the parley is unsuccessful."

"I'm aware that after me and the Admiral-General, you're probably the ranking officer here," Svarteper replied. "Well, maybe your friend Rohan even if he isn't more than half Rendelian. Leaving that aside, it's my duty to go out and talk to the renegades, see what they have to say."

"Then take me with you, as your guard."

"No," Patin said, joining them. "If anybody should accompany the Marshal, it should be me. Takes an Aslaugor to beat down another Aslaugor, so the saying goes."

Svarteper thought a moment. "You'll both go, and a picked group of Sea-Rover archers will step just outside the barrier, bows at the ready." He grinned. "No need taking unnecessary risks. Daresay the other side will have bows drawn, too."

In a few moments, these preparations having been made, the three men started across the frozen ground to where the Aslaugor renegades were waiting for them. Snow was beginning to fall again.

In the Castle of Fire and Ice, life went on much as before Einaar's announcement concerning the Arikarin. After all, the beast had not come into sight yet, nor was there report of it, and until the menace was made real most people preferred to try to put it out of their minds as much as possible.

If anything, the entertainment in the evenings was gayer than before—a touch feverish, Einaar thought. Perhaps it was the twinight, coupled with the brilliant curtains of lights in the sky, sending no clear signal that day had ended, that contributed to the air of unreality.

He began to change his manner, but subtly, when the Duchess Ysa was present, assuming almost an air of arrogant command for her benefit. From time to time he would catch her looking at him with approval. But she did not come to him with more honeyed words about plans in the event of something unfortunate happening to the NordornKing and the NordornQueen.

Most likely, Royance told him, the Duchess considered her work well under way, his ambition kindled and needing nothing more from her at present. "She'll return to the subject when she thinks necessary," Royance said.

This playacting represented a minor diversion from the press of worries that beset the Lord High Protector from all sides. In consultation with Lord Royance, Einaar determined to make the preparations for any coming battle with the Arikarin as invisible as possible, so as not to alarm the inhabitants of Cyornasberg any sooner than necessary.

After all, it was still possible that the beast would not trouble the Castle of Fire and Ice, but realistically, Einaar knew that this was a wan hope at best.

He began paying more open court to Lady Elibit, even to seating her next to himself at meals and monopolizing her company. If he dared—

Of course he dared. This was the lady he wanted by his side permanently. Under ordinary circumstances, he would, of course, have petitioned Ashen NordornQueen's permission to wed one of her ladies. But these were far from ordinary circumstances.

A sudden, wryly amusing thought struck him. The Duchess Ysa was precisely the one to take over this matter. What better way to convince her that she had the managing of the Duke's affairs in the palms of her very capable hands—all his affairs—than to put her to planning his wedding.

Lord Royance, when Einaar informed him of this, laughed aloud. "You have told me that you sometimes indulge in inappropriate humor," the old gentleman said, "but in this instance I find it highly amusing and in nowise objectionable. By all means, if you fancy the lady, turn the matter over to Ysa. I have heard that there are other weddings in the offing. Such is always the way, among young men, when war is staring us in the face."

"That should keep her well occupied, I hope."

"As do I. At the very least, it will keep all of your people busy and give them something better to contemplate than watching out of the corners of their eyes in case the Arikarin is slinking up on them."

Fourteen

Half a day's travel past the little stand of trees just north of the village, the appearance of the countryside changed. Gaurin pushed ahead as swiftly as he dared over the broken land.

A ridge of high mountains, many of them leaking smoke, confronted him. Here, despite the frequent snowfall, the drifts were not deep and in many places had melted and refrozen. Steam escaped through rifts in this uneasy surface, and hot springs bubbled to form occasional pools in places where molten rock had flowed beside rivers of ice. From time to time the ground trembled as fire mountains stirred, and the stench of brimstone was ever thick in the air. It didn't look very promising as an area where the Mother Ice Dragon would have her lair.

Fortunately for the inhabitants of Pettervil, the general slope of the land was west, toward the sea, and away from the inhabited areas. This had made it possible for the villagers to carve out meadows on the eastern slopes, where they could keep livestock and expect that the animals would not freeze in a sudden storm. The group of travelers had already spotted two *seters*, probably erected for the use of herdsmen.

Having gotten such a late start, the company paused at one of these to spend the night. They kindled a small fire in the little hearth in the middle of the floor, set a pot of stew to cooking, and heated water in another so they could have some meat broth to drink as they sat on the stone benches. The war-kats disappeared to hunt their own food, but padded back for their share of the broth.

"I have a question," Lathrom said, stroking Keltin's ears. "In the great war, we had many war-kats with us. But on this journey there are only the four. I wonder why."

"I have wondered that, too," Gaurin responded. "I think they realize this is not a war but the tracking and disposing of a single great, mysterious peril. And so they have come to us from curiosity, perhaps, and even affection, for lack of any better term for it."

At that moment, Bitta and Finola playfully charged at the NordornKing and knocked him over, wrestling with him so realistically that Lars Svartepersson moved to intervene.

"Let them alone," Öydis said. "Nobody is getting hurt."

Rajesh began grappling with Keltin, and the two females left off their game with Gaurin and joined their mates instead, rolling around on the hard floor with abandon.

Gaurin straightened his disarranged clothing, examining it for rents inadvertently inflicted by the war-kats' boisterous play. "How much farther do you judge we must travel?" he asked their Fridian guide.

"Must go around ridge of fire mountains, then you find her," Ueli told Gaurin. He pointed northeast. "If she lets you." He hawked and spat. "What you going to do with her then?"

Gaurin laid his hand on the hilt of the Rinbell sword. "I am sworn to put an end to the menace to my land," he replied.

Ueli merely grunted.

Öydis was more vocal. "You got that hilt wrapped in leather?" she said. "It's going to freeze to your hand." She hefted her battle-ax, a fearsome thing longer than a man's arm, with the blade fastened to a sturdy wooden haft. "This is a proper Aslaugor weapon," she declared proudly. "Nordorn weapon, too. Or a mace, like Svarteper uses. We've got a bundle of throwing spears on the sled, but I wish we had some long spears as well. Spears are good. Only place metal touches skin is on your enemy and he's not likely to care for long. You lived in the south too long, NordornKing. Also, remember the legend."

"I have not forgotten," Gaurin responded, "but in the absence of the Dragon Blade, I must rely on this. A Rinbell sword served me well in the late war, and it will do so again."

"Have it your way," Öydis said, with a shrug. "Better wrap your hand, too."

Lars Svartepersson grinned, brandishing his own battle-ax, scarcely less impressive than Öydis's. "Da can have the mace. I like to use a blade. This is for me."

"Well, I'm not bad with a spear," Lathrom said. "But I daresay I couldn't win a thing from either of you if it came to a contest."

Öydis laughed. "Not so much as a bag of groats!"

Dordan spoke up. "Hah. I beat you both with my bow. No metal to freeze to my hand, and I can get off three shots while you're lining up one cast of a spear!"

"Better keep your bowstring warm, though," Öydis said, adding a rustic comment as to the best place to put it, and everyone laughed.

"This silly talk too much," Ueli declared.

He left the shelter, spoke to the dogs, and settled them for the night.

The next morning, without waiting for breakfast, he started immediately toward the northeast. The others hurried to catch up with him. "If you go straight north, we keep sled, maybe hire more. Over there, not," the guide told them, gesturing eastward. "Country where big thing live too rough for sled, hard on dogs. I know good place to leave, take maybe one pack dog."

"The sled was a great help in quickly getting us as far as we got," Gaurin told him. "We are grateful for it. I cannot shake the feeling that time is drawing short, and the sooner we dispatch the—the big thing, the better for all of us."

"I have learned to rely on Gaurin NordornKing's instincts," Lathrom observed.

Around midday, Ueli led them to a lone steading that clung to the side of a hill, nearly out of sight of any traveler—or, Gaurin thought, a marauding dragon. The Aslaugor owner made his living by supplying those who passed through with fresh teams of dogs. Prudently, Gaurin left the war-kats well outside the area, with instructions for them to stay put.

There were no good pack dogs to be had at present, so the company left the other dogs and the sled, loading what they needed on their own backs.

The man seemed happy with the gold coin Gaurin gave him, enough so that he shared his midday meal with the travelers. "Was a good bargain to begin with, NordornKing," he said, "sled, these new dogs and all, and no trade. But I thank you and wish you good fortune in your quest."

They retraced their route for what Gaurin judged to be the balance of the afternoon though time was hard to determine accurately in the long twi-night, passing another ridge of mountains to their right. No fire erupted from these, though the ground was riven and scarred with icy crevasses deeper than a man was tall. To the north, the landscape appeared similar. This was, Gaurin thought, surely the edge of the Mother Ice Dragon's Desolation, and he wanted to face it with everyone well rested.

"We will stop and make our camp at the next stand of trees," he told his companions, "unless we find a *seter* beforehand. There we will sleep and perhaps realize our objective tomorrow."

"Is *seter* back there," Ueli said, pointing to the right, behind them, "but no good. Made of wood, not stone, now ruins. Walls but no roof. Tomorrow we rest a while, use camp as base to take look, see if we find sign of big thing."

Gaurin nodded agreement, knowing that the Fridian scout was master here as surely as Öydis, in his own way.

A short time later, the company came upon a sizeable cluster of trees. Here, the snow had melted slightly and refrozen several times, forming a hard surface. Despite this slight drawback, it was as good a spot as they hoped to find and the trees offered materials for building lean-to shelters. The six people dropped their packs and began to make preparations for the night. The war-kats lolled at their ease, watching.

Suddenly the four animals' heads all turned in the same direction, and they began to growl deep in their throats. Gaurin swung around just in time to see two Ice Dragons emerging from the trees. He had time only to think that they were much smaller than the ones he had fought before, when they were upon them.

"Hatchlings!" Ueli shouted.

An arrow whistled through the air, striking one of the Dragons just below the eye. It reared and began to claw at the missile, seeking to dislodge it. Two more arrows lodged in the beast's underside. Lars Svartepersson was already charging toward the creatures, roaring a challenge, his battle-ax raised. Öydis was only a step behind him. Gaurin drew his sword, and it rang like a cold bell in the frigid air.

"You take the wounded one," he shouted to Lathrom, "and I'll take the other!"

The war-kats sprang to their feet, snarling their own throaty challenges. The younger pair made straight for the wounded Dragon. They sprang onto its flanks, biting and clawing. Only a heartbeat behind them, Rajesh and Finola sped toward Gaurin and the creature he was facing.

The wounded Dragon uttered a loud squall of pain and leaped into the air, snow cascading from under its leathery wings. The war-kats clung to its sides as long as possible, inflicting as much damage as they could, before being forced to jump to safety. Lars Svartepersson shook his battle-ax, bellowing in frustration as the Dragon flapped its way into the sky and disappeared over the tops of the trees.

Lathrom was already pounding across the snow to join Gaurin. Öydis and the NordornKing flanked the second Dragon, unable to attack because Rajesh and Finola were in the way. The Dragon tried unsuccessfully to shake off the war-kats, but they only clung that much more fiercely.

"Dordan!" Gaurin shouted.

For answer, the Sea-Rover archer loosed another arrow, his aim truer this time. It hit squarely in the Dragon's eye, making it pause as had the other one.

"That's not going to blind it!" Öydis shouted, assessing the situation at once. She dropped her battle-ax and made for the sheaf of throwing spears. Lars was in her way, and she grabbed him, nearly pulling him off his feet. "Here, you!" She tossed a couple of spears to him. "You were quick enough to brag. Now let's see how good you are!"

The two warriors ran toward the place where the Dragon thrashed and writhed, rearing and bellowing, flapping its wings, but not yet trying to lift into the air. Lathrom and Gaurin continued to circle the beast, seeking an opportunity to deliver a blow.

Lars paused long enough to launch a spear. It struck the Dragon in the midsection only to slide off again, causing no harm.

"No, you fool!" Öydis shouted. "The eyes! We have to take out its eyes!"

Suiting words to deed, she hurled one of her spears, hitting the Dragon's left eye squarely in the center. The light spear did little more than lodge in the tough tissue, but it was enough to distract the reptilian beast. The Dragon dropped to all fours again and turned away, as if bewildered. It seemed to be trying to escape its attackers and the damage they were inflicting on it. The war-kats squalled and dug in even more fiercely, biting and clawing.

With the Dragon's movement, Gaurin saw his opportunity. Remembering the tale Rohan had told, of how he had dispatched a much larger Dragon from the natural saddle just behind its head, the NordornKing scrambled up the beast's back. Clinging to the spiney protuberances, he climbed hand over hand along its neck until he reached what seemed to be the right spot. The saddle on this immature Dragon was much too small for him to sit in, but he managed to wrap his legs around the creature's neck firmly enough to give him sufficient purchase for his next action.

Holding the Rinbell sword in both hands, he plunged the blade into the little depression just at the base of the skull. It went in like a hot knife through butter, taking him by surprise. Acting on sheer instinct, he joined Rajesh and Finola as they leaped away. Even so, he was almost caught under the Dragon as it collapsed, dead instantly.

For a moment, the combatants just stared at the Dragon as if unable to believe the suddenness of their victory. Then all four of the war-kats sent up a yowl of triumph, sat down, and began to wash.

"Well now," Lars said. "That wasn't so bad."

Gaurin, Lathrom, Dordan, and Öydis stared at him disbelievingly. Ueli sniggered behind his hand.

"You really are a fool," the Chieftain declared. "This was just a baby, no more than a season out of the egg. The farmers had great trouble with its nest-mates because they didn't have weapons, let alone Gaurin's pets to contend with. Give it a year, maybe two, and we would have had equal difficulty." She turned to the Nordorn-King. "I should quit calling them pets," she told him. "They proved themselves this day."

"So they did," he replied. "Lars Svartepersson, you speak from ignorance for you have never faced Ice Dragons before. There are those here who have, and I tell you now that you must be guided by us. Your ill-cast spear could have spelled disaster, had not Öydis known where to take her aim. We were lucky because we faced an inexperienced hatchling, but we cannot hope for such good fortune every time we encounter one of the Mother Ice Dragon's spawn."

"Your pardon, NordornKing," Lars said, abashed. He kicked at the Dragon's belly and, to everyone's surprise, something red and glittering fell from where it had been lodged under one of the Dragon's pearly, iridescent scales. He kicked again, and several more tumbled out from similar places of hiding.

Lathrom picked up the largest of the objects and held it up in the wan light. "No wonder Lars's spear did no damage!" he exclaimed. "This looks like one of the gems in your crown, Gaurin, only raw and unworked."

"A fire-stone," Gaurin said, taking it from him. "How unusual."

"Not really," Öydis told him. "My stronghold is on the northeast slope of that fire-mountain range we passed. I know of fire-stones. Come, let's start making our camp, and I'll tell you about these red gems and Ice Dragons."

These gems were sometimes found, she told them as they

worked, embedded in molten rock or clumps of ash thrown out by fire mountains, and had always been much sought after. They had never been plentiful, but had become very scarce of late. "The farmers who managed to kill the other hatchlings—four of 'em if I remember right—said there were a lot of these red stones stuck around on the bodies. I suppose Ice Dragons have a fancy for these gems, even from the egg."

"But there were no fire-stones found on any of the ones we killed during the war," Lathrom pointed out.

Öydis laughed. "There are at least half a dozen farmers who are wealthy landowners now," she said, "after selling what they looted off the hatchlings. What makes you think the ones you faced hadn't also been looted well before they were taken into battle? How do you expect Baron Damacro paid his soldiers?"

"No wonder they fought so well, if this was their reward. You are a wise woman, Öydis, and what you say makes sense," Gaurin said. "Perhaps, if we can find more of the hatchlings, we can all have a share of fire-stone wealth."

"Makes you wonder what kind of glittering armor the Mother Ice Dragon sports," Lathrom commented.

A sobering thought. Without further comment on the hoarding habits of Ice Dragons, young and old, the six finished their camp. Then they prepared and ate their meal and sought their beds. The war-kats, as was their custom, disappeared, to return much later and crowd their way into Gaurin's shelter to sleep.

The dawn of the next day—not so much an actual dawn but rather a lightening of the twi-night—brought sullen skies and the promise of more snow. The men arose tired and heavy-eyed, to find Öydis stirring a pot of porridge. She, alone of them all, seemed in fine fettle.

"Gathered wild grain at the edge of the woods," she told them. "There's plenty. Snowberries, too. We won't starve, anyway. Now, eat up. If we're to wait out a blizzard, we need to make the walls of our shelters proof against wind and snow."

Lars and Dordan went into the woods with axes, cutting and gathering boughs and bringing them back to the campsite. Gaurin and Lathrom laid the heavy greenery along the exterior walls of the lean-to shelters. Ueli absented himself from the camp, ostensibly to go scout out the countryside and what might still be lying in wait for them, though Gaurin thought privately that he might be escaping the arduous labor Öydis had set them to.

Suddenly he stopped in the midst of his task. Like a man who had no command over his actions, he gazed back in the direction from which they had come.

"There is trouble—" he said.

Ashen and her companions traveled as fast as Goliat would allow.

"You are in delicate condition, my NordornQueen," he told her firmly. "Too brave for your own good, I think. Soon we find a *seter* and rest for the night."

"We've only just started!" Ashen protested. "I had hoped to put a good distance behind us before we stop."

Nevertheless, the big man wouldn't budge and Ashen had to promise that if they came across a *seter*, they would halt there. Zazar was no help to her at all, merely watching with a highly amused expression on her face.

"Nasty country," the Wysen-wyf commented from where she rode behind Ashen, indicating the range of fire mountains they were approaching. "But at least they are natural. Ahead, I sense— Well, empty it may be, but most unpleasant, where that beast lives. Let's take a look at that map of yours, girl. See if we can locate ourselves on it."

Ashen rummaged in the pile of belongings just in front of her on the sled and found the wooden box. She hadn't opened it since leaving Cyornasberg. The two silver diadems, each set with a firestone, gleamed in the dim twi-night. The map still lay under the irridescent stone bracelet. The sled hit an unexpected bump and the bracelet nearly jounced out of the box. Ashen picked it up and slipped it on, lest it be lost, then removed the map from the box and unfolded it. Zazar peered over her shoulder.

"I think this is supposed to be Pettervil," she said, pointing to a spot marked by a drawing of a little fort. "Trees aren't marked, but mountains are." She gazed around. "Looks like there's a long history of fire-mountain activity here, so that's nothing new. But look—just ahead, there's another ridge of peaks. That looks promising. Especially when you consider this."

"This" was the spot marked on the map, indicating where the Mother Ice Dragon's lair was supposed to lie.

"So close," Ashen murmured. "Dangerously near."

"It didn't matter, as long as she was asleep," Zazar pointed out. "Now that she's awake, though, the people suffer."

"Take us in that direction," Ashen told Goliat. She pointed toward the harsh mountains in the distance, off to the right.

"That's going to be hard going," Goliat said.

"If I have to get out and walk, that's what I'll do," Ashen retorted. Then she relented a little. "I know you're sworn to protect me, and there will undoubtedly be plenty of opportunity to do so, but you must allow me to fulfill my duty as well. All our lives might depend on it."

The big man bowed his head. "As you say, my NordornQueen."

He cracked the whip in the air over the dogs' heads and shifted their course in the direction Ashen indicated. Soon, the ground became so rough the sled could go no farther. Ice-lined crevasses yawned before them.

"I must continue," Ashen told her companions, "but I promise it will be just long enough that I can determine this is the place we are seeking. Wait here for me, and I will go ahead on foot."

"Not without me," Goliat stated.

"Very well, you may accompany me. Zazar, you stay with the sled."

"I didn't have any intention of doing anything else," the old Wysen-wyf said. Weyse poked her head out of the coverlet tucked around Zazar's body and whimpered a little. "Oh, hush," Zazar told her. "We're just stopped for a little while."

"I have the feeling that Gaurin may have gone past this place, unknowing."

"Possible." Zazar sniffed the air. "It's also possible—even probable—the Mother Ice Dragon isn't home," she said. "I don't sense her presence. Go if you must, to make sure we're on the right track, but if you see claw or scale or feel Dragon breath, or smell it, you turn around and get yourself back here. It isn't your mission to take on that creature by yourself."

"How will I know if I smell it?"

"You'll know. Now promise."

"I do," Ashen said.

She clambered out of the sled, grateful to stretch her cramped limbs, and with Goliat accompanying her, began her descent into one of the rifts in the frozen ground. There, as she suspected, she could go without being sighted except from directly overhead.

Goliat walked ahead of her, making the way as clear as he could. It was not an easy task for the bottom of the crevasse was littered with boulders and—as they went further—detritus of a different kind. Any doubts Ashen might have had that they had reached their objective disappeared when they began to find malodorous fragments of blue shell such as the ones Öydis had brought to Cyornasberg—how long ago? It seemed years.

They passed the discarded bones of a large animal, judging from the horned skull, and then other bones that could only have been human. They all bore tooth marks.

"Don't look, my NordornQueen," Goliat said. "It is not fit."

"I've seen bones before," Ashen said, but her voice was not as steady as she would have liked.

The crevasse grew deeper and more difficult to traverse. Ashen was on the verge of turning back when they picked their way around a corner and the mouth of a cave loomed directly ahead.

She surveyed the sky, trying to get her bearings. The trench they were in was deep enough that a few stars showed faintly in the dim twi-night overhead. "If I have my directions correct, this would be hidden from view by anybody passing along the unbroken ground above," she said. "No wonder it has gone undiscovered for so long."

"Let us go back now, NordornQueen," Goliat said.

"I promised to go if I saw Dragon sign," Ashen said, as she nudged a large cast-off scale with the toe of her boot. "I don't think this counts." Then she stared at what had lain under the scale, and bent down to pick it up.

It was a fire-stone, as big as any that she had ever seen, even though it was rough and had never known the jeweler's skilled touch.

"Please, my gracious Majesty, you have found the lair and you have found treasure. We must go back now." Goliat looked ready to pick her up bodily and carry her if necessary if she demurred.

"Very soon. I promise."

Tucking the fire-stone into her bodice, Ashen moved past Goliat, toward the dark, gaping entrance to the cave. The floor of the crevasse sloped upward until it was level with a clear area outside the opening.

A blast of fetid air hit her, colder than ice, shocking her into reality. What, she thought, am I doing? The Mother Ice Dragon could be waiting just inside, and that would be the end of Ashen NordornQueen. She stopped, listening closely, inhaling to catch the scent Zazar had warned her about. There was no sound except that of a slight wind moaning through the crevasses, no rank stench other than the staleness of the air. Surely if the cave held its dreadful inhabitant she would be sensing more than this. Emboldened, she went forward.

At the entrance of the cave, she found a tunnel that bent sharply to the left, then right again, creating a natural barrier. There were, she thought, plenty of places for a person to hide, if need be. She ventured a few more steps. Goliat was beside her. She glanced up at him, grateful for his bravery, which shored up her own faltering boldness. Now, if only there were some light—

A glow reflecting on the cave wall in front of her lured her onward. Cautious and shaking, she sidled along the tunnel, to discover that it opened into a vast, echoing cavern. An area at the far end was ablaze with a cold light she had seen before—glowing bones such as she had first encountered in the ruins of Galinth, when she had been little more than a child.

Her heart was beating so hard it seemed almost to burst through her chest. She could scarce believe she was in the Mother Ice Dragon's lair. The lighted area must be the very heart of it. However, unlike Galinth, here the very air seemed to throb with crimson, and everything the light touched was washed with the same bitter tinge.

Ashen looked around once more to make sure the beast wasn't crouching, hidden, in one of the less well lighted sections, then began making her way toward the source of the radiance. Despite Goliat's presence, she felt very much alone.

As Ashen approached the source of the coruscation, knowing that if the Mother Ice Dragon chose that moment to reenter her home she was doomed, she realized that the crimson color was coming from a great carpet of fire-stones. Though the glittering radiance reflected from the light-bones made it hard to pick out details, she could see a depression as if a vast body had lain there. This, then, was the Mother Ice Dragon's bed—a fabulously rich one. It was worthy, Ashen thought, dazedly, of a creature out of fable herself.

So far, the map had held true. If it continued to be reliable, the Dragon Blade must be close by. Reluctantly, she tore her gaze away from the incredible wealth in front of her and gazed around, only to see nothing that looked like a sword nor even where one might be hidden. Then another flicker of crimson caught her eye and she looked up, over the bed.

There it was, in full view, displayed with the arrogance of one who held herself to be invulnerable.

What Ashen had glimpsed, she now saw, were more fire-stones, set in the hilt of the Dragon Blade. She felt dizzy, as if she might faint, and drew in a deep breath in an attempt to calm herself.

"In that niche on the wall," she murmured to Goliat, pointing.

He nodded, and began to climb the rough wall of the cavern. When he got level with the niche he reached in and lifted out the weapon. It had not been fastened there, but rested, upright, on the point of the blade, as if waiting to be used. There was no sign of scabbard or belt.

"Shall I drop it to you, gracious Majesty?" he whispered.

The thought of the noise and clatter it would make, falling, caused Ashen to shudder. "No," she said. "Please."

He nodded, and climbed back down, his descent made more difficult because of having to hold on to uncertain rocky prominences with one hand while gripping the Dragon Blade with the other.

Ashen wondered why he didn't slip it into his belt. When he reached the relative safety of the cavern floor, she asked.

"Look at the sword, my NordornQueen," he said.

Gazing at the weapon, she remembered the description from the ancient document she had found hidden in the silver casket given to her as a coronation present. A brave knight had conquered the ancient male Ice Dragon in battle, dying in the effort. To honor this knight, smiths versed in the magical arts had fashioned a fabulous sword from the creature's scales—the sword that Goliat now held. A legend made real.

"Touch the edge, Majesty, but carefully," he said.

She ran her gloved fingers over the broad surface of the sword blade. It was incredibly beautiful. The scales glowed like slices of moonstone, or perhaps pearl. They graduated in size, each layer annealed to the one below, going from large and sturdy in the center of the blade to delicate, thin ones along the outer portion that created a deadly, serrated edge. A slight pressure, the merest stroking of bare fingertips, and it would draw blood—

She looked up at Goliat. "We can't carry it like this," she told him. "We would wound ourselves badly on it before we had gone a league."

"I think I saw something over in yon corner while I was up high," he said.

He searched through a pile of rubble and emerged with a scabbard, mother-of-pearl over silvered steel, bearing a fire-stone decoration. He inserted the blade into the sheath, and it fitted so perfectly Ashen knew it had been constructed for just this purpose.

"I reckon the Mother Ice Dragon didn't have use for it, but couldn't bear to throw it away," he commented.

"Dragons hoard all sorts of things, both treasure and trash," Ashen replied.

She and Goliat smiled at each other foolishly, the import of what they had done just now becoming real to them.

"We must go back now, Majesty," Goliat said.

"At once," Ashen agreed. "Now that we have what we came for."

He gazed at the pile of fire-stones.

"Pick up a few for yourself," Ashen told him. "You've earned them."

Gratefully, he scooped a handful from the great heap and dropped them into the pouch at his belt. Then he fastened the scabbard of the Dragon Blade beside the pouch, and the two of them made their way out of the cavern. As quickly as they could, they retraced their steps along the crevasse, thence back to where Zazar waited in the sled. To their astonishment they discovered her sleeping, wrapped in her snow-thistle silk, Weyse in her arms. The dogs were curled up, asleep as well. All were snoring.

It was such an incongruously peaceful scene, given the circumstances, that Ashen had to stifle a fit of giggles, brought on by the sudden easing of tension. She shook the old Wysen-wyf awake.

"Eh?" Zazar said, in a sleep daze. "What is it?"

"How can you sleep, with your companions venturing into danger!"

"Don't be silly. We were all tired, the dogs most of all. Anyway, I told you I didn't smell the Mother Ice Dragon. Was I wrong? Is she upon us?"

"No, be easy. We found something else," Ashen said. "The Dragon Blade."

"No," Zazar said. "Really?"

"Really. Show her, Goliat."

The guard pulled back his cloak, revealing the scabbard. He pulled the blade a little way out, then resheathed it.

"Well, I'm impressed," Zazar commented.

"The entrance to the lair is only a little distance from here, hidden on the other side of a notch in the mountain," Ashen said. "The Dragon wasn't home, but she might return at any moment.

We need to put distance between us and here, and we can't afford to tarry. Soon we'll find a place where we can rest, and all of us can sleep for a while."

"Then stop wasting time with all this nattering and get in the sled," Zazar said. "Kick those dogs awake, Goliat."

The Wysen-wyf pulled the coverlet aside so Ashen could climb into the sled. Gratefully, she savored the instant warmth of it, realizing that she had become chilled bone deep in the icy cavern and hadn't realized it before now. Before she tucked the cover back around herself, Goliat slipped the Dragon Blade into a space beside her, where it was well hidden from view. She put her hand on the hilt, feeling the fire-stones under her fingers.

Once all was settled, Goliat spoke to the dogs. They roused themselves and, fresh from their nap, began to run at their best speed. Once back on easier ground, he took the lay of the land and guided them north and west of this dangerous spot, where the depth of the snow made for swifter travel.

Fifteen

*S*varteper, *flanked by Patin and Cebastian*, marched across the plain until he was almost nose to nose with the two-man delegation from the renegades. The snow swirled around them. "And who might you be?" Svarteper demanded of the Aslaugor standing in front of him, the one bearing the truce banner.

"I am Rodolf, second-in-command to Asmal, leader of the Aslaug army," the man replied with more than a trace of bravado.

Svarteper turned to Asmal. "I know a certain woman who would dispute that claim," he said.

"Öydis? She is nothing," Asmal said. He spat on the ground. "She makes treaty with the enemies of the Land of Ever Snow, and consorts with the usurper who calls himself king."

"The usurper, as you call him, is the rightful NordornKing, acknowledged by all save you. Come, man, be reasonable. The war is ended. The horror that awoke and wrought such havoc from here to the southernmost parts of a land you cannot even imagine is dead. Most of those who marched under his command are dead. Your late commander, Baron Damacro, is dead. Give over, or you will be dead as well."

"We fight on," Asmal returned from between gritted teeth. "We come here only to give you terms for surrender."

Svarteper uttered a sharp bark of laughter. "Surrender? To

you? Not likely. Give over now, while there is still breath in your body. I'll see to it that you're forgiven, and you can join the NordornKing's army if you still want fighting."

"Hah," Asmal said. "I can count even if you can't, and I see few men on your side, many on mine. You give over."

Patin spoke up. "No." He favored the Aslaugor leader with an insolent grin. "Many men chase me, and I'm still here. I'll be here when you're stretched on the cold ground."

"So you say."

"Why did you call the parley if you won't even consider what we are offering?" Cebastian said.

"To tell you what we do to you when we win. We stake you out where crossed-horn woolly beasts trample you. Ice-snakes bite you. Snow-foxes eat your flesh. Ice-toads drag your bones away and drop them in deep water. If you surrender, we just kill you clean."

"That's supposed to convince us to put ourselves into your hands?" Svarteper said. He glanced at his companions. "If it comes to that, we'd rather die in battle. But we won't."

"So you say."

"I do say." Svarteper snorted. The parley had ended as he thought it might. Too bad. A lot of lives could have been saved, except for Asmal's intransigence. "We will fight. Do your best, as we will," he told the Aslaugor leader.

Asmal and Rodolf both turned and made their way back to the lines of renegades waiting Asmal's signal to attack. Some of them fingered their weapons, scowling, and Svarteper knew they would break the truce in an instant if they thought they could.

"Never fear, sir," Cebastian murmured in his ear. "Our archers are covering us well. Nobody will try anything dishonorable and live to tell of it."

The three men returned to the village safely. It seemed they had barely gotten inside the barricade when a shout went up from the attackers, followed by a flight of arrows.

The battle had begun.

The Duchess Ysa, Einaar noted, was in her element with all the weddings in the offing, especially when she discovered that he had not as yet made a formal proposal of marriage to Lady Elibit.

"I will carry your message to her!" she exclaimed happily. "Not that she would dream of declining. After all, you're the best catch in all the NordornLand. There's just one problem."

"What problem, my lady Duchess?"

"Dear little Bitteline is a sweet child, of course, and I'm fond of her. But she's without any family connections to speak of. She's from minor nobility even for Westerblad, and I doubt that she will bring much in the way of a dowry from that forsaken place. Are you sure you wouldn't prefer a higher-ranked lady than she? I could find you a brilliant match."

"Her family or her connections mean nothing to me, nor do I care for any wealth she might bring me. As the brother of the NordornKing, his Lord High Protector and guardian of the heir, and his chief minister both in his absence and when he is in his residence, I have good enough prospects for any lady in the land, and the one I choose is Elibit."

"Then so be it," Ysa replied with a shrug.

Her upraised eyebrow, however, clearly told Einaar that she thought he was throwing himself away on a nobody.

Let her so think. Einaar knew where his heart lay, and in times such as these, this was much more important than any match Ysa might devise, be it ever so brilliant.

He sought Royance's company, as had become his habit after an interview with the Duchess.

The elderly gentleman chuckled when Einaar related Ysa's reaction to his proposed marriage.

"Elibit? The one called Bitteline? The dainty little one with the soft brown hair and eyes? She's quite a morsel. I tell you, if I were only a few decades younger—" He stopped with a grimace. "Actually, Ysa has gotten so much into the spirit of things, managing all these wedding plans, she has even lined up a prospective bride for me!"

Einaar sat back in his chair. "No!" He laughed heartily, for the first time in days.

"It's true. Many of the families of the nobles are coming into Cyornasberg where it is, presumably, safer than staying at home. At first, Ysa was pushing me for marriage to Lovisa—she's Tordenskjold's daughter—to help cement relations between our two countries. When I pointed out that she was young enough to be my granddaughter, she immediately turned her attention to another lady just come into the city from County Mithlond."

"And who might that be?" Einaar inquired, fascinated.

"Lady Mjaurita. She's Mjødulf's aunt."

"I have not as yet had the pleasure of meeting her."

"That will be remedied at meat tonight," Royance said. "And it will be a pleasure, I assure you. Intelligence runs in the family." He laughed. "She's perfectly aware of Ysa's meddling and matchmaking, and is as amused by it as I. One of the advantages of maturity. Of course, nothing is apt to come of it."

Indeed, Einaar thought. *Is the gentleman smitten and preferring to pretend otherwise?*

"I'm far too old to consider taking another wife. After all, I have been a widower for—it must be forty years by now."

"Then allow me to advise you," Einaar said, smiling. "Enjoy the lady's company, and don't think about anything beyond the moment."

"In ordinary times, that would be good advice," Royance replied. "These, however . . ."

"Any news of the Arikarin?"

"Not yet, but people are beginning to trickle into town from the east. There's something that's stirring them, and my guess is they think to avoid something bad coming their way."

"I'll double the patrols we're sending out. We have no way of knowing how fast this slime-troll can travel. Else, we could predict its arrival."

"My guess is that it will get here within the week. I base this on nothing but years of experience in other matters entirely unrelated to slime-trolls." He laughed a little to himself, and the thought of Ysa sprang into Einaar's mind.

"Sir," the Duke said, "to me your opinion is as reliable as a sighting with my own eyes. I'll also double the guards and lookouts on the castle walls."

"Always a good idea." Royance arose to take his leave. "Now I must go and make myself presentable for Lady Mjaurita," he said. "She has promised to entertain me with gittern music this afternoon, and then we will go in to meat together. No doubt, Ysa will think she has won a great triumph and by tomorrow will have Mjaurita's wedding gown commissioned from the seamstresses."

Einaar likewise arose and bowed to the older man. "Sir, your very presence and your wisdom hearten me enormously. I do not know what would have become of me, pitted against such a formidable opponent as the Duchess, had you not decided to accompany King Peres to Cyornasberg." He couldn't resist a bit of teasing. "Not to mention this discussion of plans for your forthcoming wedding."

Royance snorted, but good-naturedly, and left Einaar's chamber. The Duke's smile lingered a moment before fading.

What a show they made, as if trying to pretend that Court life went on untroubled by any hint of danger approaching. And yet, why not? Perhaps the Arikarin had fallen asleep again, or lost its way. Perhaps it had fallen into a pit or a scarcely frozen-over lake and drowned.

In his heart of hearts, however, Einaar knew that none of these possibilities had any great likelihood of coming true.

The diversion Lord Royance's budding romance with Lady Mjaurita looked to provide was almost eclipsed that evening in the Great Hall. The platters were yet to be brought in, and people were still milling about, calling out greetings, finding their places, exchanging pleasantries. The Duchess Ysa ascended the dais and rang a small silver bell for everyone's attention.

"Hear me! I have splendid news for one and all," she announced in the resulting silence. "This day, the Lady Elibit of Westerblad has graciously consented to marry our lord Duke Einaar, brother to the NordornKing, Head of the Council—"

The remainder of her recital of Einaar's various titles was drowned in a general hubbub of approving laughter and applause.

King Peres, suddenly boyish under his mantle of sober kingship, shook Einaar's hand enthusiastically. "What grand news!" he exclaimed. "You are a fortunate man, dear Uncle."

"Long life and prosperity!" someone called from one of the lower tables, and the cry was taken up throughout the Hall.

Ysa led Elibit to the high table and, before the company, placed her hand in Einaar's. It signaled their betrothal.

He raised her fingers to his lips, happy at the presence of the delicate lady who was smiling tremulously, gazing at him with eyes brimming with unshed tears. "Long life indeed," he said. "Lady, will you join me here and share my platter as a precursor to sharing my life?"

"With all my heart," she replied.

Einaar glanced at Royance, standing at his place just below Peres. He had a maturely handsome woman at his side. She was dark-eyed, and only a few strands of silver showed in her raven locks. She wore the dark blue Court garb Ysa had instituted, and around her neck was the badge of Mithlond on a gold chain. A few fine lines showed around her mouth and the corners of her eyes.

"Come, sir, make me known to your companion," Einaar said.

"With pleasure, sir. But she is well able to make herself known without my help."

The lady curtseyed. "Your Grace," she said. "I am Mjaurita, Mjødulf's kinswoman, lately come to the city."

Einaar kissed her fingertips as well. "Then I know you already. Or I know of you. Your kinsman is one of the most able members of the Council."

"Your Grace is too kind."

Einaar turned to Ysa. "Thank you for your good offices," he said. "You must be persuasive indeed to convince my lady to wed me without a question or moment's hesitation."

"Not persuasive enough, I think," Ysa said, looking past Einaar toward Royance.

She would have said more, but Einaar nodded to Nalren, who,

in turn, signaled the staff of stewards to begin serving the meal. Ysa was forced to go and find her place at the table where, by Einaar's orders, unattached ladies were seated. As ranking nobility, she was at the head of it, but she was plainly none too pleased to be excluded from the high table, where she had formerly occupied a prominent position.

"Is Granddam Ysa at her plots and schemes again?" Peres asked as he served himself a piece of broiled fish.

"I fear she is, sire," Einaar said. He took some fish for Elibit, and for himself a slice of meat, dripping with juices. "The marriages already contracted for aren't enough for her. She would put Lord Royance on the list."

"No, truly?" Peres said. He glanced at Royance, more than a trace of mischief on his face. Then he turned back to Einaar. "Should I add my voice to the plot?"

"Please don't, Your Majesty," Royance said. "Frolic if you will, while there's still time, but leave me and Lady Mjaurita out of it." His tone was good-natured, but Peres dropped the subject at once.

"Perhaps I should have asked Hegrin to accompany me," the Rendelian king said to Einaar. "She loves this sort of thing almost as much as Granddam Ysa does."

"It serves as good diversion from our current woes." Einaar stared at the succulent slice of meat on the platter he was sharing with his lady. He wondered how his brother was faring, if he were cold or hungry, and his appetite abruptly departed.

Lady Elibit laid her hand on his sleeve. "What troubles you, good my lord?" she asked.

"Reality," he said, turning toward her. "How can we eat and drink and frolic as if we had no care in the world, when—when—" He broke off, unable to continue.

"We do as we must, good my lord," Elibit said gently. "It heartens the people to see their king's brother with a light spirit. It tells them there is nothing to worry about, even when the brave men who protect us know there is. You are doing a good deed."

She gazed at Einaar, her heart in her limpid brown eyes, and he wished he had a fraction of the bravery she thought he possessed.

"Aren't we going out of our way?" Ashen asked. "Our path lies north and east—or should."

"We will turn soon," Goliat assured her. "We needed to get to country where the sled can go quickly and easily. We'll catch up to Gaurin NordornKing faster than you can imagine."

Indeed, they seemed to be making excellent progress through the day, and Ashen's anxiety lessened when, true to his word, Goliat did begin to guide the sled more toward the east.

Behind her, Weyse chirped, the first time in days, and Zazar chuckled. "If you needed any more assurance, there it is," she said. "Weyse senses we're headed for her 'mama,' and we should be there anytime."

"Another day, at the most," Goliat promised. "You'll be with your husband, my NordornQueen, or I'm not the biggest member of your own House Troops!"

At that, Ashen had to smile. She guessed that Goliat could claim that title from the bulk of the entire Nordorn army. It was a tribute to the design of the sled and how it distributed weight and also to the stamina of the dogs that they could handle the load as easily as they did.

She had begun to doze a little, lulled by the smoothness of their flight over the fresh new snow, when Zazar nudged her awake.

"Look, ahead," the old Wysen-wyf said. She turned to Goliat. "That's one of those houses anybody can use, isn't it?"

"Aye, Madame, what we call a *seter*," Goliat responded. "I had hoped to reach one soon, so we can rest and feed the dogs. We'll stay there for the night and get a good start in the morning."

He whistled and guided the sled in the direction of the thatch-roofed stone building that lay ahead. When they arrived, the three people all helped unload it and take their belongings inside. The dogs seemed to want to stay outside, but Goliat insisted that they, too, get under cover.

"Never know what might be roaming around out there," Goliat commented.

Ashen had knelt beside the central hearth to kindle a fire, raking up the leavings of an earlier blaze. "The ashes are still warm, underneath the top layer," she said, looking up at Zazar and the guardsman. "Now I know we're on the right trail, and we're very close! Gaurin and his companions must have stayed here not more than two nights ago!"

She hugged herself, happy for the first time in what seemed to be weeks. With the morning, surely they would catch up with him. A longing to look on his beloved face overwhelmed her. How could she leave him, once she had found him again?

"Here, let me take over," Zazar said. "You're all lovesick again." She gazed at Ashen sharply. "Or is it another kind of sick?"

"No, I'm just eager to see him," Ashen said. "Truly."

"Nevertheless, you'll be getting an extra dose of herb tea," the Wysen-wyf responded. She began unpacking her supplies. With quick efficiency, she hooked one kettle of stew for the people over the rod that spanned the hearth and another for the dogs. She filled a small pot with water and set it at the edge of the fire to heat.

The dogs got served first. They hungrily ate all the contents of their kettle and then curled up in a heap in one corner to go to sleep. The three people and Weyse enjoyed their meal in a more leisurely fashion, but they, too, were more than ready to sleep as well by the time they had finished.

"This floor is too hard, my NordornQueen," Goliat said fretfully. "I'll go see if I can find some pine branches to soften it for you."

"You'll do no such thing," Ashen retorted. "The things that might be outside prowling in the night are a danger to you as well as to the dogs. I've slept on hard ground before."

Zazar snorted. "Told you she was no fragile ice-lily," she said to Goliat. "We'll make out just fine."

He moved his bedroll into a corner to give the women more privacy, and soon was snoring loudly enough to drown out the dogs. Ashen and Zazar took a spot close enough to the dogs to take some advantage of the warmth they gave off, despite Weyse's protests. Before any of them realized it, morning had arrived.

"We'll finish off the stew and be on our way," Zazar said. She peered into the kettle. "Never mind. I see that during the night somebody has been kind enough to do it for us."

"We can eat later," Ashen said, "when we're there."

Goliat retrieved the sled from where he had covered it with blocks of snow and stashed it behind the *seter*. He packed it again, taking the opportunity to inventory the amount of food they had left. "There's enough for us to get back to Pettervil if we manage to find something else to help make it last," he told the women. "Tonight, when we are at Gaurin NordornKing's camp, we set snares and maybe catch something good to eat." He grinned. "Even not so good. The dogs won't care."

Tonight, at Gaurin's camp. Ashen laughed, delighted anew. Though the leaden, overcast sky promised a coming blizzard, she didn't care. Soon she would be with her husband, the Dragon Blade would be in his hands, and the Mother Ice Dragon would be no more.

Goliat whistled to the dogs, and they were off over the uneven ground. He wanted to shorten the distance to their objective as much as possible, should the approaching storm catch them before they arrived. The first big flakes began to fall.

"Hurry!" Ashen urged. She glanced down at Weyse, who had moved into her lap as if by that change of position she was that much closer to her beloved Finola. "We're almost there, I know it!"

"Maybe not," Zazar said. "Look up."

A grim shape flapped overhead. It was impossible to tell how far away it was, or how big it was, until it folded its wings and stooped toward them.

"Ice Dragon!" Goliat shouted. "It's a young one, but still dangerous. We must get you under cover, NordornQueen." He gazed around, seeking a place of concealment. "Over there. It's another *seter*. Hold on tight."

For the first time he took a long whip from its socket and sent it curling over the backs of the dogs. It didn't touch the animals, but made a sharp *crack!* that caused them to redouble their efforts. The sled veered to the right and fairly flew toward the shelter.

As they approached, Ashen could see that this *seter* was old and roofless. Apparently the wooden structure had been abandoned when the one in which they had spent the night was constructed. However, ruined though it was, it offered at least a little protection from the winged horror that was almost upon them.

The women tumbled out of the sled. Hardly stopping to think, Ashen grasped the Dragon Blade and, with Zazar carrying Weyse, the women scrambled for the gaping door.

Goliat paused only long enough to try, futilely, to slash the traces and release the dogs. But the young Ice Dragon had landed. It stretched its leathery wings, snow falling from under them, and walked forward. Goliat was forced to flee, dropping his battle-ax. Inside the ruined *seter* he picked up the Dragon Blade.

"My first duty is to you, Ashen NordornQueen," he said resolutely. "Get back, please."

Outside, there was a yelp, then another as the Ice Dragon began to feed. He moved to block the sight from the women. "It will be slowed only a little," he said. "But maybe that's the time we need."

He drew the Dragon Blade from its sheath. The thin scales along the edge seemed to take on an opalescent glow. A last cry from outside, and the Ice Dragon was peering down at them from over the roofless wall. There was no way to get at this far tastier meat from that angle, and so the beast poked its head into the doorway as far as it could go.

Goliat swung the Dragon Blade—and the weapon dropped from his hand to clatter harmlessly into a corner. He stared at it in disbelief.

Ashen was equally dumbfounded. How could this be? Goliat was a worthy guardsman, skilled in weapons use, dedicated to protect her even at the cost of his own life. He would not throw away such a worthy weapon. . . . Then some words swam into her mind, a couplet she had heard from the Aslaugor Chieftain:

> *Naught but Nordorn-crowned*
> *can wield sword of Dragon spawn.*

Goliat seemed a man in a trance. The Ice Dragon, as if selecting a dainty from a tray, picked him up in its jaws. Unable to watch, Ashen closed her eyes. When she opened them again, the beast had moved back a step. Now it uttered a loud screech, flailing its wings.

It would be only a question of time before it decided to tear away the rotten wooden walls. Then the rest of the people who had fled to this inadequate shelter would be its for the devouring.

Ashen's arm felt unexpectedly warm. It was the opalescent bracelet she had put on lest it be lost, and had forgotten she still wore. She twisted it on her wrist. Knowing that she would be dead long before he could reach her, she called to him anyway.

"Gaurin," she murmured, too softly to be heard by Goliat or Zazar. "Oh, Gaurin . . ."

Sixteen

S *varteper could stay atop* the wall no longer. He grasped the ladder with hands and feet and slid down, charging toward the enemy before he had fairly touched the ground. In a moment he was in the thickest of the battle, laying about with his war mace.

"Guard yourself, Lord Marshal!" a boyish voice shouted.

But before Svarteper could turn, the enemy who had slipped up behind him staggered forward and almost knocked the Marshal off his feet as he collapsed. Svarteper glanced up to see Hod, the trumpeter, brandishing a slingshot with which he had brought down the renegade.

"See? I can fight, too!" Hod called.

"Well, fight from behind cover!" Svarteper roared in return, and plunged back into the conflict. He found himself grinning with more than his usual enjoyment of a good fight. The boy showed promise.

These quarters were too close. Around him, men grappled with each other, unable to maneuver. But with his battlefield experience, Svarteper could sense that the fight was beginning to go in his favor, though not without cost. Even as he slammed his mace into an enemy with a satisfying crunch of ribs breaking, two of his soldiers, an Aslaugor and a Nordorner, fell. Villagers also had come to join the battle, armed with whatever they could find that would serve as a weapon. He couldn't see the archers anywhere but the whine of arrows told him that some of them, at least, had found vantage points from which to shoot.

This was the hardest sort of warfare—house-to-house, often hand-to-hand fighting. Such always favored the defenders, but the renegades had the advantage of greater numbers. Slowly but inexorably, Svarteper's forces were being forced back toward the village square as the invaders continued to gain ground.

He caught sight of Cebastian catching his breath in a rare moment of respite after dispatching the man he had been fighting. "Go and start rallying the men!" he called to the young leader of the House Troops. "Push the enemy back, and we'll make a run for it to the old fort!"

Cebastian nodded and ran to do as he was ordered. The armsmen redoubled their efforts and, with archers covering them, gained the relative safety of the fortress walls. Svarteper was already planning the next phase of the battle. From the fortress, they could regroup and mount a more organized defense. The archers, stationed along the old, blunt towers, would be able to pick off the invaders almost at their leisure. Then, if the makeshift gate held, the others could hold off any attempts to scale the walls until the enemy grew weary and went away, or surrendered. Either option, as the Marshal saw it, would give him the victory.

A retreat would mean only that Svarteper would be returning to Pettervil with a larger army to subdue the renegades even to annihilation. If they surrendered, they would be turned over to the justice that Gaurin NordornKing saw fit to administer. That his own forces might be overwhelmed or surrender—or that Gaurin NordornKing might not return from his own perilous mission—was something that Svarteper refused to consider.

He caught sight of Rohan, leaning on his sword, panting as men dashed past him into the square. "What are our casualties?" he demanded.

"Still tallying, Lord Marshal." Rohan straightened up and wiped battle grime from his face. "Admiral-General Tordenskjold is collecting all the information as the men come in. We didn't get through untouched but I think we gave better than we got."

Svarteper nodded. "And the villagers?"

Rohan grinned. "Snow-bears for fighting," he said.

"Have your archers cover them and make sure they get inside the walls as well."

"Yes, sir." Rohan saluted and trotted off toward the makeshift gate. "Here comes the rear guard!" he called over his shoulder.

Svarteper could now see that there were village men pouring into the square. They were, he realized, the rear guard Rohan had mentioned. His respect for the villagers went up a notch.

Already the Nordorners were setting up a makeshift field hospital just outside the Blue Snogpus. There those men who were not badly hurt could have their wounds bandaged and return to the fight. A thought occurred to Svarteper.

"Hod!" he bellowed. "Hod, where are you?"

"Here, my lord," the young trumpeter called.

"Get your worthless hide over here!"

The lad appeared, grinning. He still had his slingshot in his hand. "Far from worthless this day, my lord!" he retorted with an impudence that would have made Svarteper laugh on an ordinary occasion.

"And how many did you hit with that thing?" the Marshal asked.

"Everyone I aimed at."

"Well, I hope you aimed at the enemy, not any of our men. Now, get yourself over to the Blue Snogpus. You'll be of more use there than hanging off the wall pegging renegades, where you'll just make yourself a target." Forestalling the boy's protest, he added, "No argument. Go."

Hod paused only a moment, then ran off to do the Marshal's bidding.

A good lad, Svarteper thought. I'll make sure he grows up to be a fine soldier. Then he turned back to ordering this stage of the battle. He decided to have his black standard bearing the silver devil-tree run up on the tallest tower, where it would wave defiantly in the slightest breeze.

The Lady Mjaurita, Einaar noted, fitted into Court society with scarcely a ripple. Her friendship and association with Lord Royance might have been the topic of conversation for a day or two, but the gossips abandoned it quickly in favor of a more exciting— even an alarming—topic.

Scouts had brought word to the Castle of Fire and Ice that the Arikarin had been sighted some two days' riding distance from the walls. How long it would take the creature to reach them at its own pace, nobody knew. Einaar's estimate was that it would arrive within a week. So far, there was no panic. That, he knew, would come later, when the troll-slug was actually sighted and at last became real for the people of Cyornasberg.

"Wedding dress or no, Lady Elibit and I will wed now," he told Ysa. "I am sorry if this upsets your plans for gay parties and celebrations."

Ysa looked as if she had slept poorly, with dark circles under her eyes and a certain haggard expression on her face. "There are many who feel as you do," she replied. "Esander tells me that there has been a constant stream of couples into the Fane on an identical errand. Even our Chatelaine and Seneschal, so rumor has it."

"When this is over, we will hold fetes and festivals for a week," Einaar said, "and honor Ayfare and Nalren especially. But for now, please be good enough to bring Esander and Lady Elibit to my private chamber. We will do it now, today."

"As you wish." Ysa straightened, and only then did Einaar realize that her shoulders had been stooped. "King Peres should be in attendance, of course," the Duchess continued, "and Lady Rannore."

"I will be honored if they agree to stand witness to the union. The marriage papers are already prepared and will be waiting to be signed."

Ysa bobbed an uncharacteristically awkward curtsey. "My lord."

She is afraid, Einaar realized, *as she has never known fear before.* Better to keep her busy, even as her elaborate plans for his wedding crumpled and wilted like paper flowers in the rain. In the long run, disappointment was easier on her than fear. On impulse, he sent word also to Lord Royance and Lady Mjaurita. Perhaps, he thought with a trace of his old humor, they would become inspired. . . .

Within an hour, both priest and prospective bride had arrived to find the witnesses and prospective bridegroom waiting. A table with food and drink had hastily been prepared, and servants stood waiting. Ayfare hovered in the background, with Nalren not far distant.

Einaar took Elibit's tiny hands in his.

"Lady, will you wed today?" he asked.

"Good my lord, I have heard the rumors. On the chance that they are true, yes, with all my heart." Elibit managed a small, brave smile. "Even if they aren't true, I would still wed today."

Einaar looked up at the people who had come to attend the ceremony. "My ladies, my lords, you see how blessed I am. Priest, pray begin. We are ready."

Esander had them kneel while he said the words over them. "Arise, my lord Duke," he said, when he had finished, "and my lady Duchess."

Einaar folded his bride in his arms and kissed her on the lips. Then he turned to the gathered assembly. "Give greetings to the Duchess Elibit once of Westerblad, now of Åsåfin and the NordornLand, Baroness of Asbjørg and premier lady of the land, second only to Ashen NordornQueen. As my duchess, she will henceforth not be known by her affectionate diminutive." He turned to her, smiling. "That is reserved solely for me."

The gentlemen in the room bowed, and the ladies swept deep curtseys, though Einaar caught a flash of startlement cross Ysa's features before she made her obeisance. Apparently it had only now occurred to Ysa that the new Duchess had supplanted her as the premier lady at Court.

"Long life and health, good my uncle," King Peres announced, "and also to you, my beautiful new aunt!"

With that, everyone in the room began adding their own happy exclamations and wishes of felicity, even, belatedly, Ysa.

King Peres took Lord Royance's hand, then Lady Mjaurita's. "Shall we celebrate any other unions this day?" he asked, deceptively serious.

"Not this day. We would not take away even the slightest luster of the Duke and Duchess's happiness," Mjaurita said, not the least bit ruffled by the young king's impertinence. "By your good leave, of course."

What might have been a tense moment passed without incident. As Royance was filling a small plate for Mjaurita, Einaar found occasion to murmur in his ear, "You could do worse than that lady. Far worse."

"I told you intelligence runs in the family," Royance murmured in return. "If ever I am moved to wed, she would be the one I would think of first."

"With that shall all be content."

Einaar turned back to his guests. To his amusement, he discovered that Ysa had already begun planning a sumptuous feast in the Hall that evening, at which the marriage would be announced.

Another evening of diversion. But the Arikarin loomed virtually just over the horizon, and soon enough he and those with him would have to devise a way to kill it or subdue it. Or leave his new bride a widow before her time. He moved to Elibit's side and put his arm protectively around her waist.

The young Ice Dragon tore at the rotten wood, and a large chunk came away in its jaws. Another moment, and it would have the entire wall down.

Then Ashen heard a sound she had never thought to hear again—the snarl of an enraged war-kat. The Dragon staggered back and, through the rents in the wall, she saw a war-kat fastened onto the Dragon's back, just below the neck. A heartbeat later, it was joined by a second, then a third and a fourth.

"Ashen!" a blessedly familiar voice shouted.

"Gaurin?" Ashen responded disbelievingly. "Gaurin, is it really you?"

"Stay back!"

Outside, a battle raged. The Ice Dragon reared and squalled, trying to dislodge the war-kats and defend itself against the warriors who had, beyond all hope, appeared outside the ruined *seter*. Öydis, Dordan, a Nordorner she did not recognize. Lathrom, at Gaurin's side. With brutal efficiency, they dispatched the beast. Three of the war-kats continued to claw at it, growling, but the fourth made straight for the doorway.

Zazar barely had time to set Weyse on the dirt floor before Finola reached her. The war-kat and the Wysen-wyf's unearthly companion rolled over and over, clutching each other and uttering shrill cries of joy.

Gaurin was not far behind, and he and Ashen likewise held each other tight as if they would never leave off embracing.

"I thought we were dead," Ashen gasped. "I thought you were too far away to reach us in time."

"But how did you come to be here?" Gaurin asked. "And why? Where is your guard?"

Ashen was spared, for the moment, from answering.

"So many questions," Öydis said as she entered the ruined *seter* as well, "and a storm brewing. Can you walk? You'll have to. Our camp is just over yonder hill." Her battle-ax was bloody.

Ashen felt faint, light-headed from shock. She tried to conquer it. "Yes, we can walk," she replied shakily.

"The Dragon ate all the dogs—the best parts, anyway," Öydis commented. "And most of a man, by the looks of things."

"That was—he was Goliat. My guard. Cebastian told me my guards would gladly give up their lives for me—" She stopped, choking on a sob. She pulled back a little to look into her husband's face. "I—I came to give you something, Gaurin."

Even to her ears, it sounded absurd.

"It will wait until we get to the safety of our camp," Gaurin said. "Lars Svartepersson, take what you can salvage from the sled.

Lathrom, see if you can persuade three war-kats to leave off savaging the Dragon's body. Öydis, help Madame Zazar."

"I wondered when you were going to say 'hello,'" Zazar commented.

"I was a little busy before."

"You're forgiven, then," the Wysen-wyf said. She bent down and pried Weyse out of Finola's embrace. "Come with me," she told the war-kat.

Gaurin shielded Ashen's eyes as he led her past the carnage just outside the *seter*. The wooden walls were barely standing. They surely would collapse in the coming storm, and would have done so under another assault by the dead Dragon. Their escape had been a narrow one indeed.

"We must bury—bury Goliat," Ashen said. "He mustn't be left for wild beasts to devour."

"In due time, my Ashen. The cold will preserve what is left of him until we can return to do him that honor."

Snow had begun falling in earnest. It was fortunate that they hadn't far to travel. If only they had known, Ashen thought, they might have tried to outrun or outmaneuver the Ice Dragon. But if they had done so, she acknowledged the chances were that the Dragon would have made short work of them all, even before she had a chance to call for Gaurin, using the iridescent bracelet.

In a short time, the newcomers were safe and snug in the NordornKing's shelter, their knitted coifs removed, their hoods thrown back.

"We'll all crowd in here while you tell us of how you came to be haring off after us in such dangerous country," Öydis told them. "I'll get water to heating so everybody can have something hot to drink."

"That would be most gratefully received," Ashen said.

Öydis continued ordering affairs, as practical as any Aslaugor housewife. "Zazar, you're with me. Lathrom and Lars too. Dordan, move in with Ueli. He snores to wake the dead, but that can't be helped. The NordornKing and NordornQueen—well, we know what they want." She nudged Zazar in the ribs.

"Those arrangements will do," Gaurin said. He turned to Ashen, settling her on the thick carpet of pine branches where she could be close to him. "Now, as Öydis said, you have a tale to tell us all."

She leaned against him, reveling in his nearness. "I thought you were still at least a day ahead of us. We stopped at a stone *seter* where you must have spent a night, but I thought the ashes were at least two days old."

"So they were," Gaurin told her. "From there we traveled a distance north out of our way to leave the dogs. Then we turned south again, bypassed the ruined *seter* where we found you, and made camp here."

"And flushed out a hatchling Ice Dragon doing it," Zazar commented. "Do the war-kats have a shelter as well? I saw them going into one nearby. Finola had her 'baby' with her."

"That must have been Lathrom's. The war-kats have been sleeping with me," Gaurin told her. "I daresay Ashen and I will be crowded with all four of them plus Weyse with us." He turned to Ashen and smiled for the first time. "But we will be warm."

"There were two hatchlings," Lathrom said. Without a thought for his rank, he was helping Öydis with the fire and the kettle. "We killed one, but the second escaped, only wounded."

"Wish we'd killed both, then and there," Lars commented.

"But if you had," Zazar pointed out, "you might have struck camp, or we might even have missed you altogether in the storm. This is as bad as anything we've faced so far. See there?"

Everyone glanced up, following her gesture. The wind howled, and flakes had begun swirling down through the opening at the top of the shelter, attesting to the worsening blizzard outside. Inside, though, all were snug.

"You spoke of bringing me a gift?" Gaurin said to Ashen. "What could possibly be so important as to prompt you to come all this way?"

"Something very important indeed," she told him. "Did anybody think to bring it with you when we left the *seter*?"

"Of course, I did," Zazar said. "It would have been a monstrous insult to our brave guard's memory to have left it there. Not to mention your own foolishness," she added.

From under her cloak she produced the opalescent scabbard trimmed with fire-stones and handed it across to Ashen. She presented it in turn to Gaurin.

"Here is the Dragon Blade," she said.

Everyone inside the shelter with the exception of Ashen and Zazar gasped and stared as Gaurin pulled the sword from the mother-of-pearl sheath. It fairly glowed in the light from the small fire.

"I thought it was just legend," he said, awed. "But how came you by it?"

"There was a map, discovered at Galinth. Rannore brought it to me. The map said also that the Dragon Blade was hidden in the lair. Gaurin, you would never have found it. I had come on this journey to bring this map to you, but along the way I discovered that, unknowing, you had bypassed the Mother Ice Dragon's lair. So I went in, with Goliat, and we found the Dragon Blade."

"So simply told, and yet such an awesome, dangerous undertaking," Gaurin said. He looked around at the people gathered in his shelter. Even Öydis seemed subdued for once. "Was there ever before a queen like this?"

"You promised me broth," Zazar said, breaking the spell. "Let's get warm inside and out, have something to eat if you've got it to spare, and then we'll wait out the storm to see what new grand adventure we'll be called upon to endure."

"At once, Zazar," Öydis said. "At once."

Some leagues to the north and west, the Mother Ice Dragon was engaged in her never-ending search for the red stones that pleased all of her kind so much. She staggered as one pang and, a little later, another smote her heart like sorrowful arrows. She knew that the last of her latest progeny was dead.

Three broods, now all destroyed. If her kind was to survive, there must be another and yet another. She must lay a fresh clutch of eggs as soon as possible, and for that she needed to retreat to her lair and to the sole remnant of her mate she kept so jealously guarded, directly above her bed of glittering crimson stones. Long had she slept, and when she awakened it was the first thing she had beheld. Then she had become aware of the Power that had dissolved her mystical slumber. He was small, not an ordinary sweetmeat creature, and to her surprise, he dominated her easily.

For the first time, under this Power's direction, she knew the secret magic of what remained of her mate. That first brood resulting from this magic she had relinquished to the Power, helpless to do otherwise. The hatchlings grew and flourished under his care. Then he had taken them away, and she had suffered terribly when each perished. Since then, she had produced two more broods, only to know more anguish when they had met similar fates.

In this remnant lay a mystery that she did not understand but which she accepted. When she fondled the artifact made from scales that had once adorned him, been part of him, that still bore a portion of his life, it would begin to glow. Then as she clutched it close, eyes closed in a kind of ecstasy, thinking only of him, the glow would enter and suffuse her body with its magic. She and her mate were one, their spirits, their life forces flowing freely between his remnant and herself. Later, at the proper time, instinct would prompt her to bring into her lair materials to scrape together and form a nest. Into that nest she would lay a clutch of six eggs.

Again following instinct, she had let these latest ones go free as soon as they were able to forage for food on their own. But the sweet flesh on which she fed them came from creatures who could also kill—the same sort of creature who undoubtedly thought he had destroyed her mate, so many years before.

These new hatchlings, she determined, would be better cared for than those that had gone before. Indeed, this time would be different. She would keep her young close beside her until they had grown to a size sufficient to make the sweet-meat creatures fear them and run away to hide.

The remnant bearing the last spark of life of her mate began to call to her, and she could not resist. Did not want to resist. Urgently desired to know the mystery of this spark once more.

All Ice Dragons disliked flying, the Mother Ice Dragon even more so than her progeny. She was too large and unwieldy to fly easily, and unless she flew very high, the effort generated so much heat it put her in grave discomfort. Also, she sensed a storm approaching, and storms made flight even more difficult. She remained where she was, grieving until it passed and her mounting urge to return to her lair overrode her aversion to flight. She climbed to the edge of an ice river near one of the peaks that spewed fire, where the red stones could be found. From that height, she launched herself into the frigid air.

The sooner she could know the magical singularity between her and the remembrance of her dead mate, the sooner she would begin the process of creating new young. All her thoughts, all her energies were now directed toward that goal. In her flight, she barely noticed the small camp at the edge of a stand of trees, where her hatchlings sometimes went to hunt for food, though she smelled sweet-meat creatures in it. Nor did she pay heed to the bodies of two of these hatchlings as she flew past the site.

Ice Dragons do not acknowledge death, even that of one of their own, once all life has left the body. The hatchlings were dead. The Mother Ice Dragon's mate might be gone, but he was not dead—not entirely, and certainly not to her. Helpless now in the grip of instinct and longing, she was going to join him once more.

Seventeen

$\mathcal{D}$uke Einaar, *wearing chain mail* over layers of snow-thistle silk, a mail coif over the knitted one, watched from horseback as Baron Arngrim with his sons put their mounted troops through their paces on the field below. Count Baldrian of Westerblad was with Einaar on this little hillock, along with an assortment of guards, trumpeters, messengers, and banner-bearers.

Arngrim, Thorgrim, Kolgrim. Einaar supposed it was easier for the baron to keep track of his children if all their names ended in "grim." He glanced over his shoulder. Count Mjødulf, given the responsibility for defense of the city and castle, would be atop a tower, observing the drills on the plain below.

The Castle of Fire and Ice stood stalwartly atop a steep rise, looking as formidable as the architect had planned, barring the way to the city it guarded. The walls of the outer ward extended landward as if embracing Cyornasberg. They were high and impenetrable, unless the attacker were an Ice Dragon, or the Arikarin.

Despite the gloom of the overcast skies, the towers presented a brave and gay appearance. The loftiest bore three flagstaffs—the central the tallest and split at the top. Empty now, it would fly the monarchs' emblems when they were in residence. Einaar's pennon, gold wulvine on deep crimson, floated from the mast to the onlooker's left, where it would be seen first by those approaching the castle gate. The third, only a little less lofty, bore the pennon of King Peres of Rendel, and below that, the silver burhawk on a red ground, Royance's cognizance. The Duchess Ysa's pennon, a gold Terror-bird on a lighter green ground, flew below Einaar's insignia. At least she took precedence over Royance, Einaar thought irrelevantly.

As he watched, a rocket arched from one of the lookout towers, flaming high and waking echoes from across the fjord as it exploded. It could have been coincidence—local wisdom said that shouts or other noises had no effect—but at that moment the ice river cracked, and an enormous fragment broke off and fell, sending waves big enough to reach the opposite cliff. Einaar took a moment to see that it posed no harm to Royance's yacht tied up to the buoy close by the steps leading up to the castle. The vessel seemed safe enough, out of the main stream of the sluggish current in Cyornasberg Fjord. Sailors were stationed aboard the yacht with orders to sail her out into the open sea at the first sign of danger, or at Einaar's command. If worse came to worst, Prince Bjauden would be taken down to the *Silver Burhawk* in the company of King Peres, and it would set out to sea, making directly for Rendel.

That much he had learned from the Duchess Ysa. He was prepared for calamity.

Danger, however, not disaster, was what the rocket had signaled. Einaar stood up in his stirrups, searching through the snowy dust raised by the horses' hooves for signs of Baron Gangerolf and the foot soldiers he and his sons Frederikke and Nils commanded. Baldrian's armsmen, carrying throwing spears, would be commanded by his only son, Axel. As Einaar's second-in-command on the battlefield, Baldrian's place was at the Duke's side.

Einaar wished, but only for a moment, that the two most powerful counts, Tordenskjold and Svarteper, were with him for the defense of the castle. But he knew better than to dwell on such a thought. Cities and castles could be rebuilt. But the NordornKing and the NordornQueen could not be easily replaced, nor could their heir. Tordenskjold and Svarteper were charged with keeping the monarchs as safe as possible. It was Einaar's duty to guard this place and their heir, to the best of his ability, or die trying.

A second rocket roared aloft. Baldrian touched Einaar's arm.

"The Arikarin must be in sight," he said.

"Only to those watching from the tower," Einaar replied. "We will wait here a while. I confess, after such long anticipation, I have a hunger to look upon the animal." He gave Baldrian a grin he hoped was not too shaky.

They hadn't long to wait. Arngrim had only enough time to position his mounted soldiers in a classic pattern—himself in the center, as the blue snow-fox banner showed—with his sons flanking him. He would take the brunt of the Arikarin's advance. Behind him ranged the foot soldiers, with archers to the forefront. Axel's banner, a black bear-dog on a white ground, was planted squarely in the middle, guarding the line of archers, just behind Arngrim.

"You have a brave son," Einaar commented to Baldrian. "I hope not too brave." He stood in his stirrups again, searching the plain, eyes shaded against the glare. "Where is Gangerolf?"

"Late again, my lord," Baldrian responded dryly.

"Damn him." Einaar turned to one of the messengers. "Go and see what is keeping our good baron," he said.

"At once, Your Grace." The messenger took one of the banners bearing Einaar's emblem so that all would know he was on an errand for the Duke, and galloped off.

Einaar missed seeing the Arikarin emerge from the stand of trees skirting a range of mountains forming the eastern boundary of the fjord. Possibly, he thought, stunned, it was just as well for his sanity. The stench of the thing hit him like a blow.

The Arikarin must have been more than twice the height of a man. Its tiny head was perched atop a sagging, shapeless body. The slime covering its gray skin shone sickly where the light touched it, and as it moved slowly out of the shelter of the woods it left a malodorous trail in its track.

How fortunate I am, Einaar thought numbly, to know aught of trolls. The Arikarin is surely the child of the First Troll of legend. When that one fell, his bones created the rocks and hills. His flesh created the land, and his colorless blood brought forth the rivers and the seas. As his flesh rotted, more trolls were created to crawl underground, out of the light. Here, before them, was one of those creatures. The Arikarin, Old Slimy, the Eater. The Last.

Would that the Slayer of the First had killed them all. Instead, in a mixture of mercy and cruelty, he had let them live. There were tales aplenty of brave deeds by later men who battled these children of the First. But that had been many years ago. Their deeds had passed into legend, and neither men nor legends were of help now that the Last had been awakened.

The Arikarin sighted the men ranged before it. It stopped, glaring at them out of its tiny red eyes, and bellowed a challenge. Flapping its fingerless hands, it shuffled forward, spraying slime in every direction as it advanced.

Einaar watched all this intently. "Archers," he muttered. "Set the archers on it."

At that moment, the archers, as if in answer to his words, loosed a volley of arrows thick enough to blot out the sky. Axel's men, stationed just ahead of the archers, hurled short, broad-bladed throwing spears in the arrows' wake, the missiles arching over the heads of the mounted warriors.

To Einaar's consternation, these attacks had little effect. A few weapons lodged in the slime covering the troll's body, but most simply dropped away, doing no damage, and the Arikarin stumped on undeterred.

Arngrim, whatever his other faults, was a brave man. He signaled, and his men spurred forward, brandishing long spears and swords, all uttering ferocious war cries. The Arikarin batted at the horses, sending mounts and men flying. Those who managed to slash or jab at it did no more damage than had the arrows or short spears. The slime covering the creature caused the points or edges of their weapons to slide off harmlessly.

A trumpet sounded down on the field. Those who could, struggled to their feet, and their comrades who were still mounted galloped across the field, each man offering aid to one or more of his companions as he rode.

The Arikarin stopped, but it was only to crouch over a fallen warrior. It lifted the body to its mouth, tasted it, and began to feed.

Fighting the need to be sick, Einaar turned to the trumpeter with him. "We have a moment's respite. Sound a retreat."

He wondered that he managed to remain calm enough his mind still worked. Our weapons are useless against the Arikarin, he thought. We have no chance out here in the open. When we are behind the castle walls—

Sword and spear and arrow had proved useless against this last, greatest child of First Troll. So far, legend was correct. If only they had the skill to construct a catapult, or a great crossbow such as he had heard about being used during the recent war, they might at least slow the creature's progress, but there was none. It seemed impervious, halting only temporarily, to feed. Nevertheless, he made a note to commission such weaponry, if legend continued to hold true, and they lived long enough to need it.

They yet had a weapon that could subdue the monster facing them—the might of the Great Signet rings. It was their one remaining hope, the Power he had hoped to call upon later, if all else failed, when the Arikarin had been weakened. Now he realized there would be no delay, no fighting the Arikarin's might. Only death to those who faced it in the field.

Einaar knew that the bearers of three of these rings—Ysa, Peres, Rannore—had to have been watching from one of the castle towers. By now they knew, as surely as he, that the next stage of the battle now depended on them and what they must do. They would have to summon up bravery to match that of the men who faced the Arikarin on the field, many of whom would not be returning. Many of whom were finding their last resting place in the beast's belly.

He stayed where he was only long enough to see that the retreat was swift but orderly. Off in the distance he caught sight of Gangerolf's banner, a brown ice-snake biting its tail, on an orange ground. The column of footmen veered off to join the rest of the Nordorners' retreat.

Even if Gangerolf had been prompt, the soldiers would have

been of no use, Einaar thought. He couldn't summon enough spare emotion to be angry at the tardy baron. He had the four Great Signets at hand, but one of the inheritors was absent. Now he concentrated solely on the hope that Ysa's having once worn the four Spirit Rings could boost the power of the three remaining rings sufficiently to bring down the monster—provided the wielders could find a way to use the sole weapons now left to them. They could but try. And if that failed—Einaar refused to consider that possibility. He, they, would find a way.

"Our archers are running low on arrows," Rohan reported to Svarteper. "For a while we could salvage spent arrows and fire them back at the renegades, but they aren't shooting many at us now. Perhaps their archers have been taken out of the fight."

That was both good news and bad, Svarteper thought. They could also be preparing for an assault on the walls and not firing for fear of hitting their own. "Never mind," he said. "How many do you estimate are left out there?"

"We must have diminished their ranks by at least half. Possibly more."

"Not enough. That still leaves us outnumbered at least two to one."

Rohan laughed. "For a Sea-Rover those are comfortable odds!"

Svarteper had to smile at Rohan's bravado. "Like your spirit, lad."

"Well, now what do we do, sir?"

"I think we might wait a while and see what our enemy comes up with next. Any new move must come from him now. That's siege warfare, you see."

Just then Patin scrambled down from his vantage point at the battlements near one of the towers and joined them. "There's a truce flag," he said.

Svarteper thought about this for a moment. "Genuine?"

"Maybe."

"This flag might be a ruse, considering how the last parley went. Let's let them cool their heels for a little while. See if they mean it."

Arild, one of Her Majesty's House Troops—away from his station near the Blue Snogpus, Svarteper noted with some displeasure—slid down a ladder and joined the group as well. "That fellow you had converse with, before the fighting started?" he said, a little out of breath.

Svarteper frowned, bringing the name out of his memory. "Asfal. No, that's not it. Asmal."

"He's badly hurt, according to his second, Rodolf." Arild wiped his face on his sleeve. "Rodolf's the one calling the parley."

"Well," Svarteper commented, "maybe this is genuine after all. If it turns out to be good news, I'm inclined to forgive you for being away from your post."

Arild turned red under the battle grime. "Commander Cebastian released us," he said. "It was going hard for us, staying to the rear. Anyway, there were plenty of villagers to guard the Blue Snogpus. Women, mostly. They wanted to fight, and that was the only way any of us would let them."

"I see. Well, then, brave armsman, let us go up on the wall and talk with this Rodolf." He turned to Rohan. "Have your archers gather their remaining arrows. I don't fancy falling into a trap."

"You'll be well protected, sir," Rohan promised.

Svarteper nodded and strode off toward the ladder. Despite the assurances he had received, when he reached the top he felt very exposed and vulnerable, even behind the crenelations, as he gazed down at the three men standing in front of the makeshift gate, holding a grimy truce flag.

"Which one of you is Rodolf?" he called.

"I am Rodolf."

Svarteper recognized him as the one who had accompanied Asmal at the failed parley before the battle had begun. "Are you in command now?"

"I am. Asmal is dead."

Svarteper merely grunted. "What difference is that supposed to make?"

"Great difference. Asmal was second to Baron Damacro. Damacro was a little off in the head, I think, with promises he was given when some of the Aslaugors were planning to go to war. I think Asmal had gone off in the head, too."

"And do you share in this?"

"You understand rank. Duty. I was vassal to Damacro, I had orders, no choice but go. I was a good officer, ready to leave off when the war had finished. Asmal not finished. He took my wife and my children so I would fight with him. Now he is dead, I am leader, I say all finished."

"You will surrender completely, and put yourself and your lives and those of the ones remaining in my hands?"

"One condition."

Svarteper was instantly on the alert. "What would that be?"

"Send men to Asmal's stronghold." Rodolf gestured toward the north. "Close by fire mountains. Bring back my wife, my children, other wives, other children. When I see they are all safe, then you do with me what you want."

"That sounds fair enough." He turned to Patin. "Are you and your fellows up for another ride into renegade country?"

"It'll make a welcome change from hiding behind a wall and waiting for them to come to us," Patin said, his teeth gleaming startlingly white in his dirty face. "You, Rodolf, you go with me, show me the way?"

The renegade nodded. "I go, no weapons. You might have fight, though, with guards at stronghold."

"Sounds even better."

"I leave my men with my second." Rodolf indicated the man with him. "This is Frøy. If I am false, kill him."

"If Svarteper doesn't, believe that I will." Patin turned and uttered a shrill whistle. Several men came running at the signal. "Get saddles on some horses, lads, and saddle an extra for our guide. We may have some more fun out of this adventure yet!"

Einaar found Mjødulf, accompanied by Ysa, Peres, Rannore, Elibit, and Lord Royance, in the Great Hall, having just descended from the tower from where they had been watching the abortive battle.

Retainers and guards hovered around them, and stewards rushed to prepare hot snowberry juice to warm them all. Tamkin put a fur-lined cloak around Peres's shoulders. Nearby, a tray of goblets, made of wood, waited to be filled.

Elibit ran to Einaar and embraced him. "You are safe, my lord!" she cried. "Safe—"

The Duchess Ysa sniffed audibly. Einaar knew that she disapproved of this open show of affection. He deliberately held Elibit a moment longer than propriety might allow before releasing her.

"Safe for the moment, perhaps," Ysa said, "but for how long? Why couldn't you prevail down there against that monstrosity?"

"Madame," Royance said. "What would you have him do? Spend all his men's lives uselessly, and only slow down the beast's progress by an hour?" He turned to Einaar. "I can't fault the way you and your nobles disposed the men nor their bravery and performance in the field. Not a one of them faltered. Quite impressive. Under ordinary circumstances, the battle would have gone your way. But we are up against an enemy unprecedented in all our experience."

"Our weapons had no effect," Einaar replied. "Either the Arikarin's hide or the slime that covers it is proof against anything we have available. We must use other methods."

Rannore put her hand on her son's shoulder. "That means the Great Signet rings," she said. "Peres and I are ready."

"Gentle lady," Einaar said. "Despite my preparations for it, I had hoped this hour would not come. It is more than anyone should have to request, that you expose yourself—and your son, King Peres—to the danger now threatening us all."

"And me."

Einaar turned to Ysa. "And you, gracious Duchess. You have earned your repose, your right to live out your days in peace here in the NordornLand, your adopted home. But still you are called upon to do more."

"I am no less brave than my daughter and grandson," Ysa said defiantly. She slurred the words a little. She held up her emerald. Both her hand and her voice shook, and cold fear radiated off her, even in the warmth of the Hall. "Let us go out now and put an end to this horrid monster once and for all."

Einaar suddenly realized that the woman was tipsy. She had a wine smell about her that surfaced even through the perfume, and her truculence and slurred words bespoke private use of neat spirits. Even frail Elibit showed more heart than she. Rage warred with contempt within him. If her craven cowardice caused them to fail—

No. He must think. How would Royance react in the face of this unforeseen problem? The elderly statesman would remain calm until all else failed and so, perforce, must he. More than one warrior had sought courage in the wine bottle; she was far from the first, and equally far from being the last who would do so.

If Ysa had truly turned coward, she would have fled, knowing what they faced, as she had done once before, unknowing. Also, she was a foreigner, and could not be expected to have a great depth of loyalty to her adopted land. Though Einaar could not excuse her for blanching in the face of the enemy, it did him no honor to fault her for what she could not help.

Still, his concern was justified and his anger merely set aside for the moment, far from forgotten. Would the Duchess be able to perform what was now expected of her? Would he be able to restrain himself from personally throwing her to the Arikarin if she weren't?

"Where shall we stand?" Peres asked. Despite his attempt to sound manly, his voice broke, and he flushed.

Einaar turned to his nephew, smiling gravely. The Rendelian king was brave, even if his granddam was not.

"Atop the east wall, where the beast approaches, my lord King. I have caused a platform to be built there, large enough to accommodate you and those who wish to stand with you." He glanced down at Elibit. "Stay behind, beloved heart. You are too fragile to endure this, and the rest of us would protect you from what awaits outside."

"I will obey you, good my lord." Her hand went to a dagger she had at her waist. "But be aware that—that I refuse to outlive you."

"Let that be as it may," he said. "If the legends have taught us correctly, we will all live and flourish, and have tales to tell when our NordornKing and NordornQueen return to us at last. We will dance in celebration, and sing many songs."

Royance took a wooden goblet of juice. "I think we could lace this well with spirits and be none the worse for it," he commented.

Nalren, the Seneschal, made reply. "Hot wine is waiting for those who want it," he said. He gestured, and another steward, carrying a steaming pitcher, came forward.

Mjødulf held out his goblet for his drink to be fortified, half and half as did the other men, even Peres despite his mother's up-raised eyebrow. Then thinking better of it, Rannore likewise accepted a little wine. Ysa demanded a man's share.

"After all, we three are doing a man's work," she said. "We should be prepared for it."

Hot words sprang to Einaar's tongue to denounce the Duchess for the way she had already been "preparing" herself in anticipation of the coming ordeal, well before this gathering in the Hall. He stifled his harsh outburst; Lord Royance had taught him well. Time enough for that. Nothing would be gained by letting his anger loose here, to the dismay of the company, when Ysa might yet prove herself.

Glad that his hand was steady, he raised his goblet and those gathered with him did the same. "Let us drink to the speedy completion of this 'man's work' and the elimination of the peril that faces us all."

They drank, and according to Nordorn custom when marking an occasion that was coming to an end, they all hurled the wooden goblets into the fire, never to be used again. All knew this was an undertaking from which they might not return.

"There's a storm brewing," Cebastian told Svarteper. "Look at the sky."

The Marshal squinted up at the darkening clouds overhead. "I've seen that dark slate color often enough to know you're right."

He thought a moment, then made his decision. "Go find that fellow Rodolf left in charge."

"Frøy," Cebastian supplied.

"Yes. Go find him and tell him he can get his men inside the fortress walls. They'll at least be out of the wind. They can eat and maybe put up a little shelter. Treat their wounds."

"You are generous, sir."

Svarteper gazed at the younger man. "I am practical. You heard what Rodolf said. Well, maybe you didn't. He told us his heart wasn't in the fight, that Asfal, Asmal, whoever he was, held hostages. Rodolf's wife and children, and he wasn't the only one. Now that Asmal's dead, that means his men are released, regardless of who's in command now. Daresay you'll find not so many out there as before he and Patin left to go fetch the women from Asmal's stronghold."

"Will we have to hunt them down later?"

"Maybe. But I think not. I think the fight's gone out of them now."

"Let us hope you are right, sir." Cebastian saluted and went off to do as Svarteper ordered.

As the remnants of the enemy filed in through the fortress gate, Svarteper could see that his prediction was correct. Not a hundred were left of the hordes that had faced the little army just the day before.

The villagers moved to aid them, now that it was obvious the danger had passed. Tents and awnings appeared, apparently out of nowhere, donated by shopkeepers. The village square immediately became more congested than on the busiest market day as the newcomers prepared to endure the coming blizzard. Women carried water and food to those who asked for it, and began helping the wounded to the makeshift hospital nearby the Blue Snogpus.

Svarteper watched these proceedings with a contented eye, knowing the war with the renegades was well and truly over, and that he had won—again.

Tonight he would sleep in his chamber at the Blue Snogpus. Then another thought struck him. Like his men, he had been distracted by battle. With the blizzard to enforce inactivity, every-one would stay under cover with only the most urgent treating of the wounded for diversion. The cleanup, setting all to rights, would have kept his men occupied just a little longer, and now he no longer had that diversion.

Inactive, bored men turned to talk and gossip to while away the time.

Soon, he knew, he would face the hardest part of this little campaign. His men, no longer distracted by battle, would begin asking where Gaurin NordornKing was, and also why the Nor-dornQueen whose arrival had been the occasion for much gossip also was nowhere to be found.

He wondered what he could tell them.

Eighteen

shen laid her bedding with Gaurin's on the thick layer of boughs and stretched out, grateful that Gaurin's shelter was at last relatively empty. The people who had crowded it had prepared a meal, eaten, then dispersed to their separate dwellings for the night. Ashen and her husband, with the four war-kats and Weyse, were now the sole occupants.

Knowing that the war-kats would be in the NordornKing's shelter for the night, Zazar and Öydis had put out the little fire and laid branches over it so that none of the furred creatures would be singed.

"The last thing we need now is for a war-kat to catch its fur on fire," Öydis said as she poked at the ashes once more to make sure all was well and truly extinguished. "Well, I'm for bed. Good night, all."

If Ashen peered through the covering of the doorway, she could see the glow of other fires at the peaks of the shelters. Even the smallest—presumably that of Ueli, the guide she had not as yet seen—showed signs of life within. He must have returned to the camp ahead of the growing storm, and he and Dordan were sorting out their living arrangements.

Even without the comfort of a fire, the interior of the shelter was warm. The war-kats sprawled wherever they pleased, and Ashen had to shove Keltin off the bedding she had just arranged for herself and Gaurin. "Not yet," she told him. "You can cuddle up to us later."

Gaurin sat watching, admiration in his eyes. "I should be angry at you for risking yourself," he said, "but I cannot deny that your presence here is most welcome. Especially since you have come through so many adventures alive by some miracle."

"The latest one by the miracle of this bracelet," Ashen replied. She twisted it on her arm. "You told me that you would always come to me at need if I wore this and called on you."

"There was the Dragon's lair," he observed. "You could have died there, you know."

"But I didn't. Oh, Gaurin, let's not dwell on what didn't happen and rejoice that we are here, together, safe for the moment at least, that you have the fabled Dragon Blade, and that our task is almost complete!"

"My task," he said. "You have done your part and more. Now it remains for me to finish it."

"I would be by your side."

"And that I will not allow."

There was a finality to his tone that told her it was no use arguing for now. Instead, she turned to other matters.

"Well, at least, I can give you the other things I brought with me," she said. She reached for the wooden box, took the peg out of the hasp to open it, and removed the diadems. She showed him the map.

"I can see the necessity for the map, even though you have removed the Dragon Blade from its hiding place." Gaurin accepted the folded parchment, but the light had grown too dim to make out the marks on it, so he gave it back to her to return to the box. "The Mother Ice Dragon might return to her lair, and I might have to follow her. But why bring our diadems?"

"I would have us—would have you arrayed as befits royalty when you face her," Ashen said proudly.

He fingered the silver band. "It will freeze to my head."

Ashen reached out and touched his honey-colored hair, now unkempt and in need of being washed. She knew her own must be in equally sad condition. It didn't matter, not when they were together. "I thought this all out long beforehand. You will wear your knitted coif, and the diadem over it. Even if you pull your hood close, the crystal snowflake and fire-stone set in the diadem will inform the Dragon whom she faces."

"That reminds me." Gaurin reached into a pouch at his belt and drew out an uncut crimson stone. "We found this on the other young Dragon we killed, embedded under its scales. There were more stones. I think Lathrom shared them out."

Likewise, Ashen handed him the fire-stone she had discovered in the crevasse she had followed to the mouth of the lair. "Goliat had a handful of them, taken from the cave. The Mother Ice Dragon's bed is made of them."

"Riches beyond measure!" Gaurin exclaimed.

"Perhaps we will take some back with us, when you have destroyed the creature."

"A few, perhaps," he told her. "Enough to add to the Crown jewels. A few to sell, discreetly, to foreign traders, so we can reward our brave companions and the soldiers who followed us north. If we take too many, they'll become so worthless they won't even be sought for paperweights."

Ashen laughed. "I didn't think of that."

"Perhaps these two stones are all we should carry away of what the Mother Ice Dragon has accumulated. They say such treasure is cursed."

"And perhaps not." Ashen had begun to understand how warriors could appear to be heartless and even joke about grave matters in times of danger, and how this kept them sane. "Goliat is dead and cannot tell anyone. Zazar won't care, one way or the other, about the secret of the Mother Ice Dragon's lair and its fabulous riches. This will be our treasure to use sparingly, when there is need. We will not be greedy."

"We shall see." He smiled. "Enjoy your fantasy, my Ashen. Tomorrow, if the storm has eased, you will go with Ueli to the dog-breeder where we left my sleds, and there you will wait for me."

She pretended a greater indignation than she really felt. "You would send me out into the cold and the snow when there are warm, snug shelters here where I may await you? I think not, my Gaurin."

"I apologize, Ashen. My sole thought was for your safety."

She relented at once. "I know. But with the Mother Ice Dragon out ravaging, unseen and unknown, there is no place that is completely safe. Even with you absent the camp, gone on your errand, there are those who will guard me. Far better here than in some stranger's cot, surrounded by noisy, barking sled dogs."

"Instead, we are surrounded by squirming, playful war-kats." They both smiled at Bitta, who was trying to "steal" Weyse out of Finola's grasp. The two females began tussling, not seriously, and Weyse squeaked when Finola rolled over on top of her. Keltin and Rajesh were already sound asleep, oblivious to their mates' activity.

"Let us to bed, Ashen," Gaurin said. "How I have missed having you beside me in the night."

"Nor half as much as I have missed you," she responded.

They removed their outer clothing and slipped under the snow-thistle silk bedding. With contented sighs, they shifted into their familiar sleeping positions. Ashen lay quietly, relishing the feel of Gaurin's beloved hand stroking her body.

"Ashen!" He touched the slight bulge of her abdomen. "You're—you're—"

"With child."

"And yet you came out into the wild, risking both yourself and the new one? How could you!"

"How could I not?" She extricated herself from his embrace and propped herself up on one elbow. "There is nothing for you to remonstrate with me about. I've had Zazar to look after me, and she's given me strengthening tonics every morning. I am quite well. In fact, I feel stronger than I have ever felt before."

"Nevertheless, you should have sent someone else with the map."

"So Ysa tried to tell me. And would that someone else have dared go into the Mother Ice Dragon's lair and take the Dragon Blade? No, Gaurin, even as your life thread in the Web of the Weavers has brought you to accomplish this incredibly brave deed, to put an end to the dreadful creature that threatens us all, this was mine to do. I was meant to follow you wherever you might go, even into the Dragon's jaws."

"Ashen."

He folded her into his warm embrace again. Later, they slept, still entwined.

Svarteper, accompanied by Cebastian, was making the rounds, visiting each group of Nordorn and Aslaugor soldiers, ascertaining how many they had lost, the condition of those wounded. Tordenskjold and Rohan were likewise employed, taking the tally of Sea-Rovers still in condition to fight.

Gratified, Svarteper discovered that their losses were relatively light. His small army had inflicted much more hurt on the enemy than they endured in return.

Morale was quite high, but he and Cebastian were asked, in every tent or house they entered, where the NordornKing was and why he had sent his Marshal in his place. The NordornKing had the reputation of one who would always be in the forefront of any battle, but nobody had caught sight of him during any of the fighting.

Cebastian answered for him first, and Svarteper accepted the phrasing gratefully. "Gaurin NordornKing is occupied elsewhere," the commander of Her Majesty's House Troops said. "He will be among us shortly."

But this evasion wouldn't satisfy the men for long. There were too many of high rank missing—Lathrom, Öydis, Dordan, leader of the Sea-Rovers' archers. His own son, Lars. Lars, though, Svarteper admitted, had been sent primarily for his strength and not because he was an officer.

At the moment, however, the men of the varied armies would simply have to be satisfied with what he could tell them, which was nothing. He wished he knew where Gaurin NordornKing was, and if he was safe.

Of course he's safe, Svarteper thought. With Lars Svartepersson guarding him, he had to be safe. Not to mention that hulking guard Ashen NordornQueen had with her.

A fresh worry. Soon the armsmen would begin inquiring about her, too.

The blizzard blew itself out in a day, and for the first time in a week, a wan sun rode the sky. Men came out of their tents and huts, stretching gratefully in its feeble light, and a deputation of men presented themselves to the Lord High Marshal. Their leader was the man who had had charge of the NordornKing's and the Marshal's warhorses.

"Respectfully, sir," said Rusken.

"Yes?"

Rusken looked around at those with him—Arild, Jesper, a couple of Aslaugor armsmen, Hod the boy trumpeter hovering in the background.

Arild spoke up. "Sir, we respectfully request that you tell us where Gaurin NordornKing is, and our beloved Ashen Nordorn-Queen, whom we accompanied to this place. Also, we find that the Great Chieftain of the Aslaugors is missing, and the Lord High Marshal of Rendel. Our comrade, Goliat, has not been seen since we arrived, along with others. We have fought well for you, sir, and we deserve an explanation."

Svarteper gazed past the deputation. Most of the armsmen, it would seem, had crowded close to hear.

"Well then," he said, "you will get one. Gaurin NordornKing traveled ahead, accompanied by those you mentioned—including my own son, Lars Svartepersson—to seek the Mother Ice Dragon. He knew the brave soldiers he left behind would guard him from attack by the renegades. And so you have."

Rusken and his companions digested this in silence. Then Arild spoke up again. "But what of Ashen NordornQueen?"

"She followed after the NordornKing, accompanied by your friend, and by the Wysen-wyf."

"Sir," Arild said quietly, "did you know our NordornQueen is with child?" His eyes filled with tears that he did not trouble to hide.

"I did not." Svarteper bowed his head and kept himself from wincing in anticipation of the protest he felt was sure to come, but again, the armsmen were silent. Then from back in the crowd someone began to sing.

> *Thrice-brave Ashen, valiant NordornQueen.*
> *Courage and beauty blended in one.*
> *Joins her true lover, Gaurin NordornKing,*
> *She will not have him battle alone.*

Someone else produced a music-drum. To its accompaniment, Arild, Jesper, and the rest of the House Troops began singing with Fjodor. Cebastian raised his baritone, adding its richness to the now-completed verses. One by one the other soldiers—even a few of the renegades—joined in the Song, picking up the new words haltingly, until the entire square was filled with the sound of masculine voices singing the praises of the Nordorn monarchs.

> *Stalwart Gaurin, praiseworthy NordornKing.*
> *Faces unflinching the danger unknown.*
> *His greatest weapon, steel-slender NordornQueen,*
> *They live forever in story and song.*

Now even Svarteper's eyes were stinging. He could only nod to the men in the square and retreat to the relative privacy of the Blue Snogpus. Moved as they all were by the incredible gallantry of their rulers, it would not do, he thought, for the men to see their Marshal weeping openly.

Einaar led his companions out of the southeast tower and onto the high eastern battlements of the Castle of Fire and Ice. Though the wall was thick enough for four men to walk abreast, the chest-high crenelations were designed for the protection of archers. Only a very tall defender would have a good view of anything but sky. Hence, the platform he had caused to be built, with side rails lest any of the occupants look down and grow light-headed—especially, he thought with more than a trace of cynicism, those who were a bit tipsy.

Rannore climbed the steps onto the platform, steady and with no visible trembling. Peres followed in his mother's footsteps alone, leaving an unhappy Tamkin behind. Ysa seemed reluctant to set foot on the first step. Einaar offered her his hand. The Duchess's hand was cold and clammy, but she gathered herself resolutely and, with his help, ascended to the platform.

Behind them came Royance with Mjødulf and Baldrian close behind. The platform had become crowded. Arngrim, still smelling of horse sweat, positioned himself at the wall, and Håkon joined him. As usual, Gangerolf was late. Einaar scarcely noticed.

Down below, still some distance from the castle, the Arikarin seemed to be finishing its horrid feast. It raised its head, as if sniffing the breeze. Then it howled as if it had scented something—a prey it had long sought—and began shuffling toward the walls with renewed purpose. Its cold, fetid stench preceded it.

"What do we do now?" Peres asked.

"There's nothing we can do, until it comes closer," Einaar said. His stomach was rebelling. He tried to keep himself steady, for Peres's sake if no one else's, but the quaking in his middle was sure to make its presence known before long.

"It smells me," Ysa whispered, in a strangled voice. "It wants me. Maybe it will spare the rest of you if I throw myself down to it—"

At least she was that brave to save me the trouble, Einaar thought. But was it bravery to seek a quick and easy death?

"That is foolish talk, Madame!" Royance exclaimed. "Have you learned nothing at all? The Arikarin will consider you only one particularly tasty treat among many. Contain yourself."

"It approaches," Rannore said.

Einaar looked at her. She seemed possessed of an unnatural calm, as if some Power was speaking to her. Perhaps, he thought, this Power was also telling her how to use the Great Signet rings to overcome the slime-troll that had almost reached the base of the castle wall. There, the stonework flared out, designed to give a scaling ladder no purchase and also to deflect missiles from a catapult.

The Arikarin laid one fingerless hand on the wall as if gauging how much effort it would take to tear it down. Einaar peered over the parapet. Slime was oozing freely from the troll's hand. The Duke could see it disappearing into the minute spaces between the stones.

Einaar had personally inspected the walls; he knew their strength. At the base, the builders had used little mortar in favor of ashlar construction, and the great stone slabs had been fitted together so cunningly a knife blade could not be slipped between them. The Arikarin was excreting more of its noxious slime than ever, the foul odor reaching even the lofty battlement. As Einaar watched, dismayed, the creature began to work one of the stones loose.

The slime dissolves the mortar and greases the blocks, he thought, strangely remote from the danger around him. Just a few removed, and the wall might come down entirely. Sappers tunneling under, weakening the ground on which the wall was built, could have done no better.

"Peres, Ysa, please join me now," Rannore said, still with the eerie calm that had possessed her since she had set foot outside the tower onto the parapet.

She formed her hand into a loose fist and held it out over the wall so that the great topaz in her ring could clearly be seen. The gem seemed to catch all the light available. Peres looked at his mother, a little puzzled, but moved to her side to imitate her gesture. Ysa, guided by Royance, took a step forward and shakily added the emerald to the two pointing at the troll, like weapons.

The great gems flared. A shaft of braided three-colored light stabbed downward, and the Arikarin stumbled back, dazed. It stared upward and stopped, as if trying to think. Its hand reached out tentatively toward the wall once more. The braided light stabbed again, and the Arikarin took another step backward.

The nobles ranged along the wall on either side of the platform took audible breaths. "Behold—" Håkon murmured.

"We can repel it, but we cannot subdue it," Rannore said. "We must have the fourth Great Signet."

Peres turned to his mother. "Alas, there is none to wield it," he said. "Hegrin, as Ashen NordornQueen's daughter, might, but she is in Rendel, and there is no time to send for her." He took a deep breath. "I fear we are doomed. We cannot repel it forever. It is tiring even to do this much."

"I have a distant connection to the House of Ash," Royance offered. "I can try."

Rannore smiled. "Not you, good my lord Royance. We have one who can wield the sapphire," she said tranquilly, "though I had hoped to spare him. Let the NordornPrins be sent for and brought speedily hence, with his mother's Great Signet ring."

"Surely not the NordornPrins," Einaar protested. "He is little more than an infant! He will not even know what to do!"

"Nevertheless," Rannore said, "let him be sent for at once."

She turned to look at Einaar, and again he was struck by the unnatural calm air of command she presented and the mysterious way she seemed to know exactly how to proceed, precisely what was needed.

"As you command, Lady," he said. "Baldrian?"

"I will return in full haste," the Count replied.

The three ring-wielders took the time to rest. Though Baldrian made good his promise, it seemed that hours must have passed before he led the nursemaid, Beatha, from the tower doorway, carrying Prince Bjauden in her arms. The child was scarcely recognizable as such, bundled as he was in snow-thistle silk garments and wrapped in a woolen shawl. Behind her came Ayfare, Nalren almost on her heels.

"Well, here he is, Your Grace," Beatha said to Einaar. "But why he had to be brought out in all the cold and the snow to look at that horrible nasty monster and smell it, too, he'll have nightmares for weeks, and the poor little thing is teething—"

Einaar ignored her protests. "Ayfare, do you have it?"

"Here, Your Grace." She gave the sapphire ring to him, then stepped back. She and Nalren clasped hands.

"Give me the NordornPrins," Einaar instructed Beatha. "And take off the mitten from his right hand."

"He'll catch his death of cold! And he'll freeze his poor little fingers—"

"*I command you.*"

Reluctantly, the nursemaid was compelled to obey. "Here, sweeting," she said, handing Prince Bjauden to his uncle, "it won't be but a minute and then we'll go down to plum-sugar porridge and a nice rusk of bread to chew to help those new teeth come in!" She glanced at the Duke. "It will be but a minute, won't it, Your Grace?"

"We hope so."

Einaar settled the child on his arm. With perfect aplomb, Bjauden slipped one arm around his uncle's neck as he accepted the great sapphire ring Einaar offered him. Einaar expected the child to grasp it with childish curiosity as if it were a toy but he put two small fingers through the band of the ring and clutched it in his tiny fist. There was purpose in his movement.

"I think we are ready," he told the others.

All four now moved as one to join their rings and unleash their Power. Einaar thought he would have to guide Bjaudin's little hand, but this was unnecessary. Mysteriously, the NordornPrins, no less than Lady Rannore, seemed to know exactly what was required.

Everyone save the ring-wielders gasped as the gems in the Great Signets flared into brilliant life. Four shafts of light shot up and out, twining around each other in a fantastic display of sparkling red, gold, blue, and green bright enough to hurt the eyes. They formed a tangled ball of brilliance. An explosion rocked the countryside, waking echoes from the mountains. Another huge slab of ice dropped almost unnoticed from the ice river across the fjord. The light ball poised itself high above those watching, amazed, and with another explosion a single shaft of pure white shot down. It sizzled when it struck the Arikarin, and separated into its component parts, wrapping the creature in crackling bands of colored light from which there was no escape.

The slime-troll writhed, trying to throw off its bonds. It howled again, one vast cry of rage and despair. It sank to its knees, still struggling, and finally fell at the base of the wall. One hand continued to paw feebly at the stone it had loosened. Then it, too, lay still.

The lights winked out quietly, as if they had never been. The three ring-wielders and Einaar, holding the fourth, stepped back, staring at each other.

Royance found his voice first. "That was—that was quite re-markable," he said.

"How do you fare?" Mjødulf asked. "How does Prince Bjauden fare?"

Einaar examined his nephew, and pried the sapphire Great Signet out of his chubby fist. Solemnly, Bjauden had begun to chew on it, and Einaar feared it would fall from the child's grasp. He slipped one of his own rings off and gave it to Bjauden to gnaw instead. "He seems to be perfectly all right, unharmed in any way," Einaar reported. "He didn't even cry."

"The first attempt tired me," Peres said, "but this. . . . Well, I am tired, yes, but exhilarated not drained, the way I had feared."

"I feel the same way," Rannore said. She glanced around at those surrounding her. "Actually, I feel as if I've been asleep but in a dream, if you know what I mean."

"Dream it might have been, but one in which you found the way to put the Arikarin back into the slumber from which it was awoken," Einaar told her. He raised her hand, the one with the great topaz ring on it, and kissed it.

"I—I would very much like to go in now," Ysa said in a small voice. "I would like to have some—some more strong, hot wine and go to bed."

"Your Grace has earned your rest," Einaar said courteously.

He handed Prince Bjauden to the nursemaid, who seemed too awed to speak. She occupied herself in putting the Prince's mitten back on his hand while Einaar escorted Ysa down the platform steps.

"Please return this to its resting place," he told Ayfare, handing her the sapphire ring. She was as lost in amazement as Beatha, her equally stunned husband beside her. "I think we may not need it for a while."

"Sir."

Ayfare accepted the ring, giving him a deep curtsey, and Nal-ren bowed low. Then the head servants roused themselves. Duty was duty, regardless of the astonishing events they had just wit-nessed. They were needed below, to minister to the nobles who had wrought such great work.

As the group of nobles made their way toward the tower and the steps leading down to warmth and the leisure to contemplate the mighty deed that had been accomplished that day, the Baron Gangerolf erupted from the doorway onto the parapet.

"What's going on?" he demanded. "Did I miss anything?"

The Mother Ice Dragon reached her lair. She hauled her bulk along the tunnel and into the cold light illuminating the cave. The thing she craved, the remnant of her lost mate—

—was missing!

She uttered a roar that shook the entire mountain and sent loose stones cascading down from the ceiling. Opening her nostrils wide, she snuffled, searching for the telltale scent.

A sweet-meat creature—no, two had been here—one male, the other female. Without a doubt, they were responsible for the depredation. None else would dare. What else had they stolen?

Her bed was in disarray. She knew the placement of every fire-stone that it contained, and there were stones missing. Methodically, she searched through the rest of the cavern.

No bones from those she had brought back for her hatchlings to devour had been disturbed, nor those remnants of the shells the little ones had left behind when they dragged them outside to shelter in as they grew. The cache of her precious cast-off scales was likewise untouched.

Only the remnant. The thing the entity who had awakened her called the Dragon Blade.

It had to have been the female, she decided. Only a female would know exactly the way to wound another female the deepest.

She inhaled again. The scent was familiar. She had smelled it—where? Then she knew. She made her way out through the tunnel then and, despite her reluctance to fly, launched herself into the air once more.

She was on the hunt, and she would not rest until she had found her prey. She began winging her way toward the campsite she had passed earlier. There the female awaited her fate.

Nineteen

he storm blew itself out, and six of the eight people in the camp emerged from their shelters into the cold, crisp air, glad of even the feeble sunlight that greeted them. While Dordan cleared the stone-lined fire pit and started a fresh blaze, Öydis and Zazar headed for the stand of wheat and wild snowberries the Chieftain had discovered earlier. The war-kats and Weyse bounded along after the women.

"We might as well enjoy the snowberries while we have them," Zazar remarked, her voice carrying clearly through the frigid air. "She'll have them all eaten before you can turn around."

Lathrom filled kettles of fresh snow and set them on to melt. When the water was hot enough, he carefully prepared Ashen's morning tonic from a packet of leaves Zazar had left him, with explicit instructions.

As everyone worked, a shadow passed over them from something soaring high overhead, traveling fast. They all looked up, and Ueli scowled.

"Don't like looks of that," Ueli said. "May be big thing." He took a piece of dried meat from the stores. "This enough for me. I go find Fridian village about half a day from here. We not stay here forever. Too much trouble if that was big thing, if she know we here and she come. Fridians help us maybe."

Then, tightening his hood around his face, he took off on foot, traveling northeast.

Ashen and Gaurin were later arising than the others, and Lathrom handed her mug in to her through the portal of the shelter. She drank the contents while watching Gaurin gradually rouse himself from slumber.

"I think I haven't slept well since I left Cyornasberg," he said, yawning. "I must have missed you."

"The fact that you've been heavily burdened with cares and worries beyond what even a king should bear had nothing to do with your sleeplessness, of course."

He smiled at her—his old smile, the one that made the lines at the corners of his eyes crinkle. "Well, today, I feel as if I could fight a Dragon," he said.

"Then you're going to make yourself fine before you do," Ashen retorted. "We both will."

"Proud Ashen," Gaurin said, gently teasing. "You will abide here, looking every inch the queen you are, while I go out for a morning's exercise. Shall we breakfast before, or after?"

She dissolved in laughter, happy to be with her beloved once more, gratified that he seemed so lighthearted. Perhaps he shared her feeling—that their adventure was shortly to come to its end. With the Dragon Blade in his hand, how could he fail to triumph? "Before. When we've eaten, then we'll heat more water and cleanse ourselves. Proud I may be, but you no less so. And well you know it."

Playfully she nudged him in the ribs—a ticklish spot. He grasped her, easily pinning her arms so she couldn't continue her attack. Then he kissed her.

"Quiet. What will our people be thinking?" He kissed her again and nibbled her ear.

"They will know that their rulers are full of courage and laugh at the dangers facing them." Suddenly she turned serious. "Oh, Gaurin, what would have become of you had I not followed, or found the Dragon Blade that you passed by, all unknowing?"

"As you yourself said, my Ashen, let's not dwell on what didn't happen."

Good smells coming from outside their shelter bespoke of grain porridge cooking. Gaurin hastily shoved his feet into his boots and wrapped his cloak around him. He went out to speak to Lathrom, requesting that their shares be handed in to them, along with as much hot water as possible. "My lady would bathe, and I also," he told his friend.

"As soon as can be, Gaurin NordornKing," Lathrom responded. "I think that we have all taken much heart today, with the sun coming out and Ashen NordornQueen with us, bringing the magical weapon that will put an end to the great worm that has been the source of so much trouble to both our lands." He went on to report Ueli's errand. "It may be that by the time the Dragon is dead, he will have returned. Then, with Fridian sleds and Fridians driving them, we will all be speedily transported back to Pettervil, and thence in triumph to our homes."

"And what of our people in Pettervil?" Gaurin asked. "Do you think they have fared well?"

"I do. If they had not, I think we would have felt it long ere now."

"I thank you for that."

An hour later, having breakfasted and bathed, applied comb and brush and donned fresh clothing, Gaurin NordornKing and Ashen NordornQueen emerged from their shelter, their boots squeaking a little on the hard-packed snow. They wore their cloaks about their shoulders, but the hoods were thrown back, revealing the knitted coifs they both wore and the silver diadems crowning their heads. The crystal snowflakes set with fire-stones glittered brightly in the meager sunlight. Gaurin carried both the Rinbell sword and the Dragon Blade, and Ashen wore her necklace bearing the badge of her house in plain sight.

At the sight of the Nordorn monarchs, all of their companions bowed, even Zazar and Öydis.

The ponderous sound of great wings flapping disturbed the air. Dordan glanced up, seeking whence it came. His eyes widened. "That which we seek—it approaches!" the archer cried.

Everyone looked in the direction he was pointing. A shadow flowed over the people in the campsite below, and, as they watched, the Mother Ice Dragon dropped from the sky and settled heavily onto the snow in front of them.

❧

"I think we should leave Pettervil and go searching for Gaurin and Ashen," Rohan said. "It shouldn't be difficult to pick up their trail. They are alone. They need us!"

"I concur," Cebastian declared. "We have won our war. Now let us aid our sovereigns."

Svarteper's staff of officers were gathered at one of the tables at the Blue Snogpus, bowls of stew in front of them. The Marshal glanced at Admiral-General Tordenskjold. "And you, my friend?" he said. "You, like me, are more seasoned than these eager young-sters. What say you?"

"Well," Tordenskjold said, "I, too, want to follow after them, of course. But our duties here are not finished."

"My thoughts as well." Svarteper spooned the last of his stew into his mouth and shoved his bowl aside. "We enjoy an uneasy peace at best with some of our former enemies. Discipline, gentle-men. Cebastian? Your report, please."

The commander of Her Majesty's House Troops had been placed in charge of those who had surrendered in body but not in spirit. He had the good grace to look abashed at the mild repri-mand.

"Yes, sir," Cebastian replied. "A score of them have had to be put under constant guard. They remain defiant, maintaining their loyalty to Baron Damacro's cause."

"Do you know if any of them had wives or children held hostage?"

"I think not, but will make inquiry."

"Patin has not yet returned with the hostages. Once the women and children are here, I will make a judgment as to which of the ones remaining were really coerced and now have aban-doned their revolt and can be released to return to their homes, and which should be retained for the King's justice."

"As to that," Rohan said, "each morning finds fewer of the

renegades in the village square than the night before. They melt away in the twi-night like snow."

"Did you ask Roland's second—what's his name—about it?"

"It's Rodolf, sir, his second is Frøy, and yes, I did. He tells me that with men who had no families to threaten, there were many promises made, not kept, and that their morale was very low even before our fight with them began. I think Asmal was hoping for a speedy victory against us, thinking to overwhelm us with the numbers he had, and thereby restore loyalty."

"Very good, Rohan Sea-Rover," Tordenskjold said genially. "Now you are thinking with your head and not from your fondness for your foster mother and father."

Rohan sighed. "Fondness and loyalty," he said. "Let me take the *Sea Witch*, with your permission, Marshal, and the Admiral-General's, and sail up the coast. Perhaps I can spot Patin and even lend him some aid. Get him back here faster."

"I will take some of the House Troops and make a sortie inland on the same errand," Cebastian volunteered. "Forgive me, Lord Marshal, but my concern about the NordornQueen is so great that I cannot remain behind the village walls."

"Those are good suggestions from both of you," Svarteper replied. "Believe me, I wish to have our unfinished business here completed as quickly as possible. Then and only then will we be free to journey on. Duty comes before all in this case, and it weighs on me as heavily as you, my young friends. Remember, my son Lars is with Gaurin NordornKing, and it adds more weight to my personal burden."

The officers arose from the table and went about their tasks—Svarteper to make rounds of his men, Tordenskjold to do likewise in the company of Frøy to check on those prisoners, renegades, detainees, whatever they were to be called at this point, still remaining in the village.

Rohan summoned some of his Sea-Rovers and departed without fanfare. As Svarteper crossed the square, he caught sight of Cebastian and his Troopers as they drew straws. The winners, Arild, Basse, Dunder, and Egil, mounted, and the five men moved out through the gate. The losers, glum-faced, wandered off to find other occupations.

Fjodor seated himself on one of the benches in the market-place area, took out a small stringed instrument, and began to play. Soon the strains of "The Song" filled the square. The soldier with the music-drum came and joined him. One of the villagers produced a wooden flute, seating himself on Fjodor's other side. As Svarteper watched, he could see that more of the former renegades were now singing in company with those against whom they had recently battled. He turned away. For some reason, the sound of warriors singing always made his eyes water.

Einaar called a Council meeting to discuss what to do next about their recent foe, now in deep slumber at the foot of the east wall of the Castle of Fire and Ice. The Rendelian king and Lord Royance were included, not entirely from courtesy.

"Someone do something about the body, and quickly," Ysa demanded.

"We can't really call it a 'body,'" Baldrian pointed out. "It still lives."

"Call it what you like, the awful smell is making me sick!"

"Agreed," Einaar said. "There are many complaints. But what disposition should we make of it?"

"Hack it to pieces," Arngrim declared. "Sprinkle the pieces with lime. Bury it in the mountains."

"Ordinarily, I would agree that this would be a good course, but you above all saw what happened when your brave horsemen tried to spear the thing. Can we be sure that touching cold steel to it wouldn't awaken it again?"

"No," Arngrim admitted.

"Then beat it with wooden mallets," Ysa muttered.

Esander had been invited to the meeting as well. "Is there not a less violent way of dealing with this creature than rending it asunder or hammering its head in?"

"Sir priest," Håkon said, "I have read the translation you made of the ancient book Lord Royance sent us, and I say that you speak foolishness—the kind of woolly-headed 'mercy' that prompted old Uztinov to leave it alive all those years ago and hide it under the Yewkeep."

"Perhaps," Esander responded mildly.

"No 'perhaps' about it." Håkon glanced around at those attending. "Speaking of Lord Royance and craving His Grace's pardon, we haven't heard from you, sir, nor young King Peres. Mjødulf has yet to speak, and he's the smartest of us all. Gangerolf—well, he's late as usual."

A ripple of laughter went around the table.

"I will be silent for now," Peres said, "offering no opinion and relying instead on the wisdom of my elders." He looked at Royance.

"I wish to study the matter further," Royance stated. "And perhaps reread the translation Esander was good enough to make, and consult with him."

At that moment, Gangerolf made one of his noisy entrances. "Just came from the east ward," he announced without preamble, "and a couple of the men taking down the platform on the battlement are being sick. I told them not to lean over the wall. That thing down there stinks bad enough already."

"Greetings, Gangerolf," Einaar said, "and thank you for your report. Now, we have heard from all save Mjødulf. What say you, sir?"

"Your Grace, I have no answer—only a suggestion as to a possible way to make the problem less noisome while we work out a more permanent solution."

"Then pray give us that suggestion."

Mjødulf leaned forward in his chair and, as was his habit, laced his slim, aristocratic fingers in front of him. He gazed at their reflection in the highly polished surface of the table. "It seems that, without further knowledge, attempting to move the Arikarin from its present resting place carries with it some greater danger than upsetting workmen's stomachs. Therefore, I propose leaving it there—"

The Duchess immediately uttered a sound of protest, and Einaar held up a hand to silence her.

"—yes, leave it there, and cover it over. Let us find a crew of stolid workmen with strong stomachs, and let them build a stout tent to cover over the creature, of as tight a construction as possible. Then, perhaps, the stench can be contained while we search for a way to dispose of it permanently."

"I find much merit in what you say," Einaar told him. "Are there any opposed to this course of action? No? Then let it be so. I will put Baron—" He almost named Gangerolf but changed his mind. The Arikarin, he thought wryly, needed to be put under cover as soon as possible, and with Gangerolf in charge, the project could be delayed a month or more. "Baron Arngrim is given this task, and he may call upon such men and materials as he will need so that he can accomplish it speedily."

He arose, signaling that the Council meeting was concluded, and nodded to two of the men at the table. As the Duchess Ysa swept toward the door, a perfume-soaked kerchief to her nose, Einaar moved to intercept her. He laid his hand on her arm.

"A moment, Your Grace," he said.

Royance and Esander likewise lingered. Peres cast the four a puzzled look, but departed without comment. A wise youth, Einaar thought. Royance has trained him well also. The Duke closed the door behind him.

"Now, Madame," he said, "there is aught to speak of, concerning you and the danger we have just fought to a successful, if perhaps temporary, conclusion."

Ysa looked startled momentarily, but quickly recovered. "Now that the others have departed, we four can indeed enter into the real discussion. I didn't want to mention it in front of the barons or even Counts Mjødulf and Baldrian, and, of course, to bring my grandson into it is sheer madness, but I might know of a magic spell—"

"I know that you have taken several volumes on magic from the Fane, and it is of magic spells that we wish to speak with you, Your Grace," Esander said deferentially.

"I merely borrowed them!" Ysa drew herself up with disdain and more than a hint of outrage. "How dare you imply—"

"Nobody is saying that you did otherwise, my lady Duchess," Royance told her. "It is the use we fear you propose to make of them that concerns us."

"It should be of no concern to you at all." Ysa glanced from one to another. "None."

"If what I have learned is true even to the half, it is of great concern," Einaar said. "Come, Madame, sit. There is that we must settle among us, and the first of these things is that you are to work no magics."

"None here has the authority to say me nay, if I choose otherwise. What vicious lies have you been listening to about me?"

Nevertheless, she resumed her chair, as did the others in the room.

"We'll get to what you call 'lies' in a moment, but your invoking authority is almost amusing." Royance smiled. "No authority, you say? You are mistaken, Madame. Not for the first time, I might add."

The Duchess turned on him. "You are a visitor, with no standing in the NordornLand, of which I am now a citizen, and, saving only Duke Einaar's duchess—and the NordornQueen, of course— I am the premier lady of the land."

"So you are. But you are mistaken—again—both in your estimation of me back in Rendel and of my standing here." Royance leaned back in his chair, elbows on its arms, and placed his fingertips together. "Doubtless you have forgotten, but in our youth I was a close comrade to the late King Boroth. My family was ally to the House of Oak, and though we grew apart because our temperaments differed greatly, Boroth and I never lost our friendship."

"Why do you tell me this?" Ysa demanded.

"Because I want to. And because you never knew that in addition to being Boroth's companion, I was also his kinsman, close enough that he spoke of awarding me the title of Earl of Grattenbor. That was, of course, before he became ill."

"He never gave it you."

"No, he did not, though he made note to one of his secretaries. There was no great need. I became Head of the Council, a post I hold to this day, and I felt no great urge to impress or intimidate by means of flaunting titles. King Peres, however, fulfilled his grand-father's intention a month ago and elevated me to the rank of earl. In addition, Duke Einaar, the Lord Protector in Gaurin NordornKing's absence, has seen fit to grant me equal rank in the NordornLand. I am the Earl of Grattenbor and of Åskar, the land between Sea-Rovers' Fjord and Rendel's northernmost reaches. It has been given to me to guard that territory. We are peers, Madame, both here and in Rendel."

There was a silence. Einaar watched rage flit across Ysa's fea-tures and her visible efforts to control it. He recognized how skill-fully Royance had used truth and accuracy to insult Ysa in such a way that she could not respond. Suddenly he felt sorry for her, lit-tle as he felt she deserved it.

"Each to his own, or her own, good my lord Royance, when it comes to how they wish to be known," the Duke interjected mildly. "Not all of us have your commanding presence, myself least of all."

"Of course," Royance said. "Though you underestimate your-self, as has our lady Duchess. It is her habit." He turned to Ysa. "Your history is known, Madame, both the good and the bad over the years, and there are no lies about you in it."

"I acted always in the best interests of Rendel."

"Frequently. But how much good you could have done, Your Grace, both to Rendel and to the NordornLand, had you con-tented yourself with your own great gifts and abilities and not given in to the urge to meddle in affairs that were both beyond you and none of your concern. Instead, the consequences of your thoughtless deeds have brought much discontent and danger in their wake."

Ysa had gone dead white under the layer of cosmetics on her face. "You overstep your bounds, sir," she said, in a dangerous tone of voice.

"It is a time for bluntness, Madame, and a time for you to give up these pastimes that have occupied you for years. We in Rendel were greatly relieved when you retired to Yewkeep; King Peres and

I discussed it on the occasion of my being elevated to the rank of earl. We hoped that with the fresh start you were given, you would no longer busy yourself with dabbling, meddling, but would turn to a softer, more positive life as you have richly earned, several times over. Alas, you have continued your thoughtless—even selfish— pursuits and thus endangered both Rendel and the Nordornland."

Einaar had learned much about his mentor that Royance had not deliberately taught. Unlike Ysa's husband, the late King of Rendel, Royance had not allowed any appetites to rule him. He was a fighting man by choice. Several times, he had defended his property, or what he deemed his, in full siege from neighbors too ambitious. Einaar knew also that he was the most deadly when he did not raise his voice. This was, perhaps, the most useful thing he had yet learned from the Earl. It had stood him in good stead when his anger flared at Ysa as they were preparing to face the Arikarin.

Einaar addressed Ysa. "Your Grace," he said, "I recommend that you listen to Lord Royance. He knows whereof he speaks, and he has my full authority and permission to confront you to-day. I have made independent inquiry, and what he says is true. If by some method we can contain the Arikarin again, there must be no repeat of this, or any other calamity brought forth by your magical means."

"And you, sir priest?" she said to Esander, making it a challenge. "Will you sit silent? Have you nothing to say in my defense?"

He merely bowed his head. "I am here only to witness," he told her.

"Esander is far your superior in matters both moral and spiritual," Royance said bluntly. "Do not look to him for support regarding the charges laid against you."

Silence again, as Ysa fought to control herself. Finally, she spoke. "Very well, I have freely confessed that I awoke the Arikarin, to the great discomfort of us all, and I accept full blame. But the other calamity, the Mother Ice Dragon, I had naught to do with, I swear!"

"I believe you, Madame," Esander said.

"What then shall we do about the troll, if you do not allow me to help in the only way I can, with magic?"

"We will find a way. Please consider. Magic awakened it once and might do so again. Dear Madame, for all our sakes, particularly yours, we dare not risk it." The priest's voice was as quiet as Royance's, but gentle, without the underlying steel.

"Then," Ysa said, visibly pulling herself together, "I would not endanger our lands afresh. I—I thank you for saving me from what might have been a grave mistake."

Royance glanced at Einaar and raised one eyebrow so slightly that someone not paying close attention could have missed the gesture.

"I think I speak for all when I thank you in return," Einaar said. "You are a valued member of the Nordorn Court, Your Grace, and greatly needed. Your knowledge of protocol and all the proprieties is unrivaled. We look to you—indeed, we *rely* on you—to set an example, to define the standards of diplomacy so that we will not shame ourselves, and look like wild, untamed barbarians to those from more settled realms. There is work enough and more for your hands if you will but agree."

"But of course, I agree!" Ysa exclaimed. "How could you even ask?" She arose from her chair. "And by Your Grace's good leave, I will go and take up my duties, which I am near to neglecting, with the matter of the disposal of the Arikarin interrupting all."

"With all my heart, Madame," Einaar responded, taken aback by Ysa's sudden capitulation. "The sooner we return to as normal a state as we can, the better for us all. I leave it in your capable hands."

She curtseyed and left the room.

"I too will be about my duties," Esander said.

"My thanks to you," Einaar told him. "Without your informing me of the books, we could not have challenged the Duchess and—I believe—succeeded."

"She still has the books in her possession," the priest observed. "But I will go and get them."

He bowed and followed Ysa out of the Council chamber. Einaar turned to Royance.

"I thought she might attack you physically at one point," he said.

"There was always that possibility." Royance arose and went to the table, where refreshments were always laid. "The wine's grown cold. Well, no matter. I can use a draught, whatever its temperature."

Einaar laughed. "And I. How did you dare, sir?"

Royance filled two goblets and brought them back to the table. "I've known Ysa for many years. I know her strengths, her weaknesses, her faults, and her foibles. I have seen her exhibit bravery and also pure cowardice. But most of all, I have seen that when she has no other choice, she will acknowledge what she would rather shun as unpleasant." He drank off the contents of his goblet. "And also, she knew that I spoke the truth."

"She did not promise to amend her ways," Einaar said.

Royance leaned back in his chair, relaxed. "She didn't have to, not in so many words. But she will make full effort to do as we request."

"I would rather have had her pledge on it."

Royance shook his head. "Do not," he instructed the Duke, "leave an adversary without his—or her—dignity. The Duchess offered what we required. To have insisted on a pledge from her would have caused her to immediately start searching for a way to break it in such a way you could not prove that she was foresworn."

"It is another lesson in statecraft for which I am very grateful. Your health, sir." Einaar raised his goblet to Royance and drank.

"And my lady's," the older man said. "The handsome Mjaurita awaits me. I daresay I will find it a much more pleasant interview than the one we have just concluded."

Once the Duchess Ysa had gained the privacy of her apartment, she claimed a headache, took to her bed, and let her ladies minister to her with cloths wrung out in warm, scented water. Then she sent them away, saying she wanted to sleep.

She controlled a shudder by sheer strength of will. How could she have been so careless as to blunder by mentioning that magic spell! Better by far to have tried it and then, when it succeeded, take modest credit for dissolving the Arikarin's body.

And, incidentally, creating another little flying servant like Visp. She, at least, had a great interest in learning what had become of Gaurin and Ashen, and another Visp could have winged its way northward to spy out what was happening. If they fared well, that was all to the good. If not, then despite Einaar's reluctance—and Royance's interference—events must be set in motion to ensure that the governance of the NordornLand continued in an unbroken line. Such events and such motion as only Her Gracious Highness, the Dowager Queen Ysa, once Queen of Rendel, widow of one King, mother of another, granddam of the present King of Rendel, First Priestess of Santize, now Her Grace the Duchess of Iselin, could be entrusted to administer properly.

That insulting flattery Einaar had tried to soothe her with, telling her of how invaluable her diplomatic skills were to the Nordorn Court. She recognized empty words when she heard them just as she knew the meaning of the Terror-bird badge that had been given her.

However, prudence dictated that she lay aside her magic, at least for the time. Who knew what these wild Nordorners could concoct when it came to lodging charges against her? They could actually banish her; and then where would she go?

The Yewkeep? With its fallen tower and the memory of the awakened Arikarin so fresh in people's minds? Rendelsham? Peres had made it plain that he proposed to rule alone, without her counsel. Iselin? Perhaps, though the duchy Gaurin had created lay several leagues distant from Cyornasberg, and the manor house was in need of repair and remodeling.

An idea struck her. She would rebuild that manor, perhaps live in it half the year, and thereby let it be seen publicly that her intent was to become the best of all possible members of Nordorn nobility.

In the meantime, of course, she would follow her instructions and attend to the matters of Court protocol—and by extension of diplomacy, in which she knew she excelled.

All in good time. Ysa had never yet been defeated, and so she was not now.

Twenty

he **Mother Ice Dragon had** scarcely settled onto the snow before the war-kats, screaming a challenge, sprang forward. The Dragon glared at them, and they halted, frozen in midstride. The moment of surprise having passed, Lathrom, Öydis, and Lars put hands to weapons and prepared to attack. Dordan fitted an arrow to his bowstring but before he could draw it back, the Dragon's scarlet eyes flared again and they, too, froze. Even Zazar was unable to move or even to speak.

"And you," the Mother Ice Dragon said, turning her attention to Gaurin. "You have something that belongs to me."

Ashen realized that the creature was not speaking so that the words could be heard by those who had been put under the Dragon's spell. The voice echoed in her head, and she wondered how she, too, was privileged to hear it.

"No more," Gaurin replied. "It is mine now."

"Never."

"The legends say otherwise."

"And what do they say, feeble sweet-meat creature? What do you say?"

"I say that I have come to challenge you, and to subdue you, and to kill you," Gaurin responded.

The Dragon laughed, and Ashen almost put her hands to her

ears to muffle the unheard sound. So far, the creature seemed to be ignoring her. She did not dare move, lest the Dragon notice her and bespell her as well.

"Others have tried," the Mother Ice Dragon said. "My hatchlings gnawed their bones."

"I have seen some of those bones."

"There will be more hatchlings, more bones. Now give me back what belongs to me."

Gaurin tightened his grip on both swords. "I will not."

The Mother Ice Dragon's mind-voice took on a different quality, almost a purr. "I see that you wear a diadem with a crystal snow-star, and a red stone in it."

She reared, spreading her great wings and displaying her sinuous body. Snow cascaded from under her wings, and her tail swept the ground behind her. Everywhere, her scales were studded with fire-stones both great and small, and she glittered in the weak sunlight brightly enough to hurt the eyes. A cold smell came to Ashen's nostrils, one that could only be described as "snaky."

"The stone you wear is worked like the ones on the relic you hold. I think that is a sign." The Dragon licked her lips. "Look you. You may keep your stone. I will eat those creatures with you, of course, but give my property back to me, and I will let you leave this place unharmed."

"I think you will not."

The Dragon laughed again. "You think I am trying to deceive you?"

"Yes." He hefted his weapons again. "I came not to converse or dispute with you, Madame, but to subdue and kill you even unto death."

"That is a task far beyond you, little sweet-meat creature." The Dragon licked her lips again. "You are presumptuous. Now I think I will eat you, too."

"Not while I hold the Dragon Blade."

"And what makes you think you are entitled to touch it?"

"*'Naught but Nordorn-crowned, Can wield sword of Dragon*

spawn,' " Gaurin quoted. "You see before me your doom, for I am Nordorn-crowned."

The Dragon turned wary. "You may wield the sword, but you cannot harm me with it."

"And yet shall I try."

So saying, Gaurin stepped forward, brandishing both weapons. The Dragon's eyes flashed again.

The NordornKing struck. The Dragon Blade landed solidly and lodged in fire-stone-studded scales. He shuddered and cried out. The Dragon stepped back, laughing again, her movement easily wrenching the weapon from Gaurin's nerveless grasp. There was no visible damage to the creature from his attack, but his arm hung limp.

"I said you could not harm me with what is mine—with what is *me!*" the Dragon cried. She plucked the Dragon Blade from her scales and dropped it to the ground beside her. Then she stepped forward again just as Gaurin brought his Rinbell sword up to attack left-handed.

"The legend may have proven false, but this will not betray me!" he cried.

But before he could bring his sword to bear, the Mother Ice Dragon curled her vast tail and flicked the NordornKing away. He landed with a sickening thud some yards distant, rolled over a few times, and lay very still.

Ashen stared disbelievingly, first at Gaurin's body, then at the Mother Ice Dragon. She touched her necklace with one gloved hand. He's dead, she thought. Dead—

The stab of grief she expected did not pierce her. The wound was too deep, too swift, for her to know the pain that was sure to follow. When it came it would take away her breath with its intensity, and she knew she would join her husband wherever he might be. Until that happened, though, there was that she could still do, to honor his memory.

She ran toward the Dragon Blade, where the Mother Ice Dragon had dropped it, and picked it up.

"No!" she screamed, brandishing the weapon. "I can wield the sword for I, too, am Nordorn-crowned!"

"Another stupidly brave one? How did you escape my spell? No matter. I'll enjoy chasing you before I eat you." The Mother Ice Dragon sneered. "And you are but a weak female, even less able to harm me with it than the sweet-meat creature before you!"

The Dragon glared at Ashen, and she glared back, knowing that the beast's observation was accurate. The NordornQueen was not skilled in arms, and her strength was much less than Gaurin's. Gaurin—

"Give over. Place my property where you found it. Give it back to me," the Dragon coaxed, "and you and all with you may depart in peace."

"All but my husband, whom you have slain," Ashen got out through gritted teeth. "He believed not your lies, nor do I."

"That puny creature was your mate?" The Dragon laughed. "I slew him as my mate was slain. What you hold in your hand is all I have of him. When I was awakened, the first thing I beheld was this last remnant of my mate. You are not fit to touch it."

"You were roused by the Great Foulness of evil memory," Ashen guessed.

"If you call him that. He was great indeed. He broke the spell that put me asleep, the one that had kept me so." The Dragon's tone took on a tinge of desperation. "I must have it back. I must. Give it to me now, or suffer the fate of all who have opposed me!"

The NordornQueen stood for what seemed to be a lifetime, locked in her challenge to the Mother Ice Dragon. One hand grasped the Dragon Blade, and the other was still on her necklace, clutching it as if it, too, were a weapon. "Without fire, there can be no Ash," she muttered. And then, louder, "Without fire, there can be no Ash!"

Her necklace began to grow very warm. It seemed to Ashen that some Power—perhaps the fire in the jewel's design—had begun spreading through her body, erupting through her skin, setting her ablaze.

The Mother Ice Dragon flinched. "Hot—" she muttered.

"A fire to harm you!" Ashen cried.

The Dragon was retreating, and Ashen, strangely calm, paced forward, matching step for step.

"A fire to scorch and loosen your limbs from your body. A fire to burn through you and put you to a more merciful death than any you ever granted."

The Dragon was still giving ground, as if bewildered and helpless before the column of flame Ashen had become. The fire crackled in the frigid air, the only sound to be heard.

In the relative silence, the Power infusing Ashen caused a memory to stir, a recollection of what she had read, what she had learned. . . .

In her mind's eye she saw once more the parchment from the Dragon Box—the words and drawings showing how smiths versed in the art of magic had forged the Dragon Blade.

Realization blazed up in the NordornQueen as bright as the flame enveloping her. She almost staggered from its import.

The Dragon Blade had been created not to slay the Mother Ice Dragon, but to subdue her!

She had not questioned it at the time, but now she knew with utter certainty what magic the smiths used that had wrought the spell. The clues had been there all along, if only those reading the records had known how to decipher them. She stared at the Dragon Blade, understanding at last her error—Gaurin's error, the master scholar Emmorys's error—the assumption that the weapon had been secreted in the Mother Ice Dragon's lair by her as the safest place to hide it. Instead, it had been placed in her lair by the smiths from the beginning, to keep her trapped forever.

How clear it was now. The Great Foulness of the recent war must have negated at least that much of the spell, not knowing—or perhaps not caring—what mischief he had done. He cared only for the Ice Dragons this creature would hatch, unknowing servants with which he had wreaked so much harm and which he watched being destroyed without a qualm.

The sword was the Dragon's, and she was the sword. So had the Mother Ice Dragon stated to Gaurin. Ashen gazed upon the

Andre Norton & Sasha Miller

creature once more as the final piece of the puzzle slipped into place. She knew what she must do.

Strength of arms alone would not overcome the Mother Ice Dragon. It had never been enough to overcome her. The magic must be broken.

The Dragon Blade must be broken.

She moved as if in a dream, very slowly, as she grasped the weapon in both hands and lifted it high above her head. The hilt sent a shock through the hand that gripped it, and the thin edge of the blade bit through the glove on her other hand and cut her fingers. She paid no heed but brought the Dragon Blade down sharply across her knee. The scales shattered with a sound like that of breaking crystal. The fire-stones and the shards flew in all directions, glittering, like a deadly snowfall. The ground heaved and shook.

The Mother Ice Dragon bellowed, a real sound that echoed from the hills and trees, as she writhed in agony. She staggered and crashed to the ground, twitching.

Ashen stared at the fallen beast. She thrashed again, struggling to get to her feet, and failed. Another bellow, a weak struggle; and then the Dragon shuddered and lay still.

The body appeared to collapse on itself, even as it congealed in the frigid air. Fire-stones dropped from the scales, scattering in profusion. Abruptly a mound of ice formed, crackling, over all, through which many images of the remains of the Dragon were refracted as if glimpsed in a broken mirror.

The flames that enveloped Ashen gradually diminished, then went out. In the shocked silence, the *plink!* of blood dripping from her wounded hand was all that she could hear. She dropped the hilt of the sword into the snow, unable to hold it with fingers that had lost all strength.

She was dimly aware that her companions stirred, released from the Dragon's spell. Stiffly, every hair erect, the war-kats stalked forward, growling and sniffing the air. The people likewise began to move to go to the aid of their fallen king and injured queen.

Then Ashen NordornQueen fell to the ground next to the tower of ice covering her fallen enemy, as lifeless as her husband.

She swam back to consciousness to the familiar bite of a hot drink in her mouth. One of Zazar's potions. She spluttered a little, then swallowed. She didn't know where she was. "Gaurin—" she said feebly.

"He lives, but barely," Zazar told her. "I did what I could, and now Lathrom's looking after him."

Ashen could barely comprehend that her husband yet drew breath. "The Dragon—"

"Now, that one is well and truly dead," the Wysen-wyf said with satisfaction. "How did you think to do it, girl? Breaking the sword like that."

"It was all there, so plainly. But I hadn't figured it out until I. . . . Well, I seemed to be on fire."

"So you were. Maybe that was what jarred your brain into use. Now, drink this."

The taste of the potion was different. "I want to go to Gaurin."

"All in good time. Rest now."

When next Ashen awoke, she was lying on one side of Gaurin's shelter. With Zazar seated beside him, he lay on the other, so still and white that Ashen's heart nearly failed her. She started to pull the coverlet off and sit up, and Zazar pushed her back. She was amazed at how weak she was. She seemed almost to have no bones.

"He's sleeping," the Wysen-wyf told Ashen. "Don't waken him. I even threw the war-kats out, so they wouldn't disturb you both. It wasn't easy, persuading them to go."

"How badly is he hurt?"

"Enough. His right arm is broken. Beyond that, there is a lingering paralysis that I do not know how to undo." Zazar brushed the hair back from Gaurin's forehead with unwonted gentleness. "He has some fractured ribs. I've bandaged his chest. And his knee was dislocated. But he will recover."

Ashen went limp with relief. Only now did she become aware of the bandages on her left hand and the pain from the cuts the Dragon Blade had inflicted. "Where are the others?" she asked.

"Well," the Wysen-wyf said, "Ueli had already left to go see if we could move our camp to a Fridian village while Gaurin hunted for the Mother Ice Dragon. Now we need to get there at least temporarily so he can have better care than I can give him out here in the middle of nowhere. Öydis has gone after him, and she'll return with dogsleds. Lathrom is out hunting. Lars Svartepersson and Dordan have started back to Pettervil. With any luck the fighting is over there, and they'll send help. The plan is to take you and Gaurin from the Fridian village to the seacoast, and from there sail back quickly to Cyornasberg."

Ashen digested this in silence. "Then I am content for the moment." She yawned.

"You didn't ask how you were."

"Well enough, I think. Weak."

"Sleep," Zazar advised her. "That's the best thing for you and Gaurin, and even for the one you carry. You took some unseen hurt from the Dragon as well, you know, not to mention that flame you wrapped yourself in."

"I was covered in flame before," Ashen commented drowsily. "All of us were—you, me, Ysa. And yet I took no hurt from it."

"That was the doing of our three gifts of magic. Me, with what springs from the earth, Ysa, with what comes from her books, you, with what is inborn. This time, the magic that is yours alone came to your aid, unbidden, I expect."

"I didn't call it into being. It just—happened."

"Open your eyes for a minute," Zazar commanded. "Look at this."

"This" was the jewel that had once belonged to Ashen's mother as a brooch and which had been reworked into the necklace she had donned before setting out on their journey. The design had been a flame rising from a blue vessel set with a large sapphire, surrounded by the familiar canting pun—"Without flame, there can be no Ash." Now, to her astonishment, the sapphire was gone and the circle of gold was blackened and twisted, half-melted. Only the chain and the sapphire beads from which the ornament had hung remained intact.

"I remember saying the words that were once engraved on this," Ashen murmured. She ran her fingertips over the ruined jewel. "It was my mother's, but I gladly sacrifice it to—to do whatever I had to."

"It'll be a trophy for the Hall. From what I could see, you stepped outside yourself and summoned enough Power to see what had to be done. And then you did it," Zazar said. "Not something to be repeated often. But the circumstances warranted such an action. Now, will you obey me, and go to sleep?"

Svarteper, heedless of those watching, embraced his son in an enormous hug worthy of a snow-bear. "You're safe!" he exclaimed. "And you, too, Master Archer!"

Dordan nodded, and then went off to join those Sea-Rovers still in the village, the ones who had not accompanied Rohan on his sail north.

"But where are the others?" Svarteper demanded. "Speak, boy!"

"As soon as you give me the chance, Da," Lars said. "Maybe we'd better get inside, if you take my meaning. My message is for you and your officers."

"That would be Admiral-General Tordenskjold. Cebastian and Rohan are off north, rescuing hostages. Seems that the leader of these people we were fighting kept women and children—"

"Sir, I do have news."

"Well, then, come with me."

The two entered the Blue Snogpus. Svarteper signaled Stehmar to bring food and drink. As they sat down at one of the battered tables, the Marshal fixed his son with a stern gaze. "Now, what is it that is so important it couldn't wait?"

"Gaurin NordornKing is sore wounded, and Ashen Nordorn-Queen isn't much better off. Both seemed at the very door of death when I left our camp even though the Wysen-wyf was looking after them."

Svarteper fought to keep command of himself. "And the Mother Ice Dragon?"

"Dead, dead and buried under a pile of clear ice. I saw it happen."

"And you did nothing to help?"

Lars related the circumstances of the Dragon's spell that rendered all unable to move or speak, save for the King and Queen, and how Gaurin had attacked and the Dragon had contemptuously thrown him away. "If the NordornQueen hadn't found a way to kill that beast, it would have et us all, I know it."

Svarteper frowned, thinking. Surely Lars had been mistaken. He had been under the Dragon's spell and in any case, Ashen NordornQueen was too frail to engage in such a battle.

"We must go to their aid," he said finally. "You did well to keep this between you and me. The men would have been dismayed."

"I thought so."

"Been hard enough sidestepping around their absence as long as I did." Svarteper grinned. His plan took shape rapidly. "I will leave a detachment of men here under Tordenskjold's command to look after matters. We should get to that campsite and be back before Cebastian and Rohan return."

"Yes, sir," Lars said, visibly relieved.

"You feel like another trip out in the open country?"

"It's what I came back for, sir, to guide you."

"Then we'll leave as soon as the men can get sleds and dogs ready."

Within an hour, several sleds were skimming north, under Lars Svarteperson's guidance, toward the place where the injured NordornKing and NordornQueen waited.

Öydis and Ueli arrived at the camp with three sleds and two Fridian drivers. On one conveyance they carefully placed Gaurin, and on the second, Ashen. They loaded the Wysen-wyf, Weyse, and all the belongings and equipment that would fit on the remaining sled, preparatory to heading back in a northwest direction.

"I stay here, show soldiers how to get to village," Ueli explained. "It not far."

"What about them?" one of the Fridian asked, jerking his head in the direction of the four war-kats.

"They don't need a sled," Zazar said sharply.

"I'll take charge of them," Lathrom said. "Daresay they won't be greatly welcome in the Fridian village."

"Then come on foot as fast as you're able," Zazar told him. She tucked Weyse snugly under the snow-thistle silk coverlet she had wrapped around her and placed a lumpy bundle that looked very much like her shawl down beside her knees. She glanced back at Öydis. "Now let's get going. The sooner we get these people in a warm, proper shelter, the better."

Lathrom had set off ahead of them and the war-kats were already trotting beside him, their soft, lethal paws carrying them lightly over the surface of the snow. There were a few clouds in the sky, but none promised fresh snow. The sleds quickly overtook the Rendelian Marshal. The trail—at least for now—would be easy to follow for those who would come later.

Weyse squeaked a little, then settled down. The Fridian cracked his whip in the air, and the dogs sprang into a run.

The Fridian village, as Ueli had indicated, was only a short distance by dogsled, over a couple of rises and invisible to the people who had made camp at the edge of the woods only a few days before.

Gaurin had roused a little by the time the drivers drew the sleds up at the outskirts of the Fridian village. The headman came out to greet the newcomers. His face was heavily tattooed.

"You Gaurin NordornKing," the headman said.

It didn't seem to be a question, but Gaurin nodded.

"I Chaggi."

"My former foe."

Zazar, who had been drowsing, came fully alert.

"Yes, former. Your army beat me fair. Chaggi good Nordorner now. Friend. Welcome to village."

"I'll take over, Chaggi," Zazar said as she struggled to unwrap herself and stand up. It was a feat, to avoid squashing Weyse, and also to hide the shawl-wrapped bundle in the bottom of the sled. "Show me to an empty house, if you've got one. I'll need a kettle, some clean snow melted, some—"

"You stay back," Chaggi told her, more than a little belligerently. "You just stranger-woman."

Zazar drew herself up to her full height, her aged stoop gone for the moment. "I am the Wysen-wyf of the Bale-Bog!" she said sternly. "Or was. You have the immense privilege of helping me. Stand aside."

For a moment, it looked as if Chaggi would challenge her. Then he gave ground, motioning to a couple of Fridians with him. Without further argument, they conducted Zazar to a good-sized house just outside the circle of dwellings that ringed the ceremonial center of the village.

Zazar glanced around at her surroundings before entering. The houses were conical in shape, snugly constructed of hides and thatch, with a smoke hole at the top. The entrances all bore the curved tusks of some unimaginably huge Nordorn beast, flanking the doorways and crossing at the top. In the central area of the village, frames hung with strips of drying meat stood close to a fire that, Zazar suspected, would never be allowed to go out, lest it take the life of the village with it. In many spots flat stones marked what she recognized as snow pits, where spare food was stashed in case the hunters were unsuccessful. Each stone bore a different family mark on it—the same, she judged, as the pattern each family had engraved on his or her skin. Altogether, judging from the number of houses and stones, there were more than a score of families living here. A few dogs and children stood, staring at the newcomers.

Öydis was entering another such house. She waved at Zazar, who nodded in return. She would be returning to her mountain stronghold once Gaurin and Ashen were on their way back to

Pettervil and, apparently, saw no great need for taking any kind of formal farewell.

Zazar ducked through the doorway, followed by four Fridians carrying the litter bearing Gaurin and four more with another litter carrying Ashen. Both seemed to be unconscious. Both had new streaks of white in their hair, and Gaurin in particular seemed to have aged overnight.

"Put him over here," she said, indicating a spot close to the fire where fresh boughs had been laid, "and her beside him where I can tend them both."

As the men obeyed, others were carrying bundles of their belongings into the house. Zazar pointed to a spot close by, against one of the walls that enclosed what appeared to be a kitchen area. "Pile everything else over there. I'll sort it out later."

Two women entered, bearing not a kettle, but a large earthenware pot, full of water. It would do.

One of the women shyly offered some dried meat in a smaller pot. Using gestures, she indicated that Zazar fill the pot with water, heat it, and brew some broth.

"Thank you," Zazar said. "I know how to do this, but I appreciate your thoughtfulness. Of course, you can't understand me."

Chaggi came in. "I tell her." He turned to the woman who had brought the materials for the broth and translated what Zazar had said.

The woman's face lit up, and she said something else in rapid-fire Fridian.

"She say, let her know, you need help," Chaggi told the Wysenwyf. "She the healing-woman of village."

Zazar nodded. "I just might. I'll let her know as soon as I have an idea what might be required. Tell her now to just watch out for the man following us, and give orders for the hunters to leave the warkats alone. Maybe you'd better do that part. Or leave it to Öydis."

Chaggi nodded. He spoke to the healing-woman and the other, who must have been her assistant, and the three left the house.

Zazar, seeing that Gaurin had not stirred, took the opportunity to begin sorting through the bundles of belongings, setting that which could be used in her arts to one side. The shawl-wrapped bundle she placed carefully under a mat and piled everything else—their meager store of food, their extra clothing and weapons, miscellaneous personal belongings—on top of it.

Then, knowing that she was tired beyond what she could ever remember, she settled down to watch over her charges, and to dare doze off a little herself while the water was heating to make the strengthening broth.

"Just over that rise," Lars said. "We should see the ruined *seter* where we killed the baby Ice Dragon, and then about half a league beyond that, the camp."

Svarteper stared, astonished, at the *seter*, almost demolished by the attempts of the beast to get at the NordornQueen and her companions. The Dragon lay where it had fallen, surrounded by a sled, the remains of the dogs that had once pulled it, and what was left of the man who had driven it.

"Hmmph," Svarteper commented. He motioned to Nels, one of the NordornQueen's House Troops and the driver of one of his sleds. "You, take a look over there and see if they left anything worth salvaging. Bury that man's body and catch up with us when you can."

Nels nodded, whistled to his dogs, and the sled veered off from the track followed by the others. Svarteper pushed on with the rest of his men. Presently they spotted the shelters the NordornKing and his company had erected. A Fridian waved to them.

"That's Ueli," Lars told his father. "He must have stayed behind to meet us."

Svarteper pulled his sled to a halt. "Greetings, Ueli. We've come for the NordornKing and the NordornQueen."

"They at Fridian village. I take you to them."

"We'll have to wait for one of our men," Svarteper said as he glanced over his shoulder.

They hadn't long to wait. In a few moments Nels came over the last rise and joined them. "They left a little food, but nothing much more," he reported. "And these." He showed the Marshal a handful of small fire-stones.

"Big thing like red stones," Ueli commented. "That big thing like lots of red stones." He indicated what a casual onlooker might mistake for an ice boulder. "Covered in them, hurt eyes so bright."

"Some were lying by the Dragon, but I found these beside the man's body," Nels said. "It was Goliat."

Svarteper walked over to what must have been the battle-ground of Gaurin NordornKing's great conflict with the "big thing"—the Mother Ice Dragon.

"Remarkable," he said, gazing at the body, refracted, as Lars had said, through the fractured ice. Many fire-stones still studded the beast's scales, but more littered the ground beside her. Oddly, there were none outside the boundaries of the ice that encased the body. "You sure you saw it right? The NordornKing didn't slay her with the Dragon Blade?"

"No, Da," Lars said. "I told you. It was the NordornQueen, and she never laid a touch of the sword on the beast. She broke it, and the Dragon died. We thought they'd both died, too."

"Remarkable," Svarteper repeated. He still couldn't believe frail Ashen had accomplished what Gaurin could not. Well, soon he'd get the real story from them. "Let's go."

Zazar awoke, knowing she hadn't slept long because the water for the broth was just beginning to bubble. She dropped the dried meat into the pot, too late wishing she'd thought to crumble it first. However, it seemed to be all right. It smelled good. She rummaged around in the section of the house where their goods had been placed and found some bowls. By that time the broth was boiling. She poured it into the bowls and set them aside while she awakened her charges.

"Here, drink this," she said, giving one of the bowls to Gaurin. "It will do you a world of good." Then she turned to Ashen. "Can you sit up?"

"I think so."

Zazar put her arm around Ashen's shoulders. The Nordorn-Queen was too weak to sit unassisted, so Zazar propped her up on a bundle of clothing so she could sip her broth.

"My arm doesn't work," Gaurin commented.

"Well, of course not. It's broken!" Zazar said waspishly. "I put a temporary splint on it, but we'll need to do a better job now that we're here in Chaggi's village."

"That's quite a coincidence, isn't it. Chaggi's helping us when he fought us so hard, just a short time ago."

Zazar peered at him sharply. His strong constitution was working in his favor; a little color seemed to be coming back into his face though she could see new lines that hadn't been there before. Later, when his broken bones healed, she would address the weakness that extended through his body and Ashen's as well, concentrated in his sword arm and her right arm and hand—the hands that had grasped the Dragon Blade to use it. She suspected what this meant, but put away the puzzle to solve later.

"Your knee was wrenched, and you've got some ribs that need mending, too," she told him. "But I think you'll be all right."

Now she could address the NordornQueen. She was still deathly pale. As soon as Zazar turned to her, she lifted the bowl of broth to her lips, as if fearing a scolding such as the Wysen-wyf had given her when she was a child.

"I'm going to examine you," she said. "Gaurin, you close your eyes."

He chuckled—the best sign yet, Zazar thought, though his broken ribs made him wince. "Ashen is my wife," he said, plainly amused.

"There are some things you don't need to know," Zazar retorted. Nevertheless, she began removing Ashen's clothing so she could put her hands on the NordornQueen's flesh.

The hand that had held the hilt of the Dragon Blade was icy cold. The other was warm, and Zazar unwrapped the bandage to search for any sign of infection. To her relief, there was none. The weakness she sensed. . . . The cause was still unclear.

"I believe the Dragon Blade affected both of you when you wielded it," she told them. "I wish I could have taken a look at Goliat. He tried to use it against the baby Dragon," she said in answer to Gaurin's questioning look, "but it spun out of his hand before he could strike a blow. Maybe it's just Nordorn-crowned who can take injury from it. I mean, who *took* injury."

Gaurin looked another question at her.

"You were out of the fight by then. Ashen picked up the sword and broke it into splinters."

"But I thought—"

Ashen spoke up, her voice weak. "So did we all. But I. . . . Well, I went outside myself, a little like when Zazar, Ysa, and I faced the Great Foulness. It wasn't the same, though."

"We came near our ending then."

"Well, both of you touched death a little too closely for my comfort this time," Zazar said. "Now, we have to get you two well enough to endure the trip back to Cyornasberg, and in the doing not lose the baby Ashen is carrying." She peered at Gaurin. "You do know about that, don't you?"

"Yes, Madame Zazar, I know. Foolishly brave Ashen." He gazed on his wife and managed to smile.

At his words, Zazar allowed herself to relax, just a little. Ashen seemed in no immediate danger of losing her unborn child, and Gaurin's strong constitution was going to help him recover from most of his ordeal more quickly than she had any right to expect.

Now, all they had to do was wait in this forsaken Fridian village, whose headman had once been the NordornKing's implacable enemy, until they could safely return to Pettervil, and thence to Cyornasberg, and the end of their problems.

Twenty-one

Ashen thought Admiral-General Tordenskjold and Rohan were going to come to blows over who was going to give up his cabin to the Nordorn rulers for their journey back home. Even though she and Gaurin were now settled aboard the *GorGull*, the argument continued.

"*Sea Witch* may be swift, but the good old, reliable *GorGull* is more comfortable," Rohan declared. "That's what's important now. The NordornKing and NordornQueen shouldn't be jounced around any more than is necessary."

"If there's a storm," Tordenskjold retorted, "better to get through it quickly. *GorGull* rolls like a water-spouting monster fish in even a moderate sea."

"Oh, leave off," Gaurin said, more amused than annoyed. "The captain's quarters in *GorGull* are spacious, and my Ashen and I would not be separated. Also, there is room for Madame Zazar nearby. Tell me how you have ordered our return."

"Yes, sire," Tordenskjold said, bowing. "*Sea Witch* will sail escort. We've already got Marigold on *Stormbracer,* along with as many of our men as will fit aboard her. Svarteper will take the rest—with the prisoners we have under guard—and he'll march south, the way we came, though our ships will not tarry this time, waiting for them."

"How many prisoners are there?"

"Nineteen," Rohan said. "Cebastian has charge of them."

"Only nineteen out of that army of renegades we faced. Remarkable."

"I didn't see anything but the first battle site at your camp," Ashen said, "but I glimpsed the preparations being made in anticipation of the assault on the village. I hope the people there did not suffer greatly."

"They fared better than we expected," Rohan told her. "I think by the time the enemy had to face an assault against a determined army, the fight had gone out of most of them."

"Then we can count our adventure a success," Gaurin said.

Tordenskjold snorted, then tried to cover it as a cough. "Well, sire, if you consider that both you and the NordornQueen are sore hurt and won't be riding through the gates of the Castle of Fire and Ice but carried on litters, I suppose you could call it a success. At least neither of you is dead."

"I will ride," Gaurin said, "if I have to be tied to my saddle."

"And I also," Ashen declared.

Tordenskjold smiled suddenly. "Did you know there are new verses of the Song, honoring both of you?"

"I knew some of my escort were attempting a verse, but I didn't know it had been completed," Ashen said.

"Completed, and sung frequently while we were waiting for Rohan and Cebastian to return from rescuing the hostages Asmal was holding to encourage his men to fight for him."

Ashen sighed. "There is a great deal to catch up on, it would seem."

"And no better way to pass the time while we sail south," Rohan declared. "If we ever do." He grinned at Tordenskjold.

"We'll weigh anchor at the change of the tide," said the Admiral-General. "Svarteper's sending a rider ahead with the news of our victory."

Zazar entered the cabin, bearing a tray of food and steaming hot drinks. "Everybody, out," she said. "I need to attend to these people, and I don't need to put up with sailors' quarreling over who is better organized and which ship is faster."

"So you heard that, did you?" Gaurin said. He made as if to rise from the spacious bunk he shared with Ashen, and Zazar waved him back.

"Everybody on board did," the Wysen-wyf told him. "Many of the men think it's funny. I don't."

She pulled a table over to the bunk and set a chair in place. "If you're very good, Gaurin NordornKing—" she put a somewhat derisive emphasis on his title "—you may sit up for a while, but watch that knee and have a care of your ribs. Ashen, you stay where you are. You may sit up to eat, if you're able."

Some of the weakness Ashen had experienced since breaking the Dragon Blade had lessened, though she still had difficulty flexing her unwounded hand. "I can sit up. The thought of returning home has invigorated me." She cautiously sampled the hot herb drink. "I wish Goliat were still alive. I would promote him," she said. "He deserved a reward for his unswerving loyalty."

Zazar snorted. She stood beside the table, hands on hips, as if ready to force the food down her two charges if they didn't display enough appetite. "He got a very nice reward with those fire-stones he took from the Dragon's lair even though he didn't live to enjoy it. And speaking of that—"

"What?"

"Nothing. Some other time. Ashen, besides the harm you took from handling the Dragon Blade, how do you feel?"

She put her hand to her belly. "I am well, Zazar, truly. Your potions work better than you realize."

"Of course they work. Still, I'll feel better with you both back in Cyornasberg where I can consult with the physician, Master Birger, on some things."

Zazar gazed at Gaurin's sword arm, splinted and without movement in his fingers, and Ashen knew she worried that the paralysis gripping him might be permanent.

They finished their meal and drank the herbal mixtures Zazar gave them. Then they lay down again to sleep, and when they awoke, they were at sea.

The voyage proved smoother than Tordenskjold's gloomy predictions. No storms or rough weather marred their passage.

Under Zazar's direction, Ashen and Gaurin went out on deck for fresh air each evening after their meal. This, Zazar said, was to help their digestion and also to make them sleep better. Gaurin, favoring his wrenched knee, hobbled with a crutch under one arm and Rohan aiding him on the other. His splinted arm was held in a sling. One of Ashen's Troopers, Braute, assigned to guard duty in Goliat's place, insisted on carrying her as if she were a child, setting her down very gently near the railing where she could hold on for balance and refusing to leave her side.

Ashen enjoyed watching the other two vessels, *Sea Witch* a ship's length ahead so that *GorGull* dipped a little in her wake, and *Stormbracer* toiling along behind. The first evening at sea, she and Gaurin heard for the first time the verses of "The Song" Rohan had told them about. The strains carried easily across the water, sung by the men on *Sea Witch*.

"You are brave and strong, and you deserve to become a part of it, but I feel that I am being praised without cause," she said.

"Praised with great cause," Gaurin said.

"Great cause indeed," Braute muttered. He began to hum quietly, off-key.

Gaurin leaned close to whisper in Ashen's ear. "You'd better become accustomed to this sort of thing. You may not have intended it, but you've become a national heroine, and I don't think even an order from me would stop it."

She looked up at him and recognized the twinkle in his eye when he was teasing her. "I am grateful that we came out of this horrible adventure as well as we did," she told him. "How fortunate the ones who stayed behind and were spared the danger!"

"Look," Gaurin said. "The first star tonight. Shall it be our private star, or do you want to share it with others?"

"I want to leave it for the rest of the world and go back to our cabin—Rohan's cabin—and sleep in your arms."

"Then so shall it be."

The NordornKing nodded at Braute, who came and gathered Ashen into his sturdy arms again. At rest and peaceful, gradually recovering from their ordeal, the Nordorn sovereigns slept without waking until morning.

Twenty-two

Long before they reached Cyornasberg Fjord and the Castle of
Fire and Ice, Ashen began catching a whiff of something foul,
borne by what should have been a sweet breeze blowing along the
shore. Under Zazar's supervision, she had begun walking on her
own despite Braute's disapproval, and now stood at the rail.

"What is that horrid smell?" she asked Zazar. "It's coming close
to making me sick."

"No idea." The Wysen-wyf wrinkled her nose. "There was something a little like it earlier, back in Rendel, but this is much, much
worse. I've never encountered anything to match it before. Thank
the Powers."

"Well, we're encountering it now, and it seems to be growing
stronger the closer we get to Cyornasberg. Gaurin needs to know
of this." She turned from the rail, and Braute immediately offered
his arm for her support as she returned to their cabin.

"If I didn't know better, I'd say it was troll-stink," the Trooper
told her, "only stronger than any I ever smelled. If it's this bad out
here, just think what it has to be like in the city!"

"Yes," Gaurin said when she told him of the stench, "I can smell
it even in here. I am beginning to fear that our people we left behind
did not fare as well as we hoped, and even that the triumphal

entrance we planned to make might be somewhat less important than the calamity that has caused the odor."

"I fear that Braute has told me its origin. A troll."

"We'll find out soon enough."

Both of them were on deck, at the prow of the vessel, when *GorGull* made the turn into Cyornasberg Fjord and sailed past the *Silver Burhawk*, made fast to one of the permanent buoys. Their banners—Gaurin's snogpus on a light green ground, Ashen's flaming ash-leaf circlet on a blue ground—flew bravely from the highest masts. It was obvious that the messenger from Svarteper had arrived because the walls of the Castle of Fire and Ice were lined with people shouting and waving in welcome.

At the landing at the top of the stairs leading from the floating quay at the water's edge, Ashen could see more people waiting—Einaar, Lord Royance, King Peres, Rannore, Counts Mjødulf and Baldrian, two of the barons, Håkon and Arngrim.

"Ysa is missing," Zazar commented. "Faugh! We thought that awful stench was bad at sea! It's fair enough to knock you over here."

"I don't care about Ysa." Ashen was more concerned with watching as Gaurin was lowered to one of the ship's boats to be conveyed to shore. There he could be carried up the stairs on a litter. Braute, she knew, planned to carry her himself, not trusting a litter for such an important undertaking.

Rohan, she noted, was in the boat carrying the NordornKing, and he sprinted up the stairs ahead of the litter-bearers. He greeted the nobles on the landing briefly, then disappeared from Ashen's view in the direction of the castle gate. He would, she knew, try to make the welcome there brief.

Zazar honked loudly into a rag. "Ugh. This horrible stink coats the inside of your nose so you can't get away from it."

Ashen got into the makeshift chair suspended from ropes and, swaying in the malodorous breeze, was lowered to a second boat. Braute, descending the ship's ladder, was not far behind. The boat bearing the NordornQueen reached the quay only a few strokes of the oar behind Gaurin's. Braute would have carried her up the stairs ahead of him, but Ashen forbade it.

"I would follow and see him along his way," she told him, "even though it delays my arrival."

The cheers from atop the walls diminished as the waiting crowd began to comprehend how their sovereigns had suffered. Gaurin and Ashen entered through the gates of the castle in respectful silence. As they passed, people took off their caps and held them over their hearts. The wives of the noblemen dabbed at their eyes with scented kerchiefs.

Inside the Hall, chairs with footstools were waiting on the dais, and Ayfare and Nalren stood close by if they were needed. Ayfare looked on the verge of tears as Braute carefully placed Ashen in her chair. The housekeeper rushed forward to tuck a coverlet around her mistress's feet and legs.

"Welcome back, Madame," she said.

For answer, Ashen squeezed her hand. "See to Gaurin," she said. "He is hurt far worse than I."

The NordornKing was even now being helped to his chair and his footstool placed so that he could prop his leg on it. The physician, Birger, entered the Hall, carrying a bag of medicines.

"My friends," Gaurin said, gazing around at the company gathered. "Now I am home."

At last the formalities had been observed and the people assured that their sovereigns had, indeed, returned to them.

Gaurin and Ashen visited the nursery first. Then, with help, they bathed and dressed themselves in Court garb for a meeting of the full Council. There they received the news of what had transpired in their absence. Only two of the permanent chairs at the table were empty—Ysa's and Svarteper's. Even Gangerolf, who had missed being among those nobles to greet their king and queen's return, was present.

"So the Duchess roused this horrible creature from its enchanted slumber," Gaurin said. He shook his head sadly.

"She did confess it to me," Einaar replied, "and also to Earl Royance."

"Earl?"

"I created him so, Uncle," King Peres said, "and my other uncle of Åsåfin gave him title to Åskar."

"It was well thought on," Gaurin said.

"Before I departed north the Duchess told me also of the Arikarin," Ashen said. "I had to weigh whether this looming threat was as important as my taking the map to you. I hoped, too much, that it would not become a peril before we returned." She gazed at the sapphire, now on her finger again. "I am in wonder at the use of the Great Signets, and also that Prince Bjauden could use it when the Arikarin was conquered." She turned to Einaar. "How can you stand the stench?"

"Madame, it is much lessened now, after the workmen put a covering over the thing. We have thought hard about how to rid ourselves of the creature but do not know how it could be done without awakening it anew." Einaar held a kerchief to his nose. "Many of us have begun making the perfumers rich."

"Better to get the thing gone for good," Zazar commented.

"We agree," Baldrian told her. "But again we come to the question of how to accomplish this."

"Perhaps," Arngrim offered, "we should wait until the Lord High Marshal Svarteper returns. Under his leadership, we might yet best the creature with weaponry. And there are always the Great Signets to rely on if we should fail."

Gaurin frowned and shook his head. "I will not risk losing any more of our people in such an endeavor, unless it becomes absolutely necessary."

Tordenskjold stirred in his chair. "My county, Grynet, borders the Icy Seas, and it has endured more than its share of trolls. They seem drawn to the water, especially islands and fjords, while at the same time fearing it. I've wondered sometimes about that. Now I wonder if this couldn't be turned to our advantage."

"How so?" Gangerolf wanted to know.

"Perhaps water puts them to sleep the way the Great Signets did this descendant of First Troll, as you call it. In any event, water certainly can't do trolls much good, the way they avoid it." He laughed.

"What, then, do you propose?" Gaurin inquired.

"I propose holding our noses and waiting for Svarteper and our armsmen to return. We have four ships at our disposal but I propose we use only old *GorGull* and *Stormbracer.* We must work out a way to load the thing onto one of them."

Rohan spoke up. "I don't relish having to abandon my ships because I can't get the stink off later."

"Your point is taken. We could just shove it off the cliff and into the water to let it drown, but I daresay it would poison the whole fjord for years to come. We'll rig a big net, then, and load the Arikarin into it and tow it out into the Icy Seas and drop it into the depths there. How does that suit you?"

"Better," Rohan said, "but what if it wakes up before we've got the ropes on it?"

"That's where Svarteper's forces come in," Tordenskjold said, warming to his topic. "With them in addition to the brave men who faced this troll when it first came here and the Great Signets' power, we should be able to handle it."

"Well," Royance commented, "at least getting the thing away from the castle walls would be a great relief both to castle and city. Master Birger and his assistants have worked hard, finding potions to soothe those made ill by the stench."

"My lady Elibit has been affected no less than any other," Einaar said. "On many days she cannot rise from her bed."

"Ysa's made that her excuse too, I'll wager," Zazar muttered to Ashen. "That way she doesn't have to face people who have every right to be angry with her."

"You are too harsh with her," Ashen whispered, but in her heart she knew Zazar was correct. Aloud, she said, "Einaar, I have heard that you have deprived me of the sweetest flower among my ladies. My congratulations, brother."

Einaar cast a sideways glance at Royance, then exchanged a mischievous grin with King Peres. "No apologies, and I thank you, Madame. Next, one can hope—"

"Shall we decide on your Admiral-General's suggestion?" Royance asked hastily.

There is more here than appears, Ashen thought. "I say that Tordenskjold's plan has merit. In the absence of a better suggestion, I am in favor of it."

Those around the table nodded agreement.

"Then this is what we will do. Rohan, get your men to start weaving a net of as strong rope as there is to be had in Cyornasberg. We will be ready when Svarteper and our men arrive."

Ashen began to improve, as did Gaurin. He cautiously began putting weight on his wrenched knee under the supervision of one of Master Birger's assistants, who had a real gift in dealing with injuries to bones and joints. Daily, Claus manipulated the NordornKing's leg, stretching and massaging the muscles so they would not deteriorate under this enforced inactivity.

The underlying weakness lingered in both of them, however, and the use of Gaurin's sword arm remained slow to return. Claus could not treat it until the broken bone had healed.

"I am beginning to think that his arm will never be the same," Zazar told Ashen in private. "I have conferred with Master Birger and also with Claus, and they agree with me that both your ailments go beyond the physical. Here. Grip my arm with both hands. I want to see how strong you are."

Obediently, Ashen did as requested. Even she could tell that her right hand could grip much less firmly than the left, though it was the one that the Dragon Blade had cut deeply.

"You'll never do fine needlework again," Zazar commented.

Ashen laughed aloud in spite of herself. "I never had much talent for it to begin with!" she exclaimed. "I'll not miss it. Gaurin will miss losing his strength very much. It's a small price to pay for his life, but I don't think he realizes it yet."

As prescribed by Master Birger to help them return to normal life, she and Gaurin went down to the Hall every night for their evening meal. There Ashen discovered the reason for the secret merriment between Einaar and Peres when she was introduced to

Lady Mjaurita and observed the studiously courteous attention Lord—no, Earl—Royance paid to her.

"It would be wonderful if they wed," she whispered to Rannore, lest the old gentleman overhear.

"So it would, but first we'd have to get our lord Earl used to the idea. Next, we'd need the lady's permission." Rannore smiled. "She is very content with her status as an independently wealthy widow and is not eager to change it."

Royance was looking at them, one eyebrow slightly raised. Ashen changed the subject. "How Bjauden has grown!" she said. "And Laherne and Viktor! I am glad I left my son in such capable hands."

"Thank Beatha, not me," Rannore said. "I only supervised her and that lightly. She takes her duties very seriously. In addition, I think she truly loves her charges."

"I forced myself not to think about the children while I was gone," Ashen said. "Now, I long for the day that we have the Arikarin's body removed and the air is sweet enough once more that we can take them out so they can play."

"The Lord Marshal will be back in Cyornasberg very soon." The animation left Rannore's face for a moment. "And my husband with him. Oh, yes," she said, forestalling Ashen's comment, "I understand that he and Svarteper were needed to finish affairs at the village after the battle, and I do not begrudge it. It is all part of being the wife of such a man as Lathrom."

Ashen squeezed her friend's hand.

Lady Pernille began the first notes of "The Song." Ashen leaned closer to whisper once more. "Oh, look. Royance is taking Lady Mjaurita out to dance with her. I hope Pernille doesn't sing the verses about Gaurin and me. I would have to leave the table early, from embarrassment."

"Well," Rannore observed judiciously, "you could always take heart by watching the Duchess's Ysa's face the first time she hears them."

Ashen had to smile. "And see her beginning to plot how she,

too, could earn a place in the Song. It might be worth it, if she ever leaves her sickbed."

Within a week, Svarteper and the army returned to Cyornasberg. Surprisingly, the war-kats were with them. They stalked through the castle gate, wrinkling their noses, their fur raised along their backs.

"What's that awful smell?" the Marshal asked as he dismounted from Firefly.

"All in good time," Lathrom said. Rannore ran to him, and he swept her into his embrace.

"Well, my wife was furnishing our town house when I left, so she's bound to be around here somewhere, I suppose," Svarteper said. "Oh, there she is. Aud! I've come home."

The countess, almost lost in the crowd of nobles, waved. "About time. Welcome back, old man!" she cried. "See you tonight in the Hall, at meat!"

The armsmen, being dismissed, then scattered—some to their homes in the city, others to barracks inside the castle. As they went into the castle, Count Baldrian filled Svarteper in on what had been happening while the army had been absent.

The Marshal's scowl grew deeper as he listened to the tale, then his expression lightened. "Daresay you've not had much luck getting volunteers to load up this slime thing into the net, eh?"

"Nobody wants to do it."

"I've got those nineteen prisoners with me, the last of an army of renegades that had us hopping for a while so Gaurin Nordorn-King could go off and kill that Ice Dragon. I've got a notion he might consider this a good way to teach them the unwisdom of rebelling against their rightful ruler."

Later, at a Council meeting, Gaurin concurred. "I do not relish the thought of imprisoning these men. They were brave, if misguided. Let them accomplish this task, then let them go free."

"With the NordornQueen's permission I'll put Cebastian in charge of the work detail." Svarteper turned to Ashen. "Are you sure you can't spare him? He'd make a grand second-in-command to me."

Ashen smiled. "I've been thinking of several promotions I'd like to make. I won't promise, not yet, but I agree that he has potential that could be wasted as commander of my House Troops. I will think on it, Lord Marshal."

"While you're thinking, tell me why the war-kats decided to come back with us. Our fighting was done. The Dragon was killed."

"Perhaps they are simply fond of us," Gaurin suggested. He glanced at the four animals lounging where they pleased, in the Council chamber. Finola had her beloved Weyse in her paws once more and was giving the unearthly little creature a bath.

"Perhaps they think you need them to look after you," Zazar said, more than a little derisively. "Or maybe they're ready for a life of ease."

Gaurin laughed. "They'll have that, if it's their desire."

Ashen gazed at Bitta fondly, caressing her head. The young war-kat had asked for her paw to be massaged again, and she had done so. "It isn't every Court that can boast of four war-kats in it," she said.

"Well," Mjødulf observed, "thanks to their presence, this is one court that can boast of visitors who wouldn't dream of breaching good manners in the slightest degree."

Rajesh roused himself and got up to rub against Gaurin's good leg, then to lean against Mjødulf's knee. The Count, to Ashen's amusement, sat rigid, not moving. Obviously, he was petrified and determined not to show it.

"Stroke his head," she told Mjødulf. "I think he likes you."

"Thank you, no, Madame," the Count replied stiffly. "I—I am not fond of cats. Any cats. Let him like me from a distance, and all will be well."

"You are excused, of course," she told him. She could not fault him for bravery; she had learned of how he had played his part in defending against the onslaught of the Arikarin. "Rajesh, leave him alone."

The war-kat shook his ears and stalked off. He began to wrestle with Keltin, ignoring the blandishments of Svarteper, who did not share Mjødulf's dislike of the animals.

The other Council members hid their smiles.

The Nordorn Court, Ashen thought, will surely be an interesting place in which to live now that the war has ended, the Ice Dragon slain, and the Arikarin's body soon to be disposed of.

Twenty-three

At last the net was ready, the ships pulled up as close to the cliff face as possible, and the nineteen prisoners involved in the actual moving of the Arikarin assembled with their guards.

Most of the inhabitants of the castle were at the walls, watching, and they had been joined by many of the citizens of Cyornasberg. Ysa had been persuaded to abandon her sickbed and stand ready with Peres, Rannore, and Ashen, in case the power of the Great Signets was needed again. Gaurin, still leaning on a staff, was there also, with Einaar, Royance, and the rest of the nobles and those wives who had strong stomachs.

Ashen watched the proceedings with interest. She undertook to explain what was happening to the Duchess, who preferred to keep her eyes closed and a perfume-soaked kerchief to her nose.

"They are taking away the tent covering the troll."

"Yes, I know," Ysa murmured faintly, as a strong gust of the horrid slime-stench rose from the base of the wall.

"It is even more dreadful to look upon than I imagined," Ashen went on. "Now I wonder if I would have left if I had known of the monster you had to face."

"I told you it was a fool's errand. What are they doing now?"

"They have taken long poles and are prying at it to turn it over into the net."

"Is it stirring?"

"No," Ashen said.

"It seems to be well and truly under the spell of the Great Signets once more," Rannore said. "Only magic can awaken it again. We should have known this."

"It wasn't worthwhile to take the chance," Peres said. "I'm glad I missed breakfast."

As they watched, the men lowered the net holding the Arikarin by means of several pulleys until it could be swung over and two sides be secured to the sterns of *GorGull* and *Stormbracer*—a very hazardous undertaking. At last, however, the task was accomplished, and the two vessels, under the command of Rohan and Tordenskjold, raised sail and moved awkwardly toward the entrance to Cyornasberg Fjord. From time to time the rope net dipped in the frigid waters and ice began to form on it.

"None of this would have been possible without you," Ashen told Rannore. "My dear friend, my Lady of the Rowan, you led where others dared not. How can I ever thank you or repay you?"

"You had your role to play in this," Rannore replied, "and so did I. Do you ask for repayment? Then I do not."

"You are both reckless and foolhardy," Ysa announced. "I suppose that's a function of youth though I must say I was never as giddy as either of you."

"Pray do not scold Rannore, Madame Mother," Ashen said. "We are safe today because of her." She took a deep breath. "Already the air is sweeter."

"Then with the danger behind us, I am minded to take my leave of the Nordorn Court and go to Iselin for a while." The Duchess lowered her voice confidentially. "I counsel you, keep an eye on Earl Royance. With both Grattenbor and Åskar under his command and situated as he is between the NordornLand and Rendel, he could make himself a king if he wanted to."

"And a better ally either country could never hope for," Ashen replied aloud. "You have earned a long rest away from the Court.

Your duchy must be longing for its lady's presence, and so you have good leave to go. My counsel to you is that you depart at once. At once."

The Duchess looked at the emerald ring on her finger. She opened her mouth as if she would make some retort, then closed it again. She curtseyed. "Your Majesty." The words seemed to hurt as she said them, and she swept back into the castle, presumably to prepare for her journey.

Rannore was having trouble keeping her face straight. "Alas. Now she won't hear those verses of the Song," she said.

Peres looked puzzled. "What just happened?" he asked.

"You heard," Rannore told her son. "Your granddam is leaving the Court for a while, that's all."

"There's more to it than that," Peres said. "It sounded almost like Granddam Ysa had been banished, but not exactly." His face brightened. "Royance won't tell me, but I'll ask Hegrin when we get back to Rendelsham."

"Which should not be long delayed, Your Majesty," Royance said. He looked at Ashen. "That was well done, my dear; you have learned well. I can leave Ysa with you in good conscience now."

"But with provision always that you return when needed," Ashen said.

"And there are ties between your lands and ours," Einaar added. "Will there be anyone else returning with you besides King Peres and his company?"

"Aye, my lord, please tell us!" Peres said.

To Ashen's astonishment, the old gentleman blushed.

"The Lady Mjaurita has consented to pay a visit to Rendel," he said with great dignity, "and will be sailing with us on the *Silver Burhawk*. Beyond that, I cannot tell."

"You are a fortunate man," Gaurin told him. "Cherish this most worthy lady's friendship and ask no more than she is willing to bestow."

"Your brother gave me similar advice, and I will heed it."

"Then we all hope for a good resolve to this interesting tale."

Gaurin turned to Ashen. "Let us go inside now and enjoy the company of our guests while they yet tarry."

The Rendelian visitors chose to stay until the ships bearing the Arikarin had returned, though the Duchess Ysa departed almost unremarked despite the size of the train of pack animals bearing her belongings, accompanied by her House Troops and retinue of ladies.

A few days later, *GorGull* and *Stormbracer* sailed back into Cyornasberg Fjord.

"It was the most amazing thing," Tordenskjold reported. "By the time we got out into the Icy Seas, the damned troll had melted! It squalled once, then the net was empty."

"Indeed," Rohan said. "I'm glad we didn't drop it into the waters here. Tordenskjold said it would kill the fish, and there was a trail of them floating on the surface as we sailed back." He took a gulp of hot wine. "All that work and effort and there was nothing at the end."

"Incidentally, you showed real seamanship," Tordenskjold said, "managing that net load. Tricky business. If you stayed here with me long enough, you'd learn a lot."

"No doubt, Admiral-General, but I must return to New Vold. My people are there, and my wife."

Ashen had been listening to the two men with some amusement. "Please convey my regards to Anamara. There are gifts to take with you when you sail. And also, when Harvas returns from his freebooting mission, tell the Spirit Drummer, Frode, that he was correct. He'll know what I mean."

"I will do that, Ashen NordornQueen. And I know that you will not object when I take my ships and return home on the next tide. I've been away long enough."

"I'll miss your ships, boy," Tordenskjold said genially. "But that'll give us something to do, to build more. Any chance of loaning us some shipwrights? Nobody builds ships better than a Sea-Rover, you know."

"Of course. They'll be here by return voyage."

Rohan's small fleet sailed a day ahead of the *Silver Burhawk*. All his men had been paid well for their services—something sure to please a Sea-Rover—and Rohan himself was laden with many gifts not only for Anamara and the child she was expecting, but also for himself.

Then it was time for their other guests to depart. Ashen and Gaurin gathered with the King of Rendel, the Earl of Grattenbor, the Lord High Marshal, Lady Rannore, and Lady Mjaurita in the Great Hall to bid them farewell. The Rendelian soldiers, tutors, and others who had accompanied them waited outside, even Tamkin, who normally seemed glued to his sovereign's side. It was a good thing their journey would be mercifully brief, for the *Silver Burhawk* would be very crowded.

"As Ashen told you, my lady," Gaurin said to Rannore, "we owe everything to you. If it had not been for your bravery in facing the Arikarin and your mysterious insight as how to contain it, there would have been nothing for us to return to, once the Mother Ice Dragon was no more."

"My lady constantly surprises me," Lathrom said, gazing on her fondly. "Sir. Once again, it has been my privilege to serve you."

"Let us hope that neither of us has to call on such service again, and yet hold friendship dear."

"So might it be," Peres said. He raised one of the wooden goblets the Nordorners used when marking an occasion that was coming to an end.

All drank and cast the vessels into the fire.

Gaurin's broken bones healed in time, and his wrenched knee grew strong enough that it could bear his weight though Claus warned that the joint would ever be untrustworthy. Every weather change, the physician predicted, would make its coming known, and at such times he recommended using the discarded staff.

Too slowly for Gaurin's overstretched patience to abide, his body began to regain some of its former strength, but it was the weakness in his sword arm that troubled the NordornKing most.

"How can I defend my land if I can't properly wield a weapon?" he fretted to Ashen.

"That's for Svarteper to do, and with Cebastian as his second-in-command," Ashen told him.

"Oh, so you agreed to release him from his former post?"

"He was wasted in my House Troops."

"At least he has a position that he is able to fill. Unlike me."

"Don't be so glum, my Gaurin," Ashen told him. "Kingship is not all about battles and fighting, and our battles are, we must hope, over. Now is the time for planning and building. You don't need a weapon in your hand for that."

Gaurin was not to be mollified. "All this planning and building takes gold, and we have spent almost all of what we had. Allies are allies, but they like to be paid."

"We are far from impoverished," Ashen assured him. But nothing she said could ease the NordornKing's low spirits.

Later, seeking counsel, she called Zazar into the privacy of her little presence chamber and reported the conversation to her. "He has mended only so far and no further. Now I fear he has fallen into despair," she said.

"He should be grateful he's still alive," the Wysen-wyf retorted.

"I think he almost believes he would have been better off if he'd been killed. He is very downcast that he can no longer wield a sword. I've taken away his dagger, lest—"

"Speaking of swords." Zazar rose from her chair. "I'll be right back."

In a few minutes she returned, bearing a bundle wrapped in her old shawl, and placed it on the table.

"What is that?" Ashen asked.

"Unwrap it and find out."

Hesitantly, Ashen began unfolding the shawl. To her astonishment, it held a large number of fire-stones, along with an article that looked familiar—

"The hilt of the Dragon Blade!" Ashen exclaimed. She grasped it, noting that there was none of the shock she had felt previously, when she had faced the Mother Ice Dragon.

"That's all that was left, once you shattered it," Zazar told her. "I thought it might do as a trophy to set beside your ruined necklace, so while you and Gaurin were asleep, I went out and picked it up. I also gathered those stones while I was at it, and the scabbard. Nice-looking thing, mother-of-pearl over silvered steel. It's still in my room."

"The stones are worth a fortune. But they belong to you."

"Nonsense. I don't want them. They're toys. Trinkets only." The Wysen-wyf turned serious. "Do you remember that little packet of castings from the Web of the Weavers that Nayla sent me while we waited for the ship to take us back home? The ones you kept safe for me under lock and key while we were gone? Well, you never bought me a kettle, but I found one anyway, and used it a week or so ago. Mixed the potion and used the castings. Very interesting, what it showed."

"Why didn't you do this before?" Ashen wanted to know.

"Girl, using the castings from the Web isn't something you do lightly. First I had to be sure that all was as well as it was apt to get anytime soon, with the Mother Ice Dragon dead and the Arikarin on its way out to sea."

"Then tell me what you learned."

Zazar laughed. "It isn't fortune-telling, if that's what you mean. The spell showed me what's to come, in a general sort of way, whether it's for good or for ill. You remember what Nayla told you, back in the Bog?"

Ashen searched her memory. "New things, not all favorable, coming into my life, she told me. She couldn't say if they were good or ill."

"She isn't as experienced as I am," Zazar said, with more than a touch of complacency, "even though I'm officially retired. Right now, there's ill—that's Gaurin. His pride's been hurt, and he's deeply angry."

"Anger. Not despair?"

"Anger, despair, bitterness. It's all mixed together. The tales he's heard all his life are wrong. He should have ridden out to battle on his charger and cut down the Dragon at a single blow and returned in triumph, unharmed, and it didn't happen that way. But he's strong and he's sensible." Abruptly she appeared to change the subject. "Have you told him about the weakness in your own hand?"

"No, of course not!" Ashen said, startled.

"Well, don't be a noddle-noodle!" Zazar exclaimed. "Do it! Let him see that he wasn't the only one to carry away hurt from this adventure. It will take him out of himself and help him learn wisdom in time; there's the good. You both survived, and the people will revere the two of you all the more because you were maimed protecting them. You'll have a healthy child and, if I don't miss my guess, one more."

Ashen put her hand on her swelling abdomen. "A healthy child," she repeated softly.

"But not exactly a normal one."

Ashen glanced at Zazar, startled. "Not normal?"

The Wysen-wyf leaned forward a little and took one of Ashen's hands in her own. Her tone softened, just a little. "Not exactly normal the way Bjauden isn't exactly normal. Surely you've noticed it. The child isn't young—just immature in body. Remember, you were carrying him when you and I and Ysa confronted the Great Foulness. The magic affected him."

"And this child I am carrying . . ."

"Will also be affected by the magic that enveloped you and let you put an end to the Dragon."

"Will any of this be for the good?"

"There the spell was unclear," Zazar admitted. "I think for the good, where Bjauden is concerned. I don't know about the new one. And there's another thing you need to know."

"What now?"

"Men can sire children until they're ready to fall into the tomb, but women can't. You and Gaurin have aged unnaturally, and I think this is because of the Dragon Blade and how you both had to wield it. You were touched more lightly, and I think it was because of the Power of the flame that shielded you. This premature aging is drying up your fertility at such a rate that time is running out. You will be able to have only one more child. A boy, the potions and the Web castings indicated. The one you're carrying now is a girl."

Ashen stared at Zazar, her eyes filling with tears. "Gaurin and I gave our first daughter his mother's name. We gave our son his father's name, and he was a good man. I will give our new daughter my mother's name, for she was good and brave."

"Your first daughter's and your son's name were well thought on. As for your new child, name her for your mother if you must but call her by another. Remember that Alditha was in an unlawful relationship with King Boroth, your father."

"Yes, I will do that," Ashen promised.

She reached out and touched the glittering heap of gems. Even uncut, they were beautiful. Gaurin's worry about the Nordorn-Land's financial condition now was for naught.

"These," she murmured, "and those still in the lair—"

"Only these," Zazar said. "I don't know if you remember—you were as ensorcelled in your own way as the rest of us—but when you destroyed the Dragon Blade, the ground shook."

"I do remember. I thought it was just me, or perhaps the Dragon falling."

"No, it was an earthquake. The kettle told me that the mountain where the Mother Ice Dragon's lair once was has collapsed. Now all she gathered is sealed away forever. Cursed treasure. If anyone had been in that cave, he—or she—would have been entombed with it."

Ashen could not repress a shudder. "Not all of what you have told me is comforting," she said, "but I will take your counsel. You have ever been wise."

"Good," Zazar said brusquely. "Now, take my advice. Coax Gaurin out onto the floor tonight. Show him that his knee is fit for dancing to 'The Song,' and both his arms strong enough to hold you. Let the verses that embarrass you so much be sung, for they are about him as well. Start him to healing again. Give him his dagger back. He will not use it on himself. He has much to live for—and more to come. He only needs to be shown the way."

"I hope you are right."

Zazar snorted, her old self again. "Of course I'm right!" Then she added, "If that man of yours is still sulky after you tell him he's to have yet another child with you, remind him that Hegrin and Peres are nearly old enough to start presenting you with grandchildren in this dynasty you've created. Also, we still don't know how this great romance of Royance's with Mjaurita is going to turn out. If that doesn't restore his taste for life, then I don't know what will."

Epilogue

In the Cave of the Weavers, the Youngest worked happily on the section of the Web Everlasting that had been given to her. The other two would be pleased with how well and carefully she had recorded what had occurred, and with no interference on her part. Now she would not be sent away to learn some lesson she already, on some level, knew.

How the short-lived humans had managed to untangle the fearsome snarls, large and harsh to the touch, she did not know. Nor, she told herself, was it her concern. The Eldest was right. The affairs of mortals were of no concern to her. The task of the Three was only to record, not influence or alter. As always, today had become yesterday, and tomorrow had become today, with resolution and relief for those whose lives were detailed in the weaving. "The affairs of mortals, frail and fleeting as they are, do not concern us," she murmured, not for the first time.

"It is always the same," the Eldest said. "Their lives ebb, and flow, and most pass unnoticed. To a few is given the opportunity for more, and some refuse even this."

"Now there is order," the Middle Sister observed. "Kingdoms rise and kingdoms fall, and some are reborn while others perish forever. What more is there to know?"

The Youngest told herself she had come to understand the

wisdom of never giving in to pity for the ones whose destinies they recorded. There was no mercy available for those who were doomed, and never could there be any meddling with the design. To do such would be to create a worse tangle than the one the Three had just spent so much effort in bringing into order.

And yet, and yet. . . . New strands were beginning to emerge, brightly colored and crossing at odds with the rest of the design. Could she have touched it, influenced it without intending to, to aid the ones she secretly loved? No. She put away the thought, never to be brought out again.

As always, the living would continue to believe that they were free to make decisions, to act as they believed fit, even as their threads passed through the fingers of the Weavers.